Tales of Tyriel
A Curse of Darkness

By J.S. Matthews

This book is dedicated to my wife for all of her love, support, and for always being willing to listen to my ideas. Also, a special thanks to Ramon Ford for his help and expertise, as without him this book would have had more mistakes than anyone could count.

I would also like to thank the many teachers that I had during my years in high school, as I imagine many of them are amazed that I can string together multiple sentences, let alone an entire book.

To Zach Holmes and Alec Egizi for instilling in me a love of history and learning. To Jeremy Reed for showing me the joys of writing and reading. To Bruce Casson and Cathryn Supplee for introducing me into the world of rhetoric and literature. Finally, to Carry Stedman for showing love to an obnoxious, loud, and goofy child, and for showing me what it truly means to care for your students

To each and every one of my students who took the time to read my stories, even before they were edited, I thank you for your enthusiasm and kindness.

And finally, I thank you, my readers, whoever you are and wherever you may be. Thank you for taking the time to read my books and share in this adventure. These three stories mark only the beginning of your journey into the world of Tyriel. There are more stories to tell, more adventures to be had, and I hope you will stick with me through the rest of the journey.

-J.S. Matthews

The first Night...

A Symphony of Blood

Jarrell Vorren sat at a small desk on the upper floor of the Great Library in Eldrith. He was a young man who had not yet entered his twenties, and his once wavy hair had been cut to resemble the typical look of a Keeper. He had spent the past twelve years of his life here in this library. Twelve years of studying, researching, reading, copying, and learning amongst the endless shelves of scrolls, books, and parchments. How many hours had he spent behind a desk? How many nights had he spent staying up late into the wee hours of the morning? Studying by the dim light a candle for whatever challenges the Keepers had for him the following day. They were the most meticulous, fussy, and frustrating old men that anyone could have the unfortunate pleasure of encountering. Everything Jarrell did was nitpicked and judged to some unrealistic standard, and no matter how hard he tried they always seemed to find something wrong with his work. Of course, this was the way of the Keepers.

For thousands of years these old men had been tasked with recording and safeguarding the histories of mankind, and there was now five Great Libraries across Tyriel where the Keepers performed their duties. Their entire lives were spent researching, copying, writing, and interpreting, at least until the day came when they were too old to continue and had to be replaced. That was what Jarrell was training for. He was a replacement, selected to one day take the place of one of those grumpy, picky, frustrating old men and become one himself. While other boys were off pretending to have adventures as imaginary knights and warriors, Jarrell was forced to sit inside the musty library and study, read, and write, and then endure hours of being told what he did wrong. He had been selected, he had been chosen, and now he had no choice but to follow the path that was before him.

So here he was, locked away once again in the Great Library deep in the mountains of Arendor, beginning his life of monotony and boring repetition. Two days ago, he had been raised from a Novice to an Apprentice level, and now he was tasked with copying down the writings of the Keepers and ensuring new copies of older writings were created before the old ones faded too much. It wasn't all that boring, as he did enjoy copying down the more fun stories like Ser Baradin the Brave or the tale of Skalgrim the Slaughterer, but most of the time he found himself perusing pages and pages of boring political events and uninteresting journals. Tonight, was most torturous, as he worked on re-writing an old tome detailing the important fungi and plants located in the regions of Penland and Morovia. His fingers ached and were stained with thick layers of ink that would take days to come off, and his neck and back were sore and stiff from the hours of constant writing.

Being forced to read through such tedious and uninteresting material was quite disappointing, as he had spent the past month with one of the more interesting documents that he had seen in quite some time. It was an old volume that had started to fade entitled *An Early History of Tyriel*, written by one of the first Keepers. More importantly, it had been updated by Jarrell's Master, and Jarrell enjoyed his time with the old work as it was full of grand and epic stories from all over Tyriel. It detailed the account of how the world was created, or at least how the Chronicles told it, and how the creator god forged humans. It told of the fall of Azaral, the great evil, and how five other gods followed him in his rebellion against the creator, and of his corruption of humans in the land of Arden. He read of the first Guardian, how he fought against armies of evil creatures and demons while protecting Tyriel from the influences of the evil gods, and how humans were expelled from the paradise of Arden for their sins. An interesting tale to say the least and far more engaging than reading about plants.

Suddenly, there was a commotion down below in the entrance hall and Jarrell looked up from his work to see what was causing the disturbance. He set his quill down gently on the desktop and made his way across the walkway towards the balcony overlooking the front doors. One of the Keepers was bustling in, followed by a few guards and a man in a black cloak with his hood still pulled up. Jarrell saw nothing suspicious about this as it was quite chilly outside, but the Keeper seemed to be escorting the man. Jarrell yawned as the

A Symphony of Blood

little party passed from view and returned to his copying; he had a little way to go before he could quit for the night, and he hoped to finish early and get some much-needed sleep. Slowly he made his way back over to the little desk, but just as he started working again, he heard the echo of footsteps as someone climbed up to the second floor. He dipped the quill into the little bottle of ink nearby and began to write, only to be surprised as a man addressed him from behind.

"Good evening, Apprentice," a man said in a sharp tone.

Jarrell nearly leapt out of his seat and cursed as he spilled the bottle of ink.

"I am sorry for startling you, Apprentice," the man added.

Jarrell glared at the old man who now stood behind him.

"By the gods Master Borry, did you have to sneak up on me like that?" Jarrell asked.

The old man's eyes narrowed ever so slightly.

"I do not believe that is the proper way to address your superiors, Apprentice, and therefore you owe me an essay on Keeper training and why it is so important to respect the hierarchy within the Keeper Ranks."

Jarrell sighed and hid his sneer of contempt before the old man saw.

"I apologize Master. What is it that you need of me?" Jarrell forced the words in a respectful tone.

"Much better. Now, I need you to grab your things and follow me," the old man said and turned.

"Where to? Er–Master?" Jarrell caught himself just as the old man raised an eyebrow.

"You will know when we get there, now hurry, we have no time to lose."

Jarrell packed up his things as quickly as he could and cleaned up the splotches of spilled ink that had started to stain the desk. Soon he had his little satchel already to go and Master Borry led the way towards the stairs and down to the entryway.

"I have heard some great things about you from Master Dorn; he says you are the finest Apprentice he had ever worked with," Borry said as they walked, and Jarrell shrugged.

"I do my best, and I have had good teachers."

"Modesty is commendable, but from what I have seen and heard of your work you are already well into your Apprentice training. Keep it up, and at this rate you will be the youngest Keeper to join our ranks in a thousand years."

Jarrell found himself beaming with pride, though he tried to hide it as a true Keeper remained humble when complimented about his work, as it should always be perfect.

"Thank you, Master. I shall continue to do my best."

"Of that I have no doubt, which is why, I believe, High Keeper Yorlan wishes to see you."

Jarrell almost dropped his satchel.

"The High Keeper wishes to see me?" Jarrell said and felt his stomach drop. He had only met the High Keeper once and it was a very short meeting but had been intimidating none the less.

"Yes, that is what I said," the older man repeated irritably.

"Do you know why he wants to see me?" Jarrell asked nervously but Master Borry just shook his head.

"I know, but I think he is the one who wishes to tell you."

Neither man spoke again as they continued through the entry hall and down a flight of stairs, past a silver armored guard, and to the first of the lower levels of the library. It truly was a magnificent place, with two levels upstairs and six more that stretched far below the ground. These levels were covered from floor to ceiling in shelves of books, and many doors led off to other areas where other books, scrolls, and works were stored. At the center of these lower levels was a large square chasm that passed through all the way to the lowest level, the sixth floor. Only the most accomplished Keepers were allowed down there, and Jarrell was getting more nervous the further down they went. Long, rotating stone bridges were attached to a pillar that reached up through the center of the chasm, and the sounds of the library above echoed down through the cavern.

They passed through the first of the lower levels, the second, and the third, before finally Master Borry turned and led Jarrell along one of the railings to a little door at the end of the row. He had never been down this far into the lower libraries, and the thought of having to meet with the High Keeper was gnawing at his insides. Did he do something wrong? Were they bringing him this low into the library to punish him? They approached the door and Master Borry turned to Jarrell.

"Go ahead and knock. They are expecting you, but it is still proper."

With that the Master turned and left Jarrell standing alone in front of the big oak door, wondering what lay beyond.
After summoning the courage, he gave a soft tap on the door and heard a man

A Symphony of Blood

call from the inside.

"Enter," the voice said, and Jarrell took one last deep breath to steady himself before entering.

Inside was a large circular room lined with shelves full of books. To one end was a large wooden desk that sat facing the rest of the room and at the center was a small circular table where two men sat. At one end of the table sat the man in the dark cloak that Jarrell had seen enter through the front doors, and at the other end was High Keeper, Yorlan. He was a skinny, frail old man with a wispy white beard that stuck out from his chin and fell almost to his waist. The other man unnerved Jarrell and sat silently with his face still hidden by the hood.

"Good evening, Apprentice," Yorlan said with a smile. "I apologize for disturbing your work. I know how fascinating fungi and plants can be, especially this late at night."

Jarrell heard the old Keeper chuckle, which made him feel slightly better, though not much.

"No, it is not a problem, High Keeper. What do you need of me?" he asked as respectfully as he could.

"This man here is a traveler, and he comes to us bearing a great gift." The High Keeper waved his hand, and the hooded man slowly pulled out a bound leather volume with pieces of frayed parchment sticking out in all directions.

The man slid it across the table without a word, and Yorlan motioned for Jarrell to draw nearer.

"What is it, High Keeper?" he asked as the old man undid the binding.

"That is the question I need your help to answer," he said.

"I'm not sure what you mean," Jarrell answered. Yorlan opened the leather binding and turned it so that Jarrell could read. "A journal of some sort," Jarrell muttered under his breath. He fingered through the pages, which became lighter and less stained the further into the leather-bound pages he went. "These first pages, they are old. A hundred years, at least, but the later pages are far more recent."

"A very astute observation," the High Keeper added.

"Whose is it though?" Jarrell asked. Yorlan leaned forward and shifted the pages so that the inside cover was visible. Jarrell squinted to make out what looked like a name scribbled in the corner. Three words were clearly visible, and Jarrell felt his jaw drop as his eyes passed over the slanted lettering. "It can't be."

The High Keeper chuckled.

"I see you are having a similar reaction to my own."

Jarrell stared at the name in awe.

"Gerhold of Vilheim," he read under his breath and bent down a little closer.

"If this gentleman here is to be believed, then yes," The High Keeper said. Jarrell saw the man at the other end of the table shift uncomfortably. "He claims these are the journals of the famous Gerhold of Vilheim, the greatest monster hunter in history," the High Keeper said, and Jarrell noticed the excitement in the old man's voice. "Until now, we were only able to find bits and pieces of his story."

"My mother used to tell me stories about him when I was a boy," Jarrell said excitedly as memories flooded back into his mind. Werewolves and vampires, demons and specters, the great Gerhold had fought them all, or so the stories had said.

"Yes, I am sure most children have heard the tales while growing up, but as you may also know, no one knows how that story came to an end," Yorlan said leaned back in his chair. "No one knows what happened to the once famous monster hunter. It is as if he disappeared from this world entirely. It is a question that has plagued many a scholar and bard alike: what happened to Gerhold of Vilheim?"

"And you think these may hold the answer?" Now Jarrell was sounding excited.

The tales of Gerhold always ended with how he simply disappeared from the pages of history, lost to the past. As a boy, he had always wondered what had become of the hunter. Had Gerhold been slain by a monster? Had he decided to retire from the life of slaying? If these pages were truly the journals of the mythical figure, then perhaps they held the answers.

"That is what we need to find out," Yorlan said.

Jarrell stared blankly at the High Keeper.

"Me?" he said in disbelief.

"Did I stutter?" Yorlan asked with a grin. "Most of my Keepers are either off gathering texts or recording the goings on of the realms that I have too few here to truly manage what I need to accomplish. This was an unexpected turn of events and seeing as how Mister Ernhold here is only able to remain in Eldrith for a short time, I need someone who can copy down these texts for us and ensure that they are in fact the story of Gerhold. Are you capable of such a task?"

Jarrell wasn't sure how to answer.

"Well, I am not sure what to say, sir. Would it not be proper to hand this off to an Apprentice who is closer to being raised to a Keeper?" Jarrell asked.

"I would, but most are busy, and the others are not nearly as good as you are. So, will you do this for me? Unless of course, you would rather go back to copying down the fungi and plant lists of Midland?"

"Of course not," Jarrell blurted out, almost a bit too eagerly.

"Good. If what I hear from Master Dorn is true, then you already work at the rate and quality of a fully raised Keeper." Yorlan said and Jarrell felt even more stunned. Master Dorn had never let a single scrap of his work go by without some sort of critique, but apparently, he thought highly of his newly raised Apprentice. "I would do it myself, but unfortunately, my attention must be focused elsewhere at this time."

Jarrell glanced nervously at the stack of pages and swallowed. He looked about the room, then nodded slowly.

"Yes, High Keeper, I can do it."

Yorlan nodded and stood.

"I knew you would," he said with a grin. "This is quite the rare gift, getting to read through a story that few, if any, know the ending to."

"But how do we know these are real?" Jarrell asked and picked up the first page to get a closer look. He also noticed the other man shifted, as if offended by the question. Jarrell picked through the pages, examining the ink, the wear and tear, and tried to determine the age. The more he turned through the pages, the more he noticed something strange. "Some of these pages, the ones towards the end, look no older than a decade or less."

"I have examined them myself, and so far, they appear as authentic as any other work we keep here," the High Keeper responded.

"I'm not sure I understand then. How could these be his journals if the words and pages are so recent?"

Yorlan smiled and placed his hand on the Apprentice's shoulder.

"That is the mystery you must solve."

Jarrell glanced nervously at the stack of pages as Yorlan gave him one last encouraging pat on the shoulder.

"You know, sometimes I regret taking the title of High Keeper," he said with a sad smile. "Prestige and power are rarely a fair replacement for the pursuit of knowledge and the excitement of diving into the unknown. You will find materials over there on the desk. If you need anything else you may ring the bell near the door and a fellow Apprentice will be more than happy to come and assist you," the High Keeper said and made his way towards the door.

"Thank you, High Keeper," Jarrell said.

The High Keeper dipped is head.

"Mister Ernhold has requested that he not leave until he has the documents back in his possession, so he will be remaining here while you work, if you do not mind of course."

Jarrell nodded, and then, the High Keeper was gone, and he was alone except for the cloaked man who still sat silently at the other end of the table. The Apprentice made his way around to the desk, trying not to stare at Ernhold, and began organizing his things. Carefully, Jarrell carried the open binder of pages over to the desk but before he could begin reading the man spoke.

"Be careful with those pages, Apprentice. They were not easy to come by," the man said in an icy voice that sent shivers up Jarrell's spine. This was the first he had heard the man speak and now Jarrell wished Ernhold had remained silent. "I do not suppose you know the story of Gerhold of Vilheim, do you?"

Jarrell nodded.

"I am familiar, though no one knows of what happened to him. If these are real, then this should be a very interesting tale indeed, and perhaps they can shed light on his disappearance," Jarrell answered though he wished the man had remained silent.

"They are real, I assure you. If I were you, I would start where at the first marker, since it sounds as though you already know what has happened with him before that point."

"I always start at the beginning," Jarrell said, but Ernhold scoffed and shook his head.

"Come now, you do not need to re-read everything you already know. Besides, you wanted proof that these are legitimate?" Ernhold pointed to the little black bookmark sticking out of the pile of papers.

Jarrell sighed and realized that he really did want to find out about the story. He could be the first Keeper to ever find out what happened to Gerhold of Vilheim, which sounded grand even though it really meant nothing. Still, the Keepers did know everything about the slayer's story up to the point when he disappeared, so maybe starting ahead would not be such a bad idea after all.

A Symphony of Blood

Besides, he needed proof that these were authentic. After finally convincing himself, Jarrell lifted the other pages away, glanced quickly at the hastily scrawled map on the back of a worn piece of parchment, and then started to read.

Arendor
Castle
Ravencroft
The
Greenwood
Two Rivers
South to
Vilheim
The Iron
Mountains

A Symphony of Blood

Chapter 1: A Strange Village

The little village of Two Rivers stood silent in the cool night air as a winter storm approached the remote hills and forests of central Arendor. Most of the inhabitants had already made their way home or had settled in for a drink at the tavern, leaving the snow dusted roads through town all but deserted. An old man named Oswin stood alone behind the old tavern with a large axe in hand, chopping much needed wood for the fire inside. Winters in Arendor were particularly cold, especially when living this close to the Iron Mountains, and so ample supply of firewood was a necessity to survive the months of freezing winds and snow. Oswin had owned the little tavern for years and being the only place for miles around that had a steady supply of drink, he managed to keep a consistent profit. He finished chopping the last piece of wood but paused before heading back inside. Wood was needed for the fire, but he had an ulterior reason for being out in the dead of night in the freezing cold: he was waiting for someone.

Oswin leaned against a nearby wall and pulled a folded letter out of his coat pocket. Written on it in smooth slanted letters was an order from his lord. The old man poured over the few words that had been written on the page for what felt like the twentieth time. He was looking for a man, though no description was given, only a name: Gerhold of Vilheim. He had heard of this name before in the stories told by bards and travelers alike. He was a hunter, though he sought a far more dangerous game than most who held that title. Gerhold was a monster slayer, one whose name was known far and wide, even in a remote village such as Two Rivers. Oswin was to look for this man and give him something, a similar letter to his own. For what reason, he was not sure, and he dared not ask. His lord was not one to tolerate foolish questions, failure, or disobedience.

 Oswin always thought of himself as a good man, and he did what he had to do to take care of his village and his people, as his father had done before him. There was a dark secret that was hidden beneath the surface of the little town, one that few besides those who lived in the village knew. The lord they served was not one of Arendian noble blood, nor did he have a name that was known far and wide. He was a dark lord, secretive and powerful, and Oswin dared not anger him. They did as they were asked, and if they did, then their lord would be happy, and Two Rivers would be safe. Oswin was asked to find this man, and so find him he would.

 Suddenly, he heard the soft clip-clop of hooves echoing from somewhere off in the distance and he felt his heartrate increase as a silhouette appeared in the darkness at the edge of town. A man came riding into view on the back of a dark horse. He wore a long brown coat with the hood pulled up to obscure his face. The clanking sound of a sword could be heard as he approached, and Oswin watched with keen interest as the man made his way down the snow-covered path to the front of the tavern. Was this the man he was waiting for? Without hesitating, Oswin picked up the arm load of firewood and made his way back inside his little tavern through the back door.

 As soon as the door was open, he felt the warm embrace of the tavern, and them an hung up his cloak before making his way back out to where his guests could be heard. It was a small tavern with only a few tables scattered here and there and a small bar lined with carved wooden stools. The fire roared in the corner of the room and warmed the open common area. A few men sat at the tables near the far end while a lonely minstrel played a solemn song while Oswin made his way across the room and placed the load of firewood down near the fire. Suddenly the door to the room opened and in walked the hooded man. The others in the room turned their attention to the newcomer, eyeing his strange garb as well as the silver longsword that hung at his hip. The man seemed not to mind and closed the door behind him before making his way across the room to the bar. The minstrel began his next song and Oswin waited as the gloomy tune filled the tavern.

 "Hunters asleep beneath the trees,
Hiding from the cold night's breeze.
Farmers lock their doors behind,

A Symphony of Blood

While fears all settle in their minds.

The watchmen, awake all through the night,
Fearing what lay beyond their sight.
But little they know of beasts beyond,
Closing in as the night grows on.

And the children, they huddle tight,
for whispers of beasts in the night.
Oh, they echo, both far and wide,
there's nowhere to hide.
Nowhere to hide.

Claws and teeth and glowing eyes,
they hunt men down as daylight dies.
Ghouls and ghosts and nightmares come,
They stay all night until the dawn.

But there are those that heed the call,
And come to fight the evil spawn.
And low, when the need is dire still,
The Seekers come to haunted hill.

And the folk, they flee and cry,
for the whispers of beasts in the night.
Oh, they echo, both far and wide,
there's nowhere to hide.
Nowhere to hide.

Up all night and lying-in wait,
The Seekers hunt their evil prey.
Silver swords and holy spells,
The Seekers send them to the hells.

So, when you hear the call of death,
Fear not the jaws and claws so red.

For the Seekers come to haunted halls,
And purify the world for all.

And the Seekers, they come to fight,
for the whispers of beasts in the night.
Oh, they echo, both far and wide.
There's nowhere to hide, from the Seekers' light."

Oswin tossed a few new logs on the fire and then turned to greet this new guest who was sitting alone at the bar.

"Good evening, sir," he said and moved behind the bar. "Cold night to be out travelling."

"There are times when it is not our choice when to travel," the man answered.

"So, where are you coming from?" Oswin asked.

"From the south," the man answered.

"We don't get many visitors all the way up here who aren't merchants or woodsmen," another man said suspiciously. "Strange folk bring strange questions."

"And answers that are not your concern," the man snapped back.

"If you don't mind me asking, what can I call ye?" Oswin asked, trying to hide his eagerness to hear the name.

"I am Gerhold of Vilheim," he answered, and hush fell about the room, followed by whispers.

"What did he say?" a man whispered. "Did he say Gerhold?"

"That's what I heard," another answered.

Oswin swallowed nervously.

"We heard of ye before, slayer," one of the men said and stood. Oswin recognized him as Goran, a logger. Not the brightest man but both large and strong. "And we don't need any of that around here. Things are nice and quiet in Two Rivers, and that's the way we like it."

"If that were the truth then I wouldn't be here, would I?" Gerhold answered.

Goran was hot-headed and ill tempered. He never thought more than a few seconds ahead and that usually got him into trouble. Only Oswin knew of the letter and that meant Goran and the others would try to drive Gerhold off, most likely fearing that his mere presence would anger their lord.

"And why would a man, such as yourself, be coming to old Two Rivers?" the old barkeeper asked, trying to change the subject and keep Goran out of the conversation.

"I am searching for someone, a woman," he said. "She's been taken."

"Well, I usually know most of what goes on here in town, and I haven't seen nor heard of anything like that," Oswin said.

If he could just get the slayer to leave, then he could hand off the letter without any problems.

Just then Goran stood and crossed the room.

"We don't need ye here," the big man said.

Gerhold did not answer, but Oswin could see his eyes shining from beneath his hood.

"Sit down, Goran," Oswin said. "I'll speak with the hunter."

"No need, Oswin, the slayer is leaving, now," Goran said.

Two more men stood and made their way over. Both had short swords hung at their sides, though neither appeared to be a warrior. Oswin could feel the blood rushing to his face in anger.

"I still have business here," Gerhold answered again. "Which means I am not leaving until it's finished."

"You'll leave now," Goran said and reached out to grab the stranger's shoulder.

Before Goran or anyone else in the room could even blink, Gerhold whipped around and knocked the big man's hand to the side before driving his elbow into Goran's face. Goran fell backwards, blood pouring from his nose, while the other two men reached for the swords in their belts. Before either could draw them though, Gerhold's silver sword was in his hand.

"Stop this nonsense," Oswin said and moved from behind the bar.

Goran climbed slowly to his feet, a dazed look in his eyes as he tried to staunch the flow of blood coming from his nose.

"Those won't do you much good against me," Gerhold said and pulled back his hood, revealing ebony skin and a mangy beard. His eyes were deep and cold and his brow heavy.

"There's no need for that," Oswin said and waved the other men off. "You three get out of here, go on home."

The two men traded glances, hands still on their weapons. For a few tense moments they stared at Gerhold, until finally one of them drew his weapon. Oswin knew what would come next and so he ducked behind the bar as one of the heavy wooden chairs went sailing overhead and slammed into the wall behind him. Glass bottles shattered and spilt mead drenched the wooden floor of the tavern as the sound of clanging steel echoed throughout the room, followed by a scream of pain. Oswin climbed to his knees and peered up over the edge of the bar and was met with the sight of a bloody mangled body on the floor while three other men were in the midst of a sword fight. Gerhold was a blur, his strikes fast and efficient, and a moment later, a second scream echoed out as another of the villagers was struck down. Goran held a short sword in his hand, blood pouring from his injured nose, but instead of turning and fighting the monster slayer, the big logger almost fell backwards as he ran out the door.

The tavern stood silent as Oswin slowly stood to survey the damage. Two bodies lay in the middle of the floor, blood pooling beneath them, and most of the tables had been overturned or knocked to the side. Gerhold stood in the middle of the carnage, silver sword still in hand. A moment later he turned and faced the old barkeeper.

"Strange village you have here," Gerhold said and sheathed his sword. "At least I know I'm on the right trail."

"You didn't have to kill them," Oswin muttered.

"You're right, I didn't," Gerhold answered. "Now, how about you start telling me what I want to know."

The barkeep swallowed nervously.

"I have something for you," Oswin said and reached slowly into his coat pocket. "I was told to give this to you."

"Then hand it over," Gerhold answered.

"Here, a letter," Oswin said and handed over the parchment. "We are but humble loggers and fishermen."

"On the surface, certainly," Gerhold muttered and took the letter. He read through it quickly and then stuffed it into his coat before turning his cold eyes back to Oswin. "Are you a thrall?"

Oswin raised his eyebrows and frowned.

"I'm sorry, I don't know what you mean," he said.

Gerhold's eyes narrowed.

"Then you serve by choice."

"I do what is asked of me, nothing more," Oswin said. "If you truly are

A Symphony of Blood

Gerhold of Vilheim, then you know we have no choice."

"There is always a choice," Gerhold said and pulled his hood up. "Pray to whatever gods you serve that I do not return for you."

With that, the monster hunter turned and disappeared into the cold night, leaving the door ajar behind him. Oswin felt his heart start to slow down as the sound pounding hooves faded. The old man poured himself a drink of firewash and downed the burning alcohol in one gulp before making his way up the stairs to the second floor of the inn. There was a single room here and he made sure to lock the door after entering. In the corner was a poorly made bed and a small desk, and to the left was an old window. He sat down at the desk and just as he did a small black shadow came fluttering across the room and landed nearby. Oswin looked at the black raven and sighed before picking up a pen and quill and jotting down a quick message.

The hunter is on his way.

That was all he wrote before rolling up the parchment and sliding it into the bird's talons. He opened the nearby window and in an instant the raven disappeared into the night. Oswin sat back down in his desk chair and shook his head. Another man sent to his doom in those accursed woods and mountains. He had lost track of how many he had sent and how few had returned. He had no choice though; it was either that or disappear himself. It was a terrible thing, but it was necessary for the survival of Two Rivers.

Oswin sighed and remembered that he would still have to dispose of the bodies before turning in for the night. Goran would not be missed, but it could bring unwanted attention if people continued to go missing. At least he had no family to speak of and the other two were nothing more than muscle. Still, Oswin was worried about the hunter, this, Gerhold of Vilheim. He was different than the others he had sent into the hills. He was a fighter, and a good one at that from what he had seen downstairs, but even Gerhold of Vilheim knew not who he was about to face. The Lord of the Iron Mountains was not one to be trifled with. That would be the last he would see of the slayer, Oswin was sure of it, and so he stood up and prepared to dispose of the bodies in his tavern.

Further up the road, Gerhold had slowed his horse and was waiting on a small ridge overlooking the village, his keen eyes scanning the night sky for anything out of the ordinary. Suddenly, a small black silhouette appeared amidst the stars and Gerhold watched as it soared overhead and disappeared. The barkeeper had sent a message to someone, most likely it was who Gerhold was chasing. His enemies knew he was coming, there was no denying that now, but he had no other option other than to press on. A moment later he nudged his horse forward and continued down the snow-streaked path in the direction of the mountain peaks visible along the dark horizon.

A Symphony of Blood

Chapter 2: The Challenge

-Gerhold of Vilheim, Journal Entry: December 14, 5843 of the Common Age

  It has been just over a month since Lord Friedrich came to me and requested that I hunt down the vampire that kidnapped his wife, and I have spent the time travelling far into the north, following the clues left for me by the monster. It wants me to follow, and it wants me to know where it is going, though, I know not why. Perhaps I slew a distant relation or a servant of some sorts, or maybe there is something far more sinister at play here. Whatever the reason, the monster requested Lord Friedrich hire me if he ever wanted to see his wife alive again, and so I could not turn him down.

  I am in the final leg of the journey, at least according to the directions left for me at the small village of Two Rivers. What a wretched place. It was clear from the moment I entered the little village that it was a place tainted by evil. Perhaps I should have slaughtered them all, as The Seekers would have done, but alas I cannot bring myself to do such a cruel thing. The men who attacked me deserved their fates, and I may still pay the innkeeper another visit on my way back down the mountain, as he was clearly working with the monster. However, I must keep to my true purpose, as who knows what horrors Lady Friedrich has already been subjected to.

  The weather has only gotten worse the farther I travel into these accursed mountains. I passed through an area the locals call the Greenwood, and now I climb ever higher into the peaks and crags of the Iron Mountains. The path is carved directly into the cliff sides and looks as if men have spent a lifetime building it. I can only imagine how long this filth has lived and terrorized these parts. The corruption is palatable, almost as if I can smell the stink of evil in the air.

J.S. Matthews

I know not what lies ahead, but whatever the monster has planned it will not be enough, not when he deals with Gerhold of Vilheim.

The air was frigid and deadly as Gerhold dropped his head and trudged on slowly through the knee-deep snow, shielding his face from the gusts of freezing wind and sheets of blinding snow. The Iron Mountains were treacherous even during the warmest of summers and no man would dare enter them this late in winter, but Gerhold of Vilheim was not just any man. His name was known far and wide throughout Tyriel, and there were few who did not know of his deeds. He was a hunter of beasts and monsters, demons, and specters, and here, deep in these unforgiving mountains, he sought his prey. These tall, isolated peaks were the perfect hiding spot for the monster, as the mountainsides seldom saw the light of the sun, and there was nothing a vampire hated more than sunlight.

Gerhold was a tall man with dark hair and ebony skin to go with a thick, matted beard that hid most of the stoic features of his nearly fifty-year-old face. A chiseled veteran he was, an experienced and dangerous man and a hunter of all evil things. His eyes were as cold as the snowy peaks and frozen winds that surrounded him, and his scars told the stories of a hundred battles against monsters and creatures of darkness. He wore a long, thick, overcoat with a hood pulled up over his head, and a small pack and heavy crossbow were slung over his shoulder. A silver long sword was sheathed at his side, and a shiny gold medallion dangled from his neck.

It had been a hard journey getting here and he knew that wherever he was going he needed to reach it with the strength and will to fight. He had passed through overgrown forest paths and then through the rocky crags of the hills at the foot of the Iron Mountains. These frozen and treacherous peaks had been the longest stretch of the trip so far, as he was forced to pull his horse along due to the slippery mountain roads. His interaction with the villagers at Two Rivers had all but confirmed his suspicions that this was where he would find the vampire's lair. He had encountered similar instances before. Vampires were powerful and intelligent creatures, and fear was their most effective weapon. The villagers in Two Rivers were indebted to the monster, and so they did his bidding, whether it be sending travelers into the mountains for the vampires to capture and feed on or driving away unsavory outsiders. In exchange for these deeds, they were allowed to live.

An image of burning cottages and screaming men and women infiltrated his mind, and Gerhold found himself running through the words of the song the minstrel had been singing back in Two Rivers. The Seekers come to haunted halls, to purify the world for all, he found himself muttering in disgust. He had once been a Seeker, but he found early on a distaste for their methods. If they had been in his place back in Two Rivers, the place would be a smoldering graveyard now. Gerhold was more concerned with the creature pulling their strings. Once the vampire was dealt with, the villagers would be free. He still felt anger thinking about men like the barkeeper sending travelers to their deaths or hunters into the clutches of monsters, all to save their own skins, but from their point of view it was understandable.

Gerhold pulled his long coat closer around him as he continued down the winding icy road, trying to focus on his steps and not on the freezing winds. The path he followed was a wide, flat road cut into the mountainside, but every step had to be taken with the utmost care. Driving winds stung his face and made it nearly impossible to see, while the path was slick with thick layers of ice beneath the snow. One wrong step, one slip, would lead to a long fall over the cliff and certain death. Still, he pushed on, motivated by the mission he had accepted and by his will. Finally, the path turned, and ahead he saw a large valley open, like a massive bowl filled with tall, snow-dusted pines and icy, jagged rocks. The path continued along the mountainside, twisting this way and that, until it stopped in front of a massive stone bridge.

Gerhold looked far down the valley at two huge stone spires, on top of which were built two equally large castles of stone connected by a suspended causeway. Many turrets and towers jutted upwards from the mighty fortress like sharp teeth, and dots of flickering light marked the windows throughout the fortress. A long bridge connected the castle entrance to the mountain path and was the only visible way in, so he adjusted the grey scarf around his neck to protect most of his face from the winds and pressed on towards the foreboding citadel in the distance.

As he walked, the winds began to slowly die down and the clouds opened so that patches of starry skies could be seen poking through, and by the time he had reached the foot of the stone bridge the valley was bathed in the soft, silvery light of the twin moons above. Gerhold paused and took a deep breath before hefting the large crossbow from his back and loading it with a long silver bolt, and he did the same with two smaller crossbows that were holstered on his lower back. These were designed specially for him. They were made so that the arms of the little crossbows folded in to allow easy storage but could be opened and ready to fire at a moment's notice. They were also able to hold five of the small bolts a piece before needing to be reloaded, and Gerhold found himself admiring their craftsmanship nearly every time he pulled them out. Finally, he tugged at the silver long sword that hung at his side to make sure it did not stick in the scabbard because of the frost. Many great warriors had died because they overlooked the little things, and Gerhold was never one to ignore even the slightest detail.

    The hunter pulled a little vial containing a mouthful of orange liquid from his pack and gulped it down, reveling in the warmth that spread throughout his body. It was a simple warming potion, and though Gerhold was no alchemist he understood how important even the slightest advantage could prove to be. Frozen and stiff muscles would cause him to falter in battle, and that was something that would prove fatal against a vampire. He took one more deep breath and let it out slowly while gripping the golden medallion that dangled from his neck. It had three symbols etched into it, one for each of the three Gods he served, and he gave the medallion a small kiss before taking his first step onto the stone bridge. Now that he was this close the towering castle loomed over him and its immense size and grandeur made Gerhold wonder just how long this vampire had been living in these mountains? The bridge was ten feet wide and built from solid smooth, stones, and the castle looked no less impressive as he drew nearer to the front gates. The wooden doors stood at the top of a short staircase and Gerhold did not stop or falter as he climbed the stone steps, and then stood in front of the castle entrance. Intricate carvings covered every inch of the wood, and he could pick out a few demonic and wicked ancient symbols. The golden medallion around his neck trembled slightly while is horse shifted uncomfortably as if sensing something wrong in the air.

    "Whatever evil lies behind these doors, may the strength, grace, and mercy of the Three Divines watch over and protect me. Grant me victory over this darkness. Amen," Gerhold said aloud in his low, rugged voice.

    He reached out and knocked on the thick oak doors and heard the bangs of his fist echo off the stone walls within. It only took a moment before he heard the loud scratching of metal on metal as the great doors opened inward, and the warm glow of the inner light washed over Gerhold and the front steps. The hunter gripped his crossbow a little tighter, not sure what was going to come from within the castle. Inside were three skinny men dressed in the typical garbs

A Symphony of Blood

of servants, and though they appeared to pose no immediate threat to him, the hunter rested his loaded crossbow against his shoulder and kept vigilant for anything suspicious. One of the servants started to speak and Gerhold noticed the familiar droning and hypnotic tone of the man's voice.

"Good evening sir, and welcome to Ravencroft Castle. You are Gerhold of Vilheim?" the man said in a monotone and Gerhold nodded. "That is good; my master has been expecting you. If you will follow me this way, I will take you to him."

Gerhold stared at the servant for a moment and glanced back at the long stone bridge, wondering just how much he should trust the servant at all. A moment later he nodded and stepped into the entry hall, still not releasing the strong grip he held on the crossbow, and his eyes darted every which way, on the lookout for any movement or threat. Two of the servants stayed behind, one proceeded to shut the thick wooden doors while the other led Gerhold's horse out of view. The third led on down the hall. The three men were thralls, vampire slaves, men who had their blood drained so many times by the same vampire that they had become dependent upon their master's survival and magically bonded to the monster's will. They were not as dangerous as the vampires they were enslaved to, but great numbers of the weak could overwhelm even the mightiest of warriors. Gerhold was no fool, and he knew that no matter how weak and feeble these thralls were, they were still a threat, for their very lives depended upon the life of their master.

The vampire wanted him to follow, and now he sent servants to greet him as if he were some sort of honored guest. Something was going on, something sinister for sure but Gerhold did not know the true intentions of his host. He considered killing the thralls then and there and then proceeding into the rest of the castle, but his years of experience told him to wait. To see just what this vampire had in store for him. Besides, he came here to rescue the woman, and since this vampire knew Gerhold was coming, it would certainly have something planned. For now, he had to stay his hand and be patient until the creature revealed its intentions. Only then could he strike.

Finally, they reached the end of the long hall and the servant opened another door which led into a large dining room. Three great tables lined the center of the room and along the farthest wall there stood a raised stone platform bearing a fourth table. Calling the hall grand would not have done it justice, and Gerhold examined the large stained-glass windows that covered each wall and the golden chandeliers that hung from the high, vaulted ceiling above. Every bannister, column, and door were etched with intricate carvings and designs, and even the wood tables looked as though they belonged in the hall of the High King. Music echoed throughout the hall from some other distant part of the castle, and the rumbling notes of the organ filled the dining room with an eerie, unnatural feeling. The servant opened another door which led to a smaller room with bookshelves lining the walls and thick, red, comfy chairs in the center of the room. At the far end was a large organ that was being played by a man wearing a dark cape, and even from behind, Gerhold knew this was the Lord of Ravencroft. The thin servant left Gerhold by the door as he crossed the room and whispered something in his master's ear. Immediately the rumbling music disappeared, as the vampire turned slowly to stare at his newly arrived guest.

"Gerhold of Vilheim, I presume?" the vampire said, and his smooth, airy voice echoed throughout the room. "I am glad you were finally able to make it to my estate, I do hope the journey wasn't too hard on you."

He had a thin, well-groomed mustache and black hair that was slicked back to reveal a high, noble brow. He raised his hand and beckoned Gerhold forward.

"Come in sir, come in! You and I have much to discuss and very little time in which to discuss it." Gerhold stared at the vampire with his cold eyes and then took his first step into the study.

A thrall closed the door behind him, leaving the two alone in the room.

For a moment, the two just stared at each other, the hunter and his prey, though Gerhold wondered which he was this time. The vampire was tall, handsome, and wore a long black cape and matching doublet of blood red velvet. Silver rings adorned many of his fingers and a golden handled sword hung loosely at his side. This creature was old, very old, and Gerhold could sense the aura of experience and power that clung to the creature like an evil shadow.

"You know you are not as tall as I had imagined, what with the tales of all your exploits. Even all the way up here in this untamed country I have heard your named mentioned many a time, accompanied by some outlandish tale of slaying a hundred vampires with nothing more than your bare hands," the vampire said with a small bow that Gerhold did not return. "Of course, we both know that tales tend to be embellished some, but even if they are, your reputation is more than commendable."

"So, I have heard," Gerhold answered. "Even in Two Rivers."

"Ah, so you know my connection to that pathetic village?" The Vampire asked.

"It was not much of a mystery," Gerhold said and nodded towards the raven that still sat on its perch.

"Subtlety has never been their strongest trait, I must admit."

"Nor is it mine, so let's dispense with the pleasantries," Gerhold added. "Where is the woman?"

"I think it would be more proper for me to introduce myself first," the lord said pleasantly but Gerhold's hard face never changed. "I am Lord Harkin Valakir, and Lady Friedrich is safe for the time being. Before we get to that though, I want to know more about you. Also, I would be a poor host to not offer you refreshment. Perhaps you would like a drink or some roast chicken? You must be famished after such a long journey."

"I came here for the woman, not your hospitality," Gerhold answered.

"I guess slayers lack the basics in etiquette," Harkin added.

Gerhold shrugged.

"I'm a monster hunter, not a nobleman," he said. "Besides, what does a vampire need food for?"

"Oh, it is not for me but for the thralls. They have to eat too."

"Feed them well, do you?" Gerhold asked.

"Blood of a starving wretch is never a filling meal. Also, starving worker is a poor worker, or so the saying goes."

"Where have you taken Lady Friedrich?" Gerhold continued. He did not want to spend his time bantering with this creature.

"How about we start with you instead," Harkin took a sip from his cup and leaned against a nearby shelf. "You are familiar with Lord Alnor Bram, correct?"

Gerhold's eyes narrowed.

"Somewhat, though, my sword had a far more intimate relationship with him than I."

"I knew him some time ago, though we were never very close friends," Harkin said in a haughty tone as if dismissing the notion that he would ever have been close to his fellow vampire. "He worked for me from time to time, at least, until you killed him."

"If you are waiting for an apology, you won't be getting one," Gerhold said.

Harkin waved his hand dismissively.

"An apology? No, no I was hoping you would be able to tell me the story. I've heard rumors, of course, but a firsthand account would be far more interesting than hearsay from some tavern wench or travelling bard. So, would you mind regaling me with the tale?"

Gerhold glared at the vampire. Was Harkin stalling for something? For now, the slayer decided to play the vampire's little game. For now, at least.

"I tracked a servant of his to a crypt outside Kingsport. Your kind is always overconfident."

"A trait you seem to share with us," the vampire said with a mischievous grin.

"The guards I dispatched with this," Gerhold said, ignoring the jest and raising his crossbow. "Those inside the crypt were few and fell just the same."

"And Lord Bram?" the vampire asked and raised is eyebrows.

"A silver blade through the heart," Gerhold answered. "A fate, I think, you shall share soon."

Harkin threw his head back and laughed at the threat.

"What a tale, indeed," he said. "You lack the story telling ability of a bard, but I suppose I can appreciate you getting straight to the point. Bram was a bit of a fool. He wasn't even a lord, truly. Self-appointed more like."

"And you are?" Gerhold quipped.

Harkin raised his hands and gestured the grand room.

"Look around you, Gerhold. This castle is rivaled by only a few across this entire world. Its design is flawless, its art impeccable, and its defenses impenetrable. This entire region bends to my unseen will, as you noticed in Two Rivers, and my influence has spread much further than even a slayer like you would understand. I have informants across the realms on every continent, both those of the dark curse and not. My servants are numerous and my power extensive. Lord is hardly a title befitting one of my power and status, slayer. I have existed on this world for hundreds of years, and I will continue to. So, I suppose the title of Lord is not accurate, because I am far more than that."

The vampire sneered at Gerhold and took another sip from his chalice, but Gerhold was not impressed or intimidated.

"You may grant yourself whatever title you wish, but for me, there is only one title I will grant you: prey." Gerhold responded. "And now you know that the stories of me are true, you should understand exactly how much danger

A Symphony of Blood

you are in."

"Yes, I believed as much, even before meeting you," Harkin said with a smile. "Your reputation precedes you Gerhold, a reputation as the greatest slayer in all of Tyriel. At first, I believed the stories to be exaggerations, as I said before, but after so many years of hearing tale after tale about you, I came to the realization that they must be true. It was then that I decided I had to meet you."

"Is that why you took the lady? To meet me. I would have been happy to introduce myself had you just sent an invitation," Gerhold said and patted the crossbow in threatening manner. "I am always willing to meet with your kind."

"I know you would have come, but the woman was necessary as well. You see, having you here was just not enough, I needed something else; a carrot on the end of the stick one might say."

"If you knew I would come anyway then why take the woman?" Gerhold asked again.

"She was a needed goal, a reward for my challenge," the lord took another drink. "I needed something to motivate you. It's always more fun when the hero has something to lose."

"Enough with the games, vampire, where is the woman?" This time he raised the crossbow and held it with both hands.

Gerhold had grown tired of these games, and he was not going to waste any more time bantering with the likes of Harkin. Over the years he had encountered many vampires like this one and each had died just the same, but he reminded himself that the woman must come first. Harkin stood for a moment as if contemplating something.

"You wish to know where the woman is?" the vampire asked rhetorically.

Gerhold tightened his grip on the crossbow.

"Fine, I will tell you," the lord responded and made his way out of the little study and back into the grand dining hall. He bade Gerhold to follow. "The woman is being held in the highest tower of my castle just above the clock tower." Harkin said as he marched across the empty hall.

"Then our conversation is at an end," Gerhold said and raised the crossbow again, ready to fire.

"I would not do that if I were you, not if you want to see the woman alive again," Harkin said in his smooth tone and climbed the steps to his golden throne and sat.

"Give me one reason to keep you alive?" Gerhold asked.

"Because Lady Friedrich's life depends on me," the vampire answered. "You kill me, and she dies. Our fates, as of now, are intertwined you might say."

"Tell me what you want monster. Now!"

Harkin laughed and shook his head.

"A contest, dear Gerhold, a challenge that only the greatest slayer in the world could succeed in." He took one last sip from the chalice and tossed it aside, causing the glass cup to shatter. The vampire's eyes flashed a deep black, as if consumed by the dark ravenous pupils, only to slowly fade back to their original crimson color. "I told you I needed a goal for you, and she is it. I did not simply wish to meet you, slayer, but rather I wanted to see if the rumors were true. Why else would I go to so much effort to get you here? If I wanted to kill you, I could have had a hundred vampires and servants hunt you down. No, I do not want you dead, at least not yet. I want to test you first; I want to see just how great the famous Gerhold of Vilheim truly is. What better way to see for myself than to come up with a little game for the two of us to play?"

"And what sort of a game is this?" Gerhold asked, still with the crossbow pointed at the lord.

Harkin reached into his doublet and pulled out a golden ring and held it up so Gerhold could see.

"You know what this is, slayer, do you not?"

Immediately Gerhold felt the golden medallion around his neck start to tremble again, and his eyes narrowed. The hunter did not answer right away but stared at the little ring with a look of disgust.

"Cursed gold," he said finally. "Taken from Arden thousands of years ago when humans were expelled from those lands by the Three Divines for their betrayal."

"So, you know your history," Harkin answered.

"Everyone knows the story of Arden," Gerhold said. "Of the great betrayal."

"Yes, six gods betrayed the creator, two stayed loyal," Harkin said. "Humans trapped in the middle of a war between the Divines, destined to fall as well."

"Evil men with ill intent led to the fall of man, not destiny," Gerhold added. "That is why the paradise of Arden was destroyed."

"Arden?" Harkin repeated. "The mysterious island land created to protect humans from the evils of the six Betrayers. What a fantastic tale. If you

A Symphony of Blood

know of Arden, then I am sure you know of the story that comes after."

An old poem made its way into Gerhold's mind and he started repeating the words without a second thought.

> "But evil came into their thoughts,
> And men forgot that which they sought.
> Pursuing things of power and might,
> Deceived by darkness in their plight.
> Becoming gods, that was their goal,
> And to destroy that which was old.
> Plot they did, for powers sake,
> To leave this realm and then to take,
> That which they believed was right.
> In Arden where there is no light."

Harkin laughed and clapped mockingly as Gerhold finished the poem.

"Bravo, Gerhold. A scholar and slayer? Quite impressive," he said with a smile that showed off his elongated fangs. "Hubris and pride are the greatest enemy of man."

"And monsters," Gerhold added.

"Perhaps," Harkin said. "Man rebelled against the Gods, the created against their creator, and in their hubris, they allowed evil to enter their paradise."

"And were enslaved by it for a thousand years," Gerhold continued. "Humans were only saved when they repented, and only then were they rescued by the very creator that they turned their backs on."

"But you know then, that when the Divines forced humans out of Arden, they told them to take only what they wished them to take. When some of the survivors decided to bring their gold and jewels with them, a curse was placed upon the treasures for all time. Any human who touches one of these pieces of cursed treasure will be cursed in turn, but you know all of this, do you not?" Harkin asked rhetorically and rolled the little ring between his fingers.

"I did not know creatures of evil believed in the Three." Gerhold answered.

"Even the Betrayers believe in the creator, but that does not mean they follow him. However, what I believe matters very little. You have heard this story a hundred times, I am sure."

"Why retell what I already know?"

"Because it is important. You see, dear Lady Friedrich came into possession of a piece of this lost treasure only a few weeks ago," the vampire let the words hang for a moment but Gerhold's stare did not soften.

"You cursed her?" he asked, already knowing the answer.

"She took the gift of her own free will, not knowing what it was of course, but that makes no difference," Harkin said with an evil smile.

"How long does she have?"

"A few hours at the most. Which is why you do not want to kill me just yet."

"I did not come here to banter with you, creature. What is it I need to do to save the woman?" Gerhold said angrily and fingered the crossbow trigger.

"As I said, I have a challenge for you Gerhold. A challenge that only a man of your reputation can win, if the stories are true that is." Harkin smiled again. "Lady Friedrich has only a few hours before the curse will complete its cycle. If you can reach the highest tower and the woman in time and if you can return her safely to this hall before the curse has run its course, then I will provide you with the cursed gold piece and the ability to save her from an eternity of undeath."

"That's impossible," Gerhold said. "There is no way to stop the curse once it has begun."

Harkin laughed again.

"For you, maybe, but as a vampire I have knowledge you do not. In your arrogance you forget, though a monster I may be, I have lived for far longer than you ever will. The curse can be stopped, but you need the very piece of cursed treasure to do it."

"And what is stopping me from killing you and taking that right now?" Gerhold asked and nodded in the direction of the ring.

Harkin laughed.

"Come now, slayer, I am not a complete fool. This is not the same piece I gave to her and besides, I doubt you know how to destroy it. Both the gold and the knowledge to destroy it shall remain hidden until you return with the woman. That is, if you return with her. This castle is a dangerous place, and its other inhabitants may not be as welcoming as I have been. That is your challenge, Gerhold of Vilheim, to make your way through my castle and rescue the woman. Only then will I truly believe all the tales I have heard of you. So, what do you

A Symphony of Blood

say? Do you accept this challenge, or do you leave the woman to an eternal death and become what you have hunted for so many years? The choice is yours, but I assure you, if you kill me now then she will die as well."

Gerhold glared at the vampire and pondered his words. After only a moment he slowly lowered the crossbow.

"Alright, monster, I will play your game, for now. But know this, whether she lives or not, I will be coming for your head," Gerhold threatened, and the two glared at each other for a moment.

"I look forward to it, slayer. Now, if I were you, I would get started. You have only a few hours to make your way to the highest tower, though, may I give one last suggestion?" Harkin asked and Gerhold waited before nodding. "You see I am not an unfair host and seeing how the odds are already stacked against you I have decided to give you a small bit of assistance."

"I need no help from you," Gerhold said, but Harkin waved his hand as if dismissing the response.

"Do not be a fool, you have never been to my castle before and its sheer size will ruin any chance you have of reaching her in time. As I said, I am a gracious host, and I will not have you running a race you cannot win."

"So, give me a map and be done with it."

Harkin chuckled and licked his lips.

"Actually, I have something a bit more fun in mind. If you head up the stairs and down the hall, there will be a door leading to my dungeons," the vampire said with a cryptic smile. "Inside you will meet someone. Someone who will serve as your guide."

"I will be fine on my own." Gerhold answered, but Harkin only laughed again.

"You are fool if you do not seek him out, and I doubt you will even make it past my first challenge without him. You can find this guide in the last cell in the dungeon. Now, I suggest you get started; you do not have all night after all. Compose for me a symphony of blood, slayer, and maybe, just maybe, you will leave here alive."

For a moment, Gerhold considered raising the crossbow and killing the monster then and there, but a picture of Lady Friedrich leapt into his mind and stopped him before he could even lift the weapon. He had no choice, and he was going to have to play the creature's game if he wanted to rescue Lady Friedrich. Besides, he would have time to kill Harkin after he saved her, and if he did not, then the monster would die anyway.

Without another word, Gerhold turned and made his way towards the stairs. If the creature was being honest then he only had a few hours before the gold consumed the woman's soul, and then there was nothing that could be done for her. A few hours to make his way through the castle and whatever traps and horrors lay within. He could try it alone, but then again that was not the wisest decision. If he wanted to make it to the woman in time and have a chance of saving her from the curse, then he would need a guide.

A Symphony of Blood

Chapter 3: An Unlikely Ally

    Gerhold sprinted up the stairs and then down a long hallway. The castle truly was enormous, and, as he ran down the hall, he could not help but admire the many tapestries, decorations, and paintings that lined the walls. Many of them depicted events from the fall of man and their expulsion from the paradise of Arden, while others were portraits of vampire lords and ladies. He passed by open rooms, one of which included a kitchen, and others that held more shelves of books or displays of armor and trinkets. Finally, he reached the end of the hallway and came to another open room with three doors, one across from where he stood and two more to the sides. Flanking each door were sets of finely crafted armor, and at the end of the room was another thrall.

    "Good evening, sir. Lord Harkin asked me to be of assistance if you wished to know which way you must go to reach the dungeons," the thrall said in his droning voice. Gerhold paused for a moment before nodding. "That is good; Vergil will be pleased when he finds out you are releasing him."

    "Vergil?" So that was the guide's name. "Which way then?" Gerhold asked impatiently and the man pointed to the door on the left.

    "This way. You will find Vergil in the furthest cell, but please do not disturb the other inmates."

    Gerhold did not bother to thank the man, as he knew it did not matter, and dashed to the door on his left. Thrall's had no mind of their own and no feelings beyond those to please their masters. Beyond the thick wooden door was another hallway lit by flickering torches and lined by a few small windows, and at the end of the little hall was a circular stairwell that led deep into the heart of the rock spire and to the dungeons below. Down the stairs he ran, two by two, until finally reaching the bottom and proceeding into another open room. Again, his medallion began to vibrate against his chest. At the center was a small wooden table with a brass key. Gerhold scooped up the little key and used it to unlock the door at the end of the room which led to a long corridor lined by prison cells. As soon as the door was open Gerhold was met by a cacophony of screams and shrieks.

"Feed us already! I need to feed!" A monster screamed.

"It has been days, Harkin! Where is our blood? Where is it?" Another shrieked and twenty other voices chimed in, though Gerhold did his best to ignore them as he entered the corridor, his eyes set on the last cell at the end of the hall.

"I smell something. Yes, yes, I do! Flesh! Blood!" One of the prisoners yelled and slammed hard against the thick metal door.

"I smell it too! Fresh meat it is! Fresh and juicy! Give it to me now!" Another growled and Gerhold realized the cells were filled with other vampires, starving ones by the sound of it. As he passed each cell, the inhabitant screamed and beat against the walls and metal door in an uncontrollable frenzy. Gerhold could see the glow of blood red eyes that stared through the small slot in each door, and noticed that each door was made of silver, an enchanted metal, a metal that all undead feared.

"It is! Fresh meat! Fresh blood! Curse you, Harkin! Curse you and all your house!"

Finally, Gerhold reached the end of the corridor and stopped in front of the last cell. He slid the little brass key into the lock and twisted it until he heard a click. The cell door creaked open to reveal a ten by ten-foot cell separated by a line of silver bars, and inside the cell sat a man. He wore a white button-down shirt and black pants, and a mane of long blonde hair hung low over his shoulders. But it was not the man's clothes or hair that caught Gerhold's attention; it was the tight, pale, skin that made the hunter do a double take. Vergil stood slowly and stared at the hunter for a moment before addressing him.

"You are here for the girl, aren't you?" the vampire asked and seemed to be examining Gerhold with great interest. Gerhold nodded in response. "And for my help."

"How did you know?" Gerhold asked and the man shrugged.

"Harkin came to see me a few weeks ago and explained his little game. He said I would need to help you if I wanted my freedom. So, are you here to rescue her or not?"

"I am," Gerhold said. "Harkin failed to mention what you were."

"What I am?" Vergil repeated with a smile, revealing his elongated fangs.

A Symphony of Blood

"I take it you haven't spent much time with vampires."

"I've killed enough to know you shouldn't be trusted," Gerhold answered and turned to leave.

"You will never reach her in time without my help," the vampire added, and Gerhold paused. "You leave me here, and that woman is as good as dead, and so are you."

Gerhold turned to face the creature.

"What can you offer me that I cannot get on my own?"

"Did Harkin not tell you who I am?" When Gerhold did not answer the vampire continued. "I am Vergil, the architect of this castle. I designed it and I helped build it. I know every passageway, every hall, every room, and every shortcut better than even the lord himself. I can guide you through these cold stone halls to your dear lady."

"And why would you wish to help me against one of your own kind?" Gerhold asked and Vergil laughed.

"Look at me? I have been locked in this same cell for nearly ten years. Harkin has seen fit to feed me and keep me alive just to allow an eternity of suffering. Why would I not help you?"

"What did you do?" Gerhold asked again.

"A man does not want to be a servant for his entire life, especially when that life never ends." Vergil answered with a grin and Gerhold nodded.

"You say you hate Harkin, and you are his enemy, but I do not trust vampires, not ever," he turned to leave again but Vergil called one last time.

"So, your plan is to go traipsing through the castle without a clue of where to go?" the vampire asked with a sarcastic smile and Gerhold glared at him. "You have no idea what he has planned for you. A hunter of your status should know just how much danger you have walked into by entering this castle. You are going to need all the help you can get, from whatever source. You know it."

"I will find my way well enough," Gerhold answered, though he was not sure if he believed those words.

"You will find your way, but by the time you reach your dear lady she will have already turned, that is if you can make it through whatever the lord has planned for you. Do you plan on fighting Harkin's small army by yourself?"

"I will manage," Gerhold said curtly and started making his way back out to the corridor of cells.

"If you get me out of this cell, I will help you. I swear on pain of death, and on the very gold that cursed me to this existence, that I will hold to that oath and will not betray you."

Gerhold turned back and stared at the vampire in silence, pondering the choice at hand. Should he trust this vampire? Perhaps it was a trick, a trap set by Harkin to undermine his efforts? Yet, there was only one question that mattered; did he even have a choice? He turned to Vergil who had still not moved from the center of his cell.

"How do I know you are not one of Harkin's traps? That he is planning on me trusting you?" Gerhold asked and the vampire shrugged.

"The only question you should be asking is whether you can afford to not trust me?" Vergil asked and raised is eyebrows. "I care nothing for this woman, but I have my own reasons for wanting to help you. This game Harkin has planned for you is heavily weighted in his favor. You need me as much as I need you if I am to escape this prison. Make your choice, slayer. Do you risk failing your quest, or do you release me, and have a chance to defeat Harkin Valakir?"

Gerhold stared at the monster and let out a frustrated sigh. He did not trust the vampire, but the question still stood. Could he afford to not accept the creature's help? Gerhold ground his teeth and clenched his fists, already knowing the answer to the question.

"If I free you, monster, you will help me find the woman, and if you decide to betray me, know that I will kill you without hesitation," Gerhold said and Vergil nodded.

"Agreed, though I wish to add one condition." Gerhold's eyes narrowed as Vergil leaned in against the silver bars of his cell. "Once we have rescued the lady and she is safe, then I want your promise that we will kill Harkin."

Gerhold raised an eyebrow and stared quizzically at Vergil, whose face remained unreadable.

"Is that all you want? To kill a fellow vampire?"

"That is all; if you promise me that, then I am yours until the deed is done." Gerhold stood for another moment, fighting against his instincts to kill the creature right then and there, but instead moved forward and slid the little key into the lock on the barred door.

"Hold to your oath creature, or I will be holding your head," he said and twisted the key until the lock gave a soft click. The door opened and Vergil walked forward and out of the cage.

A Symphony of Blood

"Thank you. Now, let us move on. Do you know where she is being held?" the vampire asked as they reentered the corridor lined with cells, but before Gerhold could answer another voice rang out through the hall.

"Now this is something I never thought I would see, the world's greatest slayer allying himself with a vampire. My, my, this truly is a strange world after all." High above them, Harkin stood leaning against the railing of a small balcony overlooking the line of cells. His smug, self-satisfied smile was clearly visible even from so far away. "Are you happy to finally be out of that cage Vergil? To feel free again?"

"What do you want, Harkin?" Vergil said, and the lord let out another maniacal laugh.

"Oh, come now Gerhold, you did not think I would make it this easy, did you?" he asked and motioned with his hand.

The sound of cranking metal came from the balcony, and then suddenly, the cell doors sprung open and the confused and rabid vampire prisoners came stumbling out into the hall. They looked different from Vergil and Harkin, and their faces were distorted and animalistic. Their jaws jutted outwards, their ears had grown long, their hair was mangy and twisted, and they looked as though they were more beast than man. Gerhold noticed the enlarged pupils, the creatures' eyes consumed by the black, searching for blood to satiate their unending hunger.

"If any one of you can manage to kill Gerhold of Vilheim and this other scum, then I will grant you your freedom. Not only that, but you will also receive riches and power. You will be raised to my right hand and all the boons that come with such a title. But only if you manage to kill the two of them."

The rabid and hungry prisoners turned slowly away from Harkin and their blood red eyes settled on Vergil and Gerhold at the opposite end of the hall. For a moment no one moved, and the monsters simply stared at the two men. They growled and let out hissing sounds, seemingly unhappy with being caught between serving Harkin and ending their ravenous hunger. Claws extended from the fingers of each member of the rabid throng, and Gerhold calmly watched for any signs of movement. Suddenly, one let out a terrifying screech which was echoed by the others. Neither Gerhold nor Vergil moved while Harkin stood high above, his smile growing ever wider as the horde kicked into a frenzy. One of the vampires dashed forward, but before it could move more than a few steps, a silver bolt slammed into its chest and passed directly through its heart. The creature fell to the floor, shrieking and shaking as its skin began to burn away, until there was nothing left but a charred skeleton and an empty set of ragged clothing. The other vampires stared at the burnt outline of the corpse for a moment, before letting out another scream of feral rage and charging forward.

Most men would have been terrified by the sight of a blood-starved horde of vampires, but Gerhold had already dropped his large crossbow and in a flash drew the two smaller ones that had been holstered behind his back. The crossbow arms flipped open while Gerhold fired off two more silver bolts and two more monsters fell to the ground, pierced through the hearts by the sharp, silver metal. The hunter fired off a few more shots with the small crossbows before dropping those as well and drawing his silver sword. Dodging through the small hallway he struck left and right with the blade, leaving the screaming and burning corpses of vampires in his wake while hacking off limbs and heads. Vampires were strong, but these blood deprived prisoners were no match for Gerhold. The monsters lashed out at him and even though the slayer was no longer a young man, his experience and years of battle made up for any speed he had lost over the years.

Vergil, on the other hand, lashed out with a savage ferocity, his previously human features giving way to a more beast like appearance with an elongated jaw and fangs as he leapt into the fray. Large bone-like claws extended from each of his fingers as he slashed and tore through his enemies, using his superior speed and agility to avoid the fledgling vampires. Gerhold also noticed as Vergil's nose seemed to be pulled into his face, revealing a snout like appearance that added to the animalistic form. The horde collapsed before them, crying in agony as one by one they fell to blade and claw alike, and soon the room stood silent other than the sizzling sound of burning flesh and the last vestiges of echoing screams died away. Gerhold halted in the middle of the mess of charred skeletons and bones collecting what silver bolts he could, while Vergil stood behind him, still holding the skull of a vampire whose head he had torn off. The vampire's black eyes faded back to the crimson, his snout faded as his smooth pointed nose returned, and his elongated fangs slowly slipped behind his smooth lips. Harkin still stood high above them, laughing and clapping.

"My, my, what a show. I must say Gerhold, you are already living up to your reputation, though do not get too full of yourself. There is still a full night ahead of you, and who knows what other surprises are in store."

With that the lord disappeared.

A Symphony of Blood

"Bastard," Vergil muttered and tossed the skull to one side. "Once I get my hands on him, losing his head will be the least of his concerns."

Gerhold did not respond, but rather continued to gather up the remaining bolts and reloaded his crossbows before holstering the weapons.

"Now, where is she being held?" Vergil asked.

"In the highest tower beyond the clockworks," Gerhold said and Vergil nodded.

Vergil nodded and motioned for Gerhold to follow.

"Follow me then and stay close. Who knows what else Harkin has planned for us, but you can be sure it will be tougher than a bunch of near dead fledglings," the vampire said and led the way up the stairs, leaving behind the corridor of charred bones and empty cells.

Chapter 4: The First Tests

After the battle in the dungeon, Gerhold and Vergil made their way up the circular staircase and back to the room with the three doors. Vergil took the lead and moved right on through to the opposite door and down more corridors until they reached another set of stairs. At the top was another entryway flanked on either side by more sets of pristine armor and banners bearing a black raven on a field of crimson. Vergil led him up the stairs and through a large set of carved oak doors at the top and into a large courtyard beyond. The sky was nearly clear now, but the icy winds still blew across the frozen ground. Gerhold wrapped his scarf around his face and pulled his hood up, while Vergil seemed to not even notice the change in temperature.

The courtyard was large and Gerhold could only imagine how it would have looked had it not been winter. Terraced gardens stood on either side of the yard and stone paths crisscrossed the frozen ground. At the center was a large circular wheel and at its center stood a massive metal sculpture made of rings and iron spheres. Vergil mumbled something to himself as they stared at the barred gate at the end of the courtyard and then the vampire turned and made his way over to the metal sculpture.

"This gate is locked," Gerhold muttered to himself as he stared around for some hint of how to open it.

"So it is," Vergil said and began walking around the large metal rings.

"How do we open it?"

"I am not sure," the Vampire answered.

"Aren't you the architect?" Gerhold asked in a more frustrated tone. "What was the point of bringing you along if you do not even know how to get us through the first lock?"

"I did not design this," Vergil said. "Harkin must have built this when I was locked away."

A Symphony of Blood

"So how do we get through?" Gerhold asked impatiently. Every second wasted brought Lady Friedrich one step closer to undeath.

"I am working on it," the vampire said.

Gerhold watched as Vergil moved about the courtyard examining the metal contraption at the center.

"Over here," he said finally and called Gerhold to the center of the frozen courtyard.

"What is it?" Gerhold asked.

"You see?" Vergil said and pointed to the mass of metal rings. "This is an Astral Gate. It can only be opened once it is set to the right date aligns with where the moons are in the sky."

Gerhold looked up and saw the two crescent moons above, one in front of the other, and then back at the sculpture. He realized that it was a model of the moons and certain constellations in relation to their world.

"So, what do we do?"

"Grab the other handle and we'll see if we can move this a bit."

Together they pushed and pulled at the metal rigging, but nothing happened.

"The damn thing is frozen stiff," Vergil muttered.

"I'll grab a torch from the hall; maybe we can melt some of the ice," Gerhold turned to head back inside, but before he could Vergil called him back.

"Not to worry," the vampire said and in a flash a ball of fire appeared in his hand. He used it to create a ring of flames around the base of metal sculpture.

"So, you are a mage?" Gerhold asked and Vergil nodded.

"That I am," the vampire said as the hissing sounds of evaporating water became louder. "Surprised?"

"Just curious. There are few left who can harness those powers, and even fewer vampires."

"Aye, we're not a common bunch to say the least," Vergil added. "Magic is harder once you've turned. Something about losing your soul puts a bit of a damper on things. The worst part is you cannot learn new magic once you turn, part of the curse I suppose. Imagine having the desire to seek knowledge and understanding of the Arcane and then to be granted eternal life, but instead of being able to accrue infinite knowledge, you are stuck with what you already know. It is the most miserable part of the curse. I suppose it is a good thing I knew a fair bit beforehand."

"Where did you study before you turned?" Gerhold asked.

"I was an Apprentice at the college in Drethdin, the best school of magic in all Tyriel. Beautiful grounds and even better teaching. It was hard, but I loved it. That was a long time ago though. I haven't been back there since."

"So, you were a student?" Gerhold asked.

The more he learned about the monster now the better. Understanding your prey was the first step in hunting it.

"I was, though, as I said, things are a bit harder now," he said and shrugged. "I suppose I am close to where I was back then before I turned."

"How were you not able to escape from the dungeons then? Could you not have melted the bars or used another spell of some sort?"

"I could have, but Harkin's dungeons are enchanted to block any connection to the Nether, and that means no magic." The flames dissipated and left behind a ring of melted snow. "That should do it."

The sculpture was still hot to the touch but no longer covered in ice, and as soon as Gerhold pushed the handle the entire metal base began to spin.

"Keep pushing until I tell you to stop," Vergil said. "So, what about you, hunter? What's your story?"

"Not one that concerns you," Gerhold answered coldly.

"Isn't it a bit rude to ask me so many questions and then refuse to answer any in turn?" Vergil asked. "I have heard tales of you. They were quite impressive if I do say so myself."

"I do not make a habit of getting to know vampires," Gerhold added.

Together the two unlikely companions pushed the metal handles so that the base of the sculpture continued to spin, and as they did the metal rings started to move as well. It took a few rotations before Vergil was satisfied and held up his hand for them to stop. The vampire walked around the sculpture in a circle and continuously alternated his glances between the metal rings and the sky above. They pushed the handles for a few more rotations before Vergil had them stop again and checked to make sure the rings were positioned where he wanted them.

"I think that should work, or at least I hope so," Vergil muttered the second part.

The vampire made his way to the other side of the sculpture where a small metal lever stood and placed his hand on it.

"What happens if we get it wrong and the moons do not line up?"

A Symphony of Blood

Gerhold asked and Vergil raised his eyebrows.

"I am really not sure you want to know," he said ominously and pulled the lever. The metal rings began to spin again and then slowed so that all the rings lined up. Only then did Gerhold hear the clanking of a metal chain, and he turned to see the gate slowly lifting. "See? Nothing to worry about."

"What would have happened had you been wrong?" Gerhold asked again and Vergil shrugged.

"I am almost certain we would have been paralyzed by a spell, or perhaps blown up. It has been quite some time and my memories are somewhat foggy."

"Let us hope things get clearer as we go, or else we may not last long enough to meet with Harkin again."

The two ceased their conversation as they stopped in front of the gate, and Gerhold immediately felt for the medallion which had begun to tremble once more. Two shadowy figures now stood beneath the gate, baring their path to the bridge ahead. Gerhold exhaled slowly and watched as neither of the silhouettes moved.

"Now this is where things get a bit more difficult," Vergil said. "I hope you are up to the challenge, old man."

Suddenly, the two figures darted forward with frightening speed. Before the others could even blink, Gerhold had already drawn one of his crossbows and sent a silver bolt in the direction of one of the attackers, who dodged to the side and avoided the shot. The second bolt caught the attacker in the shoulder. Before Gerhold could get off another, the vampire had closed in on him with his sword drawn. Gerhold quickly dropped his crossbow and drew his blade to deflect a powerful blow from his attacker. He felt his arms shiver from the force of the strike and spun the blade around the deflect another. This was a true vampire, one who could move faster and swing harder than most humans could, but the slayer had faced many battles just like this and relied on his experience to counter the superior physical abilities of his opponent. Gerhold kept his eyes locked on to the vampire as it dashed back and forth and snarled from behind its elongated fangs and feral crouched form.

He parried another strike and then went on the offensive with a series of quick blows that the vampire dodged and blocked easily, and Gerhold could see the arrogant grin on the monster's face as it lashed out with another attack. The slayer rolled smoothly to the side and sent his blade straight towards the creature's chest, and though the vampire was able to avoid the fatal strike, the silver blade dug deep into its side. The monster stumbled and let out a roar of pain and ran towards Gerhold in a fury, but the calm, old hunter just rolled nimbly to the side once more to avoid the strike, and this time his blade struck true. In a howl of surprise and pain the vampire fell to the ground. Gerhold swung his blade a second time and drove the silver tip into the creature's heart. The vampire fell backwards, twitching as his skin and muscles burned away until there was nothing left but a smoldering pile of bones amidst the snowy courtyard.

Gerhold turned just in time to see Vergil send a jet of flames at the other attacking vampire. The creature screamed in terror and rolled about in the snow, trying to quench the flames that ate at his flesh. Vergil showed no mercy and continued to pour on the magical fire until the vampire stopped moving entirely and joined his comrade in true death, the vampire's eyes consumed by a dark rage until the flames finally ceased. Gerhold picked up his crossbow and sheathed his sword as Vergil made his way back over in front of the gates.

"You can fight, old man. I am starting to believe the stories I heard about you," Vergil said with a smile, his elongated fangs gleaming briefly in the moonlight.

Gerhold did not return it.

"I have killed many of your kind. One is no different than the other, and you would do best to remember that," he responded and started walking towards the bridge.

"Not a very kind way to respond to a compliment," Vergil said.

"You're right, it wasn't, vampire. Because you are what I hunt, you and everything like you. For now, we are allies, but only by necessity, not by choice." Gerhold was not yelling, nor did he sound angry. He was calm and cold like always. "Understand this, once we finish our dealings here tonight, when Lady Friedrich is safe, and after we have killed Harkin, do not think for a moment that I will not come after you. You are my prey, vampire, nothing more, and for now, a means to an end."

Vergil sneered at the remarks and shook his head.

"Fine, but we can at least keep things civil in the meantime."

"I'll do my best," Gerhold answered.

"I understand you hate my kind, and I know why. But not all vampires are like Harkin, some of us just wish to live in peace."

Gerhold scoffed.

"You drink the blood of the innocent to keep your immortality. You feast on the living like cattle, and you enslave men to your will. Tell me, creature, what, if any of that, sounds peaceful?" With that the slayer turned and stalked off across the bridge, heading for the second and larger section of the castle.

"Not all of us are like Harkin," Vergil repeated, and then followed Gerhold across the bridge.

The bridge was long and narrow, and to either side Gerhold could look down and see a drop of hundreds of feet to the valley floor below. The winds were strong and made walking across the slick, icy stones even harder, and by the time they reached the other side both men were ready to be off the path and inside the safe walls of the castle. The solid oak doors swung open and Gerhold hurried inside followed by Vergil, who still looked as though the cold had not bothered him at all. The entry hall had vaulted ceilings and great columns that lined the walls; each intricately carved and decorated with depictions of gargoyles and demonic inscriptions. Symbols of the six evil gods, the betrayers, were carved into the stone floor and flickering torches cast a strange orange light and shifting shadows across the hall. Gerhold took a few steps before Vergil reached out and called for him to stop.

"Is something wrong? Another trap?" Gerhold asked but Vergil only shook his head.

"No, it's something else. He has changed something about the castle. There used to be a door straight ahead that led to the upper towers, but it's gone," the vampire said in a confused voice and stepped forward to take a closer look.

"Perhaps your memory is worse than you initially feared," Gerhold responded gruffly but the vampire said nothing until he reached the wall. There was a small alcove with a lamp inside and Vergil stared at it in frustration, until he noticed an envelope that had been sealed and placed just beneath the lamp. He took it and stared at it for a moment before handing it over to Gerhold.

"It seems this is addressed to you," he said and passed it over. Gerhold broke the wax seal and opened the parchment to see a smooth, slanted writing across the page.

Gerhold,
By now, Vergil has realized that I have modified his original design, all for the important reason of adding a little fun to our game. You now have two ways to reach the clock tower, to the left and to the right. Choose wisely as both will hold their own surprises.

J.S. Matthews

-Lord Harkin Valakir

"So, left or right, architect?" Gerhold asked and handed him the paper. Vergil's eyes narrowed as he read the small message, and as soon as he finished, the paper burst into flames.

"Modified my design! The puffed-up son of a whore wouldn't know what to do with this castle if I spent a lifetime teaching him," Vergil said angrily. "Well, it seems as though this may be a little more difficult than I had originally thought. I can only wonder what else he has done to the place. He is ruining one of the greatest architectural feats in the world!"

"What is up that way?" Gerhold asked and motioned towards the doors on the left at the top of a flight of stairs, ignoring the vampire's tirade entirely.

"Up there? That will take us through the green house and then to the base of the clock tower."

"And the other?" he asked again, and Vergil rubbed his chin.

"That would take us through the living quarters and the second dining hall," Vergil added. "I am not sure we want to go that way though; it is likely we will run into a few more of our friends."

Gerhold seemed to agree.

"What is in this green house?" he asked, and Vergil raised his eyebrow as a wry smile crawled across his lips.

"I am guessing plants," Vergil responded sarcastically.

"I meant is there anything we should be worried about?"

"Not to my knowledge, but it has been ten years so who knows what Harkin has done to the place," the vampire answered and shook his head. "Well, this is your little quest so you choose, and I will follow."

Gerhold stared at the vampire for a moment before answering.

"I don't think passing through the living quarters is such a good idea. I do not relish the thought of running into an entire pack of vampire spawn. Let us go through the gardens."

"To the greenhouse then," Vergil nodded towards the stairs to the left.

"You first," Gerhold said.

"Still struggling to trust me, I see," Vergil said and started up the steps.

"I would never turn my back on a monster," Gerhold answered.

"Why do you call me that? Monster," Vergil asked.

"It is what you are."

A Symphony of Blood

Vergil laughed.

"But are there not men who are also monsters? Murderers, rapists and the like. Surely you would describe them as monsters as well, would you not?"

"Men can be monstrous, yes, but that is by choice," Gerhold answered. "They are still men though. They still have a soul. You do not."

"Seems a bit more complex to me," Vergil said.

"I think it is quite simple," Gerhold said. "Monsters need killing, and I am good at the task."

"But monster is just a term."

"It describes what you are, nothing more," Gerhold answered.

"Oh, but it is more," the vampire continued. "Words are a powerful thing. They can build a grand cathedral or convince others to tear one down. Words can make something sacrosanct or heretical. In short, words have the power of creation and destruction, of life and death. Let's consider the word, monster, for a moment. Its true goal is to set something, or someone, apart from the rest. To demonize said person or thing. It dehumanizes."

Gerhold snorted.

"There is nothing human about you, vampire. Nothing beyond your resemblance to what you used to be."

Vergil raised a finger excitedly.

"Ah, you, see? That is my very point. You call me and my kind a monster, and why?"

"Because that is what you are," Gerhold answered. He did not understand what sort of game the vampire was playing with him, but he would have none of it. "You drink the blood of the innocent and devour their souls. You can call yourself whatever you wish, tell whatever lies you want, but you cannot change what you are."

Vergil chuckled.

"You do it because it detaches you, and in turn it allows you, the hunter, feel good about what you do, no matter who or what you kill. Bounty hunters do the same. You can feel pity for a man who stole to feed his family, or a slave who has fled from bondage, but you feel no pity for a bandit or an escaped prisoner. Words and titles can change how we feel about something, or, in this case, lack of feeling. So, that begs the question: is there a difference between a monster hunter and a bounty hunter? One hunts monsters of the magical and fantastical variety, the other hunts monsters of the humankind. You collect money for blood, same as any mercenary or assassin would. So, from that perspective, bounty hunters may in fact be even more moral than yourself. At least they have the option bringing their charge in alive."

"If you are looking for sympathy, you will find none with me," Gerhold answered.

"You know I did not choose to become like this," Vergil said, but Gerhold remained silent. "I was an adventurer and a scholar, studying ancient buildings near the borders of Dalaran. While exploring, I fell into a cavern and found a whole room full of gold, silver, rubies, jewels, ancient texts, and the like. It was quite the find and I assumed all my troubles were over." The vampire gave a bitter laugh as they approached the door at the top of the stairs. "What I did not know, was that my troubles were only beginning. I took a handful of old coins and a few jewels to help pay for someone to help me move the treasure and then sealed up the hole so that I could find it again, only that night something changed. Something in my head, somewhere deep in the darkest corners of my mind was stirring. A sound, a music of some sort, at least that's what I thought it sounded like."

"Most say it is the most beautiful and terrifying thing they have ever heard." Gerhold commented and Vergil nodded in agreement. "A music so beautiful it makes you sick to your stomach and more elated than on your wedding day, all at the same time."

"Yes, sickening, beautiful, and eerie," Vergil said. "It was a terrifying sound though, and at first I thought it was just noise or perhaps a song that had gotten stuck inside my head. The following day though, the sounds grew louder, and louder the next, and the day after as well until all I could hear was the haunting melody. No one else could hear it though and I thought I was going mad, or maybe it had been some sort of magic placed upon the treasure trove I had found. I returned to the sealed room a week later, the music was so loud I could not even make out my own thoughts. I returned the gold and the jewels, but it was no use, the sound just kept growing louder and louder, until I was writhing on the ground in pain. Suddenly though, it just stopped."

Vergil said and snapped his fingers.

"And so did everything else," Gerhold continued. "Never again would you feel the warmth of the sun nor the sting of the cold, no more could you hear the soft and subtle melodies of music, you had no reflection, and you had no soul, as the gold had taken them from you."

A Symphony of Blood

"It's worse than that I am afraid," Vergil said. "There was something else there, like a splinter in the back of my mind. This horrible sickening shadow that only seemed to grow until it was all consuming, until there was nothing but the shadow in my mind. That is what it feels like when starved of blood. It's as if there is some sort of creature taken residence up in my very thoughts, squirming its way through them, consuming them, until all that remains is that beast. That insatiable craving for blood."

The vampire sounded guilty, as if remembering some purposefully forgotten memory.

"It devours what is left of your humanity," Gerhold added.

Vergil grunted.

"Humanity?" he repeated. "I suppose, but what little humanity we are left with after the turning is stripped away by our first feeding. When you turn, your first instinct is to feed. The feeling is uncontrollable. In fact, I would not even remember it if it were not for waking up next to a body covered in blood. She was a fellow student. I had seen her in classes from time to time. Then, she was dead."

"Murder is a crime against one's soul," Gerhold said. "It is the final stage of the turning, the final removal of that last bit of your true self."

"That is why so many vampires embrace it. The turning breaks them." He stared off into the distance out one of the windows and a pitiful smile made its way across his lips. "It has been nearly five hundred years since I was last able to hear the sound of an organ, or a harp, or even a flute. Five hundred years of unquenchable thirst, insatiable appetite, and a constant feeling of being cold and empty. Five hundred years of practicing the same spells over and over again, which is truly the worst of it. I was a mage, a student of magic, and now, I can learn nothing new. That's not he worst of it though. When you turn, something else happens, you lose who you were and something else replaces it. Something that isn't you. It's like some mindless beast has taken over part of your very being, leaving you a slave to its whims. That is why feeding is of the utmost importance, it keeps the beast at bay. Some think immortality is a blessing, but it is not. It is a constant struggle to maintain what small bits and pieces of your shattered self that you can, while fighting an ever more difficult battle against the beast within struggling at all times to break free. It takes all my strength just to remember what I already knew, who I really was…"

Gerhold listened with great interest as Vergil trailed off. He had hunted vampires, werewolves, and all manner of strange creatures his entire life, and never had he met one that seemed so full of regret and sadness. Beneath Vergil's stoic and jovial demeanor lay the heart of a grieving man. He was a vampire yes, but he still held onto some strand of his humanity, something Gerhold had never seen before. Was this something, perhaps, that he had overlooked? Maybe Vergil was more than just a monster, and if he was, then perhaps there were more out there like him. Had Gerhold maybe killed some that were still clinging to their humanity, trying desperately to fight against the dark curse that had been laid upon their lives? Vergil had contracted the curse through luck, very bad luck. It was not his choice to become what he was, as much as it was Gerhold's choice to become a slayer. Did the vampire deserve to die because of that? Gerhold said nothing of these thoughts as they continued through the hall.

To his right, the wall was lined with rows of doors and more tapestries, and to his left were many windows that bathed the long corridor in soft, silvery moonlight. Gerhold kept one hand on his sword as they walked and the other ready to reach for his crossbow. He was sure that at any moment more vampires would come hurtling out of the rooms and surround them. None came though, and by the time they reached the end of the long, diagonal corridor he relaxed his grip and said a silent prayer of thanks. They passed through the tall wooden door, and both men stopped beyond the threshold, as what was ahead startled even the architect.

The room ahead opened with a massive glass ceiling that formed a half dome over the green house, and the twin moons were clearly viewed through the clear roof. Ahead though was a mass of plants, trees, vines, hedges, wooden ramps, stairs, and platforms. Everything had a geometric pattern to it, and everything moved in straight lines. It was a maze, a maze that was made up of multiple levels that climbed up and through the canopy of the taller trees. Both men stared at the room, unable to really figure out where to go or where to start.

"Well, this is a bit different," Vergil said.

"I am guessing it is going to be a lot harder than just cutting our way through." Gerhold said and took a swipe at the nearest hedge wall, which immediately grew back into place as if nothing had happened.

"We are going to have to find our way through here," Vergil said and took a few steps forward and rubbed the back of his head. "This used to be the most beautiful garden. It took years to plan it out so perfectly and many more to build. The man has started to take apart everything I built, piece by piece."

A Symphony of Blood

"I wonder if we can climb it," Gerhold said but as soon as he started pulling himself up the side of one of the hedges, the plants started to reach up, growing higher and higher to match every foot he climbed.

"Well, looks like we only have one choice then," Vergil said. "Straight on through. I doubt it will be as simple as it looks."

"Then let us get moving. We have just over an hour or so before we cannot remove the curse, and after that—" Vergil finished his thought.

"She will be just like me," he said and Gerhold nodded.

Gerhold led the way into the eight-foot-tall hedges and did his best to keep track of which turns they made and when. The maze was large and the walls of green and brown loomed over the two men, and not being able to see beyond the thick branches and leaves of the hedges made it seem even larger. Soon they were taking one of the wooden staircases up to the second level, and here there were more rows of thick hedges and thin wooden catwalks that turned this way and that, up and down, and eventually all the way to the ground below. The air was slightly cooler the higher they went, but the thick and choking feeling of the humidity could still be felt and made taking deep breaths more difficult. They picked up their pace, making sure not to lose track of how many turns they had made, and soon they were climbing the second tower of wooden catwalks. Suddenly, Gerhold held up his hand for Vergil to stop, and both men halted at the center of one of the catwalks. He put his hand inside his shirt and pulled out the golden medallion that was vibrating ever so slightly.

"What is it?" Vergil whispered and Gerhold shook his head. They stood in silence for a just a few moments until a low growl was heard, somewhere off in the hedge maze below. Another minute passed by before another sound was heard, but this time there were the heavy sounds of padded feet to go along with the low, rumbling growls and finally a blood curdling howl pierced the air.

"We are not alone in here," Gerhold said and Vergil nodded his head.

"Do you know what it is?" Vergil asked and Gerhold drew his large crossbow.

"Aye, a werewolf."

The two stood in silence for a moment as both began to realize the danger they were now in. Werewolves were powerful creatures, cursed, much like vampires, but while vampires could avoid becoming feral by feeding, many werewolves would turn permanently.

"Sounds like it's below us for now," Vergil said and both men craned their necks to try and pinpoint just where the snarls and growls were coming from.

"Yes, but is it coming from in front of us or is it following our trail?" Gerhold said and began creeping forward once again. "We need to keep moving, but quietly. We will know soon enough if the beast is on our trail or not, and if it hasn't found it yet, I would rather not give it an easier way of tracking us."

The two men moved on with Gerhold in the lead and the deeper they went into the maze the closer the sounds of growling and snarling got. Sometimes they seemed distant and other times it sounded as if the beast was right on top of them, but still they pressed on through the heavy, damp air and through the unending maze. With every step Gerhold could feel his heartbeat quicken, and every time he peered around a corner it nearly stopped as he expected to see a snarling beast charging towards him. Suddenly, the sounds stopped, and Gerhold held up his hand for Vergil to halt.

"What's wrong?" Vergil asked and Gerhold shook his head. The medallion was starting to vibrate violently. Just then another howl pierced the air and both men turned to see a hulking figure creeping around the corner behind them.

The werewolf was crouched and walking on all four of its massive paws while it sniffed the air. The moment the creature saw them, it let out another howl and dashed in their direction, barking and snarling as saliva dripped from its gaping jaws. Gerhold reacted on instinct and shot a silver bolt at the werewolf, who howled in pain as the silver metal dug deep into its right leg. The monster was only slowed briefly and seemed even angrier than ever at the burning wound that sizzled and issued puffs of smoke. Before Gerhold could load a second bolt into his large crossbow the creature slammed into him and he was sent flying into the side of one of the hedges. The werewolf closed in, opening its jaws wide to reveal rows of razor-sharp teeth, but before it could bite Gerhold, a wave of hot fire slammed into the creature and its fur went up like kindling.

The creature danced around and slashed at the burning patches of flames that clung to its skin, and it was distracted long enough for Gerhold to regain his balance. In a flash the silver long sword was in his hand and slashed at the beast once and then twice. Grey smoke poured from the gaping wounds caused by the magical metal, and the werewolf howled once again in pain as it lashed out at Gerhold. He was ready for the attack and rolled to the side while slashing the creature across its already wounded leg, and just managed to dive backwards as a fresh wave of flames engulfed the monster. The werewolf tore off back in the direction it had come, limping, and whining in pain until it disappeared around the corner of the maze. Gerhold stood and cleaned his blade on a small rag he had pulled from his pocket, while Vergil stood behind him, ready to send another jet of flames if the creature decided to return.

"That was a close one," Gerhold said and shook his head. "Let us hope there are no others."

"There are more," Vergil answered. "Harkin kept them deep in the castle. Every so often he would feed one of his servants to them if the servants got out of line, or a thrall if they failed to serve him well enough. I imagine they'll be around here somewhere."

"Then we need to move, before another shows up," Gerhold said. "They have every advantage in these close quarters, and the beasts are hard enough to deal with on favorable ground."

Gerhold led on through the maze, listening for any sound of the werewolf. It had been a half an hour by the time they started climbing the third and final section of the maze, and in their push to make up time and put as much distance between themselves and the werewolf, they got turned around and nearly lost more than once. They were making their way down when the thumping sounds of heavy padded footfalls returned but this time the sounds came from both sides.

"Two of them?" Vergil said and started conjuring his magical flames.

"One for each of us. You have enough in you to fight two more?" Gerhold asked and Vergil shrugged.

"Possibly, but a werewolf bite is fatal to vampires, and as you saw it takes a lot more than a bit of fire to put one of those things down. I doubt I can stop one before it gets too close, but I can slow it down enough this time for you to kill it with that," He said and pointed to Gerhold's crossbow. "There is still a chance we can outrun them."

"No, we are being hunted. They have our scent." Gerhold seemed to be looking around for something and then motioned for Vergil. "Right here! I can see the exit through the hedge, see?" he said and pointed through a small hole in the thick branches. Down below were the last few twists and turns of the maze and Vergil seemed confused.

"So where do we go? There is already one ahead of us."

"We go straight through and climb down," Gerhold said and started hacking at the hedge. It was at least a thirty-foot drop from where they were, but if they could just get through the thick hedge they could climb down with ease and make it to the exit before the werewolves caught up with them.

"We've already tried that, remember?" Vergil said and turned around in a panic when a loud snarl echoed through the greenhouse from below.

"We just need to be able to fit the two of us through! Use your fire and burn it while I cut it away."

Vergil shook his head and then sent a stream of fire into the hedge. The little branches twisted and burned and Gerhold hacked as hard as he could and as quickly as his arms would move until a large enough hole appeared for one of them to fit through. Before either of them could make it through, one of the werewolves came tearing around the corner at full speed. It let out a terrifying howl as soon as it laid eyes on them, and the beast charged forward. Vergil directed a streak of fire in the creature's direction. Immediately the wooden supports and branches went up in flames and the werewolf leapt back with a whimper of pain, scratching, and clawing at the burning patches of fur. Gerhold fired one of his crossbows and heard the creature roar as the wound began to hiss and issue puffs of grey smoke.

Finally, the hole was big enough and Vergil climbed through. He sent another stream of fire from the opposite side as he hung by the hedge until Gerhold was able to make it onto the other side. Just as he did, a loud bark and a snarl came from the opposite end of the wooden walkway and a heavy body slammed against the hedge. Both men started climbing down as quickly as they could, and a second werewolf slammed up against the hedge, trying to claw and bite its way through, but the enchanted bushes continued to regrow and without the added fire the werewolf could do nothing but snarl and continue to claw fruitlessly at the hedge. Gerhold looked up to see much of the section now ablaze and smoke spewing from the burning wood and branches.

They reached the bottom and sprinted off into the maze once more, now hearing the two monsters barking and howling behind them as the beasts scrambled back down through the elevated part of the maze. Soon the exit was in sight and the two companions threw themselves against the door just as the two werewolves came bounding and howling around the corner. Vergil pulled Gerhold inside and slammed the door, hearing two large crashes and more snarls as the monsters scratched and clawed at the wooden door. They jogged wearily down the hall and when they turned the corner, Gerhold slumped against the wall, trying to catch his breath.

"You all right, old man?" Vergil asked and slapped him on the back.

"I'm getting too old for this," he said with a laugh.

"You are only too old when you are dead," The vampire said, and took a short walk down the hall. "I know where we are now. The clock tower should be just up this way, so come on. We are wasting time." He pulled Gerhold to his feet and the two proceeded onward.

Chapter 5: Clocks and Riddles

They ran up the flights of stairs and down another short hallway, and then stopped in front of a small wooden door. Vergil opened it and together the two passed into the very bottom of the massive clock tower. The room was hot and stuffy, despite its size, and three large furnaces stood to the left of the room from where they had entered. Great pipes carrying steam climbed up from the furnaces where the steam was used to push turbines and move the many metal gears that powered the clock tower. Gerhold stared up the remaining flights of crisscrossing steps and sighed, wishing there was another way up that did not involve so many stairs. The sounds of creaking, clanking, and scraping metal echoed throughout the tower, massive bronze gears turned and twisted, and the occasional hiss emanated from the various pipes and pistons as steam escaped. Large chains hung down through the tower and swung back and forth as the entire tower seemed to vibrate with the shifting gears and pipes.

"How far up is it to where we can get to the other tower?" Gerhold asked and Vergil smiled wryly.

"Are you sure you want me to tell you? Or would you prefer to not know?" Vergil asked, and Gerhold spat on the ground.

"Maybe it is better if you just do not say another word about it."

A minute later, both men were climbing the rickety switchback staircase as fast as they could while trying to avoid the various puffs of burning steam and shifting gears. With every step the wood creaked and groaned, and thick layers of dust shot up in the air. Thankfully the higher up they got the cooler it was as they moved further and further from the furnaces; however, the thick, humid feeling in the air stayed the same and made it hard to take deep breaths.

"So, how did one of Nurrian descent come to live in Vilheim as a monster slayer? Seems like a strange mix," Vergil asked as they climbed. "I assume you are from Nurria? Unless things have changed in the past ten years."

A Symphony of Blood

"Was the dark skin your first hint?" Gerhold asked sarcastically.

"It was a bit of a giveaway," Vergil answered with a chuckle.

"I was born in Aquib as one of the casteless, and in Nurria, if you do not belong to a caste, then you are worth little more than the dirt you walk upon. I was sold into slavery and for the first sixteen years of my life served one of Aquib's most powerful noble families. Eventually though, they had a guest, a monster slayer from the north. He needed someone to guide him deep into the jungle as he was hired to hunt a water serpent that had been plaguing the fishing villages along the rivers, and he chose me. When we returned, he purchased me and then gave me my freedom," Gerhold said, and a few images of long forgotten memories danced through his mind. "I followed him, and he trained me."

"Not many monster hunters make it on their own for so long," Vergil added.

"I wasn't alone. The man who trained me was a member of the Seekers," Gerhold said.

"Ah, yes, the Seekers. Wonderful group they are," he said sarcastically.

"They were, at one time," Gerhold answered.

"Not if you are someone like me," Vergil added. "Are you still with them?"

Gerhold shook his head.

"No. I did not see eye to eye with them on things."

"I'm not surprised," Vergil said. "I've heard of the Seekers burning entire villages to ensure all traces of monsters are gone. They think anyone even suspected of dark magic or assisting with it deserves to be purged. No one is innocent in their eyes."

"They believe the ends justify even the most horrific acts. I disagreed."

"And so, you went your own way?" Vergil added.

"It was hard, but I found allies where the Seekers could not." Gerhold looked up and decided it was a bad idea to try and count how many steps they had left. "I made my home in Vilheim after a priest took me in. I had a particularly bad run in with a Cackler demon, and he helped me."

"Demons are vicious. I'm surprised a human could handle one alone," Vergil said.

"Barely. I was young and foolish back then, but I was at least smart enough to know that I would need help. So, I made Vilheim my home, or as much as one could with how much I travel."

"You have an interesting tale, indeed, Gerhold of Vilheim. I have met few Nurrians in my life and they were likable enough. They do not seem to travel much. You do not remind me of them at all, other than in your appearance that is."

"I am a Nurrian in appearance only. I will never return to that realm."

"Was it really that bad?" Vergil asked. "I have heard tales of its great wealth and majestic cities. Massive stone pyramids and temples that stretch to the heavens. They even say that the jungles are enchanting to look at, casting a spell on visitors that can only be described as magical."

"Some have wealth, and some do not," Gerhold answered. "It is a rigid society, unmoving, unchanging. One where you are what you are born. A merchant, a noble, or a slave, you are what your parents were. I was unfortunate enough to be the least of those. I find the place detestable, though I suppose my point of view is a bit jaded."

"I can't imagine why, after being a slave and all," Vergil jested.

After a few more minutes of climbing, they heard a sound below them as the door into the base of the clock tower swung open, and in walked a line of shadowy black figures. Vergil whispered for him to halt and both men stood close to the wall, hoping against all odds that the vampires would not see them, but it took only a moment before one of the monsters pointed in their direction and said something that Gerhold could not hear. Suddenly the entire group of vampires was charging up the steps after them.

"Time to move," Vergil said, though Gerhold needed no encouragement.

"So much for a nice slow climb," Gerhold muttered.

They hurried upwards, ignoring the groaning protests of the old staircase as they sprinted up the stairs two at a time. Below, the sounds of hissing and battle cries from their pursuers could be heard. Gerhold stopped for a moment and took aim with his crossbow. The bolt struck the first vampire in the stomach, though it did very little to slow the monster and seemed to only make it angrier. The second bolt, however, caught the vampire in its forehead and sent it spinning off the staircase, where it fell forty feet to the stone floor below. A bolt to the head was not enough to kill a vampire, it had to be through the heart, but it was enough to paralyze the creature until the bolt was removed and the creature had time to heal. Gerhold knew they would not be able to outrun the monsters, and Vergil seemed to come to the same conclusion as an arrow darted right past his ear and clattered off the stone wall.

A Symphony of Blood

Vergil sent a ball of flame at the attackers, who seemed to stare at the vampire in shock, but before any of them could respond a second jet of fire struck at them and one fell back down the stairs, beating at his burning cloak. Gerhold caught another in the shoulder with a bolt before the monster was able to reach him and then dispatched the creature with a swift parry and strike. Just then, Vergil called out and pointed at the staircase above, and Gerhold turned to see two more vampires sprinting down from the upper level. The hunter turned and fired a bolt which caught one of the monsters in the leg, and the creature cried out in pain as the wound hissed and burned. The vampire leapt over his wounded comrade and charged straight for Vergil who flung himself at the creature and knocked the sword from its hand. The two vampires danced back and forth now on the rickety staircase, engaged in a brutal hand-to-hand fight, while Gerhold slung his larger crossbow behind him and leapt off the staircase just as the other two vampires reached him. He swung on one of the heavy chains in an arch and landed on of the rows of stairs below, and in one smooth motion drew his two smaller crossbows and fired a stream of bolts into the vampire that had followed.

The creature screamed in agony as one of the bolts pierced through its heart, and it fell screaming down through the tower. The only things that remained of the monster by the time it hit the stone floor was a pile of blackened bones. Gerhold had just enough time to dive under the second attacking vampire as it lunged at him from above and again his deadly bolt found its mark and the creature crumpled over the side of the staircase with a shriek. For a moment Gerhold leaned against the wall to catch his breath and looked up to see Vergil still battling the last vampire.

The two seemed evenly matched as they lashed out at each other with strong punches, kicks, and slashing claws. Vergil was bleeding from his forehead and the other creature had multiple scratches on its face and a bloody gouge along its side. They traded blows while snarling and barring their fangs at one another, the inner beast slowly clawing its way out of both. Finally, Vergil caught the creature's arm and, with great effort, snapped the bone in two, which led to the monster crying out in pain as Vergil delivered another elbow to its face and hurled the broken arm into one of the shifting gears. The creature screamed as the gears pulled it in, and the sound of crunching bones and shredding flesh could be heard over the vampire's blood curdling screams.

Finally, the shrieks stopped, and all that was left was a burning, bloody mess as the creature's flesh disappeared. Gerhold lowered his crossbow and returned to his feet, preparing to celebrate their victory, when he looked down to see more vampires flooding through the door below. He cursed at their luck and sprinted up the stairs to where Vergil was calling for him.

"Go! Up the stairs now! I have an idea," Vergil said and Gerhold dashed past him and up the next few flights of stairs.

He turned just in time to see the first jets of flame leap from Vergil's hands, and he directed the fires onto the old staircase, which went up like dry kindling and sent streams of smoke high up into the tower.

The two choked and coughed in the growing plume of black smoke until finally reaching the top of the staircase and climbing through a small door overhead. Once they were in the next level of the clock tower, they slammed the door shut and pushed a few heavy storage crates over it for good measure. Little wisps of smoke emanated from between the small slits in the door and Gerhold could hear the cries of the vampires below as they slammed against the door. Soon, the cries faded away and the banging stopped, and Vergil motioned for Gerhold to follow him out through another door at the end of the tower.

"That was a good idea, lighting the stairs on fire. We should have done that the first time we were attacked," Gerhold said and Vergil nodded.

"It would have made things a bit easier," Vergil said and chuckled. "Next time we are running from a horde of vampires through a clock tower I will remember that."

Suddenly, there was a loud *bong* that emanated from high above and down through the castle, followed by ten more as the clock marked the eleventh hour. Gerhold glanced at Vergil, who shook his head in frustration. Both men were looking forward to a moment of rest, but they were already running out of time. Together, they moved on out of the little room and left the burning clock tower behind.

Gerhold was thankful when they passed through the next door and came out of the stuffy interior of the castle. Outside now, they stood at the foot of another bridge that connected the center of the clock tower to another, the highest tower in the castle. Gerhold closed his eyes and let the freezing wind cool him and realized just how much higher they were now. Below, the rest of the castle could be seen, and even farther below the forested valley stretched out in all directions until it came to the foot of the massive peaks. He stared up at the tall tower in front of them that reached high above into the night sky. More clouds were starting to move in, warning of another approaching storm. The breather did not last long, as Vergil had already begun to make his way across the narrow bridge.

"So, is there anything I need to know about this tower?" Gerhold asked and the vampire shrugged.

"I am not sure, so far he has changed many things about this castle, so who knows what surprises lie in store for us. We must hurry though; it will not take long for our friends to make their way back around to us."

They ran across the bridge and entered the large tower through a small door. Inside was a spiral staircase that climbed through the interior of the tower, and soon they were at the top of it and passed through one last door. This room was circular and almost completely empty except for a single door at the opposite side, several small pedestals lined the curved walls of the room, and a larger pedestal at the center. Next to the center pedestal was a metal lever, and it took another moment before Gerhold even noticed the two men standing near the door at the opposite end of the room. He immediately realized they were thralls and as soon as Gerhold closed the door the two men approached.

"Good evening, sirs, my master wishes to express his congratulations for making it this far," one said.

"He also wishes to tell you that you now have less than an hour before the lady succumbs to the curse," the other added.

"And that you should increase your pace if possible else you fail in your task to save her," the first finished, and Gerhold glanced at Vergil, who gave him a worried look. Both thralls were thin and pale, and their scraggily, wispy hair gave the impression that they were wasting away.

"What is this room, thrall? What do we need to do to pass?" Gerhold asked.

"As most of the other tasks have required your physical skills, this challenge will require your wits to solve," said the Thralls.

"As you see, there is a single pedestal at the center of this room, and on it are six indentations."

"And around the room are many medallions, but only six will fit within the indentations."

"To open the door and rescue the lady, you must find each medallion and match it to the corresponding indentation."

"If your medallions do not match, then this tower will be destroyed and you with it."

Gerhold looked around the room as the two thralls finished their speech. At the center was the large pedestal with the six circular impressions and interspersed throughout the room on their own pedestals were many thin, cylindrical medallions. Near each indentation on the center alter were words carved into the stone and Gerhold stepped forward to see them a little closer. Each one was different, and each was a short riddle. He walked around the room and glanced quickly at each of the medallions which had different words imprinted on them.

"Heart, tree, sword, spear, water, shadow, wind, fire, mountain, tongue, mind, moon, and sun," Gerhold read out loud and Vergil nodded as if he understood.

"There are more over here. Thief, shield, horse, death, life, wine, time, and dreams," Vergil read and then made his way back over to the pedestal at the center of the room.

"They are riddles, and each of these medallions holds one of the answers," Gerhold mumbled to himself.

"This one, right here," the vampire said and pointed to the first of the six indentations and read the words beneath it. "I am older than the world itself and I have killed more men than any sword. What am I?"

"Older than the world…" Gerhold mumbled to himself. "Well, it is obviously not the sword," he said as he moved about the room glancing at the stone medallions.

"Perhaps a mountain?" Vergil suggested and Gerhold rubbed his chin in thought.

"Mountains are part of this world, not older than it. We need something older."

"I'd take a fight over this riddle solving," Vergil commented.

Gerhold stopped and examined each of the words and tried to fit them into the riddle. Tree, water, wind, heart, and shadow could all be ruled out as they made no sense, and surely spear was not the correct answer. Fire had killed many men but less than either a sword or spear and most of the others made no sense at all.

"Death? That makes the most sense," Vergil said and Gerhold glanced at the little stone medallion with the word on it.

"Death does not kill; it is the result of killing."

A Symphony of Blood

"None of these make sense," Vergil said irritably. Gerhold took one more walk around the room and then picked up one of the medallions warily.

"Time," he said and tossed it to Vergil who fit it into the first slot. "Time is the answer."

"Are you sure?" the vampire asked and Gerhold nodded. "Alright, if you say so."

"What is the next riddle?"

"No soul, nor flesh, nor thoughts have I, but alive I am inside. I drink and eat but have no heart. What am I?" Vergil read and shrugged.

"It's not an object, not a thief," Gerhold was thinking out loud. The riddle itself did narrow down the choices and Gerhold thought for a moment while moving around the room again, staring at the remaining medallions. Then he paused and grabbed a nearby stone.

"Did you find it?" Vergil asked

"A tree," Gerhold answered with a smile and Vergil fitted it into the second slot.

"I am sharper than any sword and can cut to the heart and soul. What am I?" Gerhold strolled around the room again, examining the stones.

"Not a sword or spear, not the mountain, and neither water nor fire cut into anything," Gerhold said aloud and continued to go through the medallions.

"Perhaps death?" Vergil said.

"That seems to be you answer for everything."

"Did I mention how I prefer fighting to these foolish riddle games?" Vergil said but Gerhold did not respond. Instead continued to move in a circle, glancing at the medallions one by one as he passed.

After another minute, Gerhold halted in front of one of the pedestals and smiled.

"A tongue," he said and picked up another medallion. "Not too hard now is it." There were only three spots left, and yet many medallions remained.

"I am the maiden all men fear but every man must dance with me, and only once may we dance. Who am I?" Gerhold walked around the room and rubbed his chin, then hesitantly grabbed another medallion.

"Death?" he said in a questioning tone. "You only get to dance with her once." Vergil placed the stone into the indentation.

"See? I knew it would be one of the answers," Vergil responded with a smile.

"We are running out of time, what is the next one?" Gerhold asked.

"There are only two left," the vampire answered and read the next riddle. "I softly whisper every day and yet only the farmers and the mountain men hear my call. Through the trees I pass unseen, and across the lands I soar. What am I?"

Gerhold chuckled and tossed another medallion to Vergil who looked at it and nodded with a smile.

"The wind, if only they were all that easy," he said as Vergil fit it into the empty slot. "And the last one?"

"I follow wherever you go and behind you cannot leave me. Whether brightest day or darkest night I will always be with thee. What am I?"

Gerhold walked around the room glancing at the medallions one last time. No one could leave behind their heart or mind but what did that have to do with a bright day or dark night? He supposed one could always have their dreams with them but that still seemed to not fit with the entire riddle. Gerhold made one more loop around the room then picked up a medallion and walked over to the pedestal.

"Wait," Vergil said and Gerhold stopped before fitting in the last medallion into its slot. "Are you sure?"

"I am." He handed the stone to Vergil who read the word inscribed upon the stone.

"A shadow," the vampire said and hesitated, only a little, before fitting it into place. "I am over five hundred years old, and if you get me killed now it will be quite the anticlimactic ending. It would be quite disappointing to be killed by such a foolish trap."

"I doubt we will have much time to be disappointed," Gerhold said as Vergil pulled on the lever.

Initially nothing happened and Gerhold held his breath. Finally, after what felt like minutes, a loud grinding sound echoed from below as the large metal door at the end of the room creaked open. Gerhold let out a sigh of relief as Vergil did the same, and the two men moved forward through the open door. Beyond was another circular stairwell that climbed up higher into the tower, and after another minute of sprinting up the stairs they stopped in front of a small wooden door.

"This should be it… the highest tower," Vergil said.

"Let us hope Harkin was not lying," Gerhold responded and opened the door.

Chapter 6: A Race against Time

    Inside was a large circular room with a small bed at one end and a desk and red armchair along the right side. There was a small fire in the fireplace that cast shadows about the room, and along the far end was an open shaft where a dumbwaiter held an empty plate and a few other dirty dishes. Sitting in a chair nearby, Gerhold saw a young woman with golden hair, seemingly staring at the crackling fire and completely unaware of their presence. The little medallion around his neck gave a slight tremor as he approached the woman.

    "Lady Friedrich?" Gerhold said and the woman did not move. "My lady, are you alright?" he said again and finally the woman turned to them, though her face was strained and unreadable.

    "Who are you and what are you doing here?" she asked in surprise. The woman shook her head slightly and touched a hand to her temple. She was young and beautiful, but there was clearly something straining her attention and Gerhold knew exactly what it was.

    "My name is Gerhold. I have come to bring you back to your husband," he said and moved closer to help her out of the chair.

    "I am sorry, I could not hear you," she said and shook her head. "Did you say you were here to rescue me?" she asked again, though there was no happiness in her voice.

    "I have. Now please, we must move as quickly as we can." He made to help her up, but she recoiled and walked to the other side of the room.

    "No, no you cannot take me. That man, that thing or whatever he is, he did something to me," she said, and her eyes were wide with fear. "I know not what, but something is happening to me!"

"You are becoming a vampire," Vergil said, and she stared at him in shock.

"I am? What is happening to me?" she said and nearly collapsed.

"Please my lady we must go, now!" Gerhold said and tried to help her to her feet.

"No! No! Nothing can help me now! He said there was nothing you could do," she said, and a small tear appeared in her eye.

"Gerhold, let me try," Vergil said and bent down near the woman. "Lady Friedrich, look at me, try to ignore the sound. You can hear it can you not?" he asked, and she looked at him with those same tearful eyes.

"Yes, yes I can! Can you not hear it? Can you not hear the sounds? I thought they were in my head, that I had some strange song stuck in my mind, but it never goes away! It just keeps getting louder, and louder! I cannot stop it! What is happening to me?" She screamed and threw her face into her hands.

"I know my lady, I understand. Please, look at me," Vergil asked again and the woman slowly lifted her eyes. "You must be strong. The sound will continue to grow until you can hear nothing else. We only have a small amount of time before the music ceases and then there will be no way to help you. If you stay here, then there will be no escaping that fate, but we can help you," he said and set his hand on her shoulder. She closed her eyes and took a deep breath to calm herself.

"Alright," she responded finally, and Vergil helped her to her feet. "What must I do?"

Gerhold was watching the other two, when suddenly he felt another, stronger vibration in his medallion. Just then another sound came from the stairwell and in walked a vampire with his sword drawn. Before the creature could move though, a silver bolt slammed into its chest and the monster fell back into the hallway shrieking in pain. Gerhold stood with one of his small crossbows in hand, and the second ready to fire.

"They have found us!" Gerhold said as a second vampire came through and fell in the same manner as his companion.

Vergil sprinted across the room and slammed the door shut as Gerhold fired another volley through the doorway. Together they moved the thick oak dresser in front of the door, but as soon as they moved away there was a loud crash against the wood. They moved the desk against the door as well, but the furniture would only buy them a little time before the vampires would be able to break their way in. Frantically, the two men searched around the room for another way out. There was single window at the end of the room, but they were far too high and there was no way to climb down. Finally, Gerhold stopped in front of the shaft with the dumb waiter and an idea popped into his head.

Quickly, he leapt onto the little shelf and started slamming his foot through the opening into the dumbwaiter. After the third kick the little metal shelf gave way and fell through the shaft. Gerhold stuck his head in and looked down. The metal chains used to pull the dumbwaiter up and down through the shaft were still there and he motioned for Vergil to grab Lady Friedrich. Another hard crash came against the door and the desk and dresser moved just slightly. Gerhold knew they only had a few seconds before the monsters would break their way in, and he called for Vergil to go down through the shaft first with the woman. Just as Lady Friedrich's head disappeared the door broke inwards, followed by a line of black clad vampires hungry for blood. Gerhold reached into his pack and pulled out two silver spheres, each with a short wick attached to the top. He thrust the wicks into the fireplace and tossed them across the room at the oncoming horde as he dove into the shaft.

There was a loud explosion and great plumes of smoke floated into the shaft from the open hole above as Gerhold gripped the chains tightly and slid down after the other two. It took only a short time to reach the bottom, where he crashed hard onto the smashed dumbwaiter. A set of strong hands reached in and dragged him out of the shaft and Gerhold found himself staring at Vergil, who was grinning.

"I hope that was not the last of our luck," the vampire said and Gerhold nodded in agreement. "What in the hells did you do up there?"

"Pyrite bombs. Nice little way to deal with more than one advisory in close quarters," Gerhold answered and pulled a third one out to show the vampire. "Silver metal casing around a small amount of pyrite oil. It makes a decent explosion and sends shards of silver in all directions. Not usually my style but it seemed like a good idea," he said and stowed the bomb in his pack.

"What about that medallion?" Vergil said and pointed to the gold necklace.

"That was made for me by a priest. It can detect a curse nearby if I am not already aware of it and has saved my life more than a few times."

"Is that how you knew they were coming?" Vergil asked and Gerhold nodded. "Thank the gods for that."

"We will have time to thank the gods later," Gerhold looked around and realized they were standing in another kitchen. "Do you know where we are?" Vergil glanced around the room for a moment.

"These are the kitchens that serve the secondary dining hall, which means we should be able to pass through straight to the living quarters and back across to the main area of the castle," Vergil said and pointed to a large door at the end of the kitchen.

"Hopefully, most of the vampires left to chase us down in the tower," Gerhold said and started heading for the door.

"They probably did, but it will not take them long to reach us here."

"Then we need to be across that bridge before they find us," Gerhold said and bent down to help Lady Friedrich to her feet. "Come my lady. We need to get moving again."

"The sounds, they are unbearable," she said through gritted teeth, and placed her hands over her ears.

"It will be over soon," Gerhold responded.

"In one way or another," he heard Vergil mutter.

"How long do you think she has?" Gerhold asked. Vergil shook his head and frowned.

"Not long," Vergil answered.

They passed into the second dining hall, which was considerably smaller than the great hall Gerhold had entered on his way into the castle, and went into a long hallway lined with doors on one side and windows on the other. He realized immediately that it was just an inverted version of the hallway they passed through on the way to the gardens, and the many doors along the corridor made him nervous as they could have been hiding anything. The group began to make their way down the hall, and due to Lady Friedrich's condition, they moved far slower than he would have liked. Every time they passed a door Gerhold expected it to burst open, so he kept his hand on the long silver dagger he kept sheathed in his belt. The small, cramped hallway would make wielding his sword a bit of a challenge, and so he readied the shorter weapon, just in case. Occasionally, Lady Friedrich whimpered slightly, cradled her head in her hands, and muttered to herself.

They reached the halfway point down the hall, and Gerhold had started to hope they would make it through the hall without any encounters. Suddenly, one of the doorhandles ahead started to turn, and out walked a tall, thin vampire wearing a finely embroidered black silk shirt. A look of shock and confusion was visible on his face as he turned and saw the three people standing in the middle of the hall. Before the vampire could even blink, Gerhold whipped out one of his crossbows and shot a bolt straight through its chest. The creature fell backwards with a moan of surprise and then cried in pain. Immediately other doors along the hall started to open as more vampires came to check on what was making such a terrible noise. Gerhold fired his crossbow a second time and then spun with a second weapon drawn and killed two other monsters, while Vergil grabbed Lady Friedrich's hand and pulled her down the hallway. Gerhold slew another vampire that was blocking their path as more came running into the corridor from behind.

Vergil sent a stream of fire behind them at the oncoming horde to try and slow the vampires down, while Gerhold fired one last volley into the attackers before turning and diving past the flames. Together they sprinted down the rest of the corridor, holding Lady Friedrich between the two of them, and ran for the door to the entry hall. Another vampire leapt out at them but Gerhold slashed the monster with his dagger and then shot it through then chest with his crossbow. Finally, they reached the end of the hall and burst through the door at the large entryway. The screams and cries of the vampires behind them died away as Gerhold slammed the door shut and leapt over the railing to the hard, stone floor below. Vergil and Lady Friedrich were already outside and by the time Gerhold reached the doorway, the vampires were already entering the hall. They sprinted across the small bridge and as soon as they reached the other side, Vergil reached into Gerhold's pack and pulled out the last of his silver bombs, then ran and laid the bomb near the center of the bridge.

"What in the hells are you doing? We need to go now!" Gerhold yelled as the doors burst open and the vampire horde came running onto the bridge.

"Just get back and stay down!" Vergil yelled and sent a ball of fire at the center of the bridge.

The flames and the horde met at the exact same spot and a massive explosion shook both sides of the bridge. There was a bright flash of light, and Gerhold was thrown backwards through the astral gate and into the courtyard. For a moment he could see Vergil being throw sideways by the blast before his view was obscured. Fire and smoke filled the air, and the sound of cracking stone and the screams of dying vampires pierced the night air as the bridge crumbled and crashed to the valley floor far below. Once the smoke had cleared, Gerhold stood up to see the extent of the damage, which was considerable, as the entire bridge was gone and only two small wedges remained sticking out at either side. A few vampires stood at the opposite end, shrieking and yelling, but Gerhold paid them no mind. The bridge had been the only way across, and now, it was gone. He turned to congratulate Vergil, but the vampire was nowhere to be seen. Gerhold moved forward slowly and leaned over the edge but could still see no sign of him. Shocked and confused, Gerhold let out a roar of rage and pulled out his large crossbow, firing off a few shots at the monsters on the opposite side. He dropped to one knee and shook his head. Vergil was gone.

A Symphony of Blood

Chapter 7: A Symphony of Blood

Gerhold was still kneeling at the edge of the cliff, staring off where Vergil had fallen or had been blown off by the force of the explosion. He had known the vampire for only a short time, and he knew very little of him, but Vergil had been a good ally and had stayed true to his word. Gerhold had never mourned over the death of a vampire before, but he now had a pit somewhere deep in his stomach and felt almost as if he might retch. He looked up at the castle area they had escaped from and noticed that the entire top of the largest tower had been blown off and that the clock tower was still on fire. The winds had already begun to pick up, and the sky had all but disappeared behind a thick layer of grey clouds. They had escaped but at a great cost, and now he had to move on by himself once again.

He stood up and realized that he had completely forgotten about Lady Friedrich, who was huddled on the courtyard ground with her knees pulled tightly to her chest. She did not shiver in the cold, and Gerhold fingered his crossbow, just in case, as he approached the woman, who was muttering under her breath. Even with the howling winds and the ringing in his ears from the explosion, he could still make out what she was saying.

"The sounds, the sounds are too loud! Too loud now! They hurt; the sounds hurt! Make it stop, make it stop please!" she shrieked and threw her hands around her ears as if trying to block out the noises.

Gerhold bent down and lifted the woman into his arms. She continued to mutter and scream about the pain, but he ignored the cries and moved as quickly as he could through the courtyard with the metal sculpture of the moons, and then up the steps to the castle. Once inside, the woman's screams echoed off the stone walls and Gerhold moved as fast as he could through the hallways and back towards the great hall. He grunted and heaved with the effort of carrying the woman and running after such a long night, and nearly his entire body ached from the various fights and falls he had experienced. Only now did he notice the bleeding wound on his left arm from a vampire's sword, the burns on the back of his hand and along the right side of his neck, and the various other scrapes and bruises he had received that made nearly every part of his body sore. Still, he had been injured far worse before, and he was so close now that the hope of victory gave him an extra burst of speed as he sprinted on through the hallways. Finally, the great hall came into view and a few moments later he was stumbling down the long flight of stairs to the dining hall, still carrying Lady Friedrich. As soon as he came into view, Gerhold could see the satisfied smile on the face of Lord Harkin, and the vampire began to slowly clap as if seeing the climax of a fine performance.

"Oh, bravo Gerhold, bravo indeed," the vampire laughed as Gerhold fell to his knees in front of the elevated throne, gasping for breath while Lady Friedrich's cries echoed throughout the room. "A masterpiece! This was truly your greatest performance, a true symphony of blood. Without any doubt, you are the greatest slayer of our age." Gerhold got slowly to his feet, still wheezing and coughing, but of sound mind enough to draw his crossbow and point it at the heart of the vampire lord.

"Where is it? Where is the gold?" he yelled and fingered the trigger.

"Of course, the gold, to remove the curse and save the fair maiden from a life of eternal suffering," the lord said with a flourish of his hand and an evil grin. "Where is dear Vergil? Did he not make it? How sad, it was so touching to see the world's greatest slayer cozying up with one of the monsters he seemed to hate so much. It was truly heartwarming."

"Where is it? Throw it on the floor now!" Gerhold yelled again, but just then the screams of terror and pain ceased, and he turned to see Lady Friedrich sitting up but with eyes wide with horror. "My lady, my lady hold on. Do not give in!" He knelt by her side and the woman's eyes drifted slowly over to him.

"Give my locket to my husband… tell him to remember me," she said in an almost hollow voice before throwing her head back and screaming in pain as her features contorted, forming the face of a maddened beast.

Gerhold leapt back and readied his crossbow but was suddenly lifted into the air and thrown across the room where he landed hard on the cold stone floor. His crossbow went spinning away and Gerhold rolled over, holding his aching side and back. He looked up to see Lord Harkin staring at him with that same smug grin, and with his hand outstretched; the lord knew magic. Harkin let out an evil, triumphant laugh as the woman continued to writhe and shriek as the curse took hold of her mind and body.

"How disappointing," the lord said and laughed. "Could this have ended more perfectly? This deserves a song, a ballad! How does it feel, slayer? How does it feel to have come so far only to fall short at the last moment? You old fool. Did you really think you would be a match for me? I played this game with you tonight to see if you were even worthy of your title, and I can see now that you are. You are the greatest hunter I have ever seen during my thousand-year life, which will make my victory all the more impressive." The lord chuckled again. "How does it feel, Gerhold? To know that you lost. To know that the woman you came here to save will be the instrument of your death."

Gerhold climbed gingerly to his feet and stared at the lord with those cold, dead eyes of his, and then at the woman who was now rising from the floor as if an invisible puppeteer was pulling her strings. Her face was similar now, at least somewhat, but there was the unmistakable hunger in her eyes and the tight, pale look of a vampire. Gerhold made no move for his crossbow, nor for his other weapons, but waited and watched as the lord continued to gloat. Two more vampires entered the room, and now it was four against one, poor odds for any vampire hunter, but Gerhold of Vilheim was not just any hunter. Sore, bruised, bleeding, and tired he was, but not yet defeated. He wished he still had Vergil with him, but no matter what, he was going to keep his promise to the vampire, whether he lived or not.

"Now, Gerhold of Vilheim, do you have any last words? I cannot promise they will end up on your tombstone, as I imagine that there will not be enough left of you to bury," Harkin said with an evil laugh.

"I made a promise, hell spawn, and I always keep my word."

Before any of the vampires could move both crossbows were in Gerhold's hands and two bolts were already in midflight. The first struck one of the vampires in the chest and through the creature's heart, while the second struck Lord Harkin in the shoulder. Before he could get off another shot, he was hit by a stream of silver light that struck him in the chest and hurtled him backwards where he slammed against the stone wall. The two crossbows flew from his hands, and Gerhold slumped against the wall, trying to fight for breath. Lady Friedrich and the other vampire ran towards him, and Gerhold lunged with whatever strength he had left and grabbed one of the fallen weapons, and then fired the last silver bolt into the attacking vampire's heart. Lady Friedrich snarled and rushed forward, realizing now that the crossbow was empty and slashed at him with her claws. Gerhold was thrown to the stone floor once again, and his side burned with pain from the deep gashes left by the vampire's claws, and when he made for his sword another strike sent him sprawling once again and the blade clanged away across the stone. He crawled to a nearby table and tried to pull himself to his feet, but the blood crazed vampire was already on top of him. She lifted Gerhold up by his throat so that he was leaning against the table and licked her lips as if savoring a coming meal. Her empty black eyes bore into him, her nose had disappeared leaving a bestial snout-like appearance, and her jaws extended to reveal the elongated fangs that would tear into his neck. Gerhold struggled for breath and could hear Harkin's laughter ringing in his ears.

"My new toy is stronger than she appears," the lord said and laughed again. "Now my lady, drain him dry and feast on his flesh."

Gerhold saw the vampire's mouth open and her razor-sharp teeth started inching towards his neck. For a moment, he thought it was all over, that he was finally about to meet his end. His body was bruised and bloodied; he was beyond exhausted, and the embrace of death was almost a welcoming thought. Suddenly, he felt something sharp poking against his lower back and reached behind where he felt the long, smooth shaft of a silver bolt. With everything he could muster, he pulled the bolt from its quiver and slammed it as hard as he could into the lady's chest. Immediately her grip loosened, and the creature threw herself backwards, clawing and tearing at the wound and the silver bolt. Gerhold fell to the floor and gasped for breath, trying to ignore the burning feeling in his lungs from the lack of oxygen. He watched as lady Friedrich fell to the floor in great spasms of pain, and in only a moment the deadly smoldering, fire crept across her skin. Finally, she lay still and all that remained was the familiar pile of charred bones and ashes. Footsteps echoed across the hall as Harkin, no longer bearing his sneer, came striding up to where Gerhold leaned against the legs of the wooden table.

"You are full of surprises, slayer," Harkin said and ripped the silver bolt from his shoulder. The wound was already smoldering and gave off a small trail of smoke. "But, as before, all your effort was for naught. You see, everything tonight was planned, planned to the very last detail. My powers stretch far beyond these measly mountains, and Lord Friedrich is the perfect example. You see, I needed a way to get you here without drawing suspicion, and the lord was more than eager to be rid of his unfaithful, whore of a wife. The perfect bait for my trap."

"It took an army of your kind to wound me, if it had not been for that, you would have already been dead," Gerhold said and grimaced in pain.

"You killed my minions, yes, but they are replaceable. You on the other hand, are not, and I intend to make you suffer for the damage you caused to my beautiful castle. You destroyed an architectural masterpiece. But now, I am going to kill you, Gerhold, I am going to rip the flesh from your body and drain the marrow from your bones. When I finish with you, there will be nothing left but the stories and the whispers of how painfully you died at the hands of–" Harkin stopped mid-sentence and his eyes bulged while his mouth fell open as if he was trying to cry out.

Gerhold watched as the tip of a silver blade ripped through the vampire's chest, right where his heart was. Harkin looked over his shoulder and gasped a single word.

"Y–You?"

"Yes, me!" Vergil yelled and slammed the blade through a second time.

Harkin screamed in agony as his flesh was devoured by flames until finally his skeleton crumbled to the ground. It took Gerhold a moment to realize what had happened, and he stared, open mouthed, at Vergil who was grinning and holding his silver sword.

"I believe this belongs to you?" he said and dropped to one knee beside the slayer.

"Vergil? I… I thought you were dead," Gerhold said through gasps of pain.

"It will take more than some fire and a short fall to kill me," Vergil responded with a grin. "Lie still now, I think I can heal some of these wounds." Gerhold bit down in pain as he felt the scratches on his side contract, and the broken ribs begin to snap back into place. After a few moments of pure agony, the flow of pain ceased and Gerhold stared at his now healed side. "That should do for now. I cannot do much more; it has already been a long enough night."

"How in the six hells did you survive that fall?" Gerhold asked, still in shock from seeing Vergil alive.

"I grabbed onto a small ledge when I fell. It took some time, but I was able to climb my way back up, and just in time too by the looks of it," Vergil nodded in the direction of Harkin's body.

"Thank you for that," Gerhold said and with Vergil's help was able to make it to his feet. "By the gods, I think I have had enough of this for tonight. I never thought I would be so thankful to see a vampire."

"I told you before; we are not all like Harkin."

"Well, you got your revenge at least."

"That I did," Vergil said with a smile.

The two stared at each other for a moment before bursting out in laughter. It was strange, Gerhold was tired, sore, and bloodied, but he still could not help the desire to keep laughing. Finally, he turned his attention to the pile of ashes on the floor nearby, and reached over to pull out a small, golden locket. It had belonged to Lady Friedrich and her last request had been for Gerhold to return it to the man who had betrayed her in the first place.

"Well, what are you going to do now?" Vergil asked and Gerhold sighed.

"I want to get out of here, and maybe camp down the road a way in a small cave I passed by. Should be warm enough to get me through to the morning and then I will start making my way back south," Gerhold said and pocketed the little locket. "What about you?" Vergil just shook his head.

"I am not sure. I want to be free of this place though, too many bad memories. I suppose I will drift for a while until I find a place where I can settle down, undisturbed. Who knows, maybe I can start on another castle?" Both men chuckled and then they just stared at one another. Gerhold swallowed hard and then stuck out his hand.

"I never thought I would see the day where I shook hands with a vampire in friendship," he said as Vergil laughed.

"Never thought I would see the day where I would be shaking the hand of a slayer." They clasped hands.

"Maybe you should come with me? There are plenty more monsters and demons that need to be hunted," Gerhold asked but Vergil shook his head again.

"No, I believe I have had enough of my kind for a lifetime." Gerhold chuckled and nodded, and then, as if nothing else needed to be said, the vampire turned and started towards the doors that led out of the castle.

"Vergil," Gerhold called and the vampire turned around. "Keep your humanity. I do not wish to have to hunt you down one of these days."

"And I would hate to have you hunting me," he called back. With that he was through the doors and Gerhold was left alone in the castle hall

A Symphony of Blood

Chapter 8: Overlooked

Gerhold of Vilheim, Journal Entry: December 16, 5843 of the Common Age

It has been a full day now since the night I spent fighting my way through the castle of Lord Harkin, and I am remaining in the camp I made within a small cave an hour from the castle. My body is still sore and even the cuts and bruises that Vergil healed hurt whenever I move too much, but I am alive and in one piece, which is more than I can say for Harkin or Lady Friedrich. I am still wondering what to do about Lord Friedrich, and whether I should just kill him myself or turn him over to his liege lord. I still plan on giving him his wife's locket as a small memento for his betrayal and for serving the creatures of darkness.

I do not know what happened to Vergil though, but I believe he will be fine. He is the first vampire I have ever encountered who seemed to have maintained a shred of his humanity, but perhaps there are more? Perhaps there are more out there like him, and maybe, just maybe, they will fight just as hard against their foul brethren. This has given me much to think about and I will continue to ponder these thoughts as I make my way back to Vilheim. It will be a long journey and I am ready to be home for at least a time, but I shall do my best to enjoy my travels while I can. I am getting old, but I have a few battles left in me still.

Gerhold closed his journal and stuffed the little notebook away in his pack. The soft sound of the crackling fire was the only noise other than the high pitched howling of the winds outside of the cave. He had spent the previous day and night sleeping in the little cave, trying to recover as much as he could before heading back out into the mountains. His joints still ached and reminded him of just how old he was getting, but not yet old enough to retire from his work. He had replayed the events of the previous night multiple times and still felt a deep regret over not saving the poor woman's life, but at least he had saved her from an eternity as one of those monsters. A small consolation, but it was something to distract him from his failure none the less.

He reached deep into his pocket and pulled out the golden locket that the woman had instructed him to give to her husband, pronouncing her undying love for the man who had betrayed her. The very thought made Gerhold clench his fists in anger, and he vowed to make the lord pay for his evil deeds. He returned his attention to the locket and realized that in his anger the little golden circle had popped open, and he pulled it apart out of curiosity. Inside was a folded piece of parchment, and thinking it was a love letter from either the lady or lord, he pulled it out and opened it. Gerhold was surprised to see that it was not a note, but rather a small painted portrait of a handsome, blonde man. Upon closer examination he realized that it was a near perfect match to Vergil, and he stared at the little painting in confusion. Why would Lady Friedrich have had a locket containing a portrait of Vergil?

He stared at the paper for another moment, and then, as if a ton of stone had come crashing down upon him, his eyes shifted to the few words written at the bottom of the page. The man in the painting looked like Vergil but scrawled across the bottom were the words *A portrait of Lord Harkin Valakir*. At first it made no sense, and Gerhold felt his headache as he tried to understand. The vampire that had died in the castle, the vampire he had thought was Lord Harkin, was not the lord at all. Words and pictures flashed through his mind as he tried to recall everything that had happened in the castle. When he had found Vergil, he had looked healthy and well, as if he had only spent a few hours in the prison. The shocked reaction on the faces of the vampires in the clock tower when Vergil attacked them with his fire and the rage in the fake lord's eyes as he spoke of all the damage caused to *his* beautiful fortress. Gerhold felt his chest tighten as he ran these thoughts through his mind, and his heart nearly stopped when he finally concluded that neither vampire was who he said he was.

Vergil, or Lord Harkin, had switched places with his most trusted servant, and used this identity to follow Gerhold, to get close to him, and to fool him into thinking he had an ally when all along it was his greatest foe standing side by side with him. But why had he done it? Why did he kill his servant after Gerhold was defeated? And why had the lord healed him even though he was his enemy? Suddenly, Gerhold's eyes grew, and he felt his stomach drop as he fingered the little golden locket. He felt around his neck and realized that his gold

A Symphony of Blood

medallion was missing, the medallion that would warn him of any hidden curses. Memories flickered into his mind. The medallion trembling slightly as he approached Lady Friedrich for the first time, and how he had assumed it was due to a vampire being too near. He saw an image of Vergil reaching into his pack to grab the bomb as they crossed the bridge, while slipping the medallion from around Gerhold's neck at the same time.

A small smile crept across his face, not a happy one, but rather one that acknowledged defeat at the hands of a worthy foe. In the dancing light of the fire, it looked only like a normal necklace, but somewhere deep in the back of the slayer's mind, a strange sound had begun to grow. He had not even noticed it at first, but now the faint sound of strange music was echoing in the distance. A terrifying and beautiful sound, that seemed to grow just slightly with each passing minute.

J.S. Matthews

Epilogue

Jarrell finally sat up and rubbed his eyes wearily. He had been reading and copying for well over two hours and had already been forced to replace the little candle on his desk. The journals were interesting though, and Jarrell ran through the story once more in his mind as he shifted the parchments into a more organized fashion. Had Gerhold of Vilheim really penned these words? Was this really the fate of the famed monster slayer: outsmarted and turned into a creature of darkness. Out of the corner of his eye he could tell Ernhold was staring at him from beneath his hood.

"So, what do you think, Apprentice? Are the journals authentic or not?" the man asked with a smile and Jarrell shrugged.

"Possibly, though I still do not know for sure," he answered, hoping the other man would not respond. Ernhold still unnerved him.

"They are real, I assure you. Perhaps you need to look past your own imagination," Ernhold said and Jarrell stared at him quizzically, not exactly sure what the man meant. "You are being warped by the tales you have heard of the great slayer. You cannot imagine that the man of the many stories you have heard would have been tricked and bested by a vampire."

"Maybe that is why I remain unconvinced. Because the man in these journals and the man from the stories are not the same."

"There is no doubt of Gerhold's accomplishments, but he was not invincible, at least not how the embellished stories lead you to believe. People create heroes Apprentice. They create them in their own minds and hold onto the stories because they want to. Do not allow your desires for this man to remain the perfect hero to cloud your judgment," Ernhold finished and stood. "I think that is enough for tonight. You are looking tired, and I would hate for you to ruin the manuscript out of weariness." The man said curtly and walked over to the desk.

"What about the copy for the library? How shall I complete it?" Jarrell asked, as Ernhold gathered up the papers and closed the leather binding of the volume.

"I shall return again tomorrow night. I have business to attend to during the day and I will not allow these out of my sight, not even in one of the libraries. I shall inform your High Keeper that I will expect you here again tomorrow just after sundown. Do not be late, for you have much work ahead of you."

"I will be here," Jarrell answered as Ernhold nodded and then, with a flourish of his cloak, he disappeared from the room and closed the door behind him.

Jarrell did not like the man, not at all in fact. Something about Ernhold unnerved him. He seemed like a merchant but there was something about the way he walked and the way he carried himself that made Jarrell nervous. The apprentice finished gathering up his things and finally extinguished the candle before leaving the room. As he passed through the now deserted corridors of the library, he could not help but dwell on the story he had just read. There was very little doubt in his mind that these were in fact the real journals, in spite of what he had told Ernhold, and he found himself wanting to finish the story. To finally discover what had happened to Gerhold of Vilheim.

The second Night...
A Curse of Darkness

The sun was already beginning to set by the time Jarrell Vorren began making his way down to the fourth lower level of the Great Library, for once anticipating the night of reading and copying. This was the first time in a long time that Jarrell had looked forward to his work and he had spent much of the day pondering the story of Gerhold, the greatest monster slayer in the history of Tyriel, or so the legends had said. It had been a long day, as he had spent most of it continuing his work from the previous night and fighting the urge to daydream as he poured over the boring lists and descriptions of alchemical ingredients he was supposed to be copying. It was hard not to spend his time running through the story he had finished the previous night. He had hardly slept because of this, which only added to the difficulty of concentrating on the boring volume of plant lists, but now it would all be worth it as he would finally get to continue the story.

He had left off with Gerhold fighting his way through the castle of Lord Harkin, a powerful vampire, in order to rescue the wife of a lord from Penland. Only after his victory did the hunter discover that he had been betrayed, and that Vergil, his only ally during the fight, was in fact the vampire lord himself. This twist of events had shocked Jarrell, and during the last journal entry Gerhold had discovered that he had fallen for the vampire's trap and was tricked into taking possession of a cursed piece of gold. Now Jarrell wondered what would happen next. How would Gerhold remove the curse? What had happened to Harkin?

These questions had plagued him during the night and all throughout the day. Every boy had heard the stories of Gerhold the slayer of evil creatures, the hunter of beasts, the invincible, but now Jarrell felt a new connection with the tales. He remembered reading about them as a child and hearing his father tell the tales of how Gerhold had fought off an entire coven of witches, or how he had burned a vampire lair to the ground after trapping the monsters inside. The man was a legend, a legend that had disappeared from history, and now Jarrell was going to solve the mystery of what had happened to the greatest slayer of all time. Jarrell felt his pace quicken as the excitement and anticipation began to grow, and down the stairs he leapt, two by two, until finally reaching the little room on the fourth level. When he entered, he expected to see Ernhold waiting at the table, that same dark hood pulled up to hide his eyes, but instead he found the High Keeper standing near the front of the wooden desk at the back of the circular room.

"Good evening, Apprentice," Yorlan said as Jarrell entered. There was another man in the room, a Battlemage, one of the guards hired to watch over the Keepers and the Great Libraries. The man was tall and wore the same silver armor and full faced helm the other guards always wore. He held a long spear in his left hand.

"Good evening, High Keeper," Jarrell responded.

"Do you know why I am here?" Yorlan asked and Jarrell shook his head.

"I assume it is to make sure my work is coming along smoothly," Jarrell answered. "I am only an Apprentice after all."

"True, you are only an Apprentice, but your work is good enough to rival even some of our more experienced Keepers. I trust that you are doing what needs to be done. What I really came for was to see how things were faring with Mister Ernhold. Has he been cooperating with you?"

"He says very little and allows me to work in silence," Jarrell answered, and the High Keeper nodded, rubbing his chin.

"Good," Yorlan said. "I understand you think he is a strange man."

"His presence is a bit unnerving," Jarrell commented and Yorlan nodded again, though the Keeper was staring off as if pondering something much deeper.

"I imagine it is, but you must understand that much of a Keeper's work is done in uncomfortable circumstances. Some of our brothers have endured sieges while others have been forced to travel hundreds and hundreds of miles into the most remote places in this world. It is a good lesson to learn how to perform your duties in an imperfect environment." Jarrell nodded as if to say that he understood. "Well then, if there is no cause for concern, I shall leave you to prepare." The High Keeper made to leave but Jarrell spoke up.

"Who is he? I am not sure that I trust him," Jarrell said, and the Keeper paused for a moment.

"As a Keeper there will be many instances when you will work closely with those you do not like or trust, but it is necessary to perform the duties that have been entrusted to us."

With that, Yorlan turned and made his way out of the room, followed by the Battlemage, and soon the wooden door closed behind the two men and Jarrell was left alone in the chilly little room.

He walked across to the desk and started laying out the things he would need for the night. A few large bottles of ink, fresh quills, and a large stack of parchment were all set on the desktop and shifted around until Jarrell was satisfied. There were no windows or clocks in the room, so Jarrell had no idea how long he had waited before finally hearing the sound of the door opening as Ernhold entered, holding the leather volume of scrambled pages close to his chest and his hood still pulled up to shield his face. He was a tall slender man, but that was all that Jarrell could really tell about the merchant's appearance. Jarrell did not like the man, in fact Ernhold was the last person he wanted to be in the same room with, but the papers and journals he had were worth the man's uncomfortable silence and strange mannerisms. He moved across the room to where Jarrell sat and carefully placed the parchments on the desk. Then he took his familiar seat at the opposite end of the table.

"Are you ready to continue, Apprentice?" the man said, and Jarrell could see a small grin on the man's face.

"I am."

"You know you are the first person, other than myself, to learn the fate of Gerhold of Vilheim? You should consider yourself quite fortunate," Ernhold said and Jarrell decided not to respond. "I think it would be best if you start where I placed the next marker."

"Why should I not continue where I left off?" Jarrell asked, flipping through the many pages he was going to skip over.

"Do you wish to find out what happened to the slayer or not? There are hundreds of entries in that binder; most are just mindless accounts of all too similar exploits. Would you not rather dig deeper into the true story?"

"I am supposed to be copying the manuscript, not just reading for my enjoyment," Jarrell answered, but with very little conviction as it was true that he wanted to sit down in a nice, comfy chair and read through the entire manuscript.

"You should be copying the most important parts of the journals, not the mundane and useless records that will end up in one of the storage rooms gathering dust," the man said in his smooth tone and flipped open the leather-bound volume to the next bookmark.

"Why here?" Jarrell asked.

"Do you think that the story of Lord Harkin and Gerhold ended that night at Ravencroft Castle? Read and learn, young Apprentice."

With that, Ernhold turned and made his way to the end of the table where he sat once more.

Jarrell stared at the pile of tattered parchments in front of him and sighed. The first page marked by Ernhold was a small, crumpled map, which bore a crude drawing of the borderlands between the realm of Geldor and the old lands of Daloran. He did not like Ernhold, and the more time he spent with the man the less he liked him. He was right though, as Jarrell did want to find out what had happened to Gerhold. He shook his head and frowned, knowing that the High Keeper was depending on him to copy down as much of the manuscript as he could before Ernhold left, but something in the back of his mind was pestering him. He wanted to find out what had happened. Deciding that the scolding he would get for not copying the entire manuscript would be worth it, Jarrell once again delved into the long-forgotten tale, unsure of where the story would take him next.

Geldor

North to Vilheim

The Alidar Mountains

The Bordertown

The Blightwood

The Forest Path

The Bog

The Ruins of Altandir

South to the Ruins of Daloran

A Curse of Darkness

Chapter 1: The Turning

Gerhold of Vilheim, Journal Entry: February 10, 5844 of the Common Age

Two more months have passed, and I am now only a day's ride from the outskirts of Vilheim. It has taken me more time than I had thought to find my way back, as my head is not as clear as it usually is. I am close to home, but I do not know how long I have.

The sounds, the sounds are everywhere. My mind aches every second and no matter how hard I try I cannot drown them out. It is horrible yet soothing; the most beautiful and terrifying music I have ever heard. It is calling to me, calling like a warm day or a summer breeze. I am fighting it, but for how long will I be able to hold my ground? Even now it grows louder, and louder. I can hear nothing else except it and the few thoughts I can manage to form and scrawl across this page. Harkin, he is the one thought I can draw upon freely. He played me for a fool, and a fool I was! Gerhold of Vilheim, the greatest of all monster hunters. The man who never overlooked even the smallest details was tricked into trusting a vampire, the very vampire he was seeking to destroy.

I will find him. I will find him, and I will make him taste the bitterness and finality of true death.

Gerhold struggled to stay upright on his horse as he rode through the nearly deserted streets of Vilheim. Snow fell softly on the rooftops of the city and hid the ground beneath a soft blanket of white. It was a large city, packed with tall buildings whose roofs hung over the city streets and gave a claustrophobic feeling to the people walking below. Most of the houses were two stories tall and made from thick stones and rough wooden frames. The snow-covered streets crisscrossed in between the buildings, bordered by skinny alleyways and wide open, empty markets. The faint cries of tavern patrons enjoying their drinks could be heard drifting through the cool air, and the soft sound of the wind passing by was only a whisper in the night.

The world was spinning when Gerhold finally reached the center of town and halted in front of an old, abandoned cathedral. He tried to dismount but fell and crashed down hard on the stone ground, as the snow was not yet thick enough to cushion his fall. His side and shoulder ached but Gerhold hardly felt anything, as the pounding in his head was growing so strong that it drowned out pain and pleasure alike. Slowly, he struggled to his feet and stumbled around to the backside of the chapel and in between the frozen gravestones of the cemetery to a little stairwell that led down to the undercroft. The door at the bottom was locked, and Gerhold pounded his fist on the wooden frame until finally a light appeared inside and he heard the lock click.

"Gerhold? By the Gods man what has happened to you?" The man who opened the door was a skinny, little priest with short grey whiskers and droopy eyes. The old man did his best to help Gerhold through the door. "Come, friend, tell me what is wrong? What has happened to you?"

The chapel undercroft was old and dusty. Ancient wooden shelves held rows of what looked like old texts, artifacts, and other odds and ends. As soon as the door closed Gerhold fell to the floor and began writhing in agony as the pain in his mind grew too great for even the song to drown out. He tried to pull himself up by grabbing hold of a nearby table but fell over once more as another wave of nauseating sounds echoed through his head.

"Armin… the, the curse, the noise!" Gerhold cried and cradled his head in his hands.

"Curse? Noise?" The priest repeated as if confused and then suddenly his eyes grew wide with both understanding and fear. "The Curse! Gerhold, my old friend, where is your amulet?"

"The noise! Only a few moments left…" Gerhold pulled out and held up the little golden locket.

Armin nodded and shuffled across the room.

The priest sifted through the rows of parchments and old artifacts, searching for something, and muttering to himself. He ran along each shelf desperately searching for something, something that could destroy a cursed piece of treasure. It was difficult to destroy any object that had been made in Arden as the smiths and tinkers of the old ages were vastly superior to their modern

A Curse of Darkness

counterparts. There were many techniques and skills that had been forgotten over time and now few, if any, knew the true mysteries behind the ancient artifacts of the lost realms. Armin was looking for a few specific things, as he had heard of only one way to destroy a cursed artifact: holy fire. At least that is what the priests called it, and it was a mixture of various alchemical ingredients that would create a flame so hot it could melt steel.

The old man grabbed a small metal bowl and a vial of silver powder. To this he added crushed pyrite stone, a drop of blessed oil, and a few dried golden flower petals. Gerhold's cries grew as the priest worked furiously to mix the ingredients together in the proper amounts, and after stirring the mixture over a small flame, he hurried over to Gerhold, who now thrashed and writhed on the cold, dirty floor of the undercroft. Armin bent low, touching a long match to the silvery paste which burst with a bright white flame. He reached for the golden necklace that sat on the ground near where Gerhold was flailing and used a short metal mixing rod to lift the amulet.

Out of the corner of his eye, Gerhold watched as the priest set the cursed necklace into the flames and waited as the seconds passed by. For nearly a minute Armin held the golden locket over the white flame, only to be disappointed when nothing seemed to happen. The priest returned the locket to the flames once again, but suddenly Gerhold's cries ceased. The slayer thrashed about for a moment, but Armin knew what had happened, and the priest reacted quickly. There was nothing that he could do now, and Gerhold only had one chance.

Armin leapt to his feet and ran across the room to another shelf of vials containing various solutions, and he settled on a small one containing a thick red liquid before sprinting back to Gerhold. The hunter felt his bones creak and ache. He let out another cry of pain as his body felt as if was being wrenched and torn. His head started to throb and spin. As soon as the priest bent down, Gerhold stopped his thrashing and suddenly all the pain was gone. The aches and burning had disappeared along with the echoing sounds, but his body still felt strange. Gerhold felt someone reach down and pour something into his mouth. Immediately he felt warmth spread through his body and his headache started to slowly subside. After a minute, the hunter opened his eyes and gasped as he stared up at the old priest who stood over him, still holding the little empty vial. He was alive! Alive, and now he felt better than he had in over a month. He sat up and noticed the strange look on Armin's face.

"You did it, old man," Gerhold said with a smile, but the grin disappeared as quickly as it came when he noticed the priest's head shaking side to side.

"No, my friend. There was nothing that I could do. I tried to destroy the amulet, but I failed. The curse has already completed its work."

Gerhold looked confused for a moment, but then he reached his hand up and touched his lips. He pulled his fingers away and looked at the vestiges of red liquid that still lined his mouth. Only then did he realize what had happened, and only then did he realize what he had become.

A Curse of Darkness

Chapter 2: The Letter

Gerhold of Vilheim, Journal Entry: February 10, 5944 of the Common Age

It has been quite some time since my last entry, at least a few months if I am correct. Time has gotten away from me over the past hundred years, as it is much harder to keep track of time when one is immortal. I have not written anything since I lost my last journal while traveling, and only now have I regained the motivation to continue with my records. It had many adventures recorded in it, at least two years' worth, and I am still quite bothered by its loss. With so much happening over so long a time it has become harder to remember everything. As much as it pained me at first, I have come to appreciate this dark gift, to some extent.

It has now been a hundred years to the day since I became a vampire, and from that moment on I could tell something was different. I felt stronger, faster, and more agile than ever before, even when I was young, but also equipped with the experience earned through nearly a lifetime of hunting dark creatures. Before, parrying the blow of a full-fledged vampire had shaken my entire body and taken every effort just to maintain a grip on my sword, but now their attacks feel no different than a humans would have those many years ago. I am now more deadly than any hunter could ever hope to be, but not everything has been better, as it is a curse for a reason.

Fighting the thirst and hunger for blood has been difficult to say the least, but it is a challenge I intend to win. Not once in a hundred years have I feasted on an innocent victim and I shall hold to that oath even if it means my death. I have written this promise many times in my journals, but each time it is a reminder of the task. The hunger is always there, hiding, or perhaps trapped somewhere deep inside the darkest recesses of my mind. It is a caged beast, clawing at my consciousness like some savage monstrosity trapped inside a slowly collapsing prison. Of course, there are worse things *than having to stave off the thirst for human blood. Not hearing music for so many years has been the most difficult to accept, and every day I long to hear the soft melody of a flute or mandolin. It is far more painful to sit in a tavern with so many happy patrons and know that only I exist in this painful silence, than to be starving from lack of blood or feeling the stinging rays of the sun.*

I suppose, though, that this curse is mine to bear for a higher purpose, and that the Gods have chosen me as a champion of light, to hunt down the spawn of evil until my last breath. Of course, I also have a more selfish goal in mind. It has been a hundred years of hunting and slaying, but I am still no closer to locating Harkin Valakir and no closer to gaining my vengeance. It is possible that he is dead, perhaps destroyed by another slayer, but I will not believe it until I find his bones or kill him myself. I will find him though, as I have until the end of this world to search. One day, I will find Lord Harkin, and on that day, he shall finally meet his end.

Gerhold closed the dusty leather journal and set it on the table next to a low burning candle. He yawned and rubbed his tongue against the elongated fangs on the top and bottom of his mouth, realizing that even after a hundred years they still felt strange to him. These fangs, along with the constant thirst for the blood of humans, had become constant reminders of what he was, the power he had, and the danger he had become to the world. Absentmindedly he tugged on the little golden chain and locket that hung on his neck, another reminder of what had happened so many years ago. Gerhold pushed these thoughts aside, as it was better to dwell on the hunger as little as possible, or at least that was one way he had found to combat the never-ending thirst.

Gerhold leaned back in his chair and stared around the room. This was the largest room in the upper level of the chapel and was a bit too large for his taste, but it did give him room to add new shelves of books or storage for equipment whenever he needed it. Despite its age, the old cathedral was still standing, and Gerhold had come to make these spacious upper areas into his living quarters and armory. These once dusty and empty rooms were now filled with racks of armor and weapons, tables covered in equipment and materials, shelves full of a century worth of books, and a few sealed barrels containing Gerhold's precious supply of blood. The priests of Mathuin, who now watched over the chapel, ensured that these barrels always stayed filled, which Gerhold was more than thankful for.

A Curse of Darkness

Before he turned, Gerhold had used this chapel as a refuge, a home if he had to say he had one, and only he and the old priest, Armin, spent any time within its musty, ancient interiors. When Armin was coming to the end of his days, the old priest invited others to come and watch over the chapel in his place, ensuring that they would also help Gerhold as he did. Surprisingly, these new priests took to the task of providing for the monster slayer with more enthusiasm than Gerhold expected, and over the past hundred years they passed down these secrets to the next generation of priests so that they too could assist him. At first, Gerhold found the group annoying as he had often valued his time alone to think and plan, and with so many of the priests coming and going there was very little time when he could be by himself. After a time though, the priests showed their worth.

One of these priests spent much of his time learning the secrets of alchemy with Armin, before the old man passed away, and proved to be a true prodigy in the subject. With this knowledge, the priest was able to create a mixture of animal and human blood, which allowed Gerhold to store a large amount of the potion at one time. Over the years this priest passed his knowledge onto another, a young boy named Nethrin, and that apprentice now worked closely with Gerhold to create new weapons and tools that he could employ during his adventures. Nethrin was a bit eccentric and prone to explosions of excitement that would make even a child shy away. He was young though, and would learn, but it also helped that Nethrin was the most brilliant alchemist and craftsman that Gerhold had ever seen. Most of the equipment that now lay scattered around on various tables and stands was designed by Nethrin, and many had saved the slayer's life more than once over the past few years.

Not only had they provided Gerhold with blood, new tools, and weapons, but they also made it possible for Gerhold to continue his work as a slayer. Being a vampire had made it far more difficult for Gerhold to interact with people, as one would imagine, and there were few, if any, who would ever hire a vampire and would sooner report him to the Paladins. This was where the priests proved invaluable, as they received hundreds of pleas for assistance a month, many of which required a slayer to do the job. Most of these requests came from people too poor to hire any of the common mercenary bands, and so the priests would collect a small sum and send Gerhold to perform the work. If they ever heard of anything from a neighboring town, chapel, or monastery, the priests were all too eager to call on the master hunter, for which he was quite grateful.

It was hard to go on for so long with no word or trace of Harkin, and it made him clench his teeth in frustration just thinking about how many years he had spent searching for the vampire. It had become an obsession and still he spent much of his spare time investigating strange stories and rumors that he picked up during his travels, hoping that one may lead him to some hint of Harkin's whereabouts. The vampire was not dead, he could not be, not one who was that cunning. Harkin had been smart enough to fool Gerhold into trusting him and tricked Gerhold into becoming a vampire himself. Neither living nor dead, a soulless creature, cursed to walk the earth until his death at the hands of an enemy or the end of the earth itself. He had to find Harkin, he had to obtain vengeance.

Just then the soft sound of footsteps came from the hallway and Gerhold turned to see the silhouette of a boy in off-white robes striding in. Nethrin was young at only fifteen years of age and had short hair to go with a broad smile that seemed to take up his entire face. He was walking at a very fast pace and Gerhold could tell the boy was excited about something, which was more common than not as Gerhold recalled a similar disturbance the previous day.

"Master Gerhold, sir? I did not mean to disturb you, but I just finished something that you must see!" The boy spoke in a winded tone as if he had just run the flights of stairs from the chapel floor to the upper levels.

"It is fine, Nethrin. What is it you wish to show me this time?" Gerhold asked.

"You are going to love this one, it might just be my best yet," the boy said and pulled a wrapped bundle from under his arm. Nethrin laid it on a nearby table and unwrapped it.

Inside was a long, finely crafted crossbow, with thick metal arms and a strong wire string. It looked magnificent and Gerhold could not help but hold it up close and examine the masterful craftsmanship. The wood was smooth, stained beautifully, and the emblems of the Three Gods, Mathuin, Uriel, and Athos, were engraved along each side.

"By the Gods, Nethrin, how did you manage this?" Gerhold exclaimed as he marveled at the beautiful weapon. "Why, this is the finest crossbow I have ever seen, let alone held."

"Took me four weeks of work. I call it the Crossblade, and she does more than just look pretty," Nethrin responded, and motioned for Gerhold to hand him the crossbow. "You see, I modified the design so that even your larger crossbow can now fold up, making it much easier to carry. But then I also had another idea. I remembered how you mentioned that you do not like having to drop your crossbow to draw your sword whenever something gets too close, so I made one more modification."

Nethrin pushed a little metal handle on the side of the crossbow and immediately the arms slid forward and came together at a point, producing a foot and a half silver blade. He then held down another metal latch and made a flicking motion with his wrist so that the blade extended a foot further. Gerhold took the weapon and held it out in front of him. It felt a little off balance but otherwise was an impressive piece of work.

"Anytime you need it to return to the crossbow just pull that latch down again and slide the arms back into place. Well? What do you think?" Nethrin asked excitedly.

"This is impressive. How did you manage to get the blade to extend so smoothly?" Gerhold asked as he practiced switching between the crossbow and the blade.

Before the young priest could answer, they heard another set of footsteps coming from the hall. Gerhold held up his hand for Nethrin to be silent. Another priest wearing similar robes came walking in, though he stopped and raised an eyebrow when he saw that both men in the room were staring at him.

"I did not know you knew that I was coming to see you, Master Gerhold," the older man said.

"You know I can hear better than most, Brother Francis," Gerhold answered, and the old man just smiled and nodded.

"Of course, but I will never be used to it. Why are you here, Nethrin? Did Brother Marrin not ask you to finish dusting the shelves in the undercroft? I highly doubt you managed it so quickly," the older man said scathingly.

"Well –er– you see, I started dusting, but then I suddenly had an idea for the new weapon I was building for Master Gerhold here, and well I…" the young boy trailed off and started shifting his feet uncomfortably.

"If you focused on your studies and meditation as much as you focus on your tinkering you would already be a Vigil," the old man said and shook his head.

"I am sorry Brother Francis, I only wished to help Master Gerhold," Nethrin responded.

"Enough, boy, we will discuss your punishment later. For now, I need you to go and finish your duties, and you better not even think about touching that forge or workshop of yours until they are done. You are dismissed," Francis finished and Gerhold saw Nethrin's shoulders slump in disappointment.

"Of course, Brother Francis, I apologize," Nethrin said glumly, and with one more longing glance towards Gerhold and the crossbow Nethrin turned and disappeared into the hall.

"I do not know what to do with that boy. He is one of the brightest followers I have ever encountered, but he gets distracted by the simplest of things. By the Gods, a mouse could run by and somehow manage to inspire some sort of new contraption in that wild imagination of his, and no sooner would he be back in his workshop tinkering with the devils know what and trying to build whatever it was that popped into his head. It is maddening I tell you. How can one teach the disciplines of patience, fortitude, and focus when the pupil cannot even concentrate long enough to sweep a hallway?" Brother Francis exhaled slowly and rubbed his wrinkled forehead.

"He is young, Francis. Give him time and he will become as boring as the rest of you," Gerhold responded with a chuckle, and absentmindedly flicked the blade of the crossbow open again. He was amazed at just how easy and simple an addition it was and was already planning out just how he would be able to use it.

"Perhaps you are right, but the boy still needs to learn some focus or he will never learn a thing," the old man sighed.

"He is good at what he does, and once you can teach him to focus that same passion into your teachings, he will come along. Boys are far too easily distracted to be cooped up in a place like this, and it only leads to more imaginings," Gerhold added.

"I suppose we can hope. I am starting to believe that the Gods are the only hope of training that boy."

"Maybe they are testing your patience. The Three often challenge us with tasks that seem impossible, but that is only so we are forced to rely on them for strength and not ourselves," Gerhold said and Brother Francis chuckled.

"I would prefer if the Gods tested someone else's patience. The boy may just drive me to my grave."

"I take it you did not come all the way up here to discuss Nethrin's study habits?" Gerhold asked, trying to change the subject.

"Ah yes, of course. I am sorry for getting distracted, that boy seems to rub off on everyone," Francis said and reached into the pocket of his robes. "This just arrived for you not ten minutes ago. It was delivered by a Paladin. I was about to send Brother Charles to come and warn you, but the man simply handed over the letter and asked us to give it to you immediately."

"A Paladin? The Vigils know I am here?" Gerhold asked suspiciously and tore open the letter.

The Paladins were holy warriors who followed the teachings of the Vigilant, the most powerful religion in Tyriel. They served the Three Gods just as Gerhold did, but all Paladins swore oaths to destroy any and all dark creatures, including vampires. This made Gerhold nervous as he knew they would not care who he was or what he did, for in their eyes he was a creature of darkness and nothing more. He pulled the folded piece of parchment and a small metal seal from the envelope and began reading the slanted handwriting.

To Gerhold of Vilheim,

I am in desperate need of your services and request an audience with you. You will find my airship at the east docks of Vilheim. The name of the ship is the Ilvarin. My Paladins have strict orders not to harm or delay you in any way. Present this seal to the guards at the entrance and they will allow you to enter. Come alone, and please tell no others of our meeting.

May the light shine upon thy path,
Pontius Urban, Vigil of Righteousness

Gerhold stared at the letter for a moment and then handed it to Francis who read through it quickly. The Vigil of Righteousness, one of the three leaders of the Vigilant, wished to meet with him? Years ago, Gerhold would have been astounded, even excited, to meet one of the holy leaders, but now it only made him nervous. Was this a plot to get him out in the open? To kill him? Gerhold rolled the circular metal seal between his fingers and stared at the symbols of the Three that were etched into its surface.

"Pontius Urban wishes to meet with you? The Vigil of Righteousness himself is in Vilheim?" Francis said excitedly.

"Apparently, he is, unless this is only a trap. I would not be surprised to see the Paladins do such a thing. They are more cunning than most realize. People look and see the armor, but not the men beneath."

"You must be cautious my friend. I have met Pontius Urban only once, but his Eminence is not a man who takes kindly to fools or foolish words. Do you intend on meeting with him?" Francis asked as he handed back the letter.

"Not sure if I have much of a choice," Gerhold answered and scanned the letter one last time. "Besides, if he serves the Three, then I should be able to trust him. He is a Vigil after all."

"Yes, he is, but he is also the commander of the Paladins," Francis added.

"Well then, let us hope, for their sakes, that his word is true." Gerhold folded the letter and stuffed it into his pocket while walking across the room. He pulled his brown overcoat from a hook on the wall and threw it over his shoulders, then he buckled his sword belt around his waist and slung the newly constructed crossbow over his back. "Tell no one of this, the letter asked that I say nothing to anyone. So, keep quiet until I return."

"I will, but Gerhold?" The slayer turned back as he was walking out the door. "Make sure you do come back."

Gerhold did not respond, but instead smiled and then disappeared into the hall.

A Curse of Darkness

Chapter 3: An Unlikely Employer

The streets of Vilheim were nearly deserted as Gerhold exited the cathedral and began making his way through the city and towards the east docks. Snow was falling gently and had already blanketed the ground and rooftops, and every so often cries or coarse laughter from a pub echoed through the calm night air. It was bitterly cold, but Gerhold noticed nothing, as vampires could feel neither heat nor cold. Instead, he felt nothing, as if he lived in a vacuum and was not truly part of the world, but during cold nights such as this it was more of a boon than a curse. Still a small part of him missed the stinging feeling of the cold air and the soft, cool wetness of the snowflakes as they touched his skin.

Gerhold walked briskly through the streets, keeping the hood of his overcoat pulled low over his face as he passed between the tall wooden and stone buildings. Vilheim was a crowded city that had been built along a small river that emptied into the North Sea and had become a very prosperous town for shipping goods to and from the central areas of Midland, the largest continent in Tyriel. During the past hundred years its population had exploded, and now the city was an unorganized mess of two- and three story houses that sometimes held four or more families. The docks were almost always crowded with traditional seafaring vessels while on the eastern side of town the skydocks were never empty. At the center of the city was a large fortress with a one-hundred-foot wall of solid stone that stood high above the other buildings. Vilheim had been Gerhold's home now for almost a hundred and fifty years, and despite all the changes it still felt like the same city he had settled in all those years ago.

After a few minutes of walking, the eastern skydocks finally came into view and Gerhold made his way towards a line of old abandoned houses along the edge of the massive wooden structures. Skydocks were tall wooden scaffolds with metal catwalks and multiple wooden bridges that stretched out at varying lengths to accommodate as many ships as possible. Airships resembled seafaring vessels but also had a large canvas filled with a number of inflated ballonets attached above it. The canvas was secured to the rest of the ship by thick steel ropes and two thick, metal pipes that pumped hot air up from the ship's furnaces and into the ballonets, which would allow the ship to rise high into the air.

Gerhold hated flying, and the past hundred years had done nothing but intensify that feeling. He had always preferred travelling by the wildest roads possible and seeing as much of the world as he could, but with an airship he felt as though he was disconnected even more so than he already felt due to the curse. Still, airships had their uses and were invaluable during the Plague Wars which had taken place hundreds of years ago and had also made traveling and shipping much easier and faster. For Gerhold though, there was no better way to travel than straight through the wilderness itself, not high above where you missed the many beautiful sights and grandeur of nature.

Gerhold pushed these thoughts aside as he made his way into one of the abandoned buildings. He was careful at first, making sure that the building was abandoned before stepping inside. The City Watch rarely patrolled this area, and so these old ruins served as the perfect place for the poor and homeless to set up residence. Gerhold made his way up the charred staircase to the second floor which looked out over the docks and pulled a small looking glass from the inside of his coat. The docks were almost empty, save for workers and a few members of the City Watch who patrolled up and down the wooden scaffolds. It took only a moment before Gerhold found what he was looking for, a large ship with the word *Ilvarin* written across the stern. Through the looking glass, Gerhold could see a few men in silver armor walking along the deck, but otherwise nothing was out of the ordinary.

Satisfied with his reconnaissance, Gerhold returned to the streets and made his way to the docks. The snow started to fall a little harder now as he approached the entrance where two guards from the City Watch stood talking. The message had said to use the front entrance but Gerhold did not trust anyone, not even a Vigil, and instead made his way around to the northern edge of the docks. The City Watch was there to protect the citizens of Vilheim, but more often than not they exploited their positions of power and were more tyrants than protectors. Gerhold did his best to avoid contact with any of them unless necessary, just in case any of them were to learn of his condition. He did not trust the City Watch, and it seemed that the people of Vilheim were actually better off with the criminals than the city guards. Power, no matter how little, always seemed to corrupt men.

He quickly scaled the wall that surrounded the compound and landed softly on the other side, then he started to make his way around the docks as silently as he could, keeping to the shadows to avoid any wondering eyes. It was easy, as there had been many times over the past years when he had been forced to sneak past vampire guards, blood crazed cultists, and necromancers. A few members of the City Watch would pose little to no trouble.

Silently, Gerhold made his way up a flight of stairs that passed along the first tall scaffold dock until he reached the second level, and then across a metal catwalk to where the Ilvarin was docked. It was a beautiful ship made from a smooth, dark stained wood with gold trim and windows made of fine glass. Clearly the Vigil enjoyed travelling comfortably, though Gerhold wondered just how much of the peoples' tithes had been used to build such a beautiful airship. Gerhold paused for a moment and listened. Footsteps echoed across the wooden walkways around him. Seven guards, all heavily armored from the heavy sounds of their footfalls, and all sounded calm by the soft rhythmic thumping of their heartbeats. He continued past the stern of the ship until he came to a long footbridge that connected the dock to the deck. He was immediately stopped by two serious looking silver-clad Paladins who stood on either side of the walkway.

"Why are you here, stranger?" the first Paladin said and held his hand up for Gerhold to halt. "No one is allowed on this wharf without his Eminence's permission or by order of the Knight Commander."

"My name is Gerhold of Vilheim, and I have come at the request of Pontius Urban," Gerhold responded and held out the silver seal bearing the mark of the Vigil of Righteousness and the Three Gods.

The two men exchanged unreadable glances. Their heartbeats quickened, though. They were nervous.

"Gerhold, you say? The Knight Commander asked to speak with you the moment you arrived and before you see the Vigil. If you will wait here for a moment, Ser Mallin will go and get him," the guard responded while the other turned around and made his way up the footbridge towards the deck.

It was only a few moments before the guard returned with another Paladin wearing similar silver armor, but with gold trimming and a long blue cloak.

"Good evening, I am Knight Commander Warrick. You are here to see his Eminence, are you not?" the man asked and Gerhold nodded. The commander motioned with his hand to follow and led the way up onto the deck. Once there Warrick rounded on Gerhold. "Before you go any further, know this; we know what you are, monster, and if you so much as move wrong, we will kill you. I do not know why his Eminence wishes to speak with you and I care not who you may have once been. Oh yes, I have heard the tales of the hunter Gerhold of Vilheim, but I do not believe that is who you are. So, mind yourself creature or I will end you."

Gerhold looked into the commander's eyes and a small smile crept to his lips, revealing the sharp extended fangs. After so many years of this sort of treatment Gerhold was not bothered by it in the least. Those many years ago when he had been human, the same words had come from his mouth more than once and with even more venom. Being on the other side had put many things in perspective but he did not begrudge the Commander for his hatred as often Gerhold did not trust himself. The hunger could set upon him at any moment and what if it were too much to control? This was the one thing that worried him more than anything else so having a Paladin nearly would only serve as another reminder to fight the urge to feed.

"I came because your Vigil requested my help, nothing more." Gerhold said but the commander's hard face did not change. Just then the door to the lower decks opened and a line of orange light spread across the deck. Gerhold turned and saw an older, slender man wearing a magnificent robe of blue and white, and a large decorative crown on his head.

"Thank you for welcoming our guest, Commander, but I think that will do for now," the elderly man said in a weak voice.

"Your Eminence, I cannot leave you alone with this creature. I request that you allow me to remain with you during the meeting," Warrick said and glared at Gerhold.

"All right, Commander, if it will keep you from mobilizing the guard at the slightest sound then yes. Come now, Gerhold, we have very little time to speak."

The old man led the way into the lighted corridor and down a short hallway to a large cabin at the end. Gerhold could feel the heat from Warrick's angry stare burning into his back but he did not mind. He was used to the treatment now and was more surprised that he had even noticed it. Once they reached the cabin the Vigil made his way to the other end of a large table at the center of the room, and motioned for Gerhold to take the seat across from him

A Curse of Darkness

while Warrick closed the door behind them.

"Now, I suppose you are wondering why I invited you here tonight?" the Vigil asked. Gerhold nodded as he sat, keeping an eye on the Knight Commander standing behind him. "Well, you were actually the entire purpose of this trip to Vilheim. I am in need of your expertise. There is an issue I need you to investigate for me, if you are willing that is."

"I think the real question is, what is the Vigil of Righteousness doing meeting a vampire in the dead of night?" Gerhold asked and the Vigil smiled at him. "That also raises the question, if you already know that I was in Vilheim, why have you not sent your Paladins to kill me?"

"We have known about you since the night you turned. Brother Armin sent a message to the Vigils a day after you returned from your journey and informed us that you posed no threat. Of course, my predecessor did not believe it at first and sent informants to investigate Armin's assertions," Pontius Urban said and gave a small cough.

"The priests of Mathuin," Gerhold muttered and shook his head. He should have known they were informing the Vigils about his escapades.

"We could not take the chance in case Brother Armin was wrong, but time has shown that he was a good judge of character. You have performed admirably, Gerhold, even with your curse. Not only that, but the priests tell me that you are a devout follower of the Vigilant, even more so than many of our own priests."

"And even when I have been hunted by your men," Gerhold added and glanced back at the Knight Commander.

"And that is why I need you. I need someone who is capable, but who is also devoted to our beliefs."

"Are there no Paladins that would meet those expectations? Why do you need me when you have an army of eager and armed warriors?" Gerhold asked suspiciously.

"If I send my Paladins, I must also report their movements to the other Vigils, and I would rather not report this issue just yet. Also, there are few who have your experience and I need the best I can find if we are to uncover this mystery. So, will you help me? I can also guarantee a significant donation to the Vilheim chapel, if that would help sway you," the Vigil finished and Gerhold paused before answering.

"That depends on what this request entails," Gerhold answered.

"Far south of Vilheim along the southern border of Geldor, is the Blightwood. You have heard of this forest, have you not?" Gerhold nodded. "It is a haunted wood, saturated in dark magic left behind from the last of the Plague Wars that destroyed the realm of Daloran over a thousand years ago."

"I know the stories," Gerhold added, a little impatiently. Being around all the Paladins was making him wary, and he wanted to spend as little time here as possible.

"Then you know that what was once a beautiful and lush wood is now shrouded in an eternal darkness. Black clouds hang over the land like an unending storm, but this darkness never grows beyond the borders of that forest, at least until now that is," the old Vigil said, and slid a piece of parchment across the table to Gerhold.

"Growing? What do you mean?"

"The darkness is spreading; it reaches beyond those accursed trees and with it many strange events have begun occurring along the border. Men and women are disappearing, animals are acting on edge and even violent, and there have been whispers of shadows emerging from the forest. Something has happened in the Blightwood, something sinister, and I need you to uncover what it is," Pontius coughed again, and took a sip from a nearby chalice to clear his throat.

"So, you want me to go into the Blightwood alone?" Gerhold asked.

"Not alone. I will send with you six of my own personal guard. They report only to me, so the other Vigils need not know of their business."

"Why not send them in, why do you need me? Pardon my suspiciousness, but you have to understand why I am wary of your intentions," the Vigil coughed again and shook his head.

"Of course, and in fact I expected nothing less from a slayer with your reputation," The Vigil said, but Knight Commander Warrick snorted in disgust.

"Reputation? He is a vampire, so even if the stories are true, then at some point he failed in his mission to destroy evil and should have taken his own life rather than endure in this world as an abomination." The Commander spat and glared at Gerhold.

"Hold your tongue Commander, or have you forgotten whom you serve?" Warrick glared at Gerhold for another moment, then he turned and gave a small bow to the Vigil.

"I am sorry, your Eminence. Forgive my lack of judgment."

A Curse of Darkness

"It is forgiven. Now, Gerhold, what do you say? Will you agree to help me?"

Gerhold paused and rubbed his forehead. He still was not sure if he could trust the man or not, and he was worried about heading hundreds of miles to the south in the company of so many Paladins who would sooner kill him than look at him. Still, if what the Vigil said was true, then something evil was brewing in the Blightwood. What sinister force could affect a massive magical phenomenon such as the one that had occurred in the Blightwood a thousand years ago? Gerhold had heard of the large battle that had taken place in the forest near the end of the last Plague War, a time when hundreds of thousands of undead had attacked and destroyed the greatest realm in Tyriel at the time, Daloran. All that was left of that once great realm was ashes, dust, and the dark forest that bordered the southern edge of the remaining realms. If the darkness of those woods was growing, then there must be something evil behind it.

"I will help you, your Eminence," he answered finally.

"Very good then. If you do not mind, I wish to depart first thing in the morning. Will you be ready by that time?" the Vigil asked eagerly. Gerhold stood and nodded.

"I will return before sunup," he said and turned to leave.

"Oh, and Gerhold?" Urban called and Gerhold turned just as he reached the door. "Thank you."

Gerhold nodded once more, and with that he was past the Knight Commander, who gave him one last scathing glare, and out onto the deck of the ship. A few minutes later he was once again on the other side of the wall that separated the airship docks from the rest of the city. He made his way back through the snow-covered streets back towards the cathedral at the center of the city. Had he made the right decision? Was he trusting the wrong men once again? He pushed these questions from his mind as he walked and focused on the one that mattered, if the darkness was growing in the Blightwood then he was needed.

Chapter 4: Flying South

Gerhold of Vilheim, Journal Entry: February 11, 5944 of the Common Age

    Last night I met with Pontius Urban. He is a powerful man, one that I am not sure if I should be trusting. The world is changing so fast that I can barely keep up with it. Perhaps it is the perspective of an immortal? The world seems to be moving and changing, while I remain unchanged. It feels like only yesterday when the Vigils were trying to hunt me down, and now they are asking for my help. I am not sure of what to make of it, but one thing is for certain: I cannot sit idly by while the evil that taints the Blightwood spreads. If what the Pontius said is true, then I have very little choice in the matter.

    I must help if I can, though I feel as though something is off. Am I walking into some sort of trap? Perhaps I am being foolish, but for now I must work with what I have. Cautious is what I must be, and not only because of the Paladins. Being away from Vilheim is a danger for me in and of itself. I always carry a large supply of blood with me, but there is always the risk that I will run out, and what will happen then? The monster lurking within the shadows of my mind is always on the prowl, always waiting for that lapse in judgement. Waiting for that one moment of weakness. What would happen if I begin to starve? To crave the blood. All those around me would be in danger, and if, Gods forbid, I did lose control, what then? What would I do if I took the life of an innocent? Would that strip me of my last vestiges of humanity? Would I become like so many others and lost what little control I have over the craving for blood?

    I do not wish to dwell on these thoughts, but they must be confronted. Immortality is a cruel thing, to know that unless I am killed or take my own life, that I will always live. That all of my triumphs, and more heavily, my failures, will continue on with me. How could I go on know that I had become what I have fought against all

A Curse of Darkness

my life? Living day after day with the guilt of feasting on the innocent is something I could not do. I will not fail. I cannot.

"Do you have everything prepared?" Brother Francis asked. Gerhold nodded and patted the small pack that lay on the ground next to him.

"I have everything I need. Will you be all right without me?" Gerhold asked with a smile.

"I am certain we will be just fine. Are you sure you have everything? Did you bring enough of the potion to last you until you return?" Francis asked again, referring to the concoction of human blood, animal blood, and few other ingredients that Gerhold relied on for sustenance.

"More than enough. Are you worried about me, Brother?" Gerhold asked and Francis frowned in response.

"I am, my friend. I am worried about a great many things. I am worried that you will run out of your potion and will be forced to resort to other means of survival, or that one of those Paladins will take it upon himself to end your life in your sleep." The old priest sighed and shook his head.

"Then you had better start praying for the Paladin that makes that decision, and that his soul is ready for eternity," Gerhold replied with another smile.

"This is not a joking matter. You need to be careful, Gerhold."

"I have been alive for over a hundred and fifty years, my old friend, and I know how to act around Paladins. I would be more worried about what is happening in the south if I were you. That is if what the Vigil said is true. If the darkness of Blightwood is spreading, then it may mean something far more sinister is at hand." Gerhold stood up from his desk, placed his leather journal in the pack, and closed it.

"If the darkness of Blightwood is spreading, then it is you that needs to worry. I am not the one climbing into the jaws of the lion." Just then the door to Gerhold's room flung open as Brother Nethrin came running in, huffing, and puffing and even more excited than the last time.

"Master Gerhold! Master Gerhold, I only just learned that you were leaving, and I have something I needed to give you before you go." The young man nearly ran over Brother Francis as he darted across the room, lugging a large, wrapped bundle that he dropped unceremoniously on the nearby table.

"By the Gods, boy! Do you not know how to knock before you enter a room?" Francis yelled and grabbed Nethrin by the scruff of his neck.

"I am sorry, Brother Francis, but I must speak with Master Gerhold before he leaves," Nethrin pleaded.

"It is all right Francis, let the boy go. Our conversation was at an end anyway," Gerhold said and put an arm on the old priest's shoulder.

Francis frowned at Nethrin before releasing him and shaking Gerhold's hand.

"Good luck, Gerhold, make sure you come back to us, and may the light guide your path." With that Brother Francis left the room and closed the door softly behind.

"I am terribly sorry to interrupt you like that, but I really must speak with you," Nethrin said excitedly.

"No apology necessary. Now, what is it that you wanted to see me about? I must depart soon so make it quick."

"Well sir, I have been working on something else along with your new crossbow. Do you like it by the way? Is it working all right?" Nethrin asked, and Gerhold could not help but chuckle at the childish level of energy that was coming from the young man.

"Aye, it works just fine, better than fine in fact. Now, what did you want to show me?"

"Well sir, you see I was thinking about how you complain about the sun when you have to travel, and well, I started tinkering with an idea." The boy undid the bundle and held up an impressive brown leather overcoat. "It is a new material I developed by mixing the cloth dye with extract from the hentrag plant. You see, many people use the oil on their skin when they know that they will be outside for long periods of time, because it absorbs sunlight and prevents it from damaging the skin. I had the idea that if I mixed it into the cloth dye and applied the mixture to the coat then it would prevent the sun from affecting you as much. It is also completely fire resistant"

Gerhold took the coat and examined it closely. It looked much like his current one, though not so worn and tattered, and had a small hood attached to the neck. The leather was thick and sturdy, though flexible, and Gerhold was once again stunned by the abilities of his young friend. For a boy who had not yet reached the age of seventeen, Nethrin exhibited skills and talents of a master smith and tailor.

"How did you manage to make something like this so quickly?" Gerhold asked and slipped the coat on.

"Well, please do not mention this to the priests, but I developed a faster way to dust the shelves in the basement using billows and piping I built. I can now do most of my chores in half the time," Nethrin said proudly.

"Why would the priests care if you found a way to do your chores more efficiently?" Gerhold asked and Nethrin shrugged in response.

"They would say that I was avoiding my duties and not learning from them. Master Endel told me yesterday that sweeping, and dusting builds good character," the young man said in a mocking tone, and even Gerhold laughed at this. They stared at each other in silence for just a moment before Gerhold stuck out his hand.

"Thank you, Nethrin, even if it does not protect me from the sunlight it is still better than that ragged old thing, I have been wearing for ten years." Nethrin beamed and shook his hand.

"I also included a layer of auroch leather. It is thick but does not weigh as much as most other materials, and it can protect you at least a little from slashing weapons."

"A little more protection is always welcome," Gerhold ran his fingers along the leather overcoat. The outside was rough and rugged, but the inside was soft and comfortable.

"Before I go, there is one other thing I wanted to give you," the young man said and pulled a black tube out of his robes. "This is a new weapon I have been testing. I call it a sunflare." Gerhold took the little tube in his hand and looked at it curiously.

"What is it?"

"Well, if you open it here," Nethrin pulled the top off the tube and delicately slid out a thin, glass tube and a round, yellow crystal. "This is a solution of pyrite oil and liquid light. Mages often use it for lamps if they do not want to have to light them continuously, but when combined with a sun crystal it creates a flash of light that is identical to what the sun produces. I have only tested it once, but I figured, if you had the chance, you could try it for me."

"If it mimics sunlight then that may not be the best thing for me– in case you have forgotten what I am," Gerhold said with a smile.

"Well, yes, but the cloak should protect you. At least, that is what I was planning," Nethrin answered.

"If I happen to find myself in need of it then I will test it for you,"

Gerhold said and replaced the little crystal and the metal tube. "Thank you again, my friend."

"Of course, sir! And good luck. I hope you can put that new crossbow to good use."

A moment later Nethrin had darted out of the room and was heading back down to his workshop to work on some new idea, at least until the priests caught him and forced him to scrub the floors of the chapel. He was an odd boy, but Gerhold liked him, and the tools that he continuously made for the hunter were more than helpful. Gerhold fingered the new coat and smiled again. He had no idea how the boy managed to make a coat that was thick enough to stop a knife and yet flexible enough so that if felt as though he wore only a cloth robe. It felt light and yet he knew it was durable and strong. After he finished admiring the young priest's handiwork, Gerhold shouldered his pack and crossbows, buckled his sword belt around his waist, and made his way out of the room.

A few minutes later he was walking through the deserted streets once again, following the same path he took earlier that night towards the eastern end of the city. The snow was thicker now but the storm had moved on and now a cool breeze passed in between the tight streets beneath the buildings and houses, not that Gerhold noticed. It was a short while before he reached the skydocks and scaled the wall in the same place, before making his way back up the large scaffold to where the Ilvarin was anchored. Two new silver clad Paladins stood at attention in front of the footbridge that led up to the deck. Before either could say a word, Gerhold held up the little metal seal and the two guards stepped back and allowed him to climb the gangplank. Both men followed and immediately hauled the little bridge up after them.

"Good to see you are at least punctual, vampire," Commander Warrick said as he approached.

"I take it we are ready to depart?" Gerhold asked, ignoring the slight, and the Commander nodded.

"We will leave as soon as we can, as long as you have nothing else to attend to." Gerhold shook his head and the commander departed without another word.

There were at least twenty Paladins on the ship, which made Gerhold even more nervous as he knew that he could fight off a few at a time, but twenty in close quarters would not end well. Unsure of where to go, Gerhold made his way to the front of the ship and looked out over the snow dusted grounds. He

A Curse of Darkness

slid the leather hood up over his head as he noticed the familiar shades of pink and orange along the horizon, heralding the coming dawn and he hoped the leather hood and coat would do the trick in protecting him from the sunlight. The sun was one of the things Gerhold hated most about being a vampire, as he missed the soft warmth of the light that he once was able to feel. Now, it caused his skin and eyes to burn, and though he had become far more resistant to it over the many years it still made him feel uncomfortable and would burn him if he stayed out in it for too long. Hopefully Nethrin was right and the overcoat would make being out in the sunlight bearable.

He had to wait only a few minutes before the deck began to bustle with activity as the crew moved about and prepared to take off. Soon the anchor lines were untied and the ship floated gracefully into the air and Gerhold felt that familiar urge to leap from the deck at the last moment as the ground and the airship dock disappeared. Takeoff was just another reminder of how much he hated flying and Gerhold did his best to ignore the sinking feeling in his stomach. Slowly the airship picked up speed and climbed higher and higher into the air until finally leveling out and sailing through the cold morning breeze.

Far below, the lands of Penland stretched out in every direction and the city of Vilheim appeared as only a small mark of mismatched buildings amid the open, snowy plains. The wind was strong this high up, and the crew had wrapped scarves around their faces and necks to avoid the biting winds, but Gerhold stood alone at the front of the ship, trying to ignore the shifting feeling that had settled in his stomach. As much as he hated flying, he did enjoy the views that came with it and took in as much of the scenery as he could.

"Excuse me, Gerhold?" a voice called from behind and Gerhold turned to see a tall, thin man in silver Paladin armor approaching him.

"What can I do for you, Ser?" Gerhold asked as the man stopped in front of him.

"I am Ser Roland. I was asked to escort you to your quarters below deck. The Vigil does not want you to be up on deck more than necessary, considering your unique circumstances," the man said and gave Gerhold a salute by touching both hands to the opposite breast.

Roland was young, barely twenty if Gerhold had to guess, and had shoulder length dark hair that moved slightly with the winds. Paladins were supposed to wear their helm at all times, all except the Vigil's personal guard or the Knight Commander. Seeing as how Roland did not wear one, it meant he belonged to one of the two groups, which surprised Gerhold seeing as how young the man looked. Roland also had a blue sigil painted on the right shoulder of his armor which clearly indicated that he was part of Pontius's personal guard.

"I would like to wait for a few minutes, if you do not mind," Gerhold responded as he wanted to see if the new cloak and hood would work.

"Would you not rather head to the lower decks? Dawn will come shortly," Roland asked curiously.

"I will be fine, for a short while at least. You look young. How old are you?" Gerhold asked as the Paladin moved next to him and leaned against the side of the railing.

"I turned twenty last month," the young man answered.

"A little young to be one of the Vigil's personal guard, are you not?" Gerhold asked and motioned towards the blue sigil on the Paladin's shoulder.

"I am the youngest Paladin to be recruited to the Vigil's guard in over a thousand years. Not sure if I deserve it yet or not, I guess we will have to find out in a few days," he said with a smile.

"Is that right? Well then, I am sure it is much deserved. The Vigils do not promote anyone to the guard unless they are worthy."

"I appreciate that," Roland said before turning and looking out at the sunrise. So far, the hood and coat were doing their job as Gerhold could only feel a little irritation on his face. "If you do not mind, are you really the same Gerhold who fought against Lord Bran and his vampire horde over a hundred years ago?" the man asked, almost a little too eagerly.

"A horde of vampires?" Gerhold responded and chuckled. It was strange how time always led to exaggeration when it came to stories.

"Well, that is what the bards say. But are you him?"

"I am he, and I have been hunting vampires, werewolves, and demons for the past one hundred years," Gerhold answered.

"My butler used to tell me stories about you before I would go to bed. He would tell me I never had anything to fear; just the tales of Gerhold of Vilheim were enough to scare away even the most terrifying of monsters."

"If only that were true," Gerhold commented. It was strange to hear words of admiration from a Paladin.

"I always wondered what happened to you, where you went off to, or if you had finally been defeated. And now, here I am talking with you," Roland shook his head and smiled.

A Curse of Darkness

"And now you find that I am what I once hunted. Not very poetic." Gerhold rested his hands on the railing and looked down at the land passing by far below, which nearly made him sick.

"Life is rarely what the bards and story tellers make it out to be."

"You are quite strange, Roland," Gerhold said and stared out at the slowly rising sun, making sure to drop his head a bit to prevent direct contact with the sunlight.

"How so?"

"I have never met a Paladin who was so eager to speak to a vampire," Gerhold responded, and Roland looked away awkwardly.

"I took a pledge to fight evil, not to fight vampires. If the stories are true, you have done more for this world than any Paladin has. I believe that it is actions, not words or labels, that make us who we are," Roland said, and Gerhold turned to the young Paladin and raised his eyebrows.

"Wise words for one so young," Gerhold said and rubbed his forehead. The sun was still low in the sky and so the hood did not offer much protection, but the rest of his head felt comfortable and cool as if there were no sunlight to worry about. Apparently, the coat and hood were doing their job.

"Common sense is not wisdom. I have met many men who come from rich and powerful families, and yet they are the type of person that even the worst of punishments would not be justice for what they have done. On the other hand, there are poor men who have more courage, honor, and faith than those who are rich, and that is despite living in such squalor. I do not judge men on their ranks or how much coin they have in their pockets, nor by whether they have been cursed. In fact, you are the first vampire I have ever met, which leads me to believe that they are not all as evil as I was taught at the Academy." Roland finished his speech and leaned against the railing once again.

"Vampires are far more complicated than I once thought," Gerhold answered. "Though it took becoming one to realize it."

"How so?"

Gerhold smiled.

"Well, what were you taught about us?"

Roland pondered the question for a moment.

"The paladins see you as evil, soulless creatures," he started. "Consuming the essence of the living in order to prolong your own existence."

"Sounds similar to what I thought I knew a century ago."

"You don't seem to fit that description," Roland added. "But I suppose the reputation of your kind is not without merit."

"Vampires are not as different from humans as many would like to claim," Gerhold said. "We are capable of both great good and evil. I came to learn, though, that once you are on the other side, things look very different."

"So, there are more like you?" Roland asked.

Gerhold paused for a moment, considering his words carefully.

"Yes, and there are far more vampires in this world than you know."

"Have you met many?"

"Once I turned, I found out a great many things I did not previously know or understand," Gerhold said. "As if a veil was lifted from the world. The shadows became in part an ally, and within them, I discovered an entirely new world, one that had been hidden from me as a living person."

"You make it sound as if vampires live everywhere," Roland said.

"They do. Many have mastered the art of remaining unseen, living within society, hidden from the consciousness of the living for fear of being annihilated. Others do it to remain sane, to hold on to some semblance of their humanity."

"So entire societies of vampires living among us?" Roland smiled. "Not exactly sure I believe it."

"You wouldn't, unless you saw it for yourself," Gerhold answered.

"Your kind does not sound as terrible as they are spoken about in the tales and songs," Roland said.

"Not as terrible? I suppose, but do not let your guard down. We are not all still in touch with our humanity. Trusting anyone you do not truly know can lead you astray. The first time I trusted a vampire, it led me to the life of undeath I now live."

"What happened to him?" the Paladin asked and Gerhold turned his back on the sunlight that was now starting to burn his face.

"He turned out to be the evilest of all, as everything he said had been a lie. My one mistake was trusting a vampire, and I advise you not to make the same one, whether it be me or some other. Trust will get you killed, or worse." Gerhold finished and motioned for the young man to lead on.

Roland stared at him for a moment, then nodded and led on across the windswept deck of the airship towards the door that led below. They walked down two flights of stairs to the bottom level where Roland turned and made his way down a long, skinny hallway. Gerhold followed until they came to the last

A Curse of Darkness

room, which Roland opened.

"Here is your room. The Knight Commander wanted you to be as far away from the rest of the crew as possible. I think he may try to lock you in as well, so you may want to watch that," Roland added.

"Thank you." Roland nodded, and without another word he was out the door and starting up the stairs.

Gerhold waited until the sound of footsteps had disappeared before closing the door to the little room and setting down his pack. It was dreadfully small and there was barely enough room for the thin cot and small desk. Still, it wasn't the most unpleasant place where Gerhold had been forced to sleep and he did enjoy the idea of having somewhere to go and be alone in case the pressure of being around so many Paladins in such close quarters proved to be too much.

He sat down at the little desk and used a match to light the lamp on the wall, then he reached into his pack and pulled out the old journal. Inside the desk was a small bottle of half used ink and an old quill that looked as though it had been used a thousand times. Gerhold took a deep breath, dipped the little quill into the ink, and then he began to write, hoping that the journey south would not take too long.

J.S. Matthews

Chapter 5: The Border Town

Gerhold of Vilheim, Journal Entry: February 14, 5944 of the Common Age

We have reached the borderlands of Geldor and should be landing within the hour. The flight south has gone well, as well as any flight could go I suppose, and only once did we have to fly through harsh weather. I will be glad once we touch down and I can finally put my feet on the ground again. The weather is beginning to change the farther south we fly and I can see the once snow covered fields and trees giving way to colors of yellow and green. It is becoming warmer, though I can only tell by the slowly disappearing snows.

Other than the storm, the trip has been quite uneventful. I have spent much of the time either roaming the deck at night under the watchful eye of at least two Paladins, or down here in this little room going over my old journals and the few maps I brought with me, hoping that there may be some clue that I have missed in my travels as to the whereabouts of Harkin Valakir. I should be focusing more on the task at hand but I find myself drawn to the old maps and revisiting my old adventures. Perhaps it is because I have had few conversations with anyone aboard the ship other than Roland.

The young Paladin has spent much of his time speaking with me and asking me to recount many of the stories that he heard as a child. I indulge him because he is the only person aboard the boat that will even speak to me, let alone look at me. He is a strange man; although it seems that the other Paladins are not very fond of him. It does not bother Roland, who I have discovered is wise far beyond his years. It seems that he is to be one of the six Paladins to accompany me into the Blightwood, which I am more than happy to hear. It will be nice to have at least one person I can speak to.

I am worried about what we may find in this forest, for whatever is there shall not stay hidden for long. I have heard rumors from the crew and from the other Paladins

A Curse of Darkness

aboard that the villages along the border have been plagued by disappearances, and some say there are rumors that the missing villagers were dragged into the forest and never seen again. I suppose I will have to wait to find out more, but I must be wary, and I must be ready for whatever is ahead.

The sun was already reaching over the horizon when Gerhold arrived on the top deck. Roland had just informed him that they would be landing within the hour and Gerhold was more than pleased with the thought of finally getting his feet back on the ground. The crew was far more active than they had been in the past few days as men ran this way and that in preparation for the landing, and Gerhold strolled to the front of the ship, doing his best to avoid the Paladins.

Gerhold had not been this far south in many years, which was strange as he traveled often, and his work took him to nearly every realm in Midland. The lands here were wild and open, dotted with primeval forests, vast expanses of untamed land, and long forgotten ruins from a thousand years ago. The southern border of Geldor was marked by the Lemonter Highlands, which they were currently flying over, and just south of these foothills was the forest of the Blightwood. There were only a few small villages along the border, mostly because of the forest and the lack of large cities this close to the border of old Daloran. The ship was on its own, off the edge of the map some would say, and now heading into these long-forgotten lands.

The ruined realm of Daloran had not been entered for many years. Merchants, adventurers, and the like avoided the region, and few even dared to fly over the area. Daloran, once the greatest and most powerful realm in all Tyriel, had been destroyed over a thousand years ago during the last Plague War. Hordes of undead poured in from the south, led by a Lich Lord, and laid waste to its cities. Only the strength of a united Tyriel could defeat the hordes, and after their defeat, the ruined and corrupted lands of Daloran were abandoned, left to rot and decay like the hundreds of thousands of bodies left over from the war. Now Gerhold was going to lead a small group of Paladins into that forsaken realm.

To his left, beyond the eastern horizon, was the endless expanse of the Eastern Ocean, a large body of water that separated the main lands of Tyriel from the exotic island nation of Udhere, and to the west he could see the foothills and peaks of the Alidar Mountains. Off to the south the first outlines of thick tall trees were coming into view, and the sky above was shrouded in dark grey clouds that swirled as if spinning like some giant top. He stared at the clouds and frowned as he had never seen anything like them. They looked unnatural, a dark and scraggly mass that blanketed the blue sky. This area was already strange to him, but the thick layer of darkness above made it even more unnerving.

Gerhold could also tell that the crew was bothered by the growing darkness, and that the clouds seemed to sap any sort of joy from the ship. Every so often one of the men would cease what he was doing and look up at the sky, only to be reminded by a fellow crewman that it was a bad omen to dwell on the clouds. Sailors were as superstitious as any priest, and even more so in most cases. When a strange cloud passed above or the wind shifted in a strange direction most people would not even notice, but to a sailor it could mean good luck or a looming catastrophe. Still, he could not blame the men when it came to these clouds.

Just a few minutes later, the airship started its slow decent and gracefully swooped in low over the rolling hills and few trees that dotted the fields of yellow and brown. Soon the ship came to a gradual halt on a hillside just outside of a small village, and the crew members tossed heavy metal anchors attached to chains over the side where they dug into the soft earth and held the ship in place. Rope ladders were lowered over the side, and Gerhold moved across the deck to stand with Roland, who was having a discussion with two other Paladins nearby.

"I still don't know why we have to bring you, boy." One of the Paladins was saying as Gerhold approached. The man had a thick blonde beard and wore the sigil of the Vigil's guard. In his right hand the man held a small golden coin that he was flipping between his fingers. The other Paladin wore a full faced helm and Gerhold could tell he was nothing more than a guard or a recently promoted apprentice.

"Does your father know that his money won't keep you alive? Not where we're going at least. Money or not, werewolves and dark mages don't give a damn and will kill you just the same," The other said and Roland chuckled.

"I will be fine gentlemen, and as for my father and his money, I doubt he would toss a copper my way if I was starving and begging," Roland said and the other Paladin smiled.

"Out of daddy's good graces, are we? Did he offer a few hundred gold to the Vigils so that you could join the Guard and then leave you on your own? My, my, that must be tough living," the bearded man said and laughed along with his companion.

Once they noticed Gerhold their laughing ceased and both men turned to stare at him.

"Well, well, well, the creature has decided to brace the mid-day sun, eh?" the Paladin with the helmet said.

"Maybe he is trying to get himself killed so we don't have to deal with him?" the other added.

"Not sure why the Vigil even allowed a piece of filth like you on board. If it were up to me, I would have had you burned alive the moment you stepped foot outside that corrupt chapel of yours. I would have done the same to those priests you live with too; no true follower of the Vigilant path would be caught dead associating with the likes of you. Even with the fresh air, your stink is revolting," the bearded man said with a sneer.

"And that would be a very grave mistake on your part, if that were to happen," Gerhold said.

"Do you think you are special because you bear the name of some long-forgotten slayer? I have killed many monsters just like you."

"Calm yourself, Ser Andyn. Gerhold is only here to help. There is no need for such insults," Roland interjected but the blonde man scoffed.

"It is good to see we now know where your true loyalties lie, Roland. Taking sides with a vampire, and just when I thought my opinion of you could sink no lower," Andyn said and spat over the side of the ship before flipping his coin into the air once again.

Before either Gerhold or Roland could respond another voice interrupted their conversation as Knight Commander Warrick came striding up, followed by two other Paladins and Pontius Urban. Gerhold had not seen the Vigil since the first time they had spoken, and now that he saw the old man in the daylight, he noticed just how weak and sickly Urban looked.

"Ser Andyn, Ser Roland, I need you both over here now, and you as well, vampire," the commander added without even looking in Gerhold's direction. Andyn gave one last glare at both Gerhold and Roland, and then he moved past them in the direction of the Commander.

"Do not be too worried about him. Andyn is all bark and very little bite," Roland said with a smile which Gerhold returned.

"I have been a vampire for a long time, and I have heard much worse. I am far more worried about the Blightwood than I am about Ser Andyn," Gerhold said as they made their way across the deck to the stern, where Warrick was standing with Andyn, two other Paladins, and the Vigil.

"Good day, Ser Roland, and to you as well, Gerhold," Urban said as they approached and stood with the others. The Commander and the other Paladins shifted sideways just a bit, as if they were afraid to stand too close to the vampire.

"May the light illuminate your path, Pontius," Roland said and gave a salute with both hands touching the opposite breast.

"Now that you are all here, I must give you a few final instructions. Once you disembark from this vessel, you will be on your own. I must head north to the town of Harlton, as I have important business there."

One of the other Paladins spoke up.

"You mean we are being left here, your Eminence? With no reinforcements?" The man glanced at his companions.

"Unfortunately, yes. This will not be an easy task, but then that is why I am sending you. Your duty is to enter the Blightwood and discover why its darkness is spreading. Find out what magic is at work here, and whether it is just vestiges of evil left over, or something else. We shall return in three days' time. Find out what you can and report back to me. I do not think I need to emphasize how important this is? If there is dark magic at work here then we must know," the Vigil finished, and the same Paladin responded again.

"And what are we to do if it is dark magic? Six Paladins? That is no army."

"I did not intend to send an army. Master Gerhold here will be the seventh member of your company, and I expect that you will find him a welcome addition. There are few alive who have the knowledge of dark creatures and spells as he does. I am placing my confidence in you, Ser Gilbert, that you will be able to manage this task," Urban answered.

"We do not need this creature to complete this task, your Eminence," Warrick said, but the Vigil waved his hand dismissively.

"I have heard enough of that, Commander. Gerhold is going with you, and that is that." The group glanced around awkwardly and nodded. "Now, can I trust that this group can accomplish this?"

"Of course, your Eminence. The will of the Vigils will be done," Commander Warrick answered and bowed.

"Good, then I suggest you get started. You have very little time, and much to investigate. I must make haste to the north." With that the Vigil waited for the men to salute him and then made his way back to the lower deck.

Commander Warrick led the group across the deck and to the rope ladders. Once all seven companions were on the ground, the anchors were hauled up and the airship took off into the sky once again. Gerhold and the others watched as it rose high above and then turned, heading north, until finally disappearing over the horizon. For a moment the group just stood on the little hilltop, taking in their surroundings and trying to calm themselves. They were on their own now, and it would be three days before the ship would return for them. Until then, they had a job to do. The six Paladins were all part of the Vigil's guard, which meant they would be able to fight, but Gerhold was worried they would not have the first clue about investigating the issue quietly.

Both Andyn and the Commander had shields strapped across their backs and a long sword at their side, while Ser Gilbert and the other Paladin, whose name Gerhold did not know, each used a mace and a shield. Roland still held his long, silver spear that he seemed to never let out of his site, though he also had a short sword strapped to his belt for close quarters. They were warriors, not hunters, and Gerhold worried what these men would do when faced with a situation where they would have to use their wits to escape rather than fighting.

"We will start in the village, see if anyone can give us any clues as to what has been happening," Warrick said and led the way down the hill.

"What are we looking for, Commander? All I expect to hear from these backwoods peasants are tall tales," Andyn commented.

"Then we listen and figure out what is truth and what is not."

It took the group only a few minutes to make their way down the hill and towards the little village. Shacks and poorly constructed wooden houses lined a few dusty paths and there were several farmhouses visible in the distance between the hills. Gerhold gave his hood a little tug to make sure it hid most of his face, though thankfully the clouds had now hidden the sun from sight. Still, he hated the burning feeling that always came when the sunlight touched his skin. As soon as the first of the villagers saw the line of Paladins walking down the road, the town began to bustle with activity as a group of twenty or so villagers came strolling out to meet them. Warrick glanced back at the rest of the group as if to warn them, and Gerhold watched as each man cautiously gripped the hilt of his weapon. Gerhold let his right-hand slide behind his back and made sure that both of his smaller crossbows were ready to be drawn at a moment's notice, in case of any surprises.

The Commander halted about ten paces from the line of villagers, and for a moment the two groups just stared at one another. Despite being peasants, the appearances of the villagers were still surprisingly disheveled. Every one of them looked worse for wear, dirty, and disheveled. Their eyes looked as though they had not slept in weeks and their clothing was unwashed and probably smelled worse than it looked. Finally, after what seemed like hours, a man stepped forward from the group and began to speak.

"Are you Paladins?" the man asked in a weak and exhausted voice. He was old and had thin, wispy hair.

"We are. With whom am I speaking?" Warrick responded.

"My name is Fallon. I am the elder here. I apologize for the state of our village. We sent a request for help nearly two weeks ago and assumed that no aid was coming," Fallon said and motioned for a small boy to step forward with a bucket of water and a small ladle. "I would offer you more, but I am afraid we have very little to give. You see, we have not harvested our crop in some time as many are afraid to even leave the safety of the village."

"What has everyone so afraid that they do not wish to step outside in broad daylight?" Ser Gilbert asked, and the villagers began muttering amongst themselves.

"Did you not receive our message? I assumed that was why you came," the elder asked, confused.

"We came because of that," Warrick answered and pointed to the swirling, black clouds above.

"Yes, the darkness! It will consume us all!" a man yelled from the back of the group of villagers, but Fallon hurriedly shushed the man.

"Be quiet, Mander, we do not need to hear your ravings, not now especially!" the old man said, and the other villagers continued to mutter. "I am sorry; we are all just a little on edge."

"Tell us what has been happening here," Gerhold asked and stepped forward. The old man sighed before answering.

"It is the forest; something is coming from that accursed wood." Fallon came in closer before continuing. "It started four weeks ago, when the dark clouds began to spread. I have lived here all my life and never had they spread beyond the borders of the woods. At first, I thought it was nothing, but then, the disappearances started. It started with a few children and we thought it was wolves, but others started to disappear. Then entire families would go missing in the middle of the night, and witnesses claimed they heard screams disappearing into the forest. A few of our younger men decided to investigate, but they never returned, and then a few days later their bodies were found hanging headless from the trees. Something evil has awakened in that forest."

"Has anyone seen anything? Has anyone seen what has been attacking you?" Warrick asked and Fallon shook his head.

"No, but we hear them. Whatever they are, they always come out at night. We can hear them shrieking and prowling through the fields and outside of our houses. They fear the light so we set out as many torches as we can before heading inside for the night. It is not always enough, though." The elder finished and shivered.

Gerhold had listened to the man's every word and had already been running through his vast knowledge of creatures. Many monsters only came out at night, but the shrieking sounds were the real clue. Warrick glanced around at the other Paladins, who only shrugged or returned his unreadable look.

"You need to make as many torches and fires as you can. If these creatures fear the light then that is your best defense," Warrick said, and the village elder gave him a confused look.

"I do not understand; are you not staying here to protect us?" he asked, and the Commander shook his head.

"I am sorry, but our business is in the forest. Hopefully, we can figure out what is happening and how to stop it."

More muttering came from the villagers when they heard these words, and Gerhold could tell that the crowd was not expecting the answer. The elder sighed and rubbed his brow while mothers pulled their children a little closer.

"Is there nothing else you can do for us?" the elder asked and Warrick shook his head.

"We have our orders, and we must attend to them. Our airship will be returning in three days. If we do not come back by that time, then they should be able to grant you passage away from here, at least to the nearest village. I am sorry, but that is the most I can do."

"I understand, Ser, thank you for trying," Fallon responded.

"Is there anything else you can tell us about the forest?" Roland asked and another villager spoke up.

"There are some old ruins deep into the woods, in the center of the forest," a woman said, and everyone turned to stare at her. "My husband once told me of them. He said he saw them only once and that they seemed to smell of evil. He never went back into that forest, not until the others wanted to go search for those who had been taken."

"You must mean the ruins of Altandir," Roland said but the woman did not seem to know the name.

"What in the six hells are you going on about?" Andyn asked.

"Altandir? It was a city that was part of old Daloran. It was at the center of the battle that took place here over a thousand years ago. The ruins are said to be haunted by the dead from that battle," Roland said and for a moment everyone stood silent.

"Well, how do we reach these ruins?" Warrick asked.

"Just follow the path, it should lead you right to it," the woman responded, and pointed to the little dirt road that led out of the village and in the direction of the forest.

"Well, that is at least a start, but we better get moving. Sunset will be here in a few hours and we only have three days to figure out what is going on here. Elder, may the light illuminate your path," Warrick said and gave the man a salute.

"You as well, Commander, and good luck. We will pray for your safe return and that you discover what is causing this darkness."

With that, the small group of Paladins bid farewell to the villagers and then started off in the direction of the forest. Gerhold looked back for only a moment to see the villagers all crowded around the elder, discussing something, most likely how they were going to make it through another night. Ahead was the first line of trees, and Gerhold exhaled slowly, knowing that for the next three days he was going to get very little rest. He needed to stay focused, though, focused, and ready for anything.

A Curse of Darkness

Chapter 6: Into the Forest

The little dirt road curved beneath the hillsides until finally disappearing into the thick trunks and scraggly branches of the forest. The trees were tall and the canopy of dark green leaves was thick enough to block out most of the sky, and only a few stray beams of light were able to pierce the blanket of foliage and reach the gloom of the forest floor. Of course, even this did not help relieve the darkness below the treetops as the clouds above already prevented most of the sunlight from passing through. It was an unnerving sight and even the Paladins slowed their pace, wary of the darkness both above and ahead of them. A slight breeze kicked up from behind and the gnarled, twisted branches creaked and groaned like some great slumbering beast drawing ragged breaths, almost as if the forest were alive and aware of the new arrivals.

"All right, men, from here on we do no more talking than is needed," Warrick said and motioned for Gerhold to step forward. "You, monster, you will take the lead. Your eyes see better than ours in this gloom, and since the Vigil wanted me to drag you along, then I might as well put you to good use. The rest of you, keep your eyes open for anything and stay on the path. No telling what is hiding in those trees."

Gerhold nodded and stepped forward, ignoring the slight. The other men either glared or sneered in his direction as he passed.

"I want Roland behind me," Gerhold said as he stopped in front of the Commander.

"And why is that? I do not recall the Vigil giving any instructions to follow your orders," Warrick replied.

"Because he is the only one of you that I trust not to try sticking a knife in my back. It would be a pity to have to kill one of your men on the first day," Gerhold said and the other Paladins laughed.

"Fine, the rich boy can go second, but watch what you say from here on out, creature. A few more of those insults and you may push one of my men too far. We are pious men but do not let that disguise the warriors that we are. I would hate to be you if that becomes the way of things," the commander added and rested his hand on the hilt of his long sword.

"And as I said before, it would be a pity to have to kill one of you."

With that Gerhold led the way along the path and past the first line of trees. The others followed, but Gerhold could hear mutterings about being led by an abomination, and how they should kill the vampire there and now and be done with it. To Warrick's credit, the commander did his best to calm the various calls for Gerhold's head and would not hear another threat or word about the vampire. Still, Gerhold did not trust the captain, and he barely trusted Roland. Perhaps the Vigil had instructed the young Paladin to befriend Gerhold to gain his trust. He had let his guard down once before and he would never make that mistake again.

The path narrowed and the trees closed in around the little road as Gerhold led the group deeper and deeper into the Blightwood. Above, the thick, green leaves impeded what little light the dark clouds did not already block out, and the shifting beams that did make their way through did very little to pierce the gloomy shadows of the forest floor. For Gerhold, it was a pleasant feeling to be able to stroll about without worry of the sun, but for the others it was a mess of tripping, cursing, and falling. Eventually, Warrick consented to letting the others light torches, and soon a little line of bobbing orange lights followed Gerhold through the darkness as he pressed on.

Gerhold shook his head and muttered under his breath as his fears were confirmed. These men were warriors, not hunters, and every good hunter knew that you adapted and did all you could to prevent your prey from discovering you. Instead, these Paladins seemed to do anything and everything they could to alert the entire forest to their presence. Gerhold had learned early in his training, that when on the hunt, comforts became a luxury that led to problems often. When tracking a beast, the hunter must be focused at all times. It was better to be cold, weary, and hungry but alert, rather than comfortable and oblivious to the danger that awaited them around every corner and behind every tree. However, Gerhold's eyes saw better than most in the dim light of the forest, and all around not a living thing stirred nor did any sounds came from the still and silent forest.

This stillness bothered Gerhold the most though, as no animals were in sight and not a single bird sang. Instead, the only sounds were the crunching of leaves and twigs beneath heavy boots, the jingling and clanking of metal armor, the soft shifting of leaves, and the creaking of branches. Every so often a breeze would rustle the canopy above, but nothing else stirred and Gerhold could not even feel the wind. He had never been in a forest such as this and it worried him as if this were some void where life ceased to exist and only silence reigned. There was also the smell, a strange aroma that lingered in the air and only grew heavier the farther they went into the trees. It was subtle, but there was no mistaking the stench of death.

After a few hours of walking, they came across the remnants of an old campsite, most likely belonging to the villagers that were killed in the forest. It was recent, maybe a month old at the most. Gerhold examined the site and found a few footprints made by heavy boots, which confused him as villagers would not be wearing heavy plate armor. There were also a few animal tracks, wolf prints by the looks of them, but slightly larger. Warrick and the others saw nothing significant and bade Gerhold to lead on without allowing him to examine any further, and after another minute Gerhold decided there was nothing else he could find and so moved on. He glanced back once as they walked away down the path, curious as to who had made the campsite.

The further the group moved into the forest the taller the trees grew and the darker the path got. Strange mosses and lichens appeared across the forest floor and even more on the trunks and branches of the trees, as if some sickness had infected the plants: root, trunk, and branch. Branches and limbs hung low over the path, weighed down by the heavy layers of black and green growths that protruded from the bark and trunk. A disease had settled over the forest, as if the evil that it contained had manifested in this grotesque physical form, and Gerhold knew that the deeper they went the worse it would become.

Still the little group marched on, a lone shrouded figure followed by a line of bobbing orange lights amidst the darkness of the Blightwood. Gerhold did his best to scout ahead when he could but even his eyes could not penetrate the gloom completely, and every so often he got the feeling as if they were being watched. Somewhere off in the distance he heard the cracking of a twig and the rustling of a few leaves, only to be followed by silence. It was possible that there were some animals living here, but Gerhold was sure it was something else. Was there something following them? Or were they being hunted? He tried to catch a glimpse of whatever it was the next time he heard the sounds, but all he could see in the blackness were the never-ending rows trunks and choking layers of leaves and branches. Something was out there, and he was sure of it.

Behind him, the line of Paladins continued without a word, and though their ears and eyes were not as sensitive as a vampire's, Gerhold could tell that they too sensed something was amiss. Occasionally, he could hear one of the men mutter under his breath or reach unconsciously for the hilt of his sword. Warrick kept switching his view side to side as if he expected something to leap out of the forest the moment he turned away, and Gilbert nervously hummed a song in a nearly inaudible tone. Roland seemed to be the only one not bothered by the darkness and the humid stuffy air, and every time Gerhold glanced the young man's way, Roland only seemed to smile and shrug as if nothing was wrong. Gerhold liked the young man but he trusted him as much as he trusted anyone else, which was very little. After his time in Harkin's castle and the turning, Gerhold found himself setting traps and alarms around his room on the upper floor of the chapel, even though he knew the only men present were the priests. He had become somewhat paranoid, but it was better to be paranoid than dead.

After hours of trekking down the claustrophobic path, the last vestiges of light began to dissipate, giving way to a night so dark that even Gerhold was struggling to see through the unnatural blackness. Soon the group was forced to stop, and Warrick set about ordering the men to set up a small fire, much to Gerhold's dislike, and prepare for watch during the night. Gerhold offered to take the entire night's watch, as he only needed to sleep once a week to remain well rested, but Warrick refused, as he believed the vampire would feed on the men during the night if left unwatched. So, after a few minutes of bickering, Roland agreed to take first watch with Gerhold, and each Paladin would rotate every two hours. Warrick had offered to take a watch as well, but his men would not allow it, as Paladin code demanded that the commanding officer only take watch when absolutely necessary.

The other men settled down around the little fire that was set up in the middle of the path and began what was sure to be a restless night of sleep, while Gerhold and Roland sat next to each other with their backs against two nearby trees. For the first half hour neither man said a thing, instead they spent their time listening intently to the sounds of the forests, or lack thereof, and Gerhold tuned his ears to see if he could hear those strange sounds again. His thoughts wandered only a little, and he found himself reminiscing about old adventures from a hundred years ago.

"Have you ever been to a forest like this?" Roland whispered to Gerhold.

A Curse of Darkness

"You mean one where the only sounds you hear are your own footsteps and the creaking branches? No, I have not," Gerhold answered and pulled out his crossbow to make sure everything was loaded and in order. He had just heard the same sound again, far off in the distance, as if something were prowling through the forest and trying to remain undetected.

"Aye, nor have I. My father used to take my brothers and me hunting in the forests that bordered Fallorn, but that was much different. Every night we would lie down beneath the stars and listen to the sounds of the wind or the howls of wolves in the distance. A bit unnerving mind you, but not as bad as this silence," the young Paladin said. Gerhold calmly loaded a long silver bolt into his crossbow. "Maybe it was just my imagination, but it feels as though we are being watched. As if the trees are alive and spying on us."

"As a Paladin you can sense magic, and these woods are full of magical energy left over from the battle that took place here long ago," Gerhold responded and made sure his two smaller crossbows were loaded.

"I know the stories, about the battle for Altandir and how the Paladins of old stood against the brunt of the undead horde and prevented the plague from spreading into the northern realms. The battle was so fierce that the Paladins and mages used whatever they could to combat the enemy, and almost tore the veil between the spirit world and our world with how many spells and magical power were being drawn upon. Those stories always seemed like fairy tales to me, as did your stories."

"Stories take on a life of their own, given enough time, so it is never wrong to question the events of the past. Just do not forget to also learn from them." Gerhold leaned his large crossbow against his shoulder and glanced over at Warrick, who was lying on his back but with his eyes open. The commander glanced suspiciously at Gerhold and pointed to his ear. Gerhold nodded and saw Warrick give a nod in return.

Roland spoke up.

"Yours were always my favorite. The stories of Gerhold the Slayer were never dull. I can only imagine the stories you have to tell after a hundred more years."

"Too many to remember. I keep journals but it is difficult to remember so much after so long. So many hunts they all seem to blend together after a time."

"If you do not mind me asking, how were you able to live for so many years as a vampire and still continue your work?" Roland asked.

"Lies and deceit became my dearest friends. One week I was a merchant travelling through town and inquiring about rumors, the next I was a vagrant or monk. Sometimes I would get so comfortable with the lie that it felt strange to let it go. False names like Dornhold became common use for me. Over time you learn how to blend in." Gerhold glanced out again into the darkness, trying to pinpoint where the sound was coming from. "Honestly, it became much like a hunt to me, instead of sneaking through caves, crypts, and castles I was sneaking through city streets and small hamlets."

"You are always on the hunt then?"

"After nearly a hundred and fifty years of being in danger you develop a constant sense for it. Especially in this silence."

"It does not feel right. I know something was following us," Roland said and pulled out his water skin.

"The first rule of hunting is to never let your prey know that you are there until you are ready to strike." Gerhold tapped Roland with his foot and pointed to his ear.

The young Paladin looked confused at first, but his eyes narrowed as soon as he heard shifting leaves and cracking branches that were growing closer. Roland reached slowly for his spear while Gerhold did his best to peer through the darkness, and even with his keen vampire eyes he could not fully make out what he was seeing due to the unnatural darkness of the forest. He caught a glimpse of something moving in between the trees not thirty feet from the fire. Suddenly, the noise stopped and Gerhold moved slowly to his feet. For a few minutes he stood with his crossbow at the ready, listening and looking for any other signs of movement. The other Paladins were up as well, their swords drawn and their shields in hand. The noise started again, only this time it grew softer and the sound drifted away as the creature withdrew into the silent blackness of the forest.

"What was that?" Roland whispered once the silence returned and Gerhold shook his head. "You think that's what has been following us?"

"Most likely, at least I would hate to think there is something else following us," Gerhold answered and lowered his crossbow.

"Whatever it was, it's gone now," Warrick said and sheathed his sword.

"It was scouting us," Gerhold responded, and the other men turned to stare at him.

A Curse of Darkness

"Scouting us? Bah! It was just some animal that was interested in the fire, that is all. You don't need to make monsters out of shadows, but of course we already have one of those in our camp, don't we?" Andyn said.

"In this forest there are only evil things, and if there is a shadow then there is something that is casting it," Gerhold said. "You are a fool if you think that was nothing more than a deer or a fox. We have been followed since the moment we stepped foot within these trees, and the only remaining question is what is following us, or rather, what is hunting us." The other men stared at Gerhold and pondered these words, while Andyn simply smirked and muttered under his breath.

"Whether shadows or not, we need to sleep," Warrick said. "Morning will be here soon enough, and we need to be ready for anything. Roland, you and the vampire are on watch for another hour. Wake us if the creature returns." With that Warrick and the other Paladins returned to their bedrolls.

For the next hour Gerhold and Roland sat in silence, listening for any sound of the creature that had followed them, but none came. Eventually, Roland made his way over to where Ser Gilbert was sleeping and woke the Paladin for his turn on watch. Gilbert avoided coming anywhere near Gerhold and settled down on the opposite side of the fire. Another hour passed by without interruption and Gerhold spent his time reading through the journal he had brought with him. It was strange to read his old adventures and recall his triumphs and mistakes over the years. He was halfway through an entry that detailed his encounter with a banshee when the same sounds returned.

Gerhold dropped the leather journal and moved to one knee, gripping his crossbow. He tried to block out the heavy breathing and snoring of the Paladins to concentrate on the sounds of movement coming from outside the firelight. Immediately he noticed that something was different, as there were more sounds and this time they came from all directions. Their little camp was surrounded, and Gerhold listened as the noises drew closer and whatever was in the forest moved in on the little ring of firelight.

At first, Ser Gilbert seemed not to notice anything, so Gerhold tossed a small stick at the sleepy Paladin and motioned for him to listen. Gilbert crept slowly over to where the other men lay and whispered in Warrick's ear. Before the commander could issue any orders, a chorus of spine-tingling shrieks echoed from all around the camp, followed by the sounds of heavy footfalls. Gerhold stood with his crossbow at the ready and took aim at the first shadowy figure that came leaping out of the darkness and fired. The creature howled in pain and crumpled to the forest floor at the vampire's feet. The monster was covered from head to toe with matted black fur, and it was roughly the size of a man, though squat and thicker. It had a smashed nose, almost like a pig, and its lower jaw jutted outwards, revealing rows of razor-sharp teeth. More of the creatures came pouring from the darkness and into the firelight just as the Paladins were able to make it to their feet and draw their weapons.

Gerhold fired off a second bolt and then held down the little latch at the bottom of the crossbow and flicked it forward, revealing the silver blade. He dashed forward and sliced at one of the beasts, sending blood spattering across the ground, then caught another monster in the chest as it leapt at him. All around the fire, shrieks and screams echoed as the Paladins battled with sword, shield, and spear, carving their way through the waves of monsters. Another leapt at the vampire, who rolled nimbly to the side and beheaded the creature in one smooth stroke. He slung the crossbow over his shoulder and drew the two smaller ones holstered on his lower back, then fired off a volley of shots into the oncoming beasts. One of the monsters managed to get close and jumped at Gerhold, claws extended, and he felt the talons dig into his shoulders. Gerhold grabbed the creature by its snout as it snapped and shrieked, trying to bite at his face, until the vampire used his strength to rip the monster's jaws in two.

Gerhold leapt to his feet and fired off more volleys of silver bolts while the Paladins fought in close quarters with the snarling creatures and sent streams of white magical fire into the throngs of attackers. Roland slashed back and forth with his long silver spear, cleaving enemies with every stroke. Warrick and the other Paladins fought back to back, staving off the open jaws and ripping claws of their attackers, while Gerhold stood by and picked them off one by one with his crossbows.

The battle was quick and bloody, and after a few minutes of combat, the last few foes turned and scampered back into the darkness of the forest. All around, bodies of the creatures dotted the ground, some still twitching or calling out in pain as the Paladins moved about to finish their work. Gerhold drove his silver long sword into one of the dying creatures and watched as it ceased moving and its screams died away. He made his way back to the fire, which was barely burning now as one of the monsters had fallen into it and scattered most of the burning logs across the campsite. The others were standing in a circle with Gilbert trying to rebuild the fire and the others trying to shake the dirt, ash, and blood from their blankets.

"Anyone hurt?" Warrick asked and the other men shook their heads. "Good, we need to clean up these bodies. Pile them somewhere off the path."

"Do not make monsters out of shadows, eh Andyn?" one of the Paladins said and chuckled while they started moving the bodies of the monsters away from the camp. Andyn scowled in response and tried to ignore the comment.

"If you see a shadow then that means something is there. Let us hope you remember that next time," Gerhold added.

"I don't need a monster telling me how to fight monsters," Andyn yelled back and glared at Gerhold. The Paladin had a hand on his sword hilt and looked ready to draw it.

"Sit down, Andyn," Warrick said and stepped between Andyn and Gerhold.

"Aye, if it was not for the vampire those things would have been on us before I could warn you. Not sure how you heard them coming," Ser Gilbert said and motioned to Gerhold.

"Vampires have heightened senses, but even these were hard to find in this darkness," Gerhold said and kicked one of the bodies. Andyn was still glaring at him, but at least the man had taken his hand off his sword hilt and had begun fiddling with his gold coin once again.

"What in the six hells are these things? I've never seen anything like them," one of the Paladins asked, and when no one else answered Gerhold responded.

"They are howlers, a necromancer creation. Foul magic and alchemy used to mix werewolf and human blood. Abominations brought forth by the evil desires and imaginations of men."

The Paladins stared at Gerhold. Some muttered curses under their breath while others said some inaudible prayer.

"Necromancers? You think that is what we are after?" Roland asked and Gerhold shrugged in response.

"The howlers could have been created recently but then again there had always been rumors of monsters inhabiting this forest." Gerhold yanked one of the silver bolts free and cleaned the blood from it before placing it back in his quiver. "The beasts could have been here for hundreds of years, and perhaps it was them that killed the villagers. Then again, howlers devoured their victims, they did not behead them and hang the bodies from trees."

"Whatever they are, they're gone," Gilbert said and stood up from the fire, which was blazing once again.

"For now, but who says they won't come back for us with more of them?" Andyn said and spat into the fire.

"We need to rest whether they come back or not. Ser Gilbert? You are still on watch for another hour with the Vampire. If you hear anything, then you wake the rest of us immediately, and do not worry about being quiet about it. If you need to yell, then do it," the Commander said and took a seat near the fire.

"If they do come back, they'll have a rude welcome waiting for them," another of the Paladins said.

"Aye, as long as we hear them coming," Gilbert responded.

"As long as Gerhold is here I do not think we have much to worry about," Roland added and the other men seemed to agree, though they did not admit it.

"Fine, the vampire and Ser Gilbert will be on watch. The rest of you, try to get some sleep," Warrick said, and with that the Paladins returned to their blankets, most mumbling about how it was going to be impossible to sleep while others commented on the horrible smell left behind by the howlers.

Gerhold spent the rest of the night with Ser Gilbert and then with Andyn, and though no other sounds could be heard from the darkness of the surrounding forest, most of the men tossed and turned in their blankets. The vampire sat calmly against the same tree and pulled out his journal again, wondering what else the trees were hiding from them.

A Curse of Darkness

Chapter 7: The Bog

Gerhold of Vilheim, Journal Entry: February 15, 5944 of the Common Age
After the howler attack, the rest of the night went by without any disturbances, though I could tell that the surviving creatures were still out there somewhere in the darkness of this accursed forest. The question that plagues me now though is where did the creatures come from? I have only ever encountered small numbers of them in the lairs of necromancers, but I have never seen so many that seemingly live out in the wild. Are they from ages long past, leftovers from the great evil that tainted these lands so long ago? Or are they the product of a new evil, and have necromancers been using this forest for their experiments?

There is much I still must learn about this place, but I know now that evil has been allowed to fester here for far too long. I can only wonder what else we will find in these woods and what lies ahead. The howlers were dealt with easily, but what else does this forest have in store for us? If there truly are necromancers or witches in these woods then we may need more than just the seven of us, and since the airship is not due to return for another two days we have no way to request reinforcements. Above all else I must concentrate on my mission, to find out why this darkness is spreading and stop it, and if that happens to involve these creatures then so be it.

The group was up early the following morning, after a restless night's sleep. The Paladins were tired but ready to move deeper into the forest and leave the mess of howler bodies behind. The stench had grown considerably during the night and now the overpowering smells of the monster corpses was strong enough to make any man cringe in disgust. After packing up their things and taking a quick look around the camp, the group was off once again, heading slowly down the thin, overgrown path through the Blightwood.

J.S. Matthews

Gerhold led the line of silver clad Paladins onward and deeper into the army of trees. He still had the feeling that something was following and watching them, and every so often his ears picked up the sounds of a cracking branch or soft footfall somewhere far off the path. Whether it was another howler or not, Gerhold did not know, but something was still following. The Paladins heard nothing, as only the acute ears of a vampire would have been able to pick up sounds from such a distance, but they could sense that something was not right. The darkness of the forest stretched out in every direction like a seemingly endless ocean of gloom, and the gnarled and twisted trees seemed to be reaching out for them to snag their cloaks and grab at the line of men as they passed.

"It has been over a thousand years since a Paladin last walked beneath these trees," Roland said absentmindedly. "Back when the eastern realms of Arendor, Morovia, and Penland marched south to Altandir to defend the city against the undead armies."

"What happened?" Gerhold asked.

"Well, after marshalling their forces, the lords moved south along the coast and then through this forest, though I imagine it looked quite different then. They were led by King Dallen Ardelon of Arendor, a proud and noble man, but more politician than general."

"They almost always are," Gerhold added.

"Dallen was a good king according to most, but he was no warrior. When the armies arrived at the valley overlooking Altandir, the king, against the advice of his generals, sent forth a procession of banners and horses with himself at the head, like some conquering hero of old come to save the city. I can only imagine the look on his face when they came into view of the already shattered gates of the city, and the undead army burst forth and attacked," Roland said and wiped sweat from his brow.

"The city had already been taken."

"Yes, it had been conquered before the king's army had even reached the borders of this forest. Dallen was killed during the first few minutes of the battle and his armies were driven back into the woods by the vast hordes of undead. These soldiers were fresh and new to the fight but were also inexperienced and few had ever faced such a relentless foe. The first day was a slaughter, but it was the only reason why they were able to win the battle."

"Sometimes the death of a king is a boon to those left behind," Gerhold commented and Roland nodded.

A Curse of Darkness

"After the king's death a Paladin Commander named Ser Barridan took over. He had fought in earlier battles against the undead in the south and was familiar with the horde's tactics. Over the next ten months, Ser Barridan rallied the troops and held the undead at bay until, finally, the enemy retreated and moved south to fight the Callorians. Many good men fell during those endless days and nights of fighting. The undead do not need rest, but men need sleep to fight effectively. The battle took its toll on the soldiers, but they never faltered after that first day, even against such a ferocious enemy," Roland finished and rubbed his neck.

"It is difficult to fight when every fallen comrade rises to join the enemy," Gerhold added.

"I read stories that say there were so many bodies that the piles were large enough to be used as defensive walls and set on fire to make sure the bodies would not rise again. The undead ran from the flames, and it gave the soldiers hope, however strange that may sound. A sad fate for the many men who gave their lives to defend against the darkness. They deserved a holy burial and ceremonies, not to be used as a wall of corpses."

"Their deaths had meaning. The Gods will reward their sacrifice, buried or not," Gerhold answered but Roland did not respond, and it was good he did not as Gerhold realized that Warrick was glaring in their direction. Gerhold found it strange that the Commander was angry with the two of them whispering but apparently did not mind the line of torches behind him.

Paladins were strict followers of the Way of the Vigilant, a code that dictated how they lived as well as died. It was said to be shameful for a man to die without a proper burial, but Gerhold did not hold to those beliefs. He followed the teachings of the three Gods, Uriel, Mathuin, and the God of Gods, Athos, but he was not one of the Vigilant anymore. To him, the Chronicles were the only source of holy law, not the words of men who demanded service and tithes in return for salvation, as he had once believed. Roland was a Paladin, and so it came as no surprise that he believed the Vigils to be divine leaders selected by the Three to guide mankind. He had seen many powerful men, both religious and not, fall prey to the corruption of power. He would not trust the Vigils; he would never trust anyone.

As they continued on, the air seemed to grow thick and humid, leaving the Paladins to huff and sweat in their thick layers of armor. Of course Gerhold hardly noticed the change in temperature, but the humid feeling in the air meant that there was water nearby. Sure enough, after a few hours of walking since they left the camp site that morning, the path came to a halt at the banks of a thick, mucky bog. The muddy mess of water, reeds, and filth stretched out as far as they could see to both the left and right, and the only way across the swamp was a three foot wide walkway made from wooden planks that passed above the still water. The trees continued on as if nothing had changed, and the thick canopy shaded the massive bog and held the warm humid air in so that it became very difficult to breath. Gerhold shook his head and spat, knowing that they had little choice but to go on.

"If this forest wasn't bad enough already," Gilbert said and then trailed off.

"Think we can make it around, Commander?" One of the other Paladins asked, and Warrick shook his head.

"The woman said that we had to follow the path, and it looks like this is the path. Besides, it could take us days to make it all the way around this bog, and that is if we make it around. I think we should keep the path as much as we can," Warrick said, and the others nodded in agreement.

"Let us hope this bog does not take us days to cross," Gerhold added before leading the way onto the rickety old wooden catwalk.

In spite of all the water and mud, the trees grew just as thick as before, and there were many times where the men were forced to duck in order to avoid low hanging branches or leap over broken spaces along the path. The bog smelled awful as well, a bubbling, slurping mess of dark muck that gave off the scent of rotting eggs and dead flesh. Gerhold did his best to avoid wondering what was hidden beneath that slimy surface, but at least none of the men had fallen in yet.

Nearly an hour after leaving the safety of solid ground behind, the group came to a little island in what they hoped was the middle of the swamp. Gerhold held up his hand for the others to stop as something on the island caught his eye, and he crept forward alone to see what it was. The little piece of land held only a few trees and what looked like an abandoned camp. An old burned out campfire sat at the center of the three trees and the remains of several small tents were strewn about the ground. Gerhold could see at least three bodies, one of which was halfway in the swamp as if something had partially dragged the man, and it only took him a moment before he realized who the men were.

"Warrick? You need to see this," Gerhold said after returning to the line of men who were crouched on the little wooden planks.

A Curse of Darkness

"What is it, something wrong?" the Commander asked as he and the others followed behind Gerhold.

"Did the Vigil tell you about any other Paladins being sent here to investigate?" the vampire asked and Warrick shook his head.

"Other Paladins? No, no we are all there is. Why do you ask?" Warrick responded, and Gerhold pointed at the first of the bodies that lay strewn about the old campsite. "What in the six hells is this?"

The other Paladins crowded onto the small island and started searching about the campsite, checking on their dead brethren and looking for any hint as to what killed them.

"Gods, this one looks like he was chewed on quite a bit," Gilbert said as he kicked over one of the bodies and examined it.

"Same here. But were they eaten before or after they were killed?" Roland asked.

"What I want to know is why there are dead Paladins in the middle of this bloody forest? I thought we were the only ones here?" Ser Dorren added while rummaging through one of the broken tents.

"This camp is less than a month old," Gerhold said suspiciously.

"You mean these men were here in the last few weeks? Why would the Vigil send two groups?" Dorren asked, but no one answered.

"This explains the camp we found yesterday. I knew those footprints did not belong to villagers. I am guessing that they started across the swamp and believed they could reach the other side before nightfall, but did not realize how long the trek would be and were forced to setup camp here," Gerhold said and bent down to examine the muddy ground. More of the same heavy boot prints that he had found at the campsite yesterday were easily visible amidst the clutter of torn tents, scattered ashes, and scorch marks. "It looks like something attacked them that night, there are tracks that come from the swamp over here," he said and followed a line of strange footprints to the edge of the mucky bog.

"I bet it was those same things that attacked us last night," Andyn said, but Gerhold shook his head.

"Howlers do not leave boot prints, nor do they live in a swamp. Besides, there would have to be a hundred to kill an entire group of Paladins, and there are no sign of howler tracks anywhere."

For a few more minutes the group looked around the campsite for any other clues as to what happened, but only Gerhold was able to find anything significant. Whatever attacked the Paladins had come from the swamp and then returned after the slaughter. There were no bodies other than what was left of the band of Paladins, and Gerhold wondered what could attack and kill Paladins without even leaving a trace. There were scorch marks from holy fire that the Paladins had tried to use to drive off their attackers, but there were no traces of whatever attacked them other than the few strange tracks. Finally, Warrick called them all together at the center of the island.

"Any idea what happened here?" he asked and the others just shrugged.

"Something, or things, came from the swamp and attacked your brothers. The scorch marks show that they at least tried to fight them off and were not killed in their sleep," Gerhold said.

"So what killed them?" the Commander asked, but Gerhold shook his head.

"No idea. I found some strange tracks coming and going into the bog, but I cannot identify them. Do you know why they were here?" Gerhold looked at Warrick, whose face was unreadable. When he received no response Gerhold repeated his question. "Why was there another group of Paladins here?"

"Perhaps they came to answer the village's summons?" Ser Gilbert answered.

"Then why did the villagers not mention anything about them? These men followed the same path we have and only a few weeks ago, so they had to have passed through the village," Warrick answered, which was exactly what Gerhold had been thinking.

"Which raises the question, why did they not mention these other Paladins?" Gerhold said and it looked as though the other men were wondering the same.

"Commander?" Roland called and the group turned to see the young man striding up from the bank of the swamp where one of the bodies lay half in the muddy water. "I think you need to see this."

"What is it?" Warrick asked as Roland handed him a muddy metal pauldron he had taken from the dead Paladin.

"Take a look at the symbol and you can tell me," Roland responded and Gerhold moved over so that he could see the dirty shoulder guard as well. Imprinted on the metal was the same symbol that the other Paladins wore, the symbol of the Vigil of Righteousness. "I think that one down there is Ser Aldrith or at least it looks like him," Roland said and pointed at the body. Warrick stared

A Curse of Darkness

at the symbol for a moment with a confused expression on his face.

"That cannot be. Ser Aldrith is in Calloria working with the Vigil of Truth," the Commander said without taking his eyes from the symbol.

"Is that what Pontius Urban told you?" Gerhold said and the Paladins looked at him suspiciously.

"What are you implying, vampire?" Warrick responded and Gerhold shrugged.

"I am implying that the Vigil was not entirely truthful with you."

"I would watch my tongue, especially when it comes to accusing a Vigil of lying," Warrick said venomously.

"Then how do you explain that?" Gerhold said and pointed to the pauldron. "Obviously he lied to you, though the reason for that may or may not be important. All I am saying is that the Vigil had already sent some of your men to investigate, and when they did not return he decided to send us."

Warrick glared at Gerhold before tossing the metal pauldron aside. The group stood for a moment, each man contemplating what was really going on. Why did the Vigil not tell them that they were the second group? And why had the villagers not said anything about the Paladins? Of course, the warriors could have slipped by unnoticed but Gerhold doubted it by how brash and obvious his current companions had been over the past day and a half. Besides, did the village elder not tell them that they had found bodies headless and hung on the edges of the forest only a few weeks ago? Perhaps there was more going on here than Gerhold had initially anticipated.

"Whatever the Vigil's reason for not telling us is irrelevant at this point. We still have a job to do and standing here is getting us nowhere closer to accomplishing it," Warrick finally broke the silence. "We need to move on, before whatever attacked our brothers decides to come for us. The ruins cannot be far now, and hopefully we can find some answers when we get there." The other men nodded in agreement.

"Well, vampire, lead on then," Andyn added impatiently.

Gerhold took one last glance around the campsite before nodding and making his way towards the raised wooden walkway. They were off once again, but Gerhold could not help but shake his head in frustration. Whatever attacked the other group of Paladins had been powerful, and now he felt exposed and unprotected walking along the little wooden planks with no idea of what lay below him in the murky waters. Every so often, he caught sight of strange ripples or bubbles in the water, and at first they seemed to be random, but as they continued on Gerhold began to notice a pattern. The little swirls and ripples became more common, appearing in nearly every direction, and with every step it felt as though the disturbances were inching closer and closer to the raised walkway. He focused his ears as best he could, only picking up sound of swishing water. Finally, Gerhold raised his hand for the group to halt and watched as one of the shifting ripples came within only a few feet of the walkway.

"What is it?" Roland whispered and Gerhold shook his head.

All around them the water seemed to be coming alive, and now even the Paladins noticed the disturbances amidst the mud and reeds. Gerhold watched as a hulking figure rose slowly from beneath the thick layer of muck, climbing to its feet. Soon a tall, waterlogged corpse of a man stood in front of them knee deep in the muddy swamp waters, and let out a terrifying moan that was echoed by other bodies rising from the mire. Hundreds of white, slimy, mud covered bodies were rising from beneath the surface and immediately started shambling in the direction of the small wooden walkway.

"Hells and hellfire," Gilbert muttered, and without hesitation Gerhold took off down the footbridge as fast as he could without losing his balance.

"Where in the six hells did these come from?" Roland called as they ran.

"Well, we're not stopping to ask!" Gilbert yelled back and sent and jet of white fire at one of the creatures as it reached out towards them with its slime ridden fingers.

The group sprinted across the little walkways as fast as they could while the old wooden bridges creaked and groaned. All around them, water-logged corpses were rising and shambling in their direction through the muddy waters. Hungry groans from the monsters echoed from every direction and mixed with the slogging sounds of the swamp. Whenever one of the creatures came too close, Gerhold or one of the Paladins would cut it down, only to see that the corpse was replaced by two more. White hot fire flew out in every direction from the Paladins, and the flames hissed and sputtered as they engulfed the sopping wet creatures.

Still, no matter how hard they ran or how many spells they conjured, there were always more corpses ahead of them. Soon the undead creatures closed in around them, moaning and reaching for the warm flesh of the living. Gerhold whipped out his crossbow and sent a bolt into the head of the nearest monster, which let out a dying cry as it fell back into the shallow waters. The Paladins sent more streams of burning fire into the throngs of undead, trying to keep the creatures from reaching the walkway and pulling the entire thing down. Cold dead hands wrapped around the rickety supports for the old bridges and started pulling at the wood, while others reached up, groping for the feet of the line of men as they ran desperately for the shore which had just come into view ahead.

Another monster came lumbering forward before Gerhold had time to reload, and instead the vampire flipped his wrist and beheaded the creature with the silver blade that had shot out of the crossbow. He drew one of his smaller crossbows and slew three more creatures before darting forward while slashing at the slimy hands that reached up for him from below. More corpses came shambling forward out of the gloom and Gerhold knew that their only hope was to run as quickly as they could for the shore. He turned again to see Roland spinning this way and that, his spear flying in all directions, and wherever it struck, a foe fell. Lines of undead melted before the young Paladin's fury, and even the old vampire admired Roland's skill.

Gerhold yelled for the others to hurry and saw as one of the Paladins was tripped and fell screaming into the horde of hungry undead. His cries echoed through the forest but fell silent as he was pulled beneath the muddy surface of the water, giving way to unending sounds of the moaning undead. Not a moment later, part of the walkway ahead collapsed as a line of ravenous corpses finally snapped the old wooden supports. Gerhold leapt over the four foot gap and over the outstretched hands of the creatures while firing a volley of shots at the horde, trying to distract them from the other men as they tried to make it over the gap. Roland, Warrick, Gilbert, and Andyn made the jump, but Ser Dorren was caught from behind just as he landed, and many sets of cold hands wrapped around his ankles before pulling him off the raised walkway.

The group stopped and sent more fire into the horde to and tried to pull Dorren away from the clawing corpses but it was no use, and Gerhold watched as the man was pulled off down and the hungry dead began to feast. There was nothing else they could do, and so the remaining survivors took off in the direction of the shore, leaving their comrade screaming as more undead closed in around him. By the time Gerhold reached the end of the walkway, Dorren's screams had faded, and he led the way to the shore and back onto the little dirt path. Behind them the last sounds of the moaning undead seemed to drift away, leaving the group in silence once again as they ran deeper into the trees.

J.S. Matthews

Chapter 8: Altandir

They sprinted along the path for another ten minutes before stopping to catch their breath. Gerhold made his way past the panting line of Paladins and walked a little way back to see if the dead were following them. Thankfully, the path was empty as far as he could see, and by the time he reached the other men, they were standing again, though Andyn and Gilbert seemed shaken.

"Hells and bloody hellfire," Gilbert muttered again.

"Is everyone all right?" Gerhold asked, but only Roland and Warrick nodded. "It does not look as though they are following us, so we should be safe here, for the moment at least."

"Of course, they're not following us! They already got their fill on Dorren and Randel," Andyn responded breathlessly and retched.

"That bloody bog was a trap. Where do you think all those undead came from?" Roland asked Gerhold, who was still glancing back down the path for any signs of movement.

"I do not know. Perhaps they were a trap set by necromancers, or they could be from the old battles long ago. I have heard of strange things such as this occurring on the old battlefields from the Plague Wars. Dark magic always leaves scars and some never heal," Gerhold answered while reloading his crossbows.

"I don't give a damn where they came from; they just devoured two of our men," said Andyn as he threw up again. Gerhold saw that he was clinging tightly to his little gold coin once again and rubbing it furiously with his fingers.

"Pull yourself together," Warrick said and leaned down next to Andyn. "We have a long way to go and I need you to be ready for anything else that comes. You are a Paladin, not some craven woman. Men live and men die. Our concern right now is living and finding out what is happening in this forest. You took an oath of courage, now hold to it." Andyn wiped his mouth and frowned. Roland took a sip of water and offered it to Gerhold before remembering that he did not need it.

"So, howlers and now an army of undead. Let us hope this forest is not hiding anything worse," Roland commented.

"It could be a coincidence, but both of those seem to point to one conclusion: necromancers," Gerhold responded and even Warrick seemed to agree with him this time.

"That's just great. First abominations and undead, and now dark mages. Why in the six hells did the Vigil send only seven of us?" Gilbert asked.

"Our mission is not to eliminate the threat, but to find out what is happening. I doubt the Vigil had any idea what we would be facing," the Commander said and sheathed his blade after ensuring it was clean.

"But he had to know something since that first group of Paladins never returned," Gerhold said, and the Commander rubbed his forehead in frustration. Gerhold could tell that Warrick knew he was right, and the Vigil had known something more than he had told them.

"We are alive; that is what matters now," Warrick said. "We will make sure that Ser Dorren and Ser Randel are remembered. It is time to move on. Night is coming and I want to put as much distance between us and that bog as we can manage," Warrick said and helped Gilbert to his feet.

After a few more minutes of rest the Commander motioned for Gerhold to lead on. It was past midday, or at least that is what Gerhold guessed by the few rays of light that happened to make their way through the thick canopy of leaves, and immediately he started on down the path. The last thing they wanted was to stay too close to the bog and be forced to camp nearby when night fell.

"Follow me then and keep your eyes open. The ruins of Altandir should be close now, and there is no telling what evils the old bones of that city may hold," Gerhold whispered and moved down the path.

One by one, the Paladins followed along after the vampire, still mourning the loss of their two comrades. Gerhold had seen many men die and in horrible ways, but it worried him that Andyn and Gilbert had been affected in such a way. Perhaps these warrior Paladins were not as strong as rumored. What would they do when they encountered necromancers or other creatures of darkness that were far worse than undead? Gerhold tried to ignore this thought and focus on the positives. They were alive and he could tell they were getting close to their goal, almost as if he could sense the evil that was ahead. This was another advantage of being a vampire, as a creature of evil he had the innate ability to sense other forms of evil, and though the entire forest felt as though it was saturated, Gerhold could still detect the strange aura coming from somewhere ahead of them. He gripped his crossbow a little tighter at these thoughts.

The path continued to wind this way and that between the trees, though Gerhold noticed that the forest began to thin and there were more rocks and boulders strewn across the landscape. Soon they came to the first of what would be many ruined foundations of ancient houses and buildings, until finally the trees opened and the sky was visible for the first time in nearly two days. A large green valley opened up before them, and in the center was the overgrown and destroyed remains of what used to be the city of Altandir. Hundreds of ruined stone buildings lay crumbled to the foundation while others looked close to coming down. Thousand-year-old pillars, walls, and collapsed roofs dotted the landscape, and at the center, along the top of a hill, was the skeleton of what had been the seat of Altandir's rulers.

The dark swirling clouds above seamed to loom over them as if they were spinning directly over the remnants of Altandir, and there was no sunlight to be seen in the black mass. Gerhold watched as Roland and the other Paladins closed their eyes and embraced the first breeze they had felt in over a day, and even though he could not feel the cooling wisps of wind, Gerhold enjoyed the open air and finally getting out from beneath the claustrophobic and stuffy atmosphere of the forest. More trees dotted the valley, though far less than the forest that surrounded the clearing, and even from this distance Gerhold could see the plants and weeds that had taken over what had once been a beautiful city. The little dirt path they had been following turned into a paved road with cracked and overgrown stones that wound down through the valley to the city's remains, passing between the hundreds of destroyed and dilapidated old buildings and houses.

"I never thought I could be so happy just seeing the sky again," Roland commented, and the other men called out their agreement.

"And would you look at that?" Gilbert said and pointed out towards the ruined city. "Gods, this place hasn't seen a living thing in over a thousand years by the looks of it."

"After the months of battle during the last Plague War, the undead armies that conquered Altandir retreated to fight the new threats from Calloria and Drethdin in the south. The battles that took place here were so fierce and so much magic was used that the mages nearly tore open a rift to the nether. The whole area has been avoided ever since," Roland said and pointed to what remained of the city's outer wall. "The city was taken by the undead, while the armies from the north and from Zumora fought for months to take it back. Eventually it was abandoned, even after the undead retreated. The magical energies left over by those battles made the area dangerous for anyone, and that was the first time the dark clouds settled over the forest."

"And only now has it started to grow," Gerhold added.

"Did you notice the clouds?" Roland said and Gerhold nodded.

"I did, they are swirling directly over the city, as if that is where the darkness is coming from."

"Which means it is the best place for us to start our search. If these ruins are anything like the rest of this forest, then we better be on our guard," Warrick said and started off down the broken stone path.

"How much do you want to bet me that this whole damnable place is going to be full of undead or some other kind of monster?" Andyn commented.

"Then we should be all the more careful," the commander answered and paused near one of the first small groups of ruined farmhouses.

"So, what do you purpose we do, Commander?" Andyn asked again and Warrick glared at him.

"Watch your tone with me, Ser. We need to start searching as soon as we can. Night should be coming soon which means we do not have much time," Warrick said and turned to Gerhold. "What is it, vampire? You look concerned."

"I am wondering what else the Vigil knew that he did not tell us about this place," Gerhold answered, and the Paladins all turned to him, obviously unhappy with his comments.

"I already told you once, keep your blasphemous thoughts to yourself, creature," Warrick said venomously.

"The Vigil mentioned nothing of these other Paladins, and I am starting to believe that he knew more about what is happening here than he led us to believe. Do you disagree?" Gerhold asked.

"The Vigils are selected by the Gods themselves. It is not my job to question the divine, nor is it yours," Warrick responded.

"You are a fool if you cannot see that he has hidden things from us." Warrick drew his sword and set it against Gerhold's throat.

"You do not utter another word," he said, but Gerhold only returned his scowl. "Do not question the Vigils in front of me. If his Eminence withheld anything from us then he had good reason to."

"Justify the lies however you wish, Commander, but you are a fool nonetheless."

The two glared at each other before Warrick returned his sword to its sheath. The other Paladins were staring at Gerhold as well, even Roland, but he had said what needed to be said, and in spite of Warrick's heated defenses, Gerhold could tell the Commander had his own doubts. Another moment passed before Warrick turned and pointed to two of the Paladins.

"Ser Gilbert and Ser Andyn will come with me. We will start at the northern end of the city, and the two of you can stay here and set up our camp."

"And what if the city is full of undead?" Andyn asked.

"Then I will be willing to tell his Eminence to send us back a full army of our brothers to conquer it. Any more questions?"

"I do not think this is a wise approach," Gerhold spoke up, and Warrick turned his glare to the vampire again.

"And why is that? You are not a military commander or a warrior."

"You are right, I am a hunter and the best thing we can do is not alert anyone to our presence, undead or otherwise. I suggest you allow me to go and scout the city first before you go blundering in." Warrick spat on the ground and rested his hand on his sword hilt.

"I will be damned the day I listen to a creature of darkness. You are alive only because the Vigil commanded me to come back with you; if it were not for that, I would have killed you myself the first time I laid eyes on you. If you wish to go and traipse about, then I will not stop you and if you get yourself killed along the way, all the better. Ser Roland, you will stay and setup our camp; Gods know you are only good for a distraction anyways. Ser Andyn, Ser Gilbert, you both follow me. We will be back by sundown." Warrick turned and, without another word, led the other two Paladins down the broken path towards the city ruins.

"That went well," Roland said with a small grin. "Warrick is a good fighter and a good leader, until he lets his emotions get the better of him. Once that happens, he makes more foolish mistakes than an angry child, just to prove he is right."

"A poor leader is one who puts his pride before the lives of his men, and it is even worse when he does not realize it," Gerhold answered as the two men stared after the three Paladins.

A Curse of Darkness

"Going straight into the city like that, the fool is going to get himself and the other two killed. You still should not have said what you did about the Vigil. We are devout men." Roland frowned.

"Devout or not, only a fool refuses to see what is abundantly clear." Roland's eyes narrowed for a moment before he turned and stared after the other three Paladins.

"What do you purpose we do then? Stay here and setup camp?" Roland asked and Gerhold turned and walked a little further into the trees.

"We wait," he said and sat down with his back against one of the thick trees.

"Wait? And then what?"

"We wait and we watch."

"Should we not follow them? Warrick is not the most pleasant Commander, but are we really going to let him get himself killed?" Roland asked as Gerhold picked up a fallen branch and started whittling.

"That fool is going to wake whatever is living in those old stone bones, and when they do, we will be able to see just what is hiding here. Wait until they reach the city ruins, then we will follow and see what this old valley has to hide."

"Or help them," Roland said.

"If a fool kicks a hornet's nest, then only a bigger fool goes running in after him," Gerhold responded and watched as Warrick and the other two made their way across the open valley towards the ruined city. At least the foolish man was not going to head straight through the front gates.

Roland took a seat next to him and pulled out a small piece of dried jerky and bit into it. Gerhold pulled one of the small glass vials from his pack that was filled with the thick, red mixture of blood, removed the little cork, and downed the contents in one gulp. He noticed the young Paladin watching him out of the corner of his eye but Roland only looked on in mild interest while humming, which Gerhold could not hear and it only sounded like a monotone buzzing sound. Gerhold listened until Roland started to sing in a low tone, barely able to make out the words of the song.

'Farewell and goodbye to the grand golden fields and trees that were once so green.
Farewell and goodbye to the rivers that flowed and the sun that seemed only to gleam.
Farewell to the hills and mountains so tall, to spring and summer, to winter and fall.
Farewell to the lands that we once held so dear, for all that is left are death and fear.
Woe to the fields of Mathenry where you find the many who've fallen,

J.S. Matthews

And woe to the men of Daloran whose time will soon be forgotten.
Farewell to the cities and buildings so grand and the farms that were so long tended.
Farewell to the lives of those now lost and to the families that shall never be mended.
Farewell to the halls and the mighty grey towers and to the streams and the brooks and the bright colored flowers.
Farewell to our kin and our ancestor's homes, to our walls and our houses and castles of stone.
Woe to the fields of Mathenry, where the dead have now made it their own,
And woe to the men of Daloran, where darkness has taken their throne."

Roland finished the words and then sat in silence. Gerhold had heard the song before, a long time ago, but it sounded strange without music and he had forgotten the words and title. It was a haunting song, a lament of the old kingdom of Daloran that had fallen into ruin during the Plague Wars. They were within the borders of Daloran and the words of the song seemed fitting.

"A sad song for a sad tale," Gerhold said finally and Roland nodded.

"A sad tale indeed."

"What is its name?" Gerhold asked.

"*The Fields of Mathenry*, by Gendren the Great. I figured it fit the mood seeing as how we are some of the first to step foot in Daloran in many years, though Mathenry is far to the south. When I was a child, I always wanted to visit that ancient field of battle, to walk where the great heroes walked. I read the tales many times, but I have always felt that songs captured the stories of old better than books and scrolls. It brings them to life."

"Music is a strange form of magic," Gerhold added.

"Magic? I suppose so, when you think about it," Roland said and inhaled slowly. The two men sat in silence for another moment before Roland spoke again. "So how did you become what you are?" Gerhold paused before responding.

"I let my guard down," Gerhold answered and started whittling again.

"I have heard that a vampire must bite you in order to turn you, but that never made much sense. There would be thousands of your kind if that were true," the young man said.

"Few other than the Keepers remember how vampirism came to be, and apparently not even the Paladins can recall those old tales now."

"I heard another rumor, that the curse is contracted through gold, cursed gold, from the lost realms of Arden long ago," Roland said and Gerhold nodded.

"Aye, cursed gold taken from Arden by those too greedy to leave it behind," he said and tugged on the little golden chain around his neck to reveal the golden locket. Roland stared at it for a moment before he realized what it was.

"Is that it?" he asked and Gerhold nodded. "By the Gods, and all you had to do was touch it?"

"I took it into my possession, not realizing what it was, of course. It was the only time in my life that I encountered a vampire and did not kill him. What a fool I was."

"Who was this vampire? Did you hunt him down?"

"I have not seen him since, though I have tried tracking him. He may be dead, but I do not believe it, not him. I have time though, time to be patient and wait for something to turn up. One day I will find him, whether it be the vampire or his bones, I will find him," Gerhold finished and set the sharpened stake down next to him, then looked out over the valley.

Though Altandir had been abandoned for over a thousand years many of the stone structures still stood with a collapsed roof or fallen wall here and there. Most of the city had been retaken by nature, and many trees grew within the fallen wall and in between the rows of abandoned buildings. Grass and thick patches of brush and weeds poked through the cracks in the stone paths and up the sides of walls and towers. The citadel at the top of the little hillside had a few fallen towers but still held a sense of awe and beauty about it. Gerhold imagined just how beautiful the white stone city would have looked a thousand years ago, before its destruction, and wondered what secrets were now hidden beneath the ruble.

There were signs all around the valley of the many battles that took place long ago, as remnants of old siege machines still dotted the land, though now overtaken by the trees and scrubs. Nearly unidentifiable remains of weapons and armor were found here and there beneath thick layers of green grass and roots, and even the stone walls and buildings bore the scars of the many conflicts. Skeletons and bones were also a common sight, and many were still clutching their broken spears and shattered shields, a reminder of the many lives lost during those terrible battles. Gerhold found this strange as most of these should have decomposed or been worn to nothing by the years but the strange magic of the forest seemed to preserve the battlefield.

"What about you, selected as a Vigil's Guard at such a young age?" Gerhold asked, once again breaking the silence.

"The youngest in quite some time. Most of the men will say it is because of my father's influence," Roland answered.

"And is that true?" Gerhold asked again.

"My father is as pious as any ruthless, selfish, and power-hungry a lord as you will meet anywhere, which means he substitutes large donations for obedience to the Chronicles and the Three Gods. My father and I have never seen eye to eye one might say," Roland shook his head. "To be honest I hated him. His cruelness, his savagery, and his egotistic lifestyle never suited me. So, at the earliest I could manage, I ran away and joined the Paladins."

"How old were you when you left?"

"Fourteen, and it took him years to track me down. Thankfully, the Paladin code says that once one joins, he gives up all titles and lands. I did not see him, but I can imagine how furious he must have been when the Vigil told him I was to stay. He had other heirs of course, but it was more that he wanted to punish me than anything else. So, to answer your question, no, my father had nothing to do with my appointment to the Guard. I fought every day to become what I am, to make my spear as much a part of me as my hand or heart, to master as much as I could as quickly as I could manage. It bothered me at first when the others would mention my father and how the only reason I rose through the ranks so quickly was because of him, and not my skills and determination," Roland shook his head again.

"Jealousy will make fools of the wisest men," Gerhold added and Roland nodded.

"They were jealous. The younger men because of how quickly I mastered the lessons and the older because of how quickly I was able to challenge them. Once during training as an Apprentice, I refused to follow the forms given by our teacher and he had me face a full-fledged Paladin in combat. It turned out not to be just any Paladin, but rather I was to face Ser Borvir. Have you heard of him?" Gerhold nodded.

"Aye, I have heard of him. They had you fight a seasoned veteran as an Apprentice?" Gerhold asked in surprise, and Roland smiled before answering.

"He wanted to teach me a lesson, but you should have seen the look on his face when I won. When I knocked Ser Borvir to the ground and held my spear tip to his chest, not one of those men said a word to me. The following day I was elevated to a Paladin, given my armor, and sent to train with the Guard. I found out later that it was Ser Borvir that recommended me for the Guard and fought with the other Commanders to have me recruited."

A Curse of Darkness

"And yet they will never let you forget your past," Gerhold said and Roland nodded.

"It matters little now. I have proved what I am and if they refuse to see it then they can wallow in their jealousy alone. Those who still doubt me are fools and are not worth my time worrying about what they think."

Gerhold looked at Roland, a young man, but a true warrior at heart. Saddled by the lives and mistakes of his kin, he used it as fuel instead of a reason to give up. His peers still judged him by who his father was rather than by his own actions. Gerhold liked Roland, but still did not trust the man. He would never let his guard down again.

"I saw you fight back in the bog and was quite impressed."

"I appreciate that, especially from you, but undead are simple to fight. They are neither necromancers nor warriors. A Paladin once told me that if you are not moving forward then you are falling back. I still have much to learn and more to practice."

"Wise words," Gerhold said and stood up. Commander Warrick and his men had just passed into the city and Gerhold motioned for Roland to follow. "Are you ready?" Roland nodded and stood.

"As long as they do not get themselves killed too quickly," he said, and followed Gerhold at a light jog as the vampire started down the valley.

Chapter 9: Through the Streets

The going was slow as Gerhold wanted to make sure they remained hidden from any prying eyes, whether they came from the city or the surrounding forest. Everything seemed quiet, and nothing but the slight whisper of the passing wind could be heard. There was something about the city that unnerved Gerhold, and he knew that there was more to the old ruins than what they could see.

As they continued, it got harder and harder to keep Warrick and the others in sight, as the three men grew more cautious the closer, they got to the ruins of the city. They started crouching and sneaking through ruined old buildings and walls, and Gerhold would lose them, only to catch a glimpse of the Paladins as they passed between the boulders, trees, and collapsed old ruins that littered the valley. Soon, Warrick, Andyn, and Gilbert disappeared beyond the half-fallen wall that surrounded the city and into the ruins of the city proper.

"Can you still see them?" Roland whispered as the two men crouched down in the ruins of an old stone building, staring out towards where they had last seen their three companions.

"No, they made it into the city, though," Gerhold responded and crept across to where part of the wall had fallen in. "If we can sneak close to those trees and make our way between the piles of rubble we should be able to make it to that small breach in the wall there," he said and pointed to a hole that had formed at the base of the half fallen city wall.

"Do we really need to be so cautious? I have not seen a single thing, in the city or anywhere else. Maybe there is nothing here after all?"

"Did you see anything before we were attacked in the bog?" Gerhold asked and Roland shook his head.

"No, I did not," Roland answered. "I suppose you are the one who has been hunting monsters for over a century, so lead on. Tell me what to do and I will do it."

A Curse of Darkness

Gerhold smiled and nodded, then crept out and across the open space to the first clump of trees. He glanced back at Roland for a moment and thought he saw something hovering above the treetops behind them. Gerhold paused for a moment but the sky was empty, and he told himself it was nothing before continuing. Slowly they made their way closer to the city until the old, ruined towers loomed above them. Off to the west Gerhold could just make out the glowing orange peaks of the mountains as the sun dropped below the swirling clouds. The clouds seemed even stranger the closer they got to the outskirts of the ancient city, and the black mass swirled in a circle directly above the citadel at the center of the ruins. Eventually they reached the wall and crept through the little gap in the stone.

Once inside they saw the ruined buildings and crumbling streets up close. Grass and tree roots crisscrossed the broken stone paths and great trees grew up between the forgotten structures. Most of the white stone buildings were still standing, though missing a wall or roof, while some had completely collapsed after the many years of wind, rain, and abandonment. There was a time over a thousand years ago when the streets would have been filled with people as merchants called out their goods and music could have been heard on every corner and in every tavern. Now only the haunted skeleton of that city remained.

Quietly, Gerhold made his way to the first line of buildings and crept inside through an empty doorframe. It was one of the few taller structures that was still standing, and the vampire moved cautiously through the old building, listening for sounds of cracking stone or anything that would signal an impending collapse. They climbed the first flight of stairs to the second floor, which resembled the one below with thick layers of dust, broken stones, and various plants that had grown in the cracks and crevices of the floor, walls, and ceiling.

"We need to make it up to the third floor so we can get a better view of the streets; maybe we can find where Warrick and the others went," Gerhold whispered and Roland nodded.

Just then, an explosion echoed from somewhere deeper in the city ruins, followed by more bangs and incoherent shouts. Gerhold and Roland exchanged worried glances before swiftly making their way up the second flight of stairs. They had to climb over piles of fallen stone and debris that nearly blocked the stairwell to reach the top, where they found that most of the roof had collapsed and scattered rubble across the third floor. Gerhold darted over to the edge of the building and stared out over the rest of the ruined city, doing his best to locate where the sounds of battle were coming from. Another explosion rang out and Gerhold caught sight of a stream of white fire briefly while more voices called out, though he could not make out what they were saying. A few more flashes of light came from somewhere between the lines of broken structures in the distance.

"Sounds like the Commander kicked the hornets' nest all right," Gerhold said and Roland spat in frustration.

"The fool should have listened to you. Should we go to the rescue?"

"If there is anything left to rescue," Gerhold responded and took off down the stairs and to the streets below.

They ran through the streets as quickly and quietly as they could in the direction of the sounds, doing their best to keep to the remaining buildings, alleyways, and piles of rubble to avoid being seen, and only crossed the large open spaces when they had no other choice. As they drew closer to the battle the sounds of spells and cries of men died away, and once they reached the last line of structures the battle had come to an end. Gerhold thought he recognized one of the voices yelling before it ceased suddenly, followed only by silence and no more cries or explosions. For more than a minute the two men crouched in a little alleyway and listened until they heard the echo of other voices, unfamiliar voices, discussing something that Gerhold could not make it out even with his keen sense of hearing. The fight was over, that he knew, and by the sound of the voices he now heard, it had not ended in Warrick's favor.

Silently the two men made their way across the last open street and climbed a large mound of broken stone to reach the second story of a building. They paused for a moment so Gerhold could listen and while most men would have continued without noticing anything out of the ordinary, the keen ears of the vampire picked up the soft sounds of voices from the street below. Gerhold motioned for Roland to follow and together they crept up the second flight of stairs to the third level, where they came to an opened doorway and Gerhold leaned over to see what lay beyond.

On the other side was a hallway with a half-missing roof and a collapsed wall that had fallen into the adjacent room. He waited a moment before moving forward, keeping low and looking for any signs of movement. Somewhere below he could still hear the echoing sounds of voices. Gerhold crept over to the side of the collapsed wall, motioned for Roland to follow and peered down to the street below. There were scorch marks across the stone streets and buildings where

A Curse of Darkness

spells had slammed into the stone. Pieces of walls had been torn away by the impact of spells, and at least seven bodies lay in the streets, all dressed in similar black robes. Ten other men in robes stood in a group around three prone forms, which Gerhold immediately recognized as Warrick, Andyn, and Gilbert. The men were speaking in low tones and Gerhold tried to listen to the conversation.

"Paladins? Here?" one of the men said in an urgent tone.

"What should we do? The master needs to hear of this right away," another added.

"We will bring news along with their heads."

"No!" a third man said, and Gerhold could tell this was another vampire. "There could be more of them hiding about and these will be more useful alive. Have them brought to the master immediately and see what he wants us to do with them. Leave a few of our hunters behind in case any others come looking for their missing companions." The other robed men nodded and started to remove the three unconscious men.

"Wait, this one here looks to be in poor health," a man said with an evil laugh and pointed to Ser Gilbert. "Looks like he took a blade to the side."

"So? He is a warrior; if he cannot take a single blow then he deserves to die."

"But what use is a dead body?"

"You fool, the necromancers can find a use for the body if it comes to that, and if the necromancers do not want it then it will be used for feeding the fledglings; now move."

Gerhold watched as the group picked up the silver clad Paladins and carried them down the winding street in the direction of the great citadel. Gerhold made sure there were no guards nearby before motioning for Roland to follow him up a pile of rubble to the roof.

"Were those vampires?" Roland whispered as soon as they reached the top, and Gerhold looked around at the other buildings nearby, checking for any other guards.

"Some were. The others were men, maybe necromancers," Gerhold answered quietly and leapt over the small gap to another roof and dropped into another room below. "I have seen this before, though, it is a cult."

"A cult? What a wonderful addition to the undead, monsters, and necromancers," Roland whispered wryly.

"We need to follow them," Gerhold said and moved to the other side of the room.

"Are there any others about? Maybe they left some guards behind," Roland asked again as he came sliding down from the roof, spear in hand, but Gerhold shook his head.

"Perhaps, but I am not sure. Either way we need to move. That group will lead us to what we seek."

"Do you mean to rescue them? The others I mean," Roland asked as they moved across the room and leapt to another building.

"I mean to discover who these cultists are and why they are here. Warrick and the others are not our main concern," Gerhold answered.

"So, we are going to let them die?" It was not an accusing question, but Gerhold could tell Roland did not approve of his response.

"Perhaps, if we must," the vampire answered again and sped off silently in the direction of the cultists.

Across the rooftops they went and then down once again into the alleyways and side streets that passed between the tightly packed and crumbling buildings. The deeper they moved into the city the taller the buildings grew, and it became easier to remain undetected amidst the ancient piles of rubble and decaying stone walls. At one point the group of robed men and vampires halted, and it looked as though Commander Warrick was waking. One of the vampires stepped forward, rested his hand on Warrick's head as the man started to move, and then muttered some strange incantation. Gerhold watched as the commander's eyes rolled back into his skull and his body went limp once again before the group continued. Gerhold had considered launching an ambush then and there, but he was not sure if there were other guards nearby or what else lay hidden in the ruins.

Whoever these men and vampires were, Gerhold had a hunch that they were behind the darkness and getting to the bottom of that mystery was more important than the lives of the three Paladins. Gerhold felt a twinge of guilt as he had suspected this might happen, and he had even planned on using Warrick and his men as bait to see what they were up against since the fool commander heeded his pride rather than the vampire's warnings. It had been done though, and he had to make the best of the situation. He would solve this riddle and discover who the men in black robes were and why the vampires were working with them. But somewhere deep inside him, a tiny spark had grown, a small hope that somewhere in these ruins he would find something more than just why the

A Curse of Darkness

darkness of Blightwood was spreading. Perhaps this master the men had spoken of was someone more than just a necromancer. Perhaps this was the break Gerhold had been waiting for during the past one hundred years? He pushed these hopes aside and continued onwards, making his way through the ancient city as quietly as he could.

Finally, the robed men reached the mangled, metal gates that led into the citadel, and Gerhold motioned for Roland to halt as they watched the group pass beneath the great stone arch and disappear into the courtyard beyond. High above him atop one of the large towers that still stood was another cultist, staring out over the ruined city for any sign of intruders. Once Gerhold was certain the man in the tower had turned away, he motioned for Roland to follow and quickly led the way across the open street and to the gates.

Gerhold peered warily around the corner and saw the group of cultists heading across the large courtyard towards a flight of stairs that led up to the inner keep. He noticed three more guards along the high walls and towers and knew that there would be others that he could not see. The line of robed men halted in front of the thick wooden doors at the top of the stairs, and the first man in line knocked. A moment later the doors creaked open, and the group disappeared from view just as the doors slammed shut once again. Gerhold crept back to where Roland was crouched beside the base of the cracked stone wall.

"So how in the six hells are we going to get in there?" Roland asked after Gerhold explained what he had seen. The hunter shrugged and shook his head.

"Not through the courtyard. We would be spotted before we made it halfway to the keep entrance, and besides, there are guards waiting inside. We need another way in."

"Maybe there is another entrance, or a passageway of some kind? Fortresses always have an escape route," Roland added.

"I doubt we will be able to find it if there is one, and even if we did it would take us hours, and night is already upon us."

"Maybe we can sneak through the courtyard after dark."

"Vampires can see as well in the dark as you can in the light. They would see us, and besides, we still have no way in," Gerhold answered and tried to rack his brain for any ideas.

"Well, whatever we plan on doing we better get started quickly; we do not have time to sit and–" Roland stopped mid-sentence and stared up at the wall above. "Wait a minute," he said under his breath and moved around the base of a nearby tower.

"What is it?" Gerhold asked and Roland pointed at the wall.

"These vines, they might be thick enough for us to climb," he whispered excitedly and gave one of the vines a tug.

"I hope you are feeling particularly brave," Gerhold said, while picturing the vines snapping and them falling from such a great height.

"They should hold us just fine. Besides, do you have any other ideas to get us inside?" Roland asked, but before Gerhold could answer the young Paladin leapt onto the twisted vines and started to climb.

"They better hold, or this is going to be a long trip up and a short one down," Gerhold muttered before beginning the climb.

"Perhaps we should have waited for nightfall," Roland added as they continued to climb.

"It will be here soon enough, and we have no time to wait. Besides, these clouds provide enough cover, and if there are more vampires along the walls, the darkness will do little to hide us."

Hand over hand, the two men scaled the wall along the rope-like vines that climbed up the ancient stone to the battlements high above. They moved faster than Gerhold had anticipated, as the vines proved easy to climb, and only once did Gerhold catch sight of a guard patrolling the battlements above. Both he and Roland huddled against the wall and prayed that the guard would pass by without noticing them. After a tense minute, the man turned and continued along the battlement as if nothing were out of the ordinary and Gerhold let out a sigh of relief as he started to climb once more. They reached the top of the wall only a few moments later, just as the last few rays of orange light disappeared over the horizon to the west.

Gerhold was the first over the battlement and quickly pulled Roland up before heading down the battlement as quietly as possible and towards the nearest tower. They made their way across to a second tower where Gerhold hid to avoid a passing guard. He realized that the other guards must be vampires, as they made excellent sentries due to their enhanced senses, but these vampires were young, and the younger the vampire the weaker it was. It took time for one to grow into the changes that came with becoming a vampire, and after a hundred years Gerhold was far more experienced and stronger than the fledgling guards. They dodged another passing guard before stopping near the end of the wall where it met a large balcony, which jutted out over the courtyard below. There were two more vampires standing watch, one near a large set of double doors and another who patrolled two nearby corridors on either side of the balcony.

Gerhold leapt forward with Roland in tow, and before the first guard could react, Gerhold was already dashing forward with his silver dagger drawn and ready to strike. A moment later both guards lay dead; one with Gerhold's dagger through its heart and the other impaled upon Roland's silver spear. It was unfortunate as missing guards would raise suspicion, but Gerhold knew they had little choice if they wanted to get inside the fortress. They pulled the bodies into one of the side corridors just as the remains began to smolder and turn to the familiar piles of ash and bone; then they made their way quickly to the nearest door. Gerhold glanced at Roland, who nodded that he was ready, and then pushed open the metal door slowly. They moved into a darkened hallway, not knowing what evils lay hidden in the bowels of the ancient citadel.

J.S. Matthews

Chapter 10: Into the Depths

The interior of the fortress was dark and musty with thick layers of dust and grime from the centuries of decay and abandonment. Ancient bones of long dead inhabitants littered the hallway between piles of fallen stone and rubble, and small crystals lined the walls and cast a dim white light. Gerhold led the way forward, relying on his keen senses to alert him of any threats that were hidden in the gloom ahead, and soon they came to another thick metal door. Gerhold only opened it an inch before the old hinges let out an ear-piercing screech as metal scraped against metal. He took a step back and reached into his pack to pull out a small vial of yellowish liquid, which he carefully poured over the hinges and rubbed with the same rag he used to clean his sword.

"What is that?" Roland whispered.

"Oil, it keeps the hinges from sticking," Gerhold answered and pushed the door, which slid open without a sound.

"Brilliant! Where did you learn that trick?"

"From an old thief I used to work with," he answered and slipped through into the next room. "You tend to meet many interesting people when forced into hiding."

This room was much larger than the cramped hallway they had come through but no less rundown. Large cracks reached up the stone walls and across the ceilings and floors like thin, crooked fingers that twisted this way and that. Old suits of rusted and dirty armor lay strewn across the dusty floors, ancient paintings hung on the walls now only faded memories of a forgotten age, and piles of destroyed books sat in the corners of the room and beneath fallen shelves and pieces of shattered wood. Ahead was another door, only this time Gerhold could see small beams of greenish light passing beneath it from the other side. He walked quietly across the room, readied one of his hand crossbows, and opened the door slowly.

A Curse of Darkness

From what he could see through the little space between the door and the frame there was a walkway that extended to both the left and right. It was a massive circular room with a high ceiling and at least a hundred feet across. Gerhold opened the door a few inches more to make sure there were no guards nearby and to get a better view of the room. A soft, sickly green light emanated from somewhere far below and cast strange, shifting shadows along the walkway and walls of the upper floor. More thick vines hung from a large hole in the ceiling and crawled along the walls and in between the remains of the stone railing that stood around the walkway. There were more metal doors all around the room lining the wall, some cracked and fallen while others still stood resolute against the unrelenting waves of time and decay. A thin beam of strange, green light rose through the center of the large room and towards the hole in the roof.

Gerhold crept forward towards the railing and peered down through the stone spindles, searching for wherever the strange light was coming from. Below, he saw two more walkways like the one which he now stood on, and even further down was the ground floor of the citadel, except there was no floor. The ground was missing entirely, and where there should have been some extravagantly designed stone tiles there was instead an enormous hole that delved down through the foundation of the building and deep underground. The circular pit was so deep that Gerhold could see the beam of green light climbing up out of the darkness but not where it was coming from. Around the outside of the hole was another walkway and the vampire's keen eyes caught sight of the cultists along the opposite side.

After making sure the next level below was free of enemies, Gerhold moved along the walkway with Roland in tow and then climbed down. Part of this second walkway had collapsed and made it easy for Gerhold to guide them down to the next balcony, the last one above the rim of the giant pit. Here he paused and watched as the group of men paused along the little wooden walkway below next to a set of three large lifts, which were run by a complex system of pulleys, ropes, and counterweights. Gerhold caught the beginning of what sounded like an argument between the vampire leading the group of cultists and another guard who stood by the lifts.

"You dare question me, thrall?" the first vampire was shouting as Gerhold and Roland crept along the lowest of the walkways.

"You should have killed all three of them; our master will not be pleased by your decision, fledgling," the thrall answered in his droning voice, and Gerhold could feel the heat of the vampire's stare even from so far away.

"You watch your mouth, filth, or I may just bleed you for the fun of it. Now, get out of the way and prepare to lower the lifts. If the master wishes me punished, then he will do it himself."

With that the group of robed men began to step onto the first two lifts. Once two of the platforms were loaded, the thrall pulled a small lever, and the sounds of scraping metal, groaning ropes, and creaking wood echoed throughout the hall as the lifts began to descend into the depths of the pit. Only the thrall remained now.

"Wait here," Gerhold whispered and took off before Roland could protest.

Gerhold leapt over the balcony and landed catlike on the floor below without a sound. He darted in the direction of the lifts and in one smooth motion leapt over a pile of rubble and fired his crossbow. The bolt found its mark and the guard standing near the lifts fell, grabbing at his throat as blood poured from the wound. Gerhold quickly finished the man with his dagger and the gurgling sounds of the dying man ceased. He dragged the body behind a pile of rubble and motioned for Roland to make his way down.

"Not a vampire?" the young Paladin asked as he came jogging up.

"No, just a thrall. Looks like he was the only guard in here," Gerhold answered in a whisper and made his way over to the lifts.

Only one of the platforms remained as the group they were following had already taken the other two. The sounds of grinding metal and creaking chains echoed from below as Gerhold and Roland examined the lifts.

"Looks like this is the only way down," Roland whispered and pointed to the one remaining lift.

"So, it would seem, but what waits for us below? These lifts are loud and clumsy, and I doubt there will be a single inhabitant down there that will not know of our presence."

"What do you suggest then? Climbing down?"

"No, I have a much better plan, but I do not think you are going to like it," Gerhold said with a smile.

A minute later the last lift was descending down the massive hole. Roland sat with his back to the metal doors made from thick iron bars, while Gerhold lay above, staying as low as he could on the roof of the lift as it clanged and clattered its way deeper into the pit. Below, he could see what looked like the

A Curse of Darkness

ruins of a large fortress that had been carved into the stone at the bottom of the hole, and many towers and turrets reached up from the depths with a single roofless keep at the center. A beam of sickly green light emanated from the keep and reached high up the through the great pit and into the citadel above. The soft, orange glow of torches dotted the darkness and made Gerhold wonder just how vast the fortress was, as well as how many enemies it held.

"This plan of yours had better not get me killed," Roland called up. "If they are vampires will they be able to hear my heart? Playing dead will not be much use if they can tell right away."

"You will be fine; the sound of the lift will distract them long enough. Besides, you do make for a good dead body," Gerhold answered but Roland only frowned.

"What happens if the whole group is down there waiting for us?"

"We improvise," Gerhold said with a smile.

"I pray you are right about this," Roland added.

"And let us hope the Gods hear your prayers."

Finally, the floor of the cavern came into view and the lift began to slow to a halt. Gerhold huddled down as much as he could as he caught sight of two more robed men and watched as Roland closed his eyes and did his best to hold still and appear as dead as he could. The two guards approached as the lift came to a halt and looked quizzically at the seemingly dead man lying in the lift before approaching with their weapons in drawn. Before either man could come within even a few feet of the lift, Gerhold leapt from above with his silver long sword in hand, and in two quick strikes both guards feel headless. A third thrall that Gerhold had not noticed, darted away towards one of the passages, but before Gerhold could draw and fire his crossbow a silver object flew past his head and slammed into the retreating guard. The thrall fell to the floor without a sound, Roland's silver spear protruding from his chest.

"That was quite a throw," Gerhold said as Roland strode past him to retrieve the spear.

"Did you expect me to play dead while you had all the fun?" Roland responded as they quickly dragged the bodies onto the lift and pulled the lever to send it back up to the surface. "Where to now?"

"This way," Gerhold answered in a whisper and then motioned to the center passage leading away from the lifts.

"How do you know?"

"The other two passages are seldom used judging by the dust and dirt on the floor, but this center one is covered in footprints and the smells of men. If that group had gone down either of the other two it would be obvious."

"Then lead on and let us hope we remain unnoticed for as long as we can. It will not be long before the guards above find the bodies of their missing comrades," Roland said and Gerhold nodded in agreement before taking off down the passageway as quietly as he could manage.

The corridor was dark and cold, and there were only a few dim torches to light the way. More corridors intertwined with it as well as many doors made of thick iron, but the tracks they followed never deviated from long hallway. Twice they had to dive into a side passage or behind a pile of rubble to avoid passing guards, though thankfully both were just thralls and remained completely unaware of Gerhold and Roland. Soon the familiar green light bathed the hallway ahead and the echoing sounds of voices could be heard from somewhere in the distance. The corridor came to an end and opened to a large room beyond, most of which was invisible to Gerhold. Two guards were posted near the entrance, and farther in Gerhold could make out a circular space and a glowing green orb at the center. Around the outside, high above the floor, there was a balcony that encircled the upper section of the room.

"Come on, this way," he whispered to Roland and darted down a nearby side passage.

"Where are we going?"

"Just be quiet and stay close!"

They moved down the smaller passage until they came to a flight of stairs that led in the direction of the larger room. At the top was a thick metal door which Gerhold picked without any issues and darted inside, closing the door behind them as silently as he had opened it. The room was a small rectangular area with only a few old rickety chairs and collapsed shelves. A pile of decayed scrolls lay nearby, and a second door stood along the opposite wall; the same green light was visible beneath the foot of the door.

"There is a balcony; this way I think. Hopefully, we can get a better vantage point and see what we are up against," Gerhold said as he crept over to the second door and began fiddling with the lock.

"And find out if the Commander and the other two are still alive," Roland answered worriedly. "You heard what they said about Ser Gilbert? He may already be dead."

A Curse of Darkness

"If he is, then it would be a far better fate than what the other two will face while alive," Gerhold answered as the lock clicked, and he opened it just a fraction of an inch to see what was on the other side.

The ancient balcony was empty. Carved from the same stone as the rest of the subterranean fortress, the walkway reached around the entire upper level of the inside of the hall only fifteen feet above the ground. After ensuring that there were no guards, Gerhold crept forward as quietly as he could and peered through an opening in the stone spindles. Above them he could see the massive walls of the pit stretching up into the darkness and interspaced around the circular hole in the roof of the room were large, clear crystal chandeliers that cast a dim white light about the room. Below, he saw a group of robed men gathered in a circle at the center, and between them, set upon a circular stone dais, was a green glowing orb. A stream of green light protruded upwards through the top of the roofless hall and into the pit above. More men were gathered in a group around three kneeling figures in silver armor, and Gerhold watched and listened to the group's discussion.

"I instructed you to kill anyone who dared venture into the city, and yet here are three men, alive and well. Why is that fledgling? Were my instructions not clear enough?" A man in black robes with a hood pulled up over his head was talking to the group that had captured the Commander.

"You did, master, but these are not just any men, they are Paladins. I assumed you meant villagers or hunters, not–"

"It is not your job to make foolish assumptions about what I order you to do, fledgling. You are to follow my commands, not make up your own as you see fit. And now you have brought three Paladins into our midst. Perhaps there are more out there, waiting for their companions to return. What will they do when these men do not?" Gerhold closed his eyes for a moment and tried to concentrate. He had heard that voice before sometime long ago, but he could not remember where.

"If we had killed them, then they still would not have returned, and we would have had no knowledge if there were others. At least this way we may discover if they are alone or not," the other vampire answered, and Gerhold could tell the leader was pleased even though he could not see the vampire's face.

"Well then, perhaps you are not as foolish as I had initially perceived," he said and moved forward to address Warrick. All three Paladins were tied and had been forced to their knees. Ser Gilbert appeared to be alive, though he seemed to wince every time he took a breath. "Now then, you are their commander judging by your armor. Perhaps you will be kind enough to explain why you and your men are here and if there are others."

Warrick said nothing and instead spat at the hooded man's feet. The vampire laughed and struck the Commander across the side of the head, sending the Paladin sprawling to the floor.

"That was quite rude, spitting at your host in such a manner. You see I was raised a noble, and I know how one should treat his host, but I suppose that I should not assume that everyone should know of such customs. Not when they are peasants and knaves." The man threw back his hood and revealed a long mass of black hair and a clean-shaven face. Gerhold immediately recognized the vampire and his heart sunk. He had hoped it would be Harkin hidden behind that hood, but instead it was the face of Lord Galen Friedrich. "Now let us try this again; are there more of your men, perhaps waiting in the forest? It will be far more pleasant for you if you speak. If there are others, my sons and daughters will find them; as you see, we are far more dangerous in this darkness than you could ever imagine."

Again, Warrick said nothing, and Lord Friedrich just shook his head and laughed again. The vampire strode down the line of kneeling Paladins until he came to a halt in front of Ser Gilbert. For a moment, the vampire just stared at the wounded man, an expressionless look on his face.

"You, Ser, are you of noble birth per chance?" Friedrich asked but Gilbert said nothing. "You are I can tell. You reek of gold and extravagance. Noble blood is rare, especially in these parts."

Without warning, Lord Friedrich slammed his fist into Gilbert's face and sent the wounded Paladin rolling across the floor. Ser Gilbert groaned in pain, and the vampire lifted him by his throat and threw him against the wall with a sickening crunch. The Paladin shook violently as he slid to the floor and gasped for breath until Friedrich moved forward and sank a dagger into his throat. Gilbert's eyes rolled and then stared blankly off into the distance as death swallowed him. Lord Friedrich stared at the dead man for only a moment and then slowly lifted the knife blade to his lips and gently licked the blood from the blade.

Gerhold watched from the balcony but he could practically smell and taste the blood that poured from the man's wound. Somewhere deep within his mind, the beast awoke from its slumber. That feeling of clawing and gnashing of imaginary teeth grated against Gerhold's consciousness as he fought to keep the blood craved beast in its cage.

"It has been many months indeed since I have tasted the blood of a noble," Lord Friedrich said in a smooth tone as he walked across the room and stood in front of Warrick. "Do you feel like talking now?"

"Not to a creature of darkness. I would prefer to run you through," Warrick said and spat again.

"I am sure you would. You, thrall?" the vampire said, and a skinny man stumbled forward. "Take this body and have it drained; I want as much of his blood saved as possible. Have a bottle of it brought to me here once you are finished. And you, fledgling, you can take these two to the dungeons below and inform our necromancers that they may have their way with them, but first they must extract as much information as possible." The vampire nodded and bowed, then motioned for the others to pull the Paladins to their feet while the body of Ser Gilbert was dragged out of sight. Warrick and Andyn were pulled to their feet and dragged through another door at the opposite end of the room.

Gerhold stared at Lord Friedrich as many long-forgotten memories flooded into his mind, drowning out the growling beast and allowing the hunter to refocus his thoughts. Somehow Friedrich had become a vampire and now he was here. If Friedrich was here, then perhaps he was still working with Harkin. And if he was, then this was the break Gerhold had been waiting a century for.

"Gerhold, come on, we are going to lose them," Roland whispered and started to make his way along the walkway, but Gerhold did not move.

He remained transfixed, frozen by the thought of finally catching his illusive quarry. It was possible that not thirty feet from him stood the key to ending his search. Galen Friedrich had been working for Harkin Valakir long ago and so it was probable that he still worked for Harkin now. Maybe he had been sent here by Harkin himself? Gerhold shifted his gaze to Roland for just a moment and saw the confused look on the young Paladin's face and realized that he needed to make a choice: should he leave Warrick and Andyn to their fate in the dungeons of this forgotten city, or risk losing the only chance he had of finding Harkin Valakir?

Gerhold stayed where he was, frozen by the battle that raged within him. Warrick was a fool, a fool who hated Gerhold. Why should he waste his only chance to find the creature responsible for his greatest failure to save the life of someone he hardly considered to be his ally? Gerhold frowned when he realized that while the Commander was being interrogated by Lord Friedrich, he had not given up Gerhold and Roland. Was he any better than Harkin or Lord Friedrich if he left the two Paladins to their fate to pursue his own selfish agenda? Deep in the corners of Gerhold's mind he could sense the shadow. That inner beast straining to be let out. He saw Gilbert's blood pooling on the floor and the crimson marks where the body was dragged away. The hunger was always there, the monster within always lurking and ready to strike. Gerhold shook his head and swore under his breath. He stared at Lord Friedrich for another moment before nodding at Roland and heading off down the walkway in the direction the two Paladins had been dragged.

A Curse of Darkness

Chapter 11: The Stairwell

The two men moved swiftly and silently around the walkway and then into another adjacent room, leaving the eerie green glow of the strange orb and the large hall behind them.

"What was that about?" Roland asked curiously as they approached another metal door.

"That vampire, I know him," Gerhold answered as the unlocked door opened slightly and both men slid inside a small hallway containing a downward sloping set of stairs.

The thought of fresh blood was still in his thoughts, but Gerhold said nothing of it. Ignore it, calm the beast, and then continue. He had done it many times before.

"Their leader? You mean the one who killed Ser Gilbert?"

"Yes, Lord Galen Friedrich. I met him a century ago when he was a nobleman ruling over a town outside of Vilheim," Gerhold responded as they made their way down the stairs —he purposefully skipped the part about Harkin.

"And now he is here," Roland mumbled as if it were an interesting detail. "What was that orb? I have never seen anything like it before. It was almost as if those men were casting some sort of spell on it."

"They were necromancers, so it is more than likely they were."

"Do you think that is what is causing the darkness to spread? Are they casting some spell?"

"Perhaps, but that would need to be an extremely powerful spell. Besides, we need to find the Commander and Andyn before our hosts get their hands on them for too long," Gerhold said and sped off down an empty hallway in the direction they had seen the group dragging the Paladins.

Ahead was another long hallway similar to the first corridor they had followed from the lifts. The fortress was built like a labyrinth, with many crisscrossing hallways and identical corridors that were meant to confuse and disorient any intruders. However, this was an old fortress, most likely dug by the undead army during the city's occupation a thousand years ago. It had no decorations nor any embellishments of any kind, as if a soulless, careless group just carved it into the rock with no thought of how it appeared. There was nothing human about this place, and the unnatural cold that inundated the entire complex was more suited for the dead than the living. Warmth represented life and goodness, while the cold represented death and darkness.

Gerhold halted for a moment to study the hallway ahead and to make sure there were no guards nearby. The ancient layers of dirt and grime that covered the floors were freshly disturbed and it would have been obvious to even the most inexperienced tracker that more than one person had been dragged through it recently. They proceeded down the hallway, carefully listening and looking for any disturbance that would warn them of an approaching enemy. Soon they came to a long spiral staircase that sloped downwards and deeper into the roots of the earth. Only a few torches lit the large circular expanse, and a pit stretched down the center of the swirling stairs. More metal doors lined the stairwell and small corridors broke off every so often, driving deeper into the thick stone walls. This stairwell was different from the rest of the fortress, as if it had been built separately. Gerhold caught sight of the group of robed men far below, marching down the steps and dragging the two Paladins along with them.

Quickly and quietly, the two men made their way down the steps, making sure they stayed far enough away to not be seen but close enough so that they could see if the group moved into any of the small passageways. The cavern smelled terrible, a mix of rotting flesh and mold that only grew stronger the deeper they went. Finally, the group stopped near one of the larger doors only thirty feet above the bottom of the pit and entered. Gerhold could see the outline of skeletons and piles of bodies that littered the floor far below and realized that was where the terrible smell was coming from as they waited until the door closed behind the company of vampires and thralls.

Suddenly Gerhold heard the faint sound of echoing voices and footsteps coming from one of the nearby passageways, and he turned just in time to see a metal door creak open. Out walked a pair of men in black robes who immediately spotted Gerhold and Roland. The first man yelled and began to conjure a magical ball of black flame to hurl at the intruders, but before he could, Gerhold's first silver bolt caught him in the chest. The man tumbled forward with a scream and fell thirty feet into the pit and joined the bodies that already littered the bottom of the hole. The second was a vampire, and she darted down the stairs towards the two men. Roland leapt forward and stabbed at the charging creature, which dodged to the side and delivered a strong kick to the Paladin's mid-section. Roland was thrown backwards against the stone wall and then crashed against the stone steps, nearly rolling off the edge into the pit.

Gerhold had already reloaded his larger crossbow and took aim. His shot found its mark and the creature tumbled to her knees in agony as the flames spread across her body, and she clawed wildly at the silver bolt protruding from her chest. Two more doors above and one right near Gerhold opened and more robed men and vampires emerged to see what was causing such a commotion. Gerhold was still reloading when the first two enemies approached, both smiling and showing their elongated fangs.

"Too bad you chose such a slow weapon," one said and dashed forward. "You will die now!"

The vampire lunged at Gerhold but underestimated the hunter's speed, and in a flash Gerhold flipped the small latch at the bottom of the crossbow causing the arms of the weapon to flip forward and the long silver blade to emerge. Before the first creature could react, the blade had already pierced its heart and its screams echoed off the stone walls. The second vampire was so stunned by the speed and skill of this challenger that before it could even ready an attack the silver blade ripped through its shoulder. A second strike finished the creature, but Gerhold had no time to celebrate as more foes came charging down the stairs. Roland was back to his feet and had already leapt past the hunter and engaged the first attacking vampire. This time he avoided the creature's first strike and drove his spear through its heart without hesitation, just as Gerhold cut down another.

"So much for the stealthy approach!" Roland yelled and attacked again.

As the fight continued, another group of guards appeared at the top of the stairs and ran to join the fray. Outnumbered and on the defensive, Gerhold called for Roland to retreat further down the stairs. One of the newly arriving vampires leapt down from the stairs above and landed behind them, sword drawn and ready to strike. Gerhold turned swiftly and parried the blow before slicing the creature's head clean off and sending the decapitated body tumbling into the pit. They sprinted down the stairs again before turning and defending against the lines of attackers once more. Gerhold realized that they were once again on the verge of being overrun, and after dispatching another foe he pulled a small white glass ball from his pack.

"Close your eyes!" he yelled and pulled Roland back before throwing the object to the floor.

Even with his eyes shut tight Gerhold could see the bright flash from the explosion and his ears burst with pain from the deafening *BOOM* that accompanied it. The sound was louder than he had anticipated even in spite of knowing it was coming, and his head throbbed with pain. For a moment he fell against the wall and shook his head, trying to regain some semblance of balance while his ears rang incessantly from the blast. He grabbed Roland, who looked even more disoriented, and used the wall to keep his balance as he led the two of them down the stairs. Their pursuers were still stumbling up and down the steps, rubbing their eyes and ears while screaming for anyone who knew where the intruders had run off to. Gerhold took advantage of the distraction to pull open the door they had seen Warrick and the others dragged through and hurl Roland inside. He slammed the door shut behind them and quickly pulled another bomb from his pack; only this time it was a larger, silver sphere with a long wick protruding from the top.

"What in the hells was that?" Roland yelled. "My whole bloody head feels like a troll used it as a drum."

"A flash bomb, now move! This one will give you more than a headache," Gerhold answered and slid the wick into the flames of a nearby torch.

He placed the bomb at the foot of the metal door and took off down the hallway after Roland, who was still stumbling and using the wall to keep from falling over. As his head began to clear, Gerhold grabbed Roland by the arm and dragged him forward and away from the door as quickly as he could. As soon as they reached the first outcropping cut into the corridor for an intersecting passage, Gerhold threw Roland into the space and dove after him just as a bone shaking explosion ripped through the hallway behind them. A plume of thick black smoke poured through the corridor and filled the cramped space in seconds. Gerhold and Roland leaned against the wall, both men heaving and still feeling the effects of the flash bomb. Behind them he could hear the distant voices of their pursuers, though the ringing in his ears made it far more difficult to hear.

"The whole passage has collapsed, there is no way through," one man yelled, though Gerhold could not make out the rest of what he was saying.

A Curse of Darkness

"Then go around; take the hall of stairs," another answered.

"The hall of stairs? That damnable place is a maze. No one goes there, you know that," the first man said again.

"Find a damn necromancer then! Maybe they can remember how to get through there."

"Why don't we just dig this thing out?" another man protested.

"Do it, or I will drain you dry," their leader responded angrily. There were no other responses, and Gerhold knew that there was no way for their pursuers to get through the debris. The pyrite bomb had been a gamble, but it had paid off.

"Got any other surprises for me?" Roland asked.

"Plenty, but hopefully we do not need them," Gerhold answered and rose to his feet, pulling Roland with him. "All right, this way."

"More tracks?"

"That, and the air smells somewhat fouler, if that is possible. Let us hope there is another way out of these dungeons though."

"At least we lost our friends for the time being," Roland added.

"For now, but who knows what else lies ahead," Gerhold responded. Still, he wondered what other secrets this terrible place was keeping from them as they continued deeper into the poorly lit tunnel.

Chapter 12: Flesh and Bone

Gerhold and Roland continued through the dark corridors and down more flights of stairs, which were lit by only a handful of torches, leaving large gaps of darkness. They moved quickly as stealth had already failed, and Gerhold leapt down the stairs two at a time with Roland in tow. The deeper they went the worse the smell of rotting flesh and death became, and both men knew the worst was still to come. Soon they reached a larger chamber lined with heavy metal doors on two levels, and both immediately recognized it as some sort of prison, but Gerhold held up his hand for them to halt.

"What is it? I don't hear a thing," Roland whispered and readied his spear.

"That is what worries me. Unless these cells are all empty, there should be some sound coming from here," Gerhold answered and moved forward cautiously.

"You have better ears than me. If you are not hearing anything then maybe they are all empty."

"They are not empty," Gerhold replied again. He could hear a strange buzzing noise coming from all around now that they had moved into the room. "Take a look at the lower level," he said and quickly moved up the stairs to the second level of cells.

The metal doors were made of thick steel, and Gerhold found himself recalling the dungeon of Ravencroft Castile. Gerhold readied his weapon and made his way to the first cell where he peered through the small, barred window and what he saw would have made him cringe had he not seen similar things before. Inside was a pile of rotting corpses and limbs, some decomposed down to the bone while others looked almost fresh, and hordes of flies buzzed around the carcasses. He checked the second cell and found a similar scene and did not bother to check the others before leaping down to join Roland, who looked as though he had never seen something so revolting. To Gerhold though, the smell of blood was invigorating, almost intoxicating. If it had been fresh the urge to consume it would have been difficult to fight, but this older blood had a pungent smell to it. Rotten, almost.

"I take it you found the same thing up there?" Roland asked and Gerhold nodded. "I found more empty cells than filled ones but even one is too many. Why in the six hells do they have locked rooms full of corpses?"

"The necromancer's perform experiments on them, and at least now we know what happened to the kidnapped villagers."

"And where that terrible smell is coming from," Roland added.

"Something tells me it will get worse ahead," Gerhold said and saw Roland cringe just at the thought. "Come on, we need to get to Warrick before he and Andyn end up looking like this."

They passed through the room of cells and then into another short hallway that ended with a metal door. As soon as they entered the corridor, the sounds of screams could be heard from somewhere far off, and Gerhold exchanged worried glances with Roland before sprinting to the door at the end of the hall. Gerhold readied his heavy crossbow, then opened the door and dove through. On the other side was a dark room illuminated by only a few torches, but even with the little amount of light both men could make out the many pieces of equipment and instruments of torture that cluttered the circular area. Gerhold kept his crossbow at the ready and moved deeper into the room but he realized that it was empty. Another scream, much louder this time, came from beyond a second door at the other end of the room, and Gerhold motioned for Roland to follow.

"That sounds like Andyn," Roland whispered.

Gerhold tugged on the door and opened it only a little so that he could see through the other side, where another circular room could be seen. It was slightly larger than the torture chamber, and the screams were much louder now that the door was partially opened. Through the crack in the door Gerhold could see Andyn, who was suspended by chains wrapped around his wrists, and two men in black robes were poking and prodding him with red hot irons. Somewhere else in the room he heard Warrick cry out in pain and could barely overhear the sinister voice of another man.

"I have never had the pleasure of experimenting with a Paladin; this is quite exciting," the man said.

"Find out what he knows first and if there are any others, then you may have whatever fun you like, necromancer," a vampire responded, the same fledgling who had argued with Lord Friedrich earlier.

"Fine, fine. Tell us what you know, holy man, and I may consider giving you something for the pain during my experiments."

Gerhold heard nothing from Warrick, who he knew would say nothing; then he heard cranking wood and metal followed by another piercing scream. The other two men in robes were questioning Andyn, who begged for them to halt their torment, which led to whoops of derisive laughter and another prod from the hot iron.

"Are there any more of you? It is a simple question," the vampire fledgling asked Warrick again, who still refused to answer.

"It will be interesting to see what it takes to break him. I will need to record every detail for my studies," the necromancer added with malevolent anticipation. Gerhold turned to look at Roland.

"Are you ready?" he asked, and Roland nodded. "You take the two near Andyn and I will take the two by Warrick. If there are others, then we deal with them as quickly as possible."

Gerhold took a deep breath and Roland readied his spear. On the count of three Gerhold rushed forward through the door and to the right while Roland peeled off to his left. The young Paladin dove forward into a roll and drove his spear through the first vampire's back and heart before either even knew he was there, while Gerhold fired off his first shot and caught a nearby thrall in the forehead. There were six more thralls in the room and at least two other vampires that Gerhold could see, and he hurled a flash bomb across the room to distract as many enemies as he could. The vampire who was torturing Warrick lunged at him, a long sword in hand and ready to strike, but Gerhold ducked beneath the vampire's first sweeping stroke and slung his crossbow over his shoulder before drawing his blade and parrying the next strike.

The two dueled back and forth, dodging and parrying with neither foe able to gain an upper hand. The vampire may have been just a fledgling, but he was skilled with a blade, and Gerhold was forced onto the defensive as the vampire drove forward with a series of quick attacks. Knowing that he had little time, Gerhold deflected another attack and then delivered a strong kick to the vampire's mid-section, sending the attacker flying across the room where he slammed hard into a table and sent splinters of wood and metal instruments in all

A Curse of Darkness

directions. Gerhold then turned his attention to two thralls that moved in to attack and dispatched both with little difficulty. Another vampire leapt at Gerhold from behind but the hunter merely rolled to the side and in a flash, he drew one of his hand crossbows and sent a silver bolt through the creature's heart.

Meanwhile Roland had already dispatched both of the vampires who had been torturing Andyn and had now leapt into the fray with Gerhold. Since most of the effects of the flash bomb had worn off, the other foes now joined in and attacked Gerhold and Roland with a renewed vigor. One of the men was a necromancer, and he sent a stream of fire at Roland, who was forced to dive on his face to avoid being burnt, and then the necromancer began raising nearby corpses to fight. Like grotesque puppets, four dead bodies began to rise as if invisible wires tugged at their limbs. Gerhold slammed his fist into a nearby thrall, shattering the man's jaw and send him sprawling to the floor, and then leapt out of the way of another fireball. The vampire he had been dueling charged at the fallen hunter again and swung his sword forward with both hands, forcing Gerhold to deflect the blow, and the strength of the strike sent Gerhold's long sword skidding across the stone floor and out of reach.

His attacker raised his weapon to deliver the killing blow, but Gerhold was too quick and rolled out of the way as the blade slammed into the ground. Both of his small crossbows were in his hands as he completed the roll, and before the vampire could bring the sword down a second time two bolts slammed into its chest and the creature fell to the floor with a cry of agony. Quickly Gerhold took aim, and before the necromancer could hurl another fireball, another bolt slammed into his chest. The mage fell to the floor, grabbing at the wound while a second projectile caught him in the shoulder. A moment later the sounds of battle ceased as Roland impaled the last attacking thrall and Gerhold stood at the center of the room looking out over the carnage. The smell of blood was heavy in his nostrils and Gerhold forced himself to ignore the pleasurable sensations.

"Roland, are you all right?" Gerhold asked.

"Fine; Andyn is still alive as well. What about the Commander?" Gerhold moved over to where Commander Warrick was chained unconscious to a torture rack. The man was covered with bruises and burns, and Gerhold could tell he had been stretched by the rack, which could mean separated ribs, muscle tears, and maybe even a few broken bones. He put his fingers on Warrick's neck to check for a pulse.

"He will live, at least for now," Gerhold answered and released the locks on the torture device so that Warrick was no longer being stretched.

"Good. Then grab him and we can start trying to find our way out of this place," Roland said, but just as Gerhold started to free Warrick from the torture rack a voice rang out from behind them.

"You fools! You dare barge into my dungeons and ruin my experiments?" Gerhold turned to see the wounded necromancer leaning against the wall at the other end of the room. He had his hand on a chain pulley which was connected to a large metal door. "Perhaps it is time for you to have a true lesson on what necromancy is capable of," the man finished and yanked on the chain.

Immediately there was a loud grinding sound of metal on metal as the large door nearby was lifted, and in the darkness beyond, Gerhold could see the silhouette of a massive creature that began lumbering forward. From the gloom emerged a huge monster that was at least ten feet tall with thick, broad shoulders and limbs like tree trunks. The ground shook with each step as the monster moved forward. It was comprised of pieces from various corpses all sewn together to form a single creature, and atop its shoulders was a grotesque head that appeared far too small for the rest of its bulky body.

"What in the six hells is that" Roland yelled.

"It's a flesh golem."

"Any idea how to kill it?" Roland asked, but the monster turned in their direction and let out a great roar.

"Nothing comes to mind," Gerhold answered as the monster charged forward.

The golem raised its hands over its head and swung down at Gerhold who leapt out of the way and darted towards the other end of the room where the dying necromancer lay cackling. The monster roared again and swung backwards, catching Gerhold in the side and sending him flying across the room where he crashed against the stone floor. Immediately he was back on his feet and fired a bolt, which struck the creature directly in the head, but the beast just bellowed again and charged, as if the silver bolt were nothing more than a fly. Suddenly a silver spear-tip burst through one of the golem's knees, and Gerhold saw Roland dash forward with a sword in each hand. Both men attacked the creature at the same time from both sides, and their strikes left large gashes in the hunks of flesh. Though the wounds issued puffs of smoke and reached down to the bone, they appeared to not even faze the creature, which continued to flail about in all directions, trying to beat off the two attackers.

The golem flung its arm sideways and caught Gerhold once again and sent him flying against the wall, knocking the wind out of him. Roland moved forward and struck the creature again, leaving a large slash that issued streams of thick gray smoke as the silver ate away at the undead flesh, but suddenly the creature turned and reached out before the Paladin could react and the cold, slimy dead hands of the golem closed around his torso and lifted him into the air. As Gerhold fought to catch his breath he noticed his silver long-sword only a few feet away, and knowing Roland was only seconds from death he darted forward, grabbed the sword, and launched himself at the golem. He raised the blade above his head and brought it down with as much force as he could muster. The silver sword bit through the undead flesh as though it were nothing, and with Gerhold's extra strength, the blow severed the creature's right arm, which fell to the floor with a sickening thud and carried Roland with it.

The creature roared in anger and stared at the stump that was once its arm, then reached with its left hand and tried to throw an entire table at Gerhold, who dodged it easily. Roland was on his feet again, silver spear in hand, but he looked weakened and tired, and even Gerhold was starting to feel the toll of the battle wearing on him. The creature attacked again, but both men avoided the swing and Gerhold dashed around to the other side of the monster near Roland.

"Can you draw him over to the furnace? I have an idea." Roland yelled and dove backwards just as the thick, fleshy hand of the monster came crashing down exactly where he had been standing.

"I can. But whatever you have planned, it had better work because we do not have time for this!" Gerhold yelled back and fired another bolt at the creature's head to get its attention.

"Just trust me!"

Gerhold lunged forward and dodged the next two attacks, but the creature seemed to never tire, and Gerhold was finding it harder and harder to avoid the constant onslaught of swings and grabs. Finally, he heard Roland yell his name, and Gerhold darted in the direction of the large furnace in the corner of the room. Roland had opened the top of the furnace and Gerhold suddenly realized what the Paladin had in mind. He drew the creature in, as close as he could, and then just as the creature raised its arm to strike, he dove between its legs and rolled through to the other side. The monster's heavy arm came crashing down directly in front of the burning furnace.

"Come on you big, slimy hunk of flesh! Come get me!" Roland yelled. The creature roared in response and raised its arm again, but just before the strike landed, Roland leapt into the air and dove over the top of the creature, driving his spear into its head, Gerhold slammed all his weight into the creature's back.

The next moment the golem's hand made contact with the furnace and shattered the iron casing, sending sparks and burning metal in all directions. Gerhold and Roland both darted to the side and watched as the dead flesh of golem burst into flames and the creature flailed about trying to extinguish the blaze. A few moments later, the golem fell to its knees and tried to crawl in their direction, before letting out a final terrifying roar and collapsing to the stone floor in a heap of charred flesh and bones. Gerhold took a moment to catch his breath, then walked cautiously over to the corpse of the golem to make sure it was dead.

"Gods, that is disgusting," Roland said. "And to think this place could end up smelling worse."

"Come on, it is dead. We need to grab Andyn and Warrick and get out of here as fast as we can. I do not want those other guards catching up to us, and we have spent so much time here already that I doubt they will be far off." Roland nodded and yanked his spear free from the burned corpse of the golem.

"All right, I can grab Andyn; he does not appear to be too badly injured."

"Can he move on his own?"

"Possibly, guess we will have to find out," Roland said and made his way over to Andyn, who was sitting against the wall.

"Come on, we need to get you up," Roland said and made to pull Andyn to his feet.

"Wait! I need to find it first," Andyn said desperately and pulled away; Roland turned to Gerhold with a questioning look on his face and shrugged.

"Come on man get up," he said again to Andyn, who was searching through a pile of rubbish for something. Gerhold's first thought was that the man had gone mad, but then he saw Andyn pause and lift a small gold coin from the floor.

"All right, I am ready," Andyn said and clutched the little coin in his palm. Roland gave the man a strange look before helping him to his feet. A moment later the two men came walking over, though Andyn was limping and obviously in severe pain, while Gerhold pulled the still unconscious Commander Warrick onto his shoulder.

A Curse of Darkness

"Can you walk?" Gerhold asked Andyn, who seemed distant and looked quite pale.

"Yes, I can walk," he answered weakly.

"Good, now we need to move. If we run into any trouble, you need to either help us fight or stay out of the way. Understand?" Andyn nodded.

"How is the Commander?" Roland asked, and Gerhold shook his head.

"He is severely injured. That necromancer was probably going to heal him before continuing the torture. He has many burns and cuts, but what worries me the most is this." Gerhold pointed to a cut along Warrick's neck that was bandaged, but on the inside of the bandage was a slimy black substance. "Unless I am mistaken, this is some kind of poison."

"What kind?"

"I do not know, but whatever it is will probably cause him incredible pain when he awakens."

"Any idea how to cure it?" Roland asked.

"Maybe, but not down here. I doubt that whatever he was poisoned with will kill him quickly; that necromancer wanted him to suffer. If we can get him out of here, then maybe I can figure out what he was poisoned with. I am no alchemist, but I have some experience with necromancy," Gerhold answered.

"Then lead on and let us see if we can still save him." Gerhold nodded and took off through another doorway at the opposite end of the hall, hoping that he was right about Warrick and that their luck would continue to hold.

Chapter 13: The Hall of Stairs

Gerhold shifted the unconscious body of Warrick to his other shoulder as they continued up a flight of stone steps. He had no idea how deep they had come, but he worried more about what waited for them ahead. The overwhelming smell of the blood and decay had long faded, allowing Gerhold to once again focus on the sounds around them. The guards they had left back at the spiral stairs had not found them, even though Gerhold remembered hearing one of the men mention another way down to the dungeons. Why had the guards not found them yet? If there truly was another way then this had to be it, and that meant he would run into more vampires sooner or later.

"How much further before we get out of this place?" Andyn asked, and Gerhold could hear the fear in the man's voice.

"I am not sure. Why do you ask? Are you having trouble walking?" Roland asked.

"You do not know where we are, do you?" Andyn stopped and his voice shook.

"We are in Altandir, Andyn, so just take a few deep breaths and we will get out of here, all right?" Roland said.

"You do not understand; this place is corrupted. The stone itself is evil!" Andyn yelled and recoiled as if just touching the wall was causing him pain. He was once again fingering the golden coin as if it were the only thing keeping him safe.

"Stone is just that, stone. That is all," Roland answered but Andyn shook his head furiously.

"No, no not in this place. This place is evil. Can you not feel it?"

"Calm down, Ser; we will get out of here," Roland said again.

"You do not understand. This whole place is evil. They made me see things. When they took me to the dungeons, they gave me visions of this place

A Curse of Darkness

and the things that happened here. It is all foul. This place was dug out many years ago, and all these necromancers have done is add to it." Andyn seemed on the verge of panic.

"Andyn, just calm down," Roland said again.

Gerhold watched both men now, his left hand resting on one of his hand crossbows sheathed on his lower back.

"I cannot! Not while we are still here!" Andyn said.

"He speaks the truth, Roland," Gerhold said, and both men turned to him.

"What do you mean?"

"You are the one who knows the stories far better than I. I can sense the evil here, any vampire could." Roland watched with interest and concern. "Evil can corrupt even the stone and the earth itself when allowed to fester for long enough. Think of the forest and the darkness above; it is only a symptom of the darkness that has been kept below."

"And now it is being forced to the surface by that vampire master and the green orb, whatever it is," Roland responded.

"Exactly, so we need to steal that stone," Gerhold said.

"Just get me out of this place," Andyn added weakly.

"We will. Once we get back up you and Roland can take the Commander and make your way to the lifts," Gerhold responded.

"And what about you?" Roland asked suspiciously, but Gerhold just turned and continued down the corridor without answering.

Another minute more and they reached the top of the stairwell, and ahead was a short hallway. Ahead of Gerhold was a huge open cavern, and there were hundreds of crisscrossing staircases that connected, passed beneath, and twisted around the others. It was a giant maze of steps and bridges built above a large pit that was deep enough that Gerhold could not see the bottom. He grabbed a nearby torch and dropped it over the edge, watching as it fell deeper and deeper into the darkness until finally hitting the floor, and a faint crack of wood on stone echoed from below. Just then Warrick began to stir, and Gerhold set the Commander down with his back against the stone wall.

"How in the six hells are we supposed to be able to find our way through this place?" Roland asked and gazed at the stairs with a look of confusion. "There must be a thousand different paths through this place."

"Well, we had better find a way or we may be down here a very long time," Gerhold added and bent down next to Warrick.

"Commander? Commander, can you hear me?" Roland said and Warrick opened his eyes slightly and grunted.

"Where am I? What happened?" Warrick asked before cringing and letting out a sigh of pain.

"Calm yourself, Warrick. Do you remember who I am?" Gerhold asked and Warrick grunted again.

"I do not forget the face of a vampire," he answered through gritted teeth. "What happened, though? Why are you here? I remember the necromancers and being dragged down the stairs."

"You were tortured, but we are getting you out of here," Roland answered.

"It feels as though my veins are on fire."

"You were poisoned, and if I am correct, it will be more painful the longer it is in you," Gerhold said. Warrick stared at the vampire and nodded.

"Is there an antidote?" he asked and gasped in pain.

"I am not sure, but I will do my best to make one once we get out of here. I will need to find out what it is first, but I doubt it was made to kill you. More than likely you will just be in intense pain for a time," Gerhold said.

"I suppose that is better than dying," Warrick answered and cringed again.

"Just do the best you can, and we will get you out of here," Gerhold responded, then stood and turned to face Roland.

"So what now?" Roland asked.

"We need to find a way out of here."

"If what Andyn said is correct, then these halls were constructed by the army of undead that conquered the city. That is why most of the interior areas are designed to look the same and confuse anyone who enters." Roland moved in front of Gerhold and bent down to examine the steps. "Undead are of a singular mind; they obey only the one who raised them, so only the Lich would have known the way through these passages. That is why the circular stairwell looked so different; it was dug by these necromancers so that they would not have to go through this maze while the rest of the fortress was built by the undead."

"And this history lesson helps us how, boy?" Warrick growled.

"If this cult found these caverns, then they must have found a way through this maze before building the larger spiral stairs," Roland answered calmly.

"I heard one of the guards mention that the necromancers knew how to find their way through, so there has to be some secret to it," Gerhold added.

"So they would not get lost when coming and going until they planned and built the spiral stairs," Roland said under his breath and started forward onto the four foot wide stone walkway. He stopped near the first fork and knelt on one knee to examine the floor while running his hand across the stone. "There is some sort of symbol carved into the floor here."

"So? How does that help us get out of here?" Andyn asked irritably.

"Wait here for a moment," Roland said and darted up the stairway that was marked with the symbol.

The others waited in silence for him to return, and Gerhold glanced every so often at the other two men. Andyn looked worried, scared even, and was breathing rapidly. Gerhold found it strange that a man who, spent much of his time only a few days ago boasting about his various exploits and courageous acts, had been reduced to such a lowly level in only a few hours. Pride was the greatest deceiver and the greatest enemy of any warrior. Warrick, on the other hand, lay huddled against the wall, anguish etched across his face and his body tight and ridged. Whatever poison he had been given was causing him a great deal of pain, and every so often he would gasp and double over.

The minutes passed and Gerhold saw Roland sprint by more than once, mumbling to himself and cursing under his breath. Gerhold glanced back down the hallway they had come from and then ahead into the maze of stairs. He could see nothing but he knew that each moment they spent waiting to figure out the riddle, the closer their pursuers would be. The Commander continued to fidget and moan in pain and Andyn stood nearby, clutching his little coin and mumbling to himself. The longer they had to wait, the more restless Gerhold felt and the more agitated Andyn became. After nearly a half an hour Gerhold was ready to try and lead them through as best he could, but then Roland came dashing back down the steps two at a time with a wide smile on his face.

"I have it. Follow me," Roland called as he came running. "The symbols are used to mark the correct path; as long as we follow them, we should be able to make it out of here with no trouble."

"And how did you figure that out? These stairs are endless. If you are wrong then we could be lost forever in this place," Andyn said and swallowed nervously at the thought of being trapped in the caverns.

"This is the clue. There are other paths that have this symbol etched on them and I am sure it is how the necromancers found their way through without getting lost." Roland answered and pointed to the small carving.

"Are you sure?" Gerhold asked and Roland nodded. "That is good enough for me; lead on. Warrick? Can you stand?" The Commander nodded and pushed himself slowly to his feet, using the wall for support. He tried to take a step but fell to knees and grunted in pain. "If you cannot walk, then Andyn will have to help you for now."

"Why me? I'm sore enough as it is. Why don't you help him?" the Paladin spat.

"These paths are thin and I need Roland at the front to lead us. Are you capable of holding off our enemies if they attack us from behind?" Gerhold asked, and Andyn licked his lips nervously. Then, without another word, he bent down and helped Warrick back to his feet, allowing the Commander to lean on his shoulder.

With that settled, Roland lead the way up the stairs, followed by Andyn and the limping Commander, and into a small tunnel which twisted upward and emerged once more to another pathway. They came to a second intersection and Roland took a moment to examine the floor before continuing to his left down another flight of steps. Time slowed to a crawl as they went up and down flights of stairs and through tunnels, all the while hoping that Roland's hunch had been correct and that they were not getting lost in the maze of stairs. Gerhold tried to keep track of every turn they took but it took only a few minutes for him to lose track. They could use the symbols to get back but what if they came to a dead end? Where would they go from there?

On and on the stairs went, twisting and turning, passing beneath one another and into the walls of the cavern. Sometimes they would climb a twisting staircase and a moment later they would be trying to inch carefully along a thin stone platform. The sheer size of the maze had shocked Gerhold initially and the further they went the more daunting it seemed. It was no wonder to him why the guards he had overheard wanted to avoid the area. More than once Roland called for them to stop. He ran on ahead and returned a minute later to lead them on or to check another path. Sometimes the symbols would be poorly carved and the Paladin could not make out if it was the symbol marking the path or if it was just a crack in the stone, and he was forced to either guess or dash ahead to check for another. The progress was slow and Gerhold continued to pray to the Three that they were going in the right direction.

At one point, Roland was bent down examining a carving when Gerhold's keen ears picked up a faint echo from somewhere up ahead. He motioned for Roland to stay with the others and he moved forward alone up a small flight of steps. The voices were not clear, which meant whoever was speaking was not nearby, so Gerhold moved further along into the darkness until he could catch what the men were saying.

"These bloody necromancers are going to get us lost for good in here. Follow Azaral's symbol if you get lost; that is what they said. An easy task they said. It would be easy if the carvings were readable," one voice said in frustration.

"The bastards probably told us that as a jest so we would get lost in here," another responded.

"Now why in the six hells would they do that? They need to catch the prisoners or deal with the Master. They would not waste their time sending us off to get lost."

"Maybe we should go back?" the second voice said again.

"That is what I am trying to do you blithering idiot! If you would help me find out which of these paths is the right one instead of acting like an aurochs ass, then maybe we can accomplish that."

The two men ceased their conversation and Gerhold darted back down the stairs to where Roland and the others were waiting.

"We have company. At least two guards somewhere up ahead. It looks like you were right about the symbol, though," Gerhold said and Roland nodded.

"Then we must be all the more cautious."

"Lead on and keep an eye out for anything. Remember, we vampires can see well than you can in the dim light." Roland nodded again and took off up a flight of stairs.

They moved at a slower pace and Gerhold kept a watchful eye for any movement. He noticed two other sets of guards and the group barely avoided another three vampires by hiding in one of the side passageways. It appeared that their pursuers were having as hard a time determining the symbols as Roland did. A few minutes later they were forced to stop again as Roland proceeded on alone to check their path. Gerhold took a deep breath and realized that the air was somewhat clearer. The foul stench of the dungeons was wavering, and he felt his spirits lift at the simple thought of being free from the smells of blood and death. These were not unpleasant scents for a vampire, which is why Gerhold wanted to get away from them all the more. Soon, they turned a corner and Gerhold caught sight of a small door lit by only two torches in the distance. Three stairwells converged in front of the door and Gerhold knew without question that it was the exit.

"Do you see it?" Roland turned around and asked excitedly.

"The exit? Yes, but it is still some ways off," Gerhold answered.

"Then we better keep moving," Roland said and continued up another flight of stairs.

They turned another corner, and Roland stopped again. This time it was not to gawk at the exit but because two robed men stood in their path. Neither seemed to notice the group initially as they both seemed to be examining the floor, and Roland dashed forward with his spear ready, catching both men unaware and impaling each in turn. Farther along Gerhold saw more men pointing and running in their direction, and the sounds of voices echoed from all around.

"Looks like we found our friends again," Roland yelled back and Gerhold nodded.

"Then we need to go, now!"

Roland nodded and took off up the stairwell while Andyn and Warrick limped along behind. Gerhold tightened his grip on the heavy crossbow and hurried the other two men along while keeping his eyes peeled for any signs of movement along the stairs that surrounded them. Another pair of cultists leapt out in front of the group, and Roland slew both with his spear in only a few quick thrusts, but more enemies appeared below them on an adjacent staircase. Without hesitation, Gerhold jumped down and landed in front of the new line of attackers. He sent a silver bolt into the closest advisory and flipped the Crossblade open, holding the weapon in a ready stance just as the next vampire charged forward. Above, Roland led the two injured Paladins through the maze as quickly as he could, spinning, slicing, and stabbing at anything that came too close.

Gerhold dodged another attack and finished off the last of the four attacking vampires with a quick thrust through the heart. He caught sight of Roland holding off two vampires, his silver spear whirling this way and that with such speed and fluidity that neither attacker could get close. Gerhold ran up a nearby stairwell and slung the heavy crossbow back over his shoulder while drawing both of his hand crossbows. Another thrall came dashing around the corner ahead but fell immediately as a silver bolt slammed into his forehead, and Gerhold leapt over a six-foot gap to another staircase. Enemies seemed to be emerging from every crack and crevice as Gerhold sprinted up the stairs, firing bolts in every direction as he leapt and fought his way away from his companions.

While Gerhold distracted the bulk of their pursuers, Roland, Andyn, and Warrick hurried along the twisting stairs towards the exit, and they had nearly reached it. Gerhold dueled two men at a time, one in front and one behind, along the thin, four-foot-wide stone bridge at the top of two sets of stairs. In one smooth motion he deflected a blow and slashed the man in front of him across the chest, then flipped high into the air and landed behind the second man. With another thrust, the second foe fell over the side, screaming in pain, and disappeared into the pit below. A fireball exploded only a few feet away and Gerhold turned to see more enemies charging at him from both directions, and after sheathing his long sword, he leapt from the top of the staircases to another path below.

Now it was a race. Balls of fire and bolts fired from crossbows exploded and bounced all around off the stairs, pathways, and walls as he hurried towards the exit where Roland and the others were waiting. Gerhold vaulted over another gap and used a nearby wall to propel himself upward to another pathway above, and after hauling himself up, he sprinted down a flight of stairs towards Roland.

"Move! Get inside!" Gerhold yelled and pulled another pyrite bomb from his pack.

He passed a nearby torch while climbing the last set of stairs and used it to light the wick and dropped the bomb on the platform in front of the exit door. Ahead he could see Roland running and after a few seconds a loud explosion ripped through the air and shook the hallway. Gerhold turned to see smoke and flames where the platform and three staircases used to be, then moved on to join the other three who were leaning wearily against the wall ahead. Warrick looked paler than ever and Andyn had his face buried in his hands.

"If I ever see another stair again, I may use one of those bombs on myself," Roland said between deep breaths.

"Well, that was my last one, so let us hope we do not need another," Gerhold answered while reloading his crossbows. He was down to his last few bolts for the heavy crossbow and his hand crossbows only had three shots a piece.

"We are almost out of here," Roland said encouragingly and helped

Andyn to his feet.

"Not yet," Gerhold said and started down the hall, heavy crossbow in hand. "Take these two and make your way to the lifts. I will meet you at the top."

"Where are you going?" Roland called. Gerhold paused and turned, his cold unwavering eyes focused on some distant goal.

"To finish what we started, and maybe a little more," Gerhold answered and moved down the hallway, hoping that Lord Friedrich was still in the fortress.

Chapter 14: A Curse of Darkness

Gerhold darted down the empty hallway towards the central chamber where he would find Lord Friedrich and the stone that he assumed was being used to spread the darkness of Blightwood. He turned the next corner and drew his long sword as the two guards watching the entrance to the central hall saw him and charged forward. They fell one after the other to two quick strikes from the hunter. Gerhold stepped over their corpses and came to a halt in front of the twin doors that led to the great hall, readying himself for whatever lay beyond. Most of Lord Friedrich's cultists were either dead or trapped below, and unless there was another way out of the dungeons whoever was left in the chamber beyond was all Galen had left.

He would walk right through the front door and confront the vampire. Galen was a vain man, vain and proud, and Gerhold would use that pride against him. The Lord would want to interrogate him, confident that he would be able to overcome whatever Gerhold had planned, and this confidence would be his undoing. Just before Gerhold moved to open the door he heard footsteps echoing from behind and turned with his crossbow at the ready to see Roland dashing around the corner.

"What are you doing here? I told you to take the others to the surface and get them out of here?" Gerhold said and darted into one of the side passages.

"I came to help you. You really think you can take on whatever is in there on your own?" Roland argued.

"I do not need your help, but Warrick does."

"Ser Andyn can take care of him, and besides your plan of walking through the front door seems a bit rash. There has to be a better way to get that stone."

"The stone is not the only thing I seek."

"Well, you will not get what you want if you get yourself killed first,"

Roland said and shook his head. "I can help you."

Gerhold stared at the young man for a moment before smiling and nodding. He did not trust Paladins, and even now he did not trust Roland fully, but he would need the help, and his initial plan was starting to seem a bit foolish and hasty. His desire to interrogate Galen Friedrich was clouding his judgment, and after a hundred years, he was not going to let his own foolish impulses ruin this chance at ending his search.

"What is the plan?" Roland asked.

"I knew Lord Friedrich once, but it has been some time; however, nobles do not change. A nobleman can rarely imagine a world in which they are bested by those they deem below them. He is arrogant and if what we saw earlier tells us anything, it is that he wants to know what is happening. He will want to know if there are any others with us and if he is still safe."

"So, we use that against him?"

"Exactly," Gerhold said and knelt to open his pack.

Both his pyrite and flash bombs were gone, used up while trying to escape the cultists, and he had only a few bolts left for his crossbow. He rummaged through the little pack for a moment before pulling out a black tube and holding it out for Roland to see. Calmly and carefully he opened the top of the tube and slid out the glass vial containing a bright, clear liquid and the tiny yellow crystal.

"What is that?" Roland asked.

"It is called a sunflare, and it is supposed to mimic sunlight when these are combined. It was made by one of my associates in Vilheim," Gerhold answered.

"Supposed to?" Roland asked skeptically.

"I have never had a chance to test it, but if it does what he said it does, then we may just have a plan. Besides, he is the one who built this," Gerhold said and patted the crossblade. "I trust him, and if he says it will work, then it will work."

"Even if it does work, what are you going to do with it?" Roland asked and Gerhold handed him the vial.

"Not me, you," Gerhold said and motioned for Roland to follow as he made his way up the staircase to the balcony overlooking the chamber. Gerhold crouched down and opened the door just a crack so that they could see through into the room beyond. "The chandeliers are made of crystal. If you can throw the sunflare into one of them, it will magnify the light and it will cover the entire room. Any vampires caught in it will be burned or at least distracted."

"What about you? Have you forgotten that you are one as well?" Roland whispered, but Gerhold smiled.

"Leave that to me. Now, I will go in and when the time is right you start the light show. Make sure your throw counts, you only get one."

"Why wait? Why not just attack now?"

"Because there is something, I need to do first. Just make sure you hit one of those crystals," Gerhold said and patted Roland on the shoulder.

"Gerhold?" Roland called. "Good luck."

"You are going to need more than I will if you are to make that throw," Gerhold responded and left the room without another word.

He made his way down the stairs and returned to the entrance to the central chamber. For a moment he waited, pulling a black scarf from his pack and wrapping it around his neck while also making sure to pull on a pair of thick leather gloves that covered his hands. Between the scarf and the cloak that Nethrin had made for him he hoped the sunflare would not affect him. Gerhold paused for another moment to take one last deep breath and say a silent prayer to the Three before pounding on the thick wooden door. He took a few steps back as soon as he heard the sound of whispers coming from the other side of the doors, then dashed forward and leapt into the air with his feet extended. His legs drove into the set of doors with such force that the wooden beam locking the pair from the other side snapped with a loud *crack* and both swung inward, slamming hard into the two guards who had been standing nearby and sending them sprawling head over heels across the floor. Gerhold stood in the doorway between the shattered wooded gates, staring down a horde of ten vampires and their thralls.

"The doors! To the doors! Kill him!" one of the vampires screamed, but before any of them could come within ten feet of Gerhold, another voice rang out.

"No, stay your weapons," Lord Friedrich called and walked forward. The cultists lowered their weapons and stepped back, but not a single one took their eyes from Gerhold. The vampire stared at him for a moment before speaking. "Who are you? Not a Paladin, no, definitely not. So, what are you doing in my fortress? Are you the one who has been traipsing about, attacking my guards, and ruining my dungeons?" Gerhold threw back his hood so that Galen could see his face.

"I am not surprised you have forgotten my face after all the years, my lord." he said. "Though, I am still a bit disappointed."

"Should I know you? After a hundred years, most faces tend to blend together, so do not take it too hard," the vampire answered smoothly.

"Still, I would have thought you would be able to recall the man whom you hired to rescue your wife." The smile faded from Lord Friedrich's face.

"Gerhold– Gerhold of Vilheim?" he muttered and shook his head. "No, no you are dead. A hundred years ago. You were killed, and I know it."

"A hundred years ago you hired me to find your wife, but you failed to mention that you had given her to the vampire. I know it was you who gave her the locket that was cursed," Gerhold responded.

"Yes, I did. You see, my dear wife struggled with infidelity, and I was tired of being humiliated by her inability to control herself. A nobleman is always judged by how well he controls those beneath him, and she was a spoiled, ungrateful whore. I take it she did not survive Harkin's trap?" he asked.

"No, she did not," Gerhold shook his head and Friedrich laughed.

"I cannot say I am unhappy about that result. She may not have survived, but you did. I must admit it is a poor fate for such a famed slayer as yourself to have become what you hated most, to become what you hunt. You escaped Harkin's trap but it looks as though someone else caught you in the end." Galen laughed again. Gerhold reached into his shirt just below the black scarf and tugged on a small chain around his neck to reveal the golden locket.

"You recognize this, do you not?" Gerhold asked.

"Of course. So, it was Harkin then? You are truly one of us now."

"I have turned, but I am not one of you. I am still the hunter, and you the prey," Gerhold answered and a few of the other vampires turned and whispered to each other.

"So, you are a kinslayer then? That is not something you want to admit here. My fledglings do not take that subject lightly." Gerhold saw the looks of anger directed at him from all around the room, but he ignored them.

"I am a hunter of all evil things; it matters little to me what dark places they choose to hide in." Gerhold placed a particular emphasis on the word dark and saw Galen raise an eyebrow.

"That is why you are here then, slayer. To find out why this glorious darkness is spreading beyond the borders of the Blightwood?" he said and made

A Curse of Darkness

his way across the room to where the circle of necromancers where gathered around the glowing green stone. "Perhaps it is good that you have come, for in your present condition you may be able to appreciate what I have been able to accomplish here." He pointed at the stone. "Do you even know what this is?"

"No, but it is what is causing the curse of the Blightwood to spread."

"The curse? Oh yes, yes, the curse is spreading. You see Gerhold, this is a very ancient artifact, a channeling stone. One of only a few relics that remain from the old realms of Arden. It is a powerful, magical object that can amplify even the most basic spells. Using this my necromancers can now use their powers to expand the curse and cover these lands in a never-ending curse of darkness. A curse of never-ending night shall fall across Tyriel and with it, those of us who live in the darkness shall finally be free to roam and to conquer." He turned back to face Gerhold; his smile even wider than before. "Darkness shall finally reign."

"I care not for your explanations, Galen. I came here to find out where Harkin is," Gerhold said and Lord Friedrich rounded on him.

"Harkin? Harkin Valakir?" he laughed again.

"If you are here, then he cannot be far behind, so, where is he?"

"You fool. I have not seen Harkin Valakir since the day I gave him that wretched excuse for a wife to lure you to his fortress. I assumed you both died long ago. Although if you are alive then perhaps, he is as well. How I would love to wrap my hands around his throat," Lord Friedrich said and rubbed his hands together.

"And why do you hate Harkin? I thought you worked for him?"

"I did, but he betrayed me. It was he who gave me the locket to hand over to my wife, and it is he who cursed me. That same locket you now possess. He left and without any warning the curse came upon me, changing me into what I am now, but I did not wallow in self-pity. No, I became greater than Harkin Valakir ever was, and now I have the power to make this world into what I want it to be." Gerhold shifted his eyes up to the balcony and saw Roland, the sunflare in hand and ready.

"A tragic tale, but unfortunately I cannot allow you to do any such thing," Gerhold said. Friedrich and the other vampires laughed.

"Really now? And why would you wish to do that? I can make this world safe for you once again, free you from the tyranny of the sun. Why would you wish for a world where you are trapped beneath the ground or in whatever dark hole you have made your home? Why would you desire to endure that when I can make it so that we do not have to hide? I can make a world where we will be the gods. Where the people worship us. Why would you not wish to help me in this endeavor?" Gerhold stared at the vampire, his cold unyielding eyes boring into his enemy.

"So that you and your ilk can enslave and feed on the innocent? So that your evil can spread beyond these borders? Never." Lord Friedrich laughed again.

"And what do you purpose to do? Even with your skills you are outnumbered. What chance do you possibly have slayer?" Gerhold pulled the hood up over his head and wrapped the scarf around his face so that only his eyes were visible.

"Your pride is your weakness, Galen, and one day it will burn you."

Out of the corner of his eye, Gerhold saw Roland move just a bit and caught the glimpse of something flying through the air, then a bright flash of light blinded him as the sunflare landed and shattered in the crystal chandelier above. Rays of burning white sunlight shot in every direction, immediately followed by the howls of pain, and screams of the vampires as the rays of light ate away at their pale skin. Gerhold felt the heat through his cloak and scarf, and the scorching light forced him to close his eyes, but he did not need to see to fight his enemies. Relying on his keen hearing, Gerhold darted forward and engaged his blinded and burning foes. A footstep here or scream marked the position of his prey as he sliced and slashed with his long sword, followed by more cries of agony as thralls and vampires alike fell to his blade.

He danced this way and that, deflecting the wild, blind attacks from his enemies while responding with precise strikes and deadly slashes. Vampires cried out in pain as the sunlight and the slayer's sword bit into their flesh, and Gerhold could hear Friedrich screaming for help. The sunlight burned at his eyelids and forehead, but the cloak and scarf made sure that the rest of his body was protected from the burning rays, but his foes were not so lucky.

A few moments later the heat began to dissipate and Gerhold opened his eyes to see the room bathed in the fading rays of the sunflare. There were still many enemies all around the hall, and he pulled out both of his remaining hand crossbows, firing off every bolt he had before returning them to their holsters and once again drawing his sword. Roland had leapt down from the balcony and was dueling three of the thralls at the other end of the room while Gerhold engaged the remaining vampires. His foes were still blind from the effects of the sunlight and were not much of a challenge as the slayer carved his way through their ranks. Finally, he whipped his blade around in an arch and deflected an incoming blow before dispatching the enemy with a swift stab through the heart.

All around the room the burning and charred remains of vampires littered the floor, and the bodies of dead thralls were interspersed throughout the carnage. The white light from the sunflare had disappeared and now the room was once again bathed in the soft green glow of the orb. Roland stood at the other end of the room, his spear covered in blood and a pile of dead thralls surrounding him. Gerhold heard a noise coming from the center of the room where he saw Galen Friedrich on the floor leaning against the wall. The vampire was whimpering in pain while he cradled his burnt face and arms.

"You– you filthy wretch, look what you have done!" Galen yelled as Gerhold approached. "I was making a world where we could bear our curse without fear! Without shame! And now you have ruined it."

"You wanted a world where you could lord over others," Gerhold said and lifted Lord Friedrich by his throat. "Now tell me, are you sure you do not know where Harkin is? Answer and I will ease your passing."

"I would not tell you even if I knew. If I had my way, I would have you both tied and set out beneath the sun to burn; it is more than either of you deserve," Galen spat.

"Then there is no reason to keep you alive. You have lived too long, my lord. It is time you were sent to the six hells where you belong," Gerhold said and rammed the blade of his silver long sword through the vampire's heart. Lord Friedrich gasped in pain and fell to his knees as his skin and muscle began to burn away, leaving only a pile of singed bones and clothing behind. Gerhold stared at the remains for a moment as Roland approached and stood next to him.

"That was quite the fight," he said finally and Gerhold nodded.

"It was."

"And we have the stone," Roland added.

"We do," Gerhold answered and shrugged, but Roland stared at him with a look of confusion.

"You sound disappointed," he said, and Gerhold bent down to pick up the vampire's charred skull.

"I was hoping to discover something more here, something that has eluded me for a century. It seems, though, that I will have to continue to search elsewhere," Gerhold answered solemnly.

"Who is Harkin? I heard you mention his name more than once," Roland asked.

"A vampire, the one who turned me."

"Then I see why you want to find him."

"I thought Lord Friedrich would know, but alas I am doomed to continue my search with nothing to go on. No hints or tracks. Nothing," Gerhold said and tossed the dead vampire's skull across the room.

He turned and stared at the glowing green stone at the center of the room and frowned. Gerhold had been across the world and seen many strange things but nothing like this. What kind of an artifact had the power to make a spell that could affect the entirety of the Blightwood?

"Have you ever seen anything like that before?" Roland asked and pointed to the stone.

"No, but I doubt Galen Friedrich could have come up with this plan on his own. He was never the smartest man," Gerhold said and bent down to search through the remnants of Friedrich's clothes.

"You think he was working for someone?"

"Yes, and I intend to find out who," Gerhold answered as he sifted through the black robes.

"Maybe he was lying? Perhaps he was working for this Harkin?" Roland proposed and Gerhold stopped what he was doing for a moment.

"Maybe, I guess I can hope for that."

"Perhaps the Gods have other plans for–" but Roland stopped mid-sentence as suddenly the green light from the stone disappeared, and both men turned to see what had happened. It took them only a second to notice that the stone was gone.

"Where is the stone?" Roland asked and hefted his spear into a defensive position. The pedestal where it had sat hovering was empty, and both Gerhold and Roland ran over to see if perhaps it had fallen off. They reached the pedestal and Gerhold caught site of someone running from the chamber and out into the hallway, and both men charged off in pursuit.

"Come on, he has the stone!" Gerhold yelled as they passed between the broken doors.

Whoever had taken the stone was making his way through the hallways towards the lifts, and Gerhold knew that they needed to catch the thief before they reached the platforms. Gerhold turned a corner and caught a brief glimpse of their quarry. Ahead of them, sprinting down the hallway with the green stone

A Curse of Darkness

in hand, was Andyn.

Chapter 15: The Plot Revealed

"What in the six hells is he doing?" Gerhold yelled as they chased after the other Paladin, who seemed to be moving much faster than an injured man should have been able to.

"I have no idea!" Roland answered as they darted around another corner.

Ahead they could see the three lifts, two of which had already been sent to the surface and a third which Andyn was heading towards. Andyn kicked the lever operating the lift and then leapt into the only remaining elevator. Then he slammed the metal doors shut as the platform began to rise. Gerhold and Roland reached the lifts just in time to see Andyn frowning at them and holding the stone.

"What are you doing, Andyn? Why are you taking the stone?" Roland asked, but Gerhold tapped him on the shoulder and pointed to the corner of the room. The body of Commander Warrick lay on the floor and his throat had been cut.

"Sorry, but he was slowing me down," Andyn called from above. Roland darted over to the levers that controlled the other two lifts and pulled them. "I jammed the chains on both of the other lifts. I am truly sorry." With that, Andyn frowned and disappeared into the darkness above. Roland was busy pulling on the levers that operated the other two lifts, but the sounds of clanking chains did not come; instead, they were replaced by the sound of grinding metal and the lifts remained still.

"Hells! These damnable things will not budge," Roland said in a frustrated tone and kicked the lever for good measure. Gerhold did not answer but instead moved over to the lifts, trying to come up with some way to get out of the massive pit. "What in the hells is he doing though? We had the stone. Why is he doing this?"

"Perhaps he wants the glory of returning it to the Vigil himself." Gerhold answered and grabbed one of the chains.

"Well we need to catch him, there has to be another way out of here!" Roland growled and kicked another lever.

"There is," Gerhold called back and motioned to Roland. "Grab onto the other chain," he said and pointed to the opposite lift. "If you break the anchor, the chain will be able to move."

Without waiting for Roland to respond, Gerhold grabbed one of the chains and jammed his sword blade between the other, snapping the link in half. Immediately the chain he was holding gave a great jerk and lifted him into the air. Gerhold tightened his grip as he was pulled upward at a great speed while the counterweight flew past him, hurtling towards the bottom of the pit. A moment later he could see the upper section of lift approaching and the counterweight slammed into the ground below, stopping the chain and twisting Gerhold around violently. As soon as the chain stopped swinging, he was able to pull himself up, hand over hand, until finally reaching the wooden balcony and hauling himself onto the walkway. His body ached from all the fighting and climbing, but he immediately started to scan the large, roofless hall for any sign of Andyn. Roland was doing his best to pull himself up, and Gerhold dashed over to help his comrade up.

"By the Gods I feel like my whole arm got ripped out of its socket," Roland said and rubbed his shoulder. "Where is he? Do you see him?" he asked as soon as he was on his feet. Gerhold ran down the wooden walkway to the front entrance, which was still closed.

"He cannot have gotten far; the front gates are still locked so he must have taken another way," Gerhold responded.

"There he is, up there!" Roland yelled and sped off towards a pile of rubble leading up to the three levels above.

Gerhold looked up and saw Andyn scrambling up to the third level, still clutching the green stone in his right hand. They ran after him, clawing their way up the piles of rubble that connected the balconies, and then saw Andyn reach the third level and head through another doorway. Relying on his superior agility and strength, Gerhold sprinted up the last pile of debris and then made his way into the same corridor in pursuit, followed by Roland. Ahead at the end of the long hallway, he saw Andyn halfway up a metal ladder that led to the roof, and by the time Gerhold reached the first rung the man had already climbed up through a trap door and slammed it shut. Gerhold climbed as quickly as he could, but the trap door had been locked from the other side.

"What is it?" Roland asked, breathlessly as Gerhold came running back down the corridor.

"The door is locked; we need to find another way to reach the roof."

"I saw some stairs back this way; follow me!" Roland yelled and dashed back to the end of the hallway and into the large hall once again.

They sprinted around the balcony to the opposite side where a small staircase stood, and Gerhold was the first to reach the top where he came to a locked metal door. He took a few steps back and then ran forward and kicked the door, causing its metal hinges to shatter from the force of the blow and the door to be thrown outward. Beyond was a long, dark rooftop that sat beneath the swirling black sky. Gerhold and Roland dashed through the doorway onto the roof where they turned to search for Andyn. The vampire's keen eyes scanned the darkness for any sign of movement until he finally caught sight of Andyn running towards the opposite end of the rooftop where, to Gerhold's surprise, they saw a large airship docked and waiting.

Gerhold immediately recognized the ship as the *Ilvarin*, the airship belonging to Pontius Urban, and he swore under his breath as they pursued Andyn across the crumbling rooftop. Gerhold was thirty feet from the airship when Andyn started climbing the gangplank, and as soon as the Paladin was on board, another crewmember kicked the walkway over the side, leaving the airship floating a few feet from the edge of the rooftop, held by a thin piece of rope connected to a metal anchor on the side of the building. Gerhold and Roland halted at the edge of the roof and stared up at the deck of the bobbing airship where both Andyn and the Vigil stood looking down at them. The Vigil bore a smug smile, his old, wrinkled face beaming with pride and drunk on the taste of victory. A line of silver clad Paladins had appeared along the side of the ship, each holding a loaded crossbow.

"Gerhold, it seems you have arrived just in time," the old man said with a crooked smile. "I would not move if I were either of you."

"I wish I could say that I am surprised to see you," Gerhold answered.

"Your Eminence, what is the meaning of this?" Roland asked in confusion. Urban laughed and shook his head.

"Come now, boy, I thought you were a smart lad. If you cannot see what is happening, then perhaps I have misjudged you."

"What do you mean?" Roland asked again.

A Curse of Darkness

"He betrayed us," Gerhold said and turned to the young Paladin, who shifted his confused gaze back and forth between the two men.

"I take it you discovered that far more quickly than the others?" the Vigil asked and Gerhold nodded.

"Yes, as soon as we found the bodies of the other Paladins you sent, I knew something was going on."

"Though you were not smart enough to stop my plan," the old man added smugly.

"So, you have been following us, have you not? I thought I saw the ship hovering above the trees at one point, but I was not sure."

"Yes, I followed you. All thanks to Ser Andyn here," Urban said and smiled at Andyn, who frowned and looked almost on the verge of weeping.

"How did you know when Andyn had the stone though? I doubt you planned this to the hour," Gerhold asked and the Vigil held out his hand. Andyn pulled something small out of his coat and placed it into the old man's palm.

"This little coin is enchanted. As long as it was in his possession, I would be able to find him, and he could communicate with me using the enchantment. Once he had the stone, all he had to do was alert me, using a chosen phrase which would activate a duplicate coin that was in my possession. This roof was to be our meeting spot, though I thought he would be alone." Urban turned and glared at Andyn. Gerhold nodded and recalled seeing Andyn constantly fiddling with the coin and the desperate look on the man's face when it was taken from him in the dungeons.

"So, you sent a group of Paladins to find the stone for you, and when they did not return, you came to me and used Andyn as your spy." Gerhold shook his head. His eyes were on Urban, but he was far more concerned with the crossbows.

"You found Ser Aldrith and his men, did you? I suppose that upset Commander Warrick. The man was always far too caring for his own good, and it was always his greatest weakness. You see, much like a game of chess, a good leader must always be willing to sacrifice his pieces if it means winning the game. The Commander never understood this, which made him less than what he could have been."

"Warrick is dead, and he killed him!" Roland yelled and pointed his spear tip at Andyn.

"Even a rook must be sacrificed every once in a while, to obtain victory."

"That is all we are to you? Pieces? Tools to be used and thrown away when no longer necessary?" Roland said angrily.

"Each of us has his place in this world; mine just happens to be far above yours," Urban answered with another laugh.

"Why do you want the stone? What is it to you?" Gerhold asked, still keeping his eye on the crossbowmen.

"You do not know what this is, do you?" Urban asked as he took the green stone from Andyn and held it up. "You see, this is a channeling stone, an ancient relic taken from Arden long ago. One of only a few magical stones to have survived the fall of those kingdoms. It allows the holder to amplify his or her magical abilities far beyond what they should be able to manage. A novice could cast spells that only the greatest master mages could conjure. A fireball can become an inferno; a lightning bolt can become a storm. With this, the holder is close to invincible."

"So, this was all about power? Strange that a pious man would wish for something so corrupt," Gerhold added and the old Vigil smiled again.

"Come now, vampire, with this in hand I can do a great many things. With this, I can control and protect. I have always believed that having three Vigils was an unnecessary and archaic tradition. It will be far more efficient to have just one leader, me."

"That is heresy! You dare to call yourself a member of the Vigilant, let alone one of our leaders?" Roland growled and twisted the silver spear in his hands.

"You fail to see the larger picture here. I am going to use this power to further the influence of the Three, to create a world that will serve and follow as it should have from the beginning. How is this not following the Path of Vigilant? If anything, I am the only one who is righteous, for I am the only one who has the dedication, zeal, and faith to act. As this cult sought to make a world of evil, I shall use this to make a world of peace. I will become what the Vigils should have always been, second only to the Gods themselves." Urban finished and shook his head. Gerhold glanced at Roland and saw the fury etched upon his face.

"You are nothing more than any other man, only more corrupt," Roland said.

"Your words mean little if anything. Now, I have a great many things to prepare for, so if you will excuse me, I will be departing now."

"You are going to leave us alive?" Gerhold asked curiously.

A Curse of Darkness

"I see no need to kill you when this forest should be adequate to do it for me."

"I will not allow you to get away with this," Roland spat.

"And what will you do? Even if you manage to escape the Blightwood, who will believe a vampire and an excommunicated Paladin who was dismissed for consorting with creatures of darkness? Who would ever believe you over me?" The old man cackled and waved his hand. "Goodbye Gerhold, I–"

Before the Vigil could finish his sentence, his eyes bulged, and his face contorted in pain as the tip of a silver blade burst through his chest. Gerhold looked on in surprise as one of the Paladins who had been standing behind Urban slammed his sword through the old man's back again. Shock and agony passed across the Vigil's face as the life slowly drained from his eyes. The Paladin slipped the channeling stone from the old man's hand before releasing him, and Gerhold watched as Pontius Urban fell forward over the side of the ship and disappeared. A few of the other Paladins looked on in shock while others turned their crossbows on their brothers and fired. It was over in a moment and soon only six Paladins remained standing along with the one who had killed the Vigil, while the others lay dead or dying. Gerhold stared back up at the assassin who still wore his thick, full-faced helmet, and Gerhold realized that this scene was all too familiar.

"When will men learn that trust is a luxury few will ever be able to afford, Gerhold?" the Paladin said and slid the helmet off, revealing a handsome grinning face and a mane of long, blonde hair. "I assumed that you would have learned that by now."

"Harkin," Gerhold muttered and stared at the vampire standing above him.

Harkin's face was the same it had been a hundred years ago, and Gerhold glared at his hated rival. Something else happened though, deep within the darkness of his mind Gerhold felt the monster awaken again, only this time it was all the more ferocious. The scratching feeling in the back of his consciousness became a roaring slashing beast fighting to break free. He wanted Harkin dead, he wanted to tear the vampire's throat out and rip his body to pieces.

"Gerhold of Vilheim, I hear you have been looking for me."

"I have," Gerhold answered and reached for his crossbow, the angry beast within him driving his desire for vengeance without restraint, but the remaining Paladins raised their weapons again.

He looked up at Harkin, rage emanating from his every pore. A hundred years he had spent searching for this vampire, searching for vengeance, and now Harkin was only a few feet away. The beast growled and snarled in the recesses of his mind, but it was still held at bay by the will of the hunter.

"Please, do not reach for your weapons; I would hate for you to die before your time has come," Harkin said, tossing the stone into the air with one hand and then catching it with the other. "You must realize that I have survived for over a thousand years by hiding in the shadows, so what made you think you would be able to find me unless I wanted you to?"

"I assumed you would not be able to resist showing yourself."

"Immortality teaches one to be patient."

"Then why turn up now? Perhaps I would have believed you were dead had you stayed hidden long enough."

"No, not you. We are very much alike, you and I. I would never believe you slain until I saw the body or killed you myself, and I know that you are the same." Harkin smiled. "Is it strange for you to use my real name? Or am I still Vergil to you?"

"There is no Vergil. That person never existed. He was nothing more than a mirage, a figment of my imagination."

"Oh, but Vergil is real, and he is standing right in front of me," Harkin laughed and pointed at Gerhold. "A vampire who turned on his own kind. One who seeks to maintain whatever shreds of his humanity remain in effort to keep his misplaced and antiquated sense of morality. You have become the persona that I invented, and that is very interesting indeed."

"Is it? Or are you more surprised by how I did not give in to the hunger and become a monster like you?" Gerhold asked and Harkin's smile disappeared.

"I assumed that once you became one of us that you would join me, but I never could have predicted that you would harness the curse and use its power. Tell me, how did you manage to resist that initial, ravenous sensation? Or did you kill to satiate your thirst?"

"There was a priest who saved me. I have never killed an innocent to satisfy the curse; nor will I ever." Harkin raised an eyebrow and paused before answering.

"Oh, but you have killed the guilty to satisfy the thirst, have you not?" Gerhold did not respond. "Now that I see you again, I realize that I should have expected as much. You have a strong will, one that is both commendable and infuriating. As I said, you and I are very much alike," Harkin said with a short bow, but Gerhold shook his head.

"No, we are nothing alike. You gave into the hunger for blood and pursue nothing other than to drain the life from others to satisfy your own. You and vampires like you are nothing more than beasts, a plague that feeds upon the people of this world, but I am the cure."

Harkin laughed again as soon as Gerhold finished.

"You are fool, Gerhold. I am not just any monster. I have existed for thousands of years, one of the oldest living vampires. You are not as unique or special as you think. Vampires have existed since history began, and I know you understand that there are so many just like you. Fools who think they can somehow maintain their humanity. I outgrew those pathetic beliefs long ago. We are not cursed, we are awakened, enlightened. We are an improvement over the mortals. We are greater than they could ever hope to be."

"We were not made to exist forever," Gerhold said. "You know as well as I that immortality is no blessing."

"I have built cathedrals of stone in places where no man has set foot yet, I have explored the uncharted regions both above and below, and I am the one who fooled the greatest hunter in history." Harkin smiled again. "I have seen things that these poor humans could only dream of, but there is still truth in what you say. Immortality is a fickle thing."

Gerhold pushed the beast away again, ignoring the siren call for violence and clearing his mind.

"You are quite proud of an accomplishment that did nothing more than make me stronger, faster, and more aware. You took the greatest slayer in history and gave him powers to match your own and made him immortal. So, no matter how many times you escape me, I will always be there to renew the hunt."

"Perhaps you should thank me for cursing you," Harkin paused, but Gerhold did not respond. "No? I thought not. You chase after me, not due to your misplaced sense of right and wrong, nor religious fervor, but because you are compelled to do so. You hunt me because you want revenge for what I did to you, for defeating you as no other has. Pride is why you hunt me, Gerhold, the greatest of man's weaknesses. Pride, and need for a reason to exist. You see, that is the worst of immortality. For without purpose, we are nothing. Your purpose, for now, is Vengeance."

"Vengeance? Yes, one day I will have that for what you did to an innocent woman a hundred years ago, and for whatever other crimes you are guilty of," Gerhold answered.

"I could kill you right now if I wished. Between these useful fellows here and this," he held up the stone. "I could destroy you both with little effort. However, as I said, it is not your time just yet. I have other plans for you. Purpose, Gerhold. That is why you will live."

Gerhold took a step forward and glared at his fellow vampire.

"There will be a day, whether a year or ten from now, that I will find you, and on that day, I will not extend the same courtesy." Gerhold took a step forward. "I will stab you through the heart without hesitation and without mercy."

Harkin grinned and gripped the stone a little tighter.

"No, you would never kill me. Without me, without that fire and desire for revenge to drive you forward, you are nothing. Nothing but another foolish, cursed man. A man who has nothing but to live out the remainder of his years as the last vestiges of his humanity slip between his fingers, trying desperately to maintain a thread of his former life. You feel it, don't you? All our kind do. The ravenous beast that lurks within. The insatiable hunger. Without me, Gerhold, what would you use to distract yourself from the unending desire to feed? Without purpose, you would be nothing, and without purpose, the beast would consume you. It would be a pathetic and ill-suited end for a man such as you. You need me, slayer, as much as I need you. Our battle is one that will continue for ages. An unstoppable force and an immovable object, as it is said."

"Why are you here, Harkin? Was the Vigil working for you?"

"In a way he was, though he did not know it. You see, Ser Andyn here is a thrall. I fed on him long enough so that he would obey my orders while still maintaining his charming demeanor, so that no one would suspect where his true loyalties lie. A perfect spy if I do say so myself." He turned to face Andyn, who looked frightened but did not move. "You did well, Andyn. You have been a loyal servant and have delivered the stone to me as I ordered. However, you have served your purpose, which means I have little need of you now."

"Please, m-my lord–" Harkin stabbed Andyn through the heart and let the man's body fall over the side of the airship.

Gerhold felt a twinge of empathy for Andyn, knowing that the man had no choice in what he did.

"Pawns are never to be mourned," Harkin said with a smile and wiped the blood from his blade.

"Why, Harkin? Why are you here? For the stone?"

"The stone," Harkin said and tossed it again into the air. "Ah yes, I have been searching for this artifact for many years, even before we met for the first time. I made many plans over the years involving this relic. Galen learned of my search and my plots involving the stone during his time in my service, and he decided to follow through with my ideas after he assumed that I was dead."

"Then why did you not seek him out?" Gerhold asked.

"I would have, but as it turned out, he was not fond of my turning him into a vampire, and so I could not come to him. He had become somewhat powerful and held the loyalty of his fledglings and the necromancer cult, but I had only myself. After our wonderful little game, I had few resources and I knew that you would be hunting me, so I disappeared and waited, biding my time while the world continued to turn. Once I was sure the stone had been found and was in his possession, I devised the plan of using the Vigil and the Paladins to obtain the stone for me. It was rather simple. I had Andyn here subtly inform the Vigil that a powerful artifact was in the hands of a cult hiding in the Blightwood. Urban was as power hungry and selfish as any other man would be in his position, and so he could not resist a chance such as this one."

"And he sent a group of Paladins to investigate, but they disappeared. Is that why you had him send for me?"

"Of course. Who else would have been able to succeed where the Paladins failed? You see, Gerhold, I have been tracking you for many years now, watching and waiting. I knew that if I ever hoped to get my hands on that stone then I would need your help, but of course you would not give it willingly. Deception has always been one of my more refined tools. I had Andyn convince the Vigil to use you to get to the stone. Urban thought that Andyn was secretly working for him; when all along, they were both pawns in my game. These Paladins here for instance, they are all mine."

The Paladins pulled off their helms and revealed that each was a vampire.

"So now you will use the stone to spread the darkness of Blightwood, just as Lord Friedrich tried? Why stop him in the first place if he was following your plan?" Harkin tilted his head back and roared with laughter.

"Do not sell me so short, Gerhold. As you know, my plans are far more sophisticated."

"What then? What are you planning?" Gerhold asked again.

"Something that will change the world, but more importantly, it will allow us to finish our game. You see, I thought that once you turned, you would become like the rest of us, but alas I, like so many others, underestimated you. As it turned out, I had not defeated you; our battle ended in a draw, and the world's greatest slayer would continue his work."

"So, this is about me?" Gerhold answered. The anger had boiled inside of him to the point where he was not sure if he could keep it in.

"It is about us! You and I!" Harkin stared at Gerhold with a strange intensity. "I have a new test for you, Gerhold, a gauntlet that will test your will as well as your skills, and then we shall see if you are still deserving of your title."

"Run all you want, but it will make no difference. In the end, it will be my hands that will send you onto the next world."

"Who do you think you are speaking to, Gerhold? You look at me and what do you see? Just another vampire, albeit one who is more formidable, but a vampire none the less. You clearly do not understand just who you are dealing with, so allow me to open your eyes for a moment. A hunter is hired to kill a vampire or werewolf and does so without thought, as if slaying the creature has become second nature, and you think the same of me. You think that I will fall like every other foe has before you, that it is you who is controlling your destiny. You think you are the hunter, but in reality, it is you who are the prey. I am the one who is hunting you!"

The two vampires stared at each other, and neither one blinked. Gerhold wanted so desperately to reach for his crossbow, but Harkin's guards were ready to fire if he so much as moved a finger.

"I am going to find you," Gerhold said threateningly.

"I am planning on it, and by the end of this, the world will know which of us is greater; the slayer or the monster."

With that, one of the vampires cut the rope holding the airship, and Gerhold glared at Harkin as he slowly drifted up and away into the dark sky. He watched as the ship rose high into the air, a small silhouette against the black clouds, and neither he nor Harkin broke eye contact until the ship finally disappeared into the night. Gerhold stared at the spot in the sky where he had lost the ship and felt the sinking feeling of losing his quarry once again. Harkin was gone again, but this time Gerhold knew it was only a matter of time before he would reappear. Gerhold turned to Roland, who had been staring off at the same spot, and started to make his way back towards the stairs.

A Curse of Darkness

"What do we do now?" he asked and Gerhold turned to face the young Paladin. "I mean, the Vigil is gone, that vampire is gone, the stone is gone, I have been excommunicated, and now we are here with no way back save the way we came."

"We make our way out of this cursed city, then we make our way out of the forest. We will hunt down Harkin, kill him, and destroy the stone."

"There are two of us now, not seven. How can we make it out of here alive? That bastard vampire has left us with nothing in the middle of this forest, and he now has one of the most powerful artifacts in his possession."

"That makes it all the more important that we escape this forest alive," Gerhold answered and put a hand of Roland's shoulder. "We will get out of here. Now come, we have no time to waste."

The two men walked together without saying another word, each concentrating on his own thoughts. Gerhold was angry, but there was also a new feeling, a fire that had been building within him. Seeing Harkin again had sparked that fire and now he knew that eventually, whether it be a day or a hundred years from now, he would find Harkin again, and when he did, he would take his revenge. Together, he and Roland made their way back inside, preparing for the long journey back through the forest.

J.S. Matthews

Chapter 16: The Hunt Renewed

Gerhold of Vilheim, Journal Entry: March 3, 5944 of the Common Age

It has been just over three weeks since Roland and I made our way out of Altandir and back through the forest of Blightwood. Three days it took for us to find our way around the bog and then to reach the village on the border of the forest, and though we had no encounters with undead, the howlers were still a nuisance. When we arrived at the village, I questioned the elder, who admitted to knowing about the previous band of Paladins and did not tell us at the order of Lord Friedrich. As it turned out, the elder had been offering his people as sacrifices so the cult would not raid and destroy the city, and this of course did not please the other villagers. By the time we left they had already burned the man alive and left his body out to rot, and I cannot say that I blame them.

  A week later, we reached the town of Harlton, and along the way I did my best to inquire if any travelers had seen an airship pass by from the south. Few traders even used the route due to having to fly over the Blightwood, so there was a chance that, if they did happen to see an airship, it would be Harkin. By the time we reached Harlton I had heard accounts from merchants, travelers, and villagers about seeing an airship pass by in the direction of the town, and so we immediately visited the skydock upon arrival. Harlton is a small town and not often visited by large numbers of traders, so its docks were equally empty, and to my surprise the Ilvarin was still docked there. The ship was abandoned, completely empty save for the rotting corpses of a few dead Paladins, and I knew that there would be no way for us to track Harkin. The trail was lost, and I was forced to accept that.

  I am disappointed to say the least, but I now know that Harkin is alive. A hundred years of searching for him, a hundred years of hunting and tracking any lead I could find, and when I finally found him, I was forced to stand and watch as he flew away with a powerful relic that I had worked so hard to obtain. Most would say that he

A Curse of Darkness

used me, but I, nor anyone, could have known that it was he who was pulling the strings, and we were able to stop Galen Friedrich from covering the lands in darkness. However, Harkin has the stone now, and through his cryptic messages I know that he is planning something, something that involves me. I will be prepared for whatever challenge he is planning next, though I will not give up my search for him, not now that I know he is alive.

I am afraid though, more afraid than I have been in years. Seeing Harkin caused the beast within me to come to life more than it ever has. Perhaps it is my anger, my desperation that it feeds upon. Even now I feel it, clawing at dark recesses of my mind, trying desperately to find a way out. To find a way to escape and devour my sanity. I will not allow it to though, I will not descend into madness like some crazed monstrosity. I will die first before I let that happen.

Though we lost the stone, I am still pleased with the result of this quest, although Roland has been taking the events in Altandir quite hard. He has turned to drinking and spends most of his time in silence, excluding the occasional outburst of anger. After we chartered an airship to return us to Vilheim, he discovered that the Vigil had not lied when he taunted Roland about his excommunication from the Order of the Vigilant. When we arrived back at the cathedral the priests informed him that they had received notices of his termination, and of course this only led to more drinking. It must be hard for him to accept the loss of his title, and now the loss of the creed he has put so much faith in. Still, he is a good man with a good heart, and I hope that he can recover from this soon, for I would not mind some company on my next trip when it comes.

For so long now, I have worked alone while rarely taking up temporary and tentative partnerships with other hunters or mercenaries, but I hope that Roland can become a companion that I can rely on. He can fight and having the knowledge of a Paladin could always be useful. If I am to hunt and find Harkin, then I am going to need all the help I can get, and there are few men I trust in this world as it is.

Gerhold sighed and leaned back in the old wooden chair in front of his desk while closing his dusty leather journal. He was back in his room in the upper reaches of the cathedral in Vilheim and had spent the past day resting and recording what he could remember of the adventure into Blightwood. Upon their return, the priests had informed Roland and Gerhold that they were being hunted by the Paladins now and that there had been a bounty placed on both of their heads. Thankfully Brother Francis saw to it to hide the entrance to the upper level of the chapel, which was now protected by a secret stone wall, so that they could continue to assist Gerhold and hide his belongings. Two Paladins came to the chapel one morning but left after speaking with Brother Francis. Gerhold knew that they were going to need to be far more careful when coming and going, as he was sure the cathedral was being watched.

Of course, Nethrin already had a plan to construct tunnels from the chapel undercroft to the sewers and to various caves outside of the city, a plan which Brother Francis reluctantly agreed to. That way Gerhold could come and go as he pleased with no worry of being discovered by the Paladins. The boy had already started working on the first of many passages he had planned, and the older priests were furious that he was being allowed to stay in his workshop from sunup till sundown rather than performing his duties. Nethrin had also spent time following Gerhold around and inquiring about the new crossbow and if the cloak worked as intended, all the while scribbling furiously in his little notebook anything that the vampire said.

"Master Gerhold?" A voice came from the hallway and Gerhold turned to see Brother Francis enter. "I hope I am not interrupting you."

"Of course not, Brother. What can I do for you?" Gerhold asked and placed the little journal inside one of the desk drawers.

"I thought you would want to know that we have received a letter from a nearby village, something about a specter haunting a cemetery," Francis said and handed a folded piece of paper over.

"A specter? Sounds interesting enough. Do you think it is safe to leave, though?"

"Safe enough I expect, but you have never had too much trouble remaining unnoticed," Francis said. "So, shall I tell them to be prepared for your arrival?"

"Of course, but tell them there will be two of us." Gerhold answered and Brother Francis raised an eyebrow.

"You are not thinking of taking the Paladin with you, are you?" he asked.

"I am. Roland is a good man and an even better fighter. Besides, it will be good for him to get out of this place and take his mind off things for a time," Gerhold answered and Francis shook his head.

"If you say so, but good luck getting that one to stay sober."

A Curse of Darkness

"It will not be a problem, Brother." And with that Francis nodded, gave a short bow, and then left the room.

Gerhold slowly stood and yawned, then slid the chair once again beneath the desk and made his way out of his little room. He was happy to be back in Vilheim, but for some reason he felt as though he should not be back at all. Something was pulling him away, tugging at him, as if he were needed elsewhere. His body may have been present, but his mind was always somewhere else, attempting to figure out where Harkin had gone. He had sent messages to as many of his contacts as he could think of, hoping that maybe one of them would have overheard something about the stone. Wherever the stone was that would be where he would find Harkin. It was hard to not be obsessed with the hunt now that he had found his prey again, and after a hundred years of searching with no avail, he felt unable to just sit and wait in the cathedral instead of spending all his energy in search of his enemy.

However, he knew that he must maintain his patience if he wished to find Harkin, and Gerhold also knew that there were other things that needed his attention– Roland for one. The young Paladin had become more depressed by the day and was still spending far too much of his time trying to find the bottom of a bottle than doing anything useful, and Gerhold had decided that it was time for Roland to get passed what had happened at Altandir. If he was going to locate Harkin anytime soon, Gerhold knew that having the Paladin with him would more than likely speed up the process. The young man had proved his worth in the forest and during their battle through the necromancer's fortress. Gerhold had no doubt that Roland would prove to be even more important in the coming fight.

He made his way down the stairs and through the fake wall to another room. Still deep in thought, he descended another flight of stairs that passed down to the undercroft. Below, he could hear the echoing sound of metal striking stone– most likely Nethrin and a few of the priests digging the tunnels– and he came out of the stairwell into the dusty chapel basement. Not much had changed in the past one hundred years other than Nethrin's workshop, which seemed to expand every time he visited. A few torches lit up the large open area lined with old wooden supports, and Gerhold made his way over to where Nethrin's workshop stood. A forge stood in the corner, tables lay about the stone floor covered in odds, ends, and the occasional tool, and shelves holding more scraps and junk lined the walls. Leaning against one of the shelves with a green bottle of wine in his hand was Roland, looking as disheveled and unshaven as ever and smelling even worse.

"Good to see you have not finished all of the brothers' wine," Gerhold said with a grin and pulled a chair up next to where Roland was sitting. "Having fun yet?"

"I am enjoying the feeling of intoxication, not that a vampire would understand. You cannot even remember the taste of wine, can you?" Roland spat and glared at Gerhold.

"Can you remember it? Or is vomit the only thing you can taste?"

"What do you want?" Roland asked gruffly and continued his glare.

"I want you to drop that bottle and stand up; take a bath, shave, and get ready to leave," Gerhold said but Roland scoffed.

"To the hells with you, vampire! I am content with staying where I am and drowning myself in whatever liquor I can find." Roland moved to take another swig from the bottle but Gerhold kicked it out of his hand, sending the bottle spinning across the stone floor and spilling its contents.

Roland leapt to his feet and made to swing at Gerhold who easily dodged the drunken swipe. They danced back and forth for a moment, Roland swinging wildly at Gerhold while the vampire moved side to side avoiding each strike and laughing at the foolish attempts. Roland roared in anger and swung as hard as he could, but Gerhold ducked beneath the blow and stuck out his foot, tripping Roland and sending him sprawling to the floor in a heap.

"Had enough yet?" he asked, and Roland groaned.

"Just leave me be. I have enough to deal with already without you pestering me," Roland said and tried to stand but fell awkwardly to his knees.

"Because drinking yourself into a stupor and laying about all day does not qualify as busy."

"You know nothing about me. I have lost everything, not once but twice! I gave up my title, my name, and my inheritance. And for what? To be kicked to the side by some corrupt bastard who is not even alive anymore. I have no family, no title, no faith, nothing. So, tell me, vampire, why does it matter what I do now?" Roland leaned against one of the tables still in a sitting position.

Gerhold waited for a moment before answering.

"Then it is time you found yourself a new calling. I am a pious man, Roland, but I have known for a long time that the Vigils are men, nothing more. Like all men they can be corrupted by power, and often their rules and

A Curse of Darkness

proclamations are more for their own good than for those they supposedly serve. They are men, not Gods, and they will not be the ones to judge you. As men, we are all guilty of sin, and those who enjoy pointing out the flaws in others tend to be the ones who have the most themselves. You are a better man than any of them, and you do not need a title or some Vigil to tell you that," Gerhold finished and stood. He made his way across the room to a rack of weapons.

"So, what would you have me do then? Become a hunter? I am a Paladin, a holy warrior, not some mercenary for hire," Roland said and Gerhold came striding back over, a long silver spear in hand.

"Then be one, and stop acting like drunken vagabond," Gerhold answered.

"How can you be like this? How can you be so calm as if nothing is wrong?" Roland roared. "That vampire made you into what you are, and you have spent a lifetime pursuing him, and then he forces you to watch him disappear again. How can you just stand there and act as if moving will make all of that just disappear?" Gerhold stared at the young man with a small smile on his face.

"I could let it affect me. I could roll over and wallow in my self-pity. I could get angry with the Gods for placing a seemingly endless mountain in my path and for laughing at me as I attempt to reach the summit, but I will not. You must realize that these difficulties serve only one of two purposes: to destroy us or to make us stronger. The choice is ours which path we end up taking."

Gerhold finished and placed the spear on the ground in front of Roland. The young man stared at the spear for a few moments before closing his eyes and rubbing his forehead. Slowly, Roland reached out and grabbed hold of the spear, then pulled himself to his feet and leaned against the table for support as he stared at the smooth silver weapon.

"I suppose you are right," he muttered without looking at Gerhold.

"Of course, I am. Now stop moping about and get your things together. And for the Gods' sake take a bath and shave, you look terrible with that scraggly beard."

"But I am not giving up the wine. The brothers have barely touched two bottles in a decade, and it would be a true sin to let it all go to waste in this dusty old cellar."

"You can drink when we are finished with our business. Agreed?" Gerhold said.

The young man nodded in return. They stared at each other for a moment before Gerhold patted Roland on his shoulder and turned the leave. Before Gerhold reached the stairs, though, Roland spoke again.

"Where are we going?" he asked and Gerhold smiled again.

"We have a job in a village just outside of Vilheim. That is, if you can handle being a hunter for hire," Gerhold said and Roland paused before nodding.

"Aye, I can handle it. Not like I have much of a choice," Roland responded and stood, still using the spear for support as he swayed slightly from side to side.

"Good, then get ready; we will leave at nightfall."

With that Gerhold turned and made his way back up the stairs. On his way back up to his room, he paused at the balcony overlooking the cathedral floor and smiled. He felt fresh, new, as if he had just awoken from some long sleep to feel well rested and prepared for whatever lay ahead. His solemnity had been replaced by a new sense of adventure and vigor, and he knew why. The hunt had started once again, and the scent of his prey was still fresh in his mind, the scent of revenge.

A Curse of Darkness

Epilogue

"I think that is enough for tonight," Jarrell heard someone say and looked up from the dusty torn pages of the diary he had been reading.

It took him a moment to remember where he was and who was speaking; as he blinked in the dim light of the candle and glanced up at Ernhold, who had still not moved from his seat at the end of the table. Jarrell gave a great yawn and stretched before glancing at the clock on his desk. It was nearly three o'clock in the morning and he found himself feeling even more weary just thinking about having to wake up the following morning for his lessons. Slowly he started to gather up his things and made sure to carefully close the leather-bound journal.

"I did not realize how late it was," Jarrell said as Ernhold approached.

"You have the mind of a true Keeper; once you start your work, it is as if nothing else in the world exists. That can be a good or bad thing depending on the circumstance," the man said and picked up the journal. "Did you find the tale thrilling enough?"

"I did; though I wish I could continue in spite of how tired I am."

"Tomorrow night will be our last meeting," Ernhold said as he turned to leave.

"Last meeting? But I still need to record the rest of the journals." Jarrell exclaimed, trying to think of what he was going to tell the High Keeper if he was not able to record all the stories.

"I have business elsewhere, and so I must depart the day after tomorrow. We shall have our final meeting tomorrow and you may copy whatever you can."

"But what about the rest of the entries?"

"You will record all you need tomorrow. Are you not eager to discover the ending to this tale?" Jarrell said nothing. "Of course, you are, and you shall at our next meeting. Now, good night. I promise that by this time tomorrow you will know the fate of the monster hunter, and in turn, so will all."

Ernhold turned and walked out of the room, once again leaving Jarrell alone. The Apprentice flopped down into his chair and rested his hand on his forehead. He was very tired, but he was also worried, worried that he was not going to be able to complete the task given to him by the High Keeper. What would they do to him if he failed such an important assignment, his very first assignment? Jarrell closed his eyes for a moment, trying to dull the headache that had settled above his eyes and attempted to assuage the sense of panic that had taken over his stomach. What was he going to tell the High Keeper if he could not record the journals? And what would they do when they saw that he had skipped so many entries? Suddenly the sound of creaking hinges made Jarrell jump in surprise, and he looked up to see a hunched figure entering the room.

"Good evening, Apprentice, or should I say good morning?" the High Keeper said as he entered, followed by one of the battle mages.

"High Keeper, I was just about to head up to my room. I am sorry if I was down here for too long," Jarrell said quickly and gathered up his things.

"Come now, I am not one to scold a student for spending too much time practicing. I only came to see if everything went well and if you had any concerns," Yorlan said and tilted his head. Jarrell paused for a moment before answering.

"Everything is fine, High Keeper, I have been copying everything as you asked," he answered, hoping that his tone of voice had not given away his lie. The High Keeper stared at him for a moment with a small grin.

"And what of Mister Ernhold?" Jarrell shook his head.

"He is quiet and lets me work, though I still do not like the man," he answered and Yorlan nodded.

"Very good, then I shall let you continue your work tomorrow night as well. Do you know how many more nights it will take to obtain copies of the entire journal?"

"I am not sure, but I will do my best," Jarrell answered nervously and Yorlan nodded.

"Very good. I will come and see you tomorrow again to check on your progress," the High Keeper said, and Jarrell felt his throat and stomach tighten as he nodded. "Well then, if there is nothing else, then you may leave, Apprentice."

Jarrell forced himself to his feet and picked up his things from the desktop, then made his way out of the little room, leaving just the High Keeper and his guard behind, while doing his best to avoid eye contact with Yorlan as he left. With every step he felt the nervous twisting in his stomach grow and could

A Curse of Darkness

do little to prevent the waves of nausea that were rolling over him. The High Keeper was going to check on his progress and he was still missing large gaps between the two sections he had already copied. He did his best to force the apprehensive thoughts away, but it only made him more nervous about what Yorlan was going to say about his work.

      Exhausted, worried, and trying to ignore his throbbing head, Jarrell made his way into his small dim room, his thoughts still drifting over the story that he so desired to finish. Despite all the worrying and apprehension over the copies, Jarrell could not ignore the anticipation he was feeling for the following night. Ernhold had promised that by this time tomorrow, he would discover the fate of Gerhold of Vilheim, and with that promise Jarrell drifted off into a much needed and sound sleep.

The third Night...

A Dawn of Death

Jarrell Vorren lay face down on his soft bed, breathing heavily in a deep sleep as rays of warm sunlight passed through large windows into the cramped dormitory. There were seven other beds that lined the walls on either side, though none were now occupied as their owners had been awake for some time and were now either finishing their breakfast in the dining hall or already off to their first lessons and morning duties. Jarrell, though, was still asleep, exhausted from the long hours of copying and reading late into the past two nights.

The door to the dormitory opened and in walked a young man not much older than Jarrell, wearing similar robes and looking somewhat agitated. He stopped for a brief moment and shook his head after catching sight of the sprawled form of Jarrell still lying in bed, before making his way across the room and slapping the sleeping apprentice across the back of his head.

"Oy? What in the six hells are you doing?" Jarrell yelled angrily and almost fell out of bed.

"Time to get up. Do you have any idea what time it is?" the man asked, but Jarrell just moaned.

"I do not care what time it is, Mendle. Go away and leave me be," Jarrell answered and slammed his pillow back over his head.

"You will once Keeper Bernard gets a hold of you! Now get up, it is already ten past seven," Mendle answered and tore the pillow away from Jarrell. "No one cares that you were up late working with the High Keeper."

"How do you know about that?" Jarrell mumbled while trying to cover his eyes with his arm.

"Everyone knows about it. Did you think it would not get around that he has an Apprentice working on the fourth level? Most of the older Apprentices are furious that they were passed up. In fact, you are lucky I came up here to get you. Edrin wanted to leave you here in hopes that you would miss all your lessons."

"I thought it was supposed to be a secret," Jarrell mumbled again.

"Well, it is not a secret, and there are quite a number of angry Apprentices to boot. Do you think that because the High Keeper gave you some special assignment that you get to skip your lessons and duties? You are not a Keeper yet, so get up!"

"Keeper Bernard can string me up for all I care; I have not had a decent night's sleep in nearly a week! Between copying that volume of plants and my work with the High Keeper, I was not in bed until after three the past two nights," Jarrell said grumpily and tried to yank the pillow back.

"No one cares about that, you tosspot," Mendel slapped him again and then turned to leave. "If you can get dressed quickly you may only be a few minutes late. And I expect a thank-you the next time we meet. The other Apprentices will have my head if they know I helped you."

A moment later Jarrell was alone in the dormitory again, still trying to fight a losing battle against the sunlight, and it did not help that he was worrying about what Mendle had said. If the other Apprentices knew that he had been chosen by the High Keeper over them for an important job, then they would surely be jealous. How much did they know? Did they know what he was doing? Did they know that he was copying the lost journals of Gerhold of Vilheim? Mendle was three years older than he and had been moved up to Apprenticeship only two months before Jarrell. They were friends, at least it could be called that, but very few in the library truly saw eye-to-eye with Jarrell. Most of them were scholars, dedicated solely to the crafts of calligraphy and copying manuscripts. Jarrell, on the other hand, wanted to be off on adventures and would have preferred to be anywhere other than being cooped up in the old library day after day.

Slowly he sat up and stretched, feeling his tired muscles and dry eyes cry out for more rest, all the while still troubled by thoughts of what the others knew about his nightly ventures into the lower levels of the library. Instead of yielding to the desire to simply lean back and fall asleep once more, Jarrell forced himself to his feet and began getting dressed. He had early Callorian history with Master Bernard followed by a lesson on the preservation of ancient scrolls with Master Dorn. The rest of his day would be spent reading long lists of alchemical ingredients. Not the most entertaining of plans but at least he had the night to look forward to. With his robes on and his satchel packed, Jarrell gave one last sigh while staring longingly at his bed before leaving the room.

Lethargically, he made his way through the dormitories and past the emptying dining hall, catching a brief aroma of sweet-smelling sausages, eggs, cinnamon apples, and a host of other wonderful aromas. His stomach rumbled with hunger and he forced himself to continue past the hall, leaving the delicious smells to linger behind. A moment later he was out into the library courtyard.

Weary and hungry, Jarrell made his way across the courtyard towards the large, cathedral like stone library at the center of the open area. The library was made up of a two-story building at the base of one of the mountain peaks, and it took up most of the courtyard. To the east and west were two other stone buildings; one was the dormitories and the dining hall where the Apprentices and Novices lived and worked, while the second stood opposite the main library and was home to the Keepers and Masters. A ten-foot-high stone wall surrounded the open space, and many paved pathways crisscrossed the grassy courtyard and passed in between the many tall, shady trees, planters that held bunches of red and yellow flowers that were just beginning, and around the various bushes and shrubs that dotted the grounds.

It was a beautiful place to say the least, especially in the dead of winter when a thick layer of white snow blanketed the grounds and surrounding peaks or in the summer months when most of the flowers were in bloom. Today however, Jarrell hated the walk across the peaceful grounds; it only made him wish even more to return to his soft warm bed within the dormitories. Soon he was climbing the stone steps to the library entrance, and by the time he reached the large oak doors at the top his legs felt like dead weights. The inside of the library was always the same, with its unending shelves of parchment and books and scrolls that towered overhead, the soft echo of footsteps and whispering voices, and the ever-present glow of orange torches and musty smell of ancient wood and stone. Jarrell passed between the many bookcases and desks and around the large square hole that delved deep into the foundation of the library, granting a privileged view of the six lower levels that were usually restricted to the students an Apprentices. Jarrell, of course, had been making regular trips to the fourth level basement.

The previous two nights he had spent hours down in one of those windowless and cold rooms copying and reading the lost journals that once belonged to Gerhold of Vilheim, the greatest monster slayer of all time. The man had disappeared over a hundred years ago, without a trace, and there was not a single soul alive who seemed to know what had happened to the hunter, and this held true until a merchant by the name of Ernhold brought Gerhold's lost journals to this very library two nights ago. Since then, Jarrell had spent most of his time reading and pondering the stories, even dreaming about the encounters

A Dawn of Death

that he read about. The challenge within the fortress of Ravencroft, the eerie journey through the cursed forest of Blightwood, and the battles deep beneath the bones of the ancient city of Altandir, all of these seemed to dominate his thoughts and left the apprentice with the singular desire to finish the forgotten tale.

Jarrell came to a halt outside of a closed oak door to a smaller room off the main level and sighed. He was ten minutes late and knew that Master Bernard would be unhappy with him. What horrible form of punishment would the old codger have waiting for him on the other side of that door? A hundred lines of copying the same foolish phrase? Of course, he was more worried about the hours of boring lectures than the punishments, and on top of that he was still longing to return to the pages of the journals. Slowly he raised his hand, turned the little brass handle, and entered the room.

Not four hours later Jarrell emerged from the same door griping his sore right hand and even more tired and hungry than before. He glanced behind him for a moment to see Master Bernard shredding the three pages of parchment he had finished during the session, which was supposed to be a lesson in humility for the Apprentice who, according to Master Bernard, had forgotten his place. Jarrell stalked angrily back through the library and across the courtyard to the dining hall, ignoring the looks and whispers that came whenever he passed someone. By the time he sat down at one of the long tables and took a bite out of a freshly baked roll, his stomach felt as though it had been empty for a week, and in no time he had forced down the entire roll along with a wedge of cheese and a roast chicken leg. A cup of cider and a warm slice of apple cobbler later, Jarrell leaned back in his chair and let out a great, satisfied sigh, hoping that such a delicious lunch heralded a better second half of his day.

Alas, things seemed to only get worse as his lessons with Master Borrey went late and on his way back for dinner a bottle of ink spilled inside his bag and ruined an entire section of his work on the endless lists of alchemical ingredients. Once he finally managed to reach the dining hall, the meal ended far more quickly than he was hoping and soon Jarrell found himself once again slaving away over a pile of parchment with nothing but the dim flickering light of a nearby candle for company.

The hours passed slowly until Jarrell was one of the only people remaining in the library who was not a guard, and he yawned audibly before leaning back in his chair and glancing over at the old wooden clock that stood between two nearby book cases. There were still another three hours to go before he was supposed to be downstairs to meet with Ernhold, but he was already tired of copying down the bland text. He let his head slump down onto the desk with a dull thud, dreading the next few hours. Suddenly a question he had been pondering the night before wormed its way back into his mind, and Jarrell glanced warily from side to side as if to make sure there was no one aware of his thoughts. There had been many questions plaguing his mind, but there was one that he had been considering nearly the entire day.

When Gerhold entered the necromancers' lair beneath the ruined city of Altandir, he found that the growing darkness of the Blightwood was being caused by an ancient artifact called a channeling stone which had fallen into the hands of a death cult. It was a powerful object capable of magnifying any spell, creating more powerful and deadly versions of whatever spells the wielding mage was able to cast. However, Jarrell had never heard of such a thing nor had he ever read of anything that sounded similar. It had been described in the journals as an ancient relic taken from the lost realms of Arden during the human expulsion from those lands, or at least that was what the Chronicles of Old Arden had said. Jarrell was a religious man, or as much as was necessary, and he had heard stories from priests about artifacts that had been brought back from Arden. Unlike the cursed gold and artifacts that were taken by those who were too greedy to leave their worldly possessions behind, the Gods requested that the humans take these relics with them before they fled. Most of the trinkets had significant religious meaning and were now kept under lock and key by the Vigilant, but many others went missing over the nearly six thousand years since humans first set foot on these shores. Perhaps the stone was one of those missing relics?

Were such tales even true? Jarrell stood up and slid the wooden chair back beneath the desk before making his way back down the lines of shelves behind him, searching for any books on the lost realms of Arden. *A Scholars History of Arden* by Keeper Manius, *On Arden and the Fall of Man* by Keeper Harrold, and a few other volumes were soon sitting on Jarrell's desk, but after an hour each one had been perused and then set aside. Jarrell rubbed his forehead wearily and closed the last of the heavy volumes. After all of that reading, he had found nothing, not a single mention of a Channeling Stone or anything like it amongst the seemingly endless lines of words. There were mentions of amulets and rings that could cure any illness or heal any wound no matter how grave, chalices that once filled would never run out of drink, cloaks that would render their wearer nearly invisible in the darkness or keep them from freezing even amidst the coldest weather, and other strange descriptions, but not one of them had to do with a Channeling Stone.

    Frustrated by the amount of time he had wasted, Jarrell stood and stalked back down the rows of shelves with the stack of books in his arms. Perhaps the journals were wrong, and the stone went by another name. That would make it infinitely harder to find and discover what it did, but it would explain why he was not able to find anything about such a powerful artifact, however, Jarrell also had another thought. Perhaps the journals were not real after all. Perhaps they were just a story written by a bard, or by Ernhold himself, and he was now trying to make a bit of gold off them. Was it possible that the man had fooled the High Keeper into believing the journals were real? He replaced the last book and returned to his desk once more.

    There was still another hour before he had to meet with Ernhold in the fourth level of the lower libraries and Jarrell was determined to continue his search. But where else could he look? According to the journals, the Channeling Stone was a powerful magical artifact from Arden, so perhaps he could find something about it in a different section of the library. Suddenly, Jarrell sat bolt upright and smiled. He needed a book about ancient, maybe even dangerous, magical artifacts, a book that would most likely not be kept in the upper levels of the library where just anyone, especially the Novices and Apprentices, could find it. Immediately he began packing up his things. The books he was looking for could only be found in the lower levels of the library. These were normally restricted for any novices and only available to the inducted Keepers, but since Jarrell had started working with Ernhold, the guards had been instructed to grant him access.

    Any books on enchanted or magical artifacts would be found in the history of magic section of the second level of the lower libraries, unless knowledge of the stone was extremely dangerous. In this case, the Keepers would have placed it in the lowest level of the basement sections, the sixth level, where only the most important and perilous writings were kept. Books and scrolls on the history of blood magic and necromancy, recollections and experiments from demented mages, and many other unsavory texts could be found in the sixth level, and it was equally inaccessible. If the information he sought was somewhere down there, he would never be able to find it.

    Jarrell shouldered his bag and darted off toward the stairs and then down to the ground floor. When the door to the lower levels came into view, the young Apprentice paused and took a deep breath to steady himself. One small lie was all he needed to tell. He would be heading down the fourth level early to prepare for Mister Ernhold's arrival; the guard would surely believe that. What he was about to do would go against the library rules, and if he was caught, would result in severe punishment or even expulsion from the Keepers. Jarrell had never been in any sort of trouble since he had arrived, and this would only be the first time that he had ever intentionally broken a rule. If this had been a week ago, he would not have even considered trying such a thing, but after reading the journals of Gerhold and spending so much time dwelling on them, Jarrell now desired to have his own adventure. Sneaking into the restricted sections of the library seemed to be the only way to satisfy this newly developed thirst for excitement.

    He took another deep breath and then put one foot in front of the other. The guard standing by the door nodded in his direction and opened the tall, heavy oak door without saying a word, and as soon as Jarrell was down the first flight of stairs, he let out a loud sigh of relief. His heart was pounding nervously as he slowly descended the next set of stairs and came to the first of the lower levels. A large, square open space stretched out in front of him and reached far down below to the other five levels. Above he could hear the soft echoes of the upper library. Around the square pit were hundreds of shelves stacked high with books and scrolls with various labels on each shelf, and across the large space was a pivoting bridge that would rotate from side to side to allow quick access to the various sections. On the other side of the opening Jarrell could see the next oak door that led down to the second level, and he crossed the stone bridge slowly so as to not draw attention to himself and then passed through the door.

    A moment later, Jarrell was standing on the second level of the library. A solitary guard patrolled the area and made his way through the door on the other side of the square chasm and down to the next level. Jarrell wiped the beads of nervous sweat from his forehead before proceeding quickly down the rows of shelves. He had no idea when the guard would return so he frantically searched for the section marked History of Magic, which he found along the left side of the room. In each corner along the balconies of shelves were little alcoves where one could find a comfortable chair to sit on or a desk to work at, and there were a few heavy doors lining the walkway where a Keeper could have more privacy and where the more sensitive texts were kept. Jarrell immediately set to work searching for any volumes of scrolls that caught his attention, all the while

A Dawn of Death

keeping a sharp eye on both of the doors to the second level. Soon he had four large leather-bound books in his arms and made his way over to one of the desks in the very corner of a nearby niche. After another quick glance across the balconies and the rotating bridge, Jarrell pulled a chair over as far as he could to remain out of sight and began quickly flipping through the first heavy volume.

A few minutes later he set the book on the floor and reached for another when suddenly the sound of a creaking door echoed from somewhere further down the rows of shelves. Jarrell dove beneath a nearby desk and tucked his knees up under his chin, praying silently that whoever it was would continue and not notice him. The heavy sounds of metal boots drew nearer and Jarrell's heart beat so fast he was sure whoever it was would be able to hear the pounding coming from his chest. The footsteps came to a halt on the other side of the nearest shelf and Jarrell held his breath for a least a minute before finally letting out a sigh of relief as the guard continued again. The clanking sounds of the guard's boots slowly faded and then disappeared completely with the creaking sound of a second door opening. Jarrell waited another minute before he was able to summon enough courage to emerge from his hiding place and snatch up the second book.

He read even more quickly this time, scanning paragraphs and chapters for any sign or mention of a Channeling Stone. Just when Jarrell had decided to give up, he opened the fourth and final volume, a book entitled *Artifacts, Treasures, and Weapons of the Ancient Age*, and immediately a set of words caught his attention. The sixth chapter was marked, *Rune Stones* and, after deciding this would be his last attempt, Jarrell flipped to the chapter and began to skim the words as quickly as he could.

Chapter 14: Rune Stones

Of all the ancient relics brought to our world from the forgotten realms of Arden, none are rarer or more powerful than the Rune Stones. Very little is known about these mysterious artifacts as few have ever been seen or studied since the fall of Dalloran, and the little information that was recorded is indistinct and difficult to understand. Most of these relics were kept in the possession of the most powerful leaders and mages of the age with very little, if any, knowledge of their existence outside of these owners. This is only one of the many reasons why so little information about the Rune

Stones is available for study.

　　According to the few sources we do have, Rune Stones were spherical carvings mined from the White Mountains that supposedly surrounded the ancient realm of Arden, and these stones were known to have distinct properties that allowed them to absorb and then re-emit magical energies. By themselves they were little more than beautifully smooth stones, but, if the descriptions are correct, in the hands of a trained magician they became some of the most powerful relics to ever exist in our world. It was discovered that these stones, if done correctly, could be enchanted with spells, leading to a range of powerful effects. So far, we have only come across five of these enchantments.

　　Healing Stone – A Rune Stone that was enchanted with a powerful healing spell that could heal any wound or cure any ailment. The last of these stones was reportedly in the hands of Hordrad the Healer, which should come as no surprise, I imagine.

　　Seeing Stone – A Rune Stone that was enchanted with a far-seeing spell, allowing the holder to see anywhere that he or previous holders have ever visited. The only reported version of this stone was supposedly in the hands of a pirate, though the source for this information was unreliable, to say the least.

　　Necro Stone – A Rune Stone that was enchanted with a powerful necromantic spell that allowed the wielder to summon hundreds, perhaps even thousands, of undead servants at one time. At least three of these stones have existed and were used by the Liches during their attacks on Tyriel. These events are now more commonly referred to as the Plague Wars. All have been destroyed according to the current Vigil of Righteousness, Pontius Gregor III.

　　Channeling Stone – A Rune Stone with a unique enchantment that would increase the power of the wielder's spells. Most of our information on these relics states that they are dangerous and nearly impossible to control when used for even short periods of time, resulting in the death of the wielder and wide swatches of destruction. The last king of Dalloran was rumored to have been in possession of a channeling stone, though its location was unknown and kept secret from all but the king and his closest advisors. It is even rumored that they debated using the stone to combat the undead armies before the king was ultimately slain during the Siege of Lordalion.

　　Portal Stone – These Rune Stones have only been rumored to exist as there are

A Dawn of Death

no official records or accounts of their usage. Still many scholars (though not this one) believe that Portal Stones were used to open the way to the Pits of Sargoth and led to the betrayer gods entering our world and subsequently destroying Arden, leading to the expulsion of humanity. Due to the descriptions and details from the chapter of the Chronicles on the fall of Arden, certain Keepers believe that the artifacts used to open the portal were in fact a version of a Rune Stone. Of course, this requires the belief that the stories put forth in the Chronicles are in fact the truth, rather than just a long list of ancient fairy tales, and said belief has yet to be consecrated as accurate from a scholarly point of view.

It is probable that other forms of Rune Stones exist that we have yet to discover, but without further study and investigation we cannot say for sure. Without a chance to excavate the ruins of Dalloranian cities and archives we may never be able to know for certain.

Jarrell stared at the page and felt a rush of satisfaction. From the moment he had finished the first entry of the journals he had wanted them to be real, and despite the High Keeper's confidence in their authenticity there, was always a lingering feeling of doubt. Now there were no doubts. In the journals, Lord Friedrich had found a Channeling Stone in the ruins of Altandir, one of the largest and most important cities in Dalloran. Could it have been the same stone mentioned in the book he now held? That same stone was now in the possession of Harkin Valakir, according to the last entry he had read, and Jarrell wondered what the vampire lord planned to do with the stone. What did he have planned for Gerhold? A hundred new questions sprang into his mind, and Jarrell was so deep in thought that he did not even notice the soft footsteps approaching from behind until it was too late.

"Doing a little extra reading, I see," a voice said. Jarrell felt his insides freeze with terror as he turned to see the High Keeper Yorlan staring at him with an amused smile on his face.

"High Keeper! I— uh—" Jarrell stuttered as his mind went blank, all thoughts eroded by waves of nauseous fear.

"There have only been a few instances in my life where I have seen the color drain from someone's face faster than yours just now," the old man said with a chuckle. "I take it you know you should not be here?"

Jarrell could not find words to respond as the only thoughts running through his mind were of what punishment he would receive. Would he even be allowed to finish working with Ernhold? As if reading the terrified Apprentice's mind, the High Keeper took a step forward.

"You know you are not being expelled, if that is what you are thinking," he said with a smile.

"I—I am not?" Jarrell said, and immediately some feeling began to return to his arms and legs.

"Of course not, nor are you in any real trouble, at least not with me. If another Keeper finds you down here, then I cannot promise that will be the case. However, you could just tell them you are performing necessary research for the task that I have given you. I am guessing that would not be far from the truth?" he asked, and Jarrell nodded. "In that case perhaps you should tell me what you are looking for and maybe I can help you find it. I am quite familiar with this building, seeing how it is my library."

Jarrell swallowed and took a deep breath before answering.

"I-I came across something, something in the journals. A term I did not recognize," he answered and Yorlan raised his eyebrows.

"And what term is this that was so mysterious that you thought it a good idea to sneak into the restricted section of the library to define?"

"A Channeling Stone," Jarrell said, and as soon as the words came out of his mouth, he saw a look of recognition flash across the old man's face.

"A Channeling Stone you say?" the High Keeper responded curiously, though Jarrell could tell there was something the High Keeper was not telling him.

"Yes. I searched for it in most of the volumes on Arden that I could find upstairs but found nothing."

"So, you decided to make a detour on your way down to the fourth floor?"

"Yes, High Keeper," Jarrell answered and hung his head.

"And you came across this term in Gerhold's journals, did you?" Jarrell nodded. "Hmmm, very interesting indeed," Yorlan mumbled.

"I am sorry for sneaking down here."

"Oh? Well, you should know that I was also caught down here during my tenure as an Apprentice, but I barely made it down the first flight of stairs before being caught," the old man said with a smile and hint of mischief in his eye. "It was a dare that I foolishly accepted. Your violation, on the other hand, was in the pursuit of knowledge, so how can I fault a budding Keeper for such behavior?"

Jarrell smiled and nodded.

"Now, did you find what you were looking for?" the High Keeper asked. Jarrell nodded and pointed to the open book on the desk. "Ah! An excellent read indeed. Keeper Gendry was never one to write a boring text, and it is particularly enjoyable to watch the more religiously tied Keepers ruffle at his every slight against the Chronicles. The man was as devout as they come but loved to be a nuisance to his fellow Keepers. Quite amusing if I do say so myself."

"I thought all Keepers believed the Chronicles to some degree?" Jarrell asked.

"Some do, some do not, and others are not sure what they believe," Yorlan answered with a shrug. "Now, if you do not mind, I would like to escort you down to your room on the fourth level, just in case you get a sudden mind for another detour."

"Of course not, High Keeper," Jarrell said and immediately started stacking the books and preparing to return them to their shelves, still in shock that he was not going to be punished. "Again, I am sorry."

"If we expelled every Apprentice that was caught sneaking into the restricted section, we would have very few Keepers left, and they would only be the boring ones," the old man added with a smile.

After Jarrell had finished replacing the books, the two men set out across the first floor. Distant, unintelligible voices could be heard echoing down from far above and the creaking and groaning of the rotating bridges came every so often from above and below as they walked. Jarrell and the High Keeper walked side by side with Yorlan's personal guard following close behind, the dull thud of his spear a reminder of his presence with every other step. No one spoke as they continued deeper into the lower levels and Jarrell could not help but notice the new-found fondness he felt for the High Keeper. Every Keeper he had interacted with during his time at the library had all been cold, careless, dry, and seemingly empty individuals devoid of anything other than inexhaustible wells of useless facts and stories, but Yorlan was the first he had met that seemed to be somewhat human. A few minutes later they halted in front of the large oak door that led into where Jarrell would be spending the next few hours.

"I suppose this is where we must part. Mister Ernhold informed me that this would be his last night here and that he will be moving on tomorrow as he has business elsewhere. I hope you will be able to complete your work in that time—, it would be a pity to lose such a valuable set of documents without first obtaining our own copies," the High Keeper said and began making his way back towards the stairwell.

"High Keeper?" Jarrell called after and the old man paused.

"Yes?"

"I—er," Jarrell stuttered, wrestling with himself over whether to tell the High Keeper about what he had been recording, or not. "Thank you again for not punishing me."

The High Keeper smiled and gave a small nod before turning to leave once again. Jarrell stared after until both the High Keeper and the guard disappeared and sounds of their footsteps faded away. The Apprentice felt a stab of guilt and regret for not telling the High Keeper that he had skipped most of Gerhold's journal entries, especially after Yorlan had let him off with no punishment for being caught in the restricted section. The High Keeper ignored a major offense, and in return Jarrell was going to have very little work to show. Jarrell's stomach did a backflip at the thought of having to show the old man the scattered entries that he had been copying and reading over the past two nights.

How angry would the High Keeper be with him once he saw how little of the journals Jarrell had copied? Would he decide to punish the Apprentice for sneaking into the lower levels? Jarrell felt his insides continue to squirm at the thought of having to explain himself to the High Keeper as he opened the door to the small, dark room. Tonight, he would copy as much of the manuscript as he could and ignore Ernhold's jests and his own desire to continue with the story. Perhaps, if he worked quickly enough, he would be able to make up enough time to satisfy the High Keeper.

Jarrell flopped down into his chair and sighed, knowing that no matter what he was feeling about disappointing the High Keeper it would mean very little once the journals were in front of him. He had promised the very same thing the night before, but despite his desire to not disappoint the High Keeper, Jarrell wanted to find out what had happened with Gerhold even more. Had the slayer caught up with Harkin? Perhaps he was still alive even today, still hunting monsters from the shadows. That would make for quite a tale, and if Jarrell did end up being expelled for failing to copy the journals and sneaking into the restricted section, then maybe he could travel to various towns and taverns telling the stories. The life of a bard did sound like the type of adventure he would

A Dawn of Death

enjoy.

    The next ten minutes crawled by as Jarrell unpacked his things and laid out his blank sheets of parchment, quills, and bottles of ink, while the battle in his mind raged on as to whether he should continue with whatever entry Ernhold pointed him to or instead just copy down as much as he could. Just as he finished, Jarrell heard the click of the door handle and creaking metal as the door swung open. Ernhold swept in without a word and closed the door behind him, his dark hood pulled up usual to obscure his face. The man barely even glanced at Jarrell as he carefully set the leather-bound set of journals down on the desk and then stalked across the room where he sat in his usual spot at the end of the table.

    "Good evening," he said, and Jarrell nodded.

    "And to you as well."

    "I suppose you know that this is to be our last night working together? I have other business to attend to. As a travelling merchant I rarely stay in a place longer than is necessary, as time spent in the same place is money lost. It makes life easier," Ernhold said. "Do not worry, though; you will have the end of your story before the night is through."

    "If this is to be our last night, then I should do my best to copy down what I can. The High Keeper will be checking on my progress in the morning and I believe he expects me to have most of the journals copied down," Jarrell answered, but Ernhold only waved his hand in protest.

    "A foolish thing to do indeed, Apprentice. What do you think your High Keeper wants from these journals? All the stories he already has? Stories that every wet nurse, maid, and travelling tavern bard know and tell on a nightly basis?"

    "I was commanded to copy down as much as I could and determine their authenticity."

    "Your High Keeper already knows the journals are real, as do you. I see it in your eyes. You know this is the story of the greatest monster hunter who ever lived, and the fact that you are debating whether to finish the story is incomprehensible. A true scholar would leap at such a chance."

    Ernhold stood and walked in front of Jarrell. For the first time the young Apprentice felt fear, along with the usual uneasiness, come over him as the man leaned over the desk and began sifting through the pages. He stopped at a marked page and once again returned to his seat.

    "That is where you shall begin your work tonight," he said.

"But—" Jarrell had started to protest when Ernhold interrupted him.

"But what?" The man's voice was slightly raised and agitated. "You want to know the end of the story, and so does your High Keeper. Your choice is a simple one: finish the story and be the first to venture into this new realm of knowledge or retread the very same ground already crushed and withered. Make your choice, Apprentice, but know this: the world will know of what happened to Gerhold of Vilheim, whether from you or another."

Jarrell stared at the man for a moment before turning his eyes to the crumpled, decaying pile of pages on the desk. The entry that Ernhold had selected was written on a newer piece of parchment, which, surprisingly, was dated only three years prior. The young man's mind raced as he tried to decide what to do. Slowly but surely, though, his eyes began to drift back and forth across the page, and soon he was once again delving into the forgotten story of Gerhold of Vilheim.

Vilheim
SILVER QUARTER
BRONZE QUARTER
GOLD QUARTER
CASTLE NEFFGARD
SLUMS
Voldar River
1
2
3
4
5
6
7
8
9
10
11

Vilheim Map Key

1. The Western Gate
2. Vilheim Chapel
3. The Skydocks
4. The City Watch
5. Mister Quinn's Home
6. Morvin's Warehouse
7. The Drolgin
8. The Northern Bridge
9. The Iron Horse Tavern
10. The Gold District Chapel
11. Castle Neffgard

J.S. Matthews

Chapter 1: The Shadow Stalker

Gerhold of Vilheim, Journal Entry: February 3, 5947 of the Common Age

Another layer of fresh snow fell these past few nights and with it another townsman was killed, which means the creature claimed its sixth victim. Night is beginning to fall once again over Breganwarf, and I am more than ready for the cool relief of darkness. Being in this city has made me miss Vilheim even more than I am used to. They are similar in some ways: architecture and the dress of the locals to name a few, but it is how they are different that truly matters. While Vilheim has its own problems, Breganwarf is a stinking, rotting, mess of a city. Every street is crowded and cramped with all manner of peoples, mostly the poor and downtrodden, all climbing over each other like rats. The streets are lined with clogged drainage ditches that overflow with waste whenever the snows melt, discarded possessions and refuse litter the ground, the many poor and hungry beg in the alleyways even in the coldest months, and the orphaned and abandoned children run around wherever they please causing all kinds of mischief. It is much colder here along the coast of the North Sea, especially during winter, which bothers Roland in particular.

This has been a long hunt, nearly a month now we have spent in this city, but on this night, it will come to an end. Roland and I have spent much of the past three weeks traipsing through the worst parts of this filthy city, searching for any evidence of our prey, and for the most part we found nothing of note. The creature left no trace behind whenever it killed, or at least no trace that we could find, and after the first two weeks it felt as though we were trying to catch wisps of smoke with our bare hands. All of this changed four days ago, though.

I learned from an old beggar that Emric, the count of Breganwarf, recently

A Dawn of Death

buried his wife, a young woman who fell ill and died only a day before the first killing. I immediately began to wonder if the death of this woman and the killings were linked, and so we turned our efforts towards the count. It took Roland and me only a few days to unravel the mystery after this first clue fell into place. I had already been suspicious, but after a lengthy investigation I now know that those initial suspicious were correct. The creature is a Shadow Stalker, a demon that can only manifest itself in darkness and is brought into this world when someone dies still holding onto a feeling of the deepest regret. These emotions tear a hole in the veil between our world and the spirit realm, drawing the creature out and into the physical realm. I suspected that the young countess took a very dark secret to her grave and that secret drew the demon into this world. Now it stalks the city streets at night, searching for its victims.

To understand and hunt this creature I needed to uncover what it was this woman was hiding that caused her such agonizing pain, and I found my answer a day later. We were able to speak with the beggar once again and he directed us to an old woman who lived on the edge of the slums near the docks. We were able to speak to the woman and after a few coins she was willing to tell us what she knew. Her daughter had been a maid in the count's manor and told her mother everything that transpired within the place. The countess had been with child, but when she gave birth, the baby was stillborn and had already passed from this world. The count, afraid that such a thing would ruin his reputation, had the body incinerated and forbade anyone to speak of it again, driving his wife into a fit of uncontrollable grief. For days the countess refused to eat or drink, longing for her lost child, until finally she too passed. The woman was buried the same day that she died, and that very night the first of the six deaths, the young maid with whose mother we now spoke, occurred.

A sad tale to say the least and one that only grew more tragic with each death. All six victims had been related to the birth in some way: the young maid who tended to the countess, the healer who delivered the child, the two servants who disposed of the body, and the count's brother and sister, both of whom who encouraged him to hide the event. All these individuals are now dead, with the count the only living person who knew about the stillbirth. A Shadow Stalker must carry out vengeance and satisfy the departing soul that drew it into this world before it can pursue its own desires. As soon as the deed is done the creature will be free to do as it wills and roam this world free of any bonds. I must stop the demon tonight as it will most certainly be pursuing its final

J.S. Matthews

victim: Count Emric.

I know where the demon will be tonight and with the help of Roland and Nethrin, I believe we can destroy it. The plan must work or else the demon will be free to roam these lands and will be nearly impossible to find and kill. We have spent nearly a month searching for it and the hunt will end tonight, for good or ill.

The moon hung high overhead in the night sky, blocked only by a few wisps of gray clouds that passed across the star-streaked sea of black. It was cold, and a fresh coating of powdery snow blanketed the city of Breganwarf, hiding the layers of ice, dirt, and poorly paved streets beneath. The city was nearly deserted save for a few drunkards and sailors who either did not know or did not care about the warnings posted by the City Watch about the dangers of wandering through the streets at night. Six deaths in the past four weeks had made the city inhabitants terrified to be out once the sun set, all seemingly committed by the same individual, or at least that is what the City Watch claimed. Only the priests and monks seemed to think that something supernatural could be behind the deaths.

This was not surprising as few peasants would have the knowledge of such things nor would they have even wanted to believe that something like a Shadow Stalker could exist. This demon thrived on stealth and remaining unseen, and this worked in tandem with the natural human desire to ignore and excuse those things they could not explain. The creature could only manifest physically in complete darkness, and it feared light more than any mortal weapon. Breganwarf was a maze of tightly packed tri-level wooden houses, tenements, inns, taverns, and tall stone towers, which provided an infinite number of hiding spots for such a creature. The slums were even worse with most of the streets being lit by only a few odd torches. It was a dark and sinister place to begin with, now made worse by the threat of a shadow demon stalking the cramped streets and alleyways.

Gerhold stood alone in the shadows of a small side street, listening to the sounds of voices and laughter coming from a nearby tavern. There was no music of course; he had heard nothing of the sort for over a hundred years, though the silence pained him now even more than it did the first time those many years ago. The cold winds whistled as they passed between the tightly packed buildings and

A Dawn of Death

twisting streets. Gerhold had no trouble ignoring the freezing night air, as vampires were never affected by the cold, and instead he focused his attention on the massive stone castle at the other side of the square. Breganwarf Keep, surrounded by a twenty-foot-high wall of stone, stood high above the crowded city and it was the home of Count Emric. Many of the castle windows high above were lit with the dull orange light of torches that flickered and clashed against the dark sky. The castle was a paradise when compared to the filthy town below.

The sounds of merriment grew louder and Gerhold found himself smirking at the thought of the drunken sailors and dockworkers making their way to the taverns. Most of these fools would not dare to confront even a single goblin whelp but were more than willing to brave the dangers of the night as long as they were guaranteed liquor and women. A decrepit and corrupt city indeed, he thought to himself.

Just then the vampire's keen ears picked up the sound of muffled footsteps coming from somewhere further down the street that wound its way around the outer wall of the Keep. Soon the silhouette of a man appeared in the distance and he made his way down the path in the direction of Gerhold. He was tall and wrapped in a thick grey cloak, and in his right hand he held a long silver spear that clunked heavily against the stone road with every other step. His strides were quick and strong, and the man covered the distance to the little alleyway with little effort. Soon he stood in front of Gerhold, leaning against his spear.

"You know you look a bit unnerving standing in the dark like that," the man said and threw back his hood to reveal a mane of shoulder length dark hair and a wry smile." If I did not know it was you, I would have thought you to be the one behind the murders. You match the description passed on by the City Watch almost perfectly."

"You were only able to see me because I wanted you to, Roland," Gerhold answered. "Did he take the bait?"

"Possibly. He did not seem to react much when I told him." Roland moved into the alley. "If he does not fall for it then we are going to be out to sea without a sail."

"He will take it; a man like him would not pass up the chance to ensure his reputation remains unspoiled."

"Did Nethrin move the old woman?" Roland asked.

"He should have moved her this morning, at any rate I am more concerned about whether his trap is ready," Gerhold responded and Roland scoffed.

"I am more worried about whether his plan will work or not. That boy gets distracted at the worst times."

"Nethrin will be fine. His inventions have saved your life more than once in the past year alone." Gerhold pulled his crossblade from its holster on his back and checked to make sure it was loaded and ready.

"He is a talented tinker, but I am hesitant to rely on him, especially when it comes to standing face to face with a Shadow Stalker."

"As long as the count cooperates, we should have very little to worry about," Gerhold said.

"And what if the count sends someone else to deal with this problem? What if he just stays in within his walls? What will we do then?"

"A man like Count Emric will want to deal with this problem directly," Gerhold answered.

"And what if you are wrong?" Roland asked just as a metal door that was built into the Keep's outer wall opened.

Three men stepped through the opening out into the street, locking the thick metal door securely behind them. The first two men were tall and broad shouldered, clearly soldiers or guards of some sort, and the third man was obviously overweight and wore a thick fur coat.

"See? You worry too much," Gerhold said with a smile.

He crept forward, making sure to remain in the shadows, and listened to what the men were saying.

"It's too bloody cold to be out 'ere tonight if you ask me," one of the larger men said.

"Aye, I agree. We should be drinking ale and bothering that pretty new maid you hired," the other man added.

"Will the two of you be quiet? By the gods it is far too hard to find good help these days. Instead, I must drag both of you brainless fools around with me while listening to your foolish drivel," Count Emric responded.

"I bet my piss 'ould freeze before it even hit the ground," one of the guards mumbled.

Together, the three men made their way down the street and towards the center of the city. Gerhold motioned for Roland to follow as he ducked out of the little alley and fell in twenty paces behind the count and his guards. They made sure to keep their distance as best they could to not draw attention to

A Dawn of Death

themselves while continuing down the deserted snow-swept streets. Gerhold was going to put an end to the shadow demon, but to do so he needed the count. Several hours earlier, Roland, disguised as a peasant, had gone to a local tavern frequented by one of the count's servants. He spread rumors about the death of the countess and that he had heard these rumors from an old woman who lived near the docks, rumors that the servant would then pass on to the count, which would hopefully draw Emric out of the safety of his keep. The trap had been set, and now the bait was slowly moving into place.

"So 'ow come we did not just wait 'til mornin', eh? It'd be a might bit warmer by then and we could get some decent sleep," one of the count's bodyguards complained again. "Besides, the docks ain't no place for someone of your stature, m' lord."

"With all these killings happening as of late, the morning sounds like a much better idea to me," the other added and Gerhold saw the count shake his head irritably.

"Will you idiots stop your blathering already? This business must be taken care of without delay. I thought I made myself clear on this matter before we left," Emric said in a frustrated tone.

"Well, we was only tryin' ta help ye think thin's through is all."

"If I ever need help thinking things through, you two idiots would be the last people I would ever come to. That foolish old woman, the mother of a dead servant, is spreading rumors about me, and all I need you two empty-headed, knuckle-dragging, fools for is to make sure those rumors are stopped."

"So, we are going to kill her then?" one of the guards asked, and Gerhold saw the count rub his forehead in frustration before answering.

"Yes, you barbaric buffoon. Killing is the only thing the two of you are good for."

"And scaring them shop-keepers and merchants."

"Gods help me if I ever have to rely on the two of you for anything more than that," Emric muttered under his breath as they turned a corner.

Gerhold and Roland watched as the three men disappeared around the bend and then sped up to make sure they did not lose sight of the count. They came around the corner and halted as Emric and his two guards had come to a halt and were standing only ten feet away. In front of them in the center of the poorly lit street stood a tall slender figure shrouded in darkness. It had few discernable features other than its thin spindly fingers, its stretched and distorted outline that resembled the shape of a human, and a set of black empty spaces where its eyes should have been. The blowing snow seemed to pass right through the shadow as if it were not there at all and the men seemed to visibly shiver in its presence.

"Wha's all this then?" one of the guards said and stepped forward, his hand on the hilt of the longsword that hung at his side.

It made no sound but just stared at the man. The demon raised its left hand and the shadowy outline slowly morphed from a hand and fingers to a long thin blade. The first guard drew his sword while the second man struggled to pull his free. In the blink of an eye, the creature moved, becoming one with the darkness and disappeared, only to reappear a moment later behind the first guard. Before the man could react, the creature's blade burst through his chest and he was lifted off his feet before being tossed carelessly to the side. The guard's body slammed into a nearby stone wall and collapsed in a bloody heap, staining the frost covered ground a deep crimson.

The second guard stared at the creature, his hands shaking not from the cold but from fear, while Count Emric backed away in horror. Gerhold drew his crossbow as the creature turned and faced the cowering guard, once again raising its bladed arm. The guard seemed to gather whatever vestiges of courage that remained and swung his sword with all his might. It struck the shadow, and immediately the creature vanished into the darkness, leaving behind the panting and surprised bodyguard as well as the petrified count.

"Did you kill it? Is it gone?" Emric asked in a frightened tone. "Where did it go?"

"I don't bloody know!" the guard answered and spun in place, searching for any sign of the creature. "What in the bloody hells was that?"

Just then the darkness came to life once more, and the shadow demon leapt from out of the darkness and slashed its bladed hand at the guard. He raised his sword to deflect the blow, but the creatures arm passed through the blade and beheaded the man in once swift stroke. The guard's headless body fell limply to the ground, leaving the surprised count splattered in blood and frozen by the horrifying sight of his dead protectors. Emric watched as the creature stepped over the pool of crimson blood and seemed to slither in his direction. As the Shadow Stalked drew nearer the count took a step back and fell, scrambling on his hands and knees while crying out for mercy from the creature, which only seemed to savor the moment before this important kill.

A Dawn of Death

It once again raised its arm, preparing to finish the final step in the binding magical curse that held the demon enslaved, but just before the creature could slay the count, Gerhold fired his crossbow. The silver bolt slammed into the ground between the demon and Emric, exploding with a loud *BOOM* and a flash of bright light. The vampire covered his eyes and heard the piercing shriek of rage echo throughout the streets. When he opened them, the creature was gone, once again melding into the darkness, and both he and Roland dashed forward to the blinded and disoriented count, who still lay sprawled on the ground with his back against the wall of a nearby stone building.

"Get up, you fool! That thing could be back at any moment," Roland said and dragged the confused count to his feet. Emric swayed on the spot and Roland was forced to allow the count to lean on his shoulder for support as they started down the street.

"What is going on? Who are you? Leave me be, I—I have money. I promise I can give you more gold than you can ask for if you do not hurt me," the count whined as more tears streamed down his face.

"Stop your blubbering. We are not here to harm you. Gods know I would not mind it, though," Roland said as he continued to drag the man across the street. "Do you see it?"

Gerhold jogged this way and that, leading Roland and the count through the streets, trying to make sure he kept to the well-lit paths and avoided the side streets and alleys. His crossbow had already been reloaded with a second flashbolt and he held it at the ready, his keen eyes searching for any sign of the demon.

"No, but it is out there somewhere. Keep up; we only have a few blocks to go," Gerhold said just as the shadows in a nearby alley seemed to come to life.

Immediately he turned and fired his crossbow and another explosion and flash of light ripped through the air, followed by the creature's screams of rage. Gerhold quickly reloaded his crossbow and stood at the ready as they rounded another bend. Again, the creature appeared, this time above them along one of the high arching rooftops, and again it was driven away by the hunter, only to manifest again in front of Roland and the count. Gerhold fired again, hoping he could hold off the demon long enough for them to reach the docks. He pushed the other two men onward down the street, firing off shot after shot into the darkness that surrounded them every time that he caught sight of the shifting shadowy figure. Soon the sound of ocean waves could be heard crashing against the frozen coast ahead. They turned down the next street and ran parallel to the coast as fast as they could towards a small line of dingy tenements that surrounded a small open courtyard.

Gerhold said a silent prayer, hoping that Nethrin had finished setting up their trap in time. If not, he was not sure how they would hold off the demon and keep it from killing the count. Suddenly the creature appeared in front of Roland, who was still dragging the sobbing count along beside him, and it swung its bladed arm, intent on killing the two men with a single stroke. Gerhold launched himself forward and slammed his shoulder into Roland's back, sending both men crashing to the ground, and Gerhold felt a burning pain in his shoulder as the monster's claw nicked his shoulder. He ignored the pain, and as soon as he hit the ground, Gerhold rolled over and fired his last flashbolt at the creature, forcing it to fall back into the shadows with a scream of rage.

"Get up, now!" Gerhold yelled and dragged the count to his feet.

"Where did it go?" Roland asked as they sprinted the rest of the way to the little open square.

They ran into the center of the plaza and Gerhold threw the count against the icy pavement where he sat and wept. Both Gerhold and Roland stood back-to-back, their eyes darting this way and that, searching for any sign of the Shadow Stalker.

"Do you see it?" Gerhold asked.

"No, but I am more concerned if Nethrin got the trap ready or not," Roland answered. Just then the shadows at the end of the path began to shift and change until the dark outline of the shadow demon was visible.

"Just worry about keeping this fool alive," Gerhold said and kicked the count lightly. "If he is killed, then we will have little chance of finding it again."

"We need to be alive to protect him, though," Roland added as they turned to face the creature.

The demon stood ten paces from where they were, but this time it stayed away, watching, and studying them. For a moment it just stared as if planning what to do next. They had nowhere to run now; they had trapped themselves in this place, and the only way out would be through the demon. The creature took a step forward but remained cautious of the two men.

"You are different," a hissing voice emanated from the shadowy figure. "Still, you will not keep me from my quarry. Give me what I want, and I will kill you quickly."

"If you want him, then come and take him," Gerhold responded. He

A Dawn of Death

pulled the count to his feet and held the sobbing man in front of him.

"No, no please! I beg you; do not let it take me!" the count shrieked and tried to break away from Gerhold's grip.

"Come, demon. Come and claim what is yours," Gerhold taunted again.

The creature hissed and let out a high-pitched screech. Both of its arms morphed into crescent shaped blades, and it began to slowly inch forward, the lifeless dark slits where its eyes should have been flashing with rage. Gerhold watched as the creature drew closer, waiting for the right moment to spring the trap. The demon raised its arm, the shadow blade prepared to kill.

"Now, Nethrin!" Gerhold yelled.

A second later a bright light exploded from a nearby alley, followed by a line of raging orange flames that raced forward through the courtyard. The demon let out a scream and tried to disappear, only to be cut off by the circle of blinding firelight. It dashed back and forth, trying to find some way through the wall of fire, but there was none; the creature was trapped. Gerhold threw the count backward and away from the demon as it turned and faced them. There was only one way to truly kill a shadow demon and that was with sunlight. Gerhold knew that they could not keep the creature contained until morning. Thankfully, they had already come up with an alternate solution. Gerhold reached into his coat pocket searching for a small metal cylinder that contained a sunflare, an invention of Nethrin's that perfectly mimicked sunlight. It had worked on vampires, but he had never tested it on a demon, at least until now. Gerhold fished around his coat pocket but to no avail, the sunflare was not there. He desperately checked his other pockets, hoping he had just misplaced it but they were also empty.

"Any time now," Roland yelled as the demon lurched towards them, the twin shadow scythes at the ready.

"It is not here! I do not have it!" Gerhold called back as the creature let out a terrifying screech and leapt forward.

Gerhold raised his sword and parried the blow, leaving the demon surprised and even more enraged. Silver was a magical metal and so it could deflect the demon's attacks and even wound it, but without the sunflare there was no way to truly defeat the creature. Gerhold dodged another attack, and the creature turned and swung at Roland, who leapt out of the way and jabbed at the monster with his spear.

"Where in the hells did you leave it?" Roland asked as the creature renewed its attacks on Gerhold, who lashed out at it with his blade, spinning and striking.

"I must have dropped it when we fell. You go find it! I can handle this lot," Gerhold yelled back and slashed the demon across the stomach.

Roland knew better than to argue and without hesitation the man rolled past the attacking demon and leapt through to the other side of the flames. Gerhold glared at the creature and readied his weapon once more as he was now the only thing that stood between the demon and its freedom. How long could he hold off the creature alone, though?

The demon lunged forward flailing its arms left and right as Gerhold expertly parried each strike. Had he been a normal human he would have been overwhelmed by the attacks, but Gerhold was superior to any human. His speed and quickness allowed him to match the demon, and the powerful strikes that would have forced a normal man to the ground felt like nothing more than a normal impact. They danced back and forth between the flames with Gerhold doing his best to keep the creature from reaching the count, but the fires were slowly starting to die, and if the creature escaped, there would be little he could do capture it again.

Gerhold dove to the side and avoided another wild strike from the shadow demon and briefly went on the offensive before being forced back. Slowly but surely the creature was wearing him down, and soon Gerhold faltered and the demon lashed out with a series of furious attacks that knocked the hunter to his knees. The shadow demon bore down on him with all its might and knocked his sword to the side before slashing at his head, an attack that Gerhold barely avoided as his silver blade went skidding across the frozen ground while he dove out of the way. His shoulder wound throbbed and his breathing was heavy as he rolled to his feet and turned to face the demon, which now stood between Gerhold and his sword. He pulled his crossblade from its holster and flicked the small switch near the trigger, causing the arms to flip forward and a slender silver blade to emerge just in time to parry another blow.

Gerhold was thrown off his feet and into the air by the force of the blow and came crashing down onto the frozen stone with enough force to knock the wind out of him. His head spun from the pain, but he forced himself to ignore it as best he could while slowly getting to his knees. The demon stood only a few paces away, but instead of finishing off Gerhold, it turned and started towards the count who still lay near the edge of the now-dying ring of fire. Gerhold tried to stand, but his head began to swim, and his vision blurred. Suddenly he saw the outline of a person on the other side of the shrinking wall of fire, and between the pounding of his head and the triumphant shriek of the demon he could barely make out the words the man was yelling.

"Gerhold, duck!" Roland yelled and Gerhold could barely make out the shimmering glass vial as it flew and landed at the foot of the shadow demon.

Gerhold threw himself as low as he could against the pavement and covered his head as the sunflare exploded, bathing the entire square in a blinding light. The demon let out a second scream only this time it was different, an agonizing cry that echoed through the streets. The sunflare burned for only half a minute before Gerhold felt the burning heat begin to fade, and already the ear-piercing shrieks had died away along with the searing heat. Gerhold pulled his arm back from his head and stared at where the demon had been standing, only to see a smoking pile of ash in front of the still weeping count. Gerhold felt a strong hand grab him underneath his shoulder and lift him to his feet.

"Come on; we have to go," Roland said and Gerhold grunted in response. "By the Gods, you just stood up to a shadow demon and lived. Too bad no one is going to hear that story."

"We need to get out of here before the City Watch shows up; they should be here any minute," Gerhold said between deep painful breaths.

Another set of footsteps echoed from across the square, and the two men turned to see a skinny young man running towards them. Nethrin had a large grin on his face as usual and was already mid-sentence by the time he reached them.

"Master Gerhold, Master Roland, why, that was incredible! I cannot believe the sunflare worked against a shadow demon. I mean I knew it worked on vampires, but I was not sure it would work on a demon," the young man started, but Roland cut him off.

"Not right now, Nethrin, we need to leave. Get my things."

"Oh, yes, the City Watch, I almost forgot. Where are we heading?" Nethrin asked while scrambling about, gathering Gerhold's sword and crossbows.

"To the safe house in the slums you fool! Where else would we go?" Roland answered irritably.

"Oh, yes, of course. I'll lead the way, but what about him?" he asked and pointed towards the count.

"The City Watch will take care of him. Now, to the slums, boy; lead on."

With that the young man dashed forward down the street with Roland carrying Gerhold in tow. The sounds of the City Watch could be heard approaching from the distance, and the soft sobbing sounds of the terrified count still echoing in the distance. Gerhold limped along with support from Roland, but in spite of the pain from his various wounds he felt elated, excited. The hunt was over; another monster had been slain, and he was still alive.

A Dawn of Death

Chapter 2: A New Job

Gerhold of Vilheim, Journal Entry: February 4, 5947 of the Common Age

Two days have passed since our encounter with the shadow demon, and we have spent most of our time hiding away in a dingy, must, tenement in the poorest area of the Breganwarf slums. My wounds have healed and once again I find myself thanking the Gods for this curse, as strange as that may seem. It would have taken a normal man months to fully heal from such wounds, while I am fit to fight after only a few days of rest. I usually prefer the city, but after spending so much time here in this awful smelling hole, I find myself longing for the open air and green fields. The City Watch has also stepped up their patrols ever since the count was found, and of course all of this, the murders and the count's attack, have been blamed on the poorest members of the city. Supposedly there are dark mages hiding in the slums and they summoned a creature to attack the count, or at least those are the lies being spread. No matter, though, as we will be departing as soon as we can.

Roland has gone to retrieve our payment for the job, and Nethrin is busy constructing some strange new design. Other than the smell and the constant disturbance from the City Watch raids, it has been nice to have some time to myself and gather my thoughts. I am not sure where we will head off to next, but I heard rumors of a coven of witches that is hiding in the forests of Fallorn to the east. There is rarely ever a shortage of jobs for us, not in this world. Tyriel is a place of beauty, but beneath that gilded exterior is a sick and twisted core, an unending tide of evil that seeps through like blood from an open wound. I will be fighting this tide until the end days or until I finally breath my last.

I wonder sometimes, though if I will ever succumb to that same tide. The monster inside of me has been dormant for some time, biding its time, waiting for me to be weak enough to pounce. My fight against the beast is never ending though it is good to have a respite from the mental struggle of keeping the scratching and snarling at bay. However, I am only now beginning to realize the threat this poses as I see no end in sight. I am immortal, cursed to live on until I am defeated or until I fall prey to the monster inside. How long can I fight this battle? How long can I defend against darkness of my own mind? I can fight monsters with silver, but what do I have to defend against my own insanity?

Harkin, Lord Friedrich, Pontius Urban; many men who fell to their desire and lust for power. I have read much about the now deceased *Vigil of Righteousness*, most of which paints him as a kind and caring man, at least until his later years. If such a good and pious man can fall prey to the temptations of power, then how long will I be able to last? Will there be a time when I am the one who is hunted? I try not to dwell on these thoughts, but they are hard to ignore. If I ever do turn, who will be there to stop me?

Gerhold closed the leather journal and stowed it safely in his pack before standing up and making his way over to a nearby window. Dark curtains blocked the incoming sunlight, but Gerhold could not help but pull them back every so often to catch a glimpse of what was going on in the cramped streets below. In the slums there was almost always something interesting happening, whether it was a scuffle between ruffians or between members of the City Watch and the peasants. He could only look out for a short time before the bright light of the sun began to sting his eyes and face, forcing him to once again withdraw into the dusty dank rooms of the shack. Most days during the winter were cloudy, which gave Gerhold some respite from the stinging rays of the sun, but today was not one of those days, and after only a few seconds of looking out, he felt the familiar burning sensation along his face and eyes.

With a sigh he closed the curtains and made his way back over to the little desk and pulled out a small book. Inside were hastily written notes, anything that he had heard over the past three years that may have pertained to rumors of the whereabouts of Harkin Valakir. A tale of a powerful vampire living in the hills near Fallorn, attacks on the road between Morovia and Penland, or disappearances in the city of Kingsport, all of these could hold the key to finding Harkin. He had spent a hundred years searching for the vampire and failed, but how could he stop his search while knowing the vampire was out there still,

A Dawn of Death

waiting for him? No doubt Gerhold's enemy was still planning his next move. Harkin possessed a very powerful artifact, a channeling stone, but what he planned on doing with it still eluded Gerhold. He knew that Harkin was a mage, but he did not know what a mage, could do with such an artifact.

It was frustrating to say the least, to know that his quarry was out there, somewhere, but unable to find even a trace of him. Gerhold was the greatest monster hunter in the world, and yet even he had failed to find Harkin. What hope did he have now after failing for so many years? There was one comforting thought, though, and it was that Harkin would eventually find him. No matter how long Gerhold went without finding the vampire, eventually they would meet again, and he would make sure it would be their last. Just then the sound of footsteps came echoing from the hallway, and Gerhold turned to see Nethrin striding through the doorway.

"Good day, Master Gerhold," the young man said as he came darting into the room.

"And to you, Nethrin. Has Roland returned yet?" Gerhold asked and the young man nodded.

"Yes, he just got back a few minutes ago. However, I wanted to speak to you. I have been doing some research on Channeling Stones, as you requested, and I thought you would want to hear what I have discovered so far."

"Indeed, what have you found?" Gerhold asked as Nethrin laid out a set of extremely old books across the desk.

"Well, there really was not much to go on, and to be honest I found very little of note other than these two volumes," he said and pointed to the two books. "These both mention a few things about ancient relics taken from Arden called Rune Stones. Apparently, these were pieces of rock that could be enchanted with any number of spells to bolster their effects or create new magic entirely. It is some very interesting reading, but there was nothing about any channeling stones, at least not by that name."

Gerhold bent down to examine the texts as the pages were frayed and smudged from years of use. After a moment, the hunter shook his head and sighed in frustration.

"Three years and this is all we have to go on," he added. "You would think that such a powerful artifact would have some sort of record."

"Well, if it is as powerful as you believe then perhaps the information was hidden intentionally."

"Perhaps, but I hope we can find something. I do not like the idea of running into Harkin and not knowing what we are going to face." Gerhold shook his head.

"Hopefully, by then, we can learn more about it. I will keep looking, and if I have my way, we will have a few tricks of our own for him," Nethrin said and patted Gerhold's shoulder. "Anyway, I think Roland wanted to see you."

"I imagine so. Thank you, Nethrin, and let me know if you find anything else."

"Of course," the young man said excitedly and gathered up the books before leaving the room.

Gerhold smiled and shook his head, contemplating just how little Nethrin had changed over the past few years, as he was still the ever-excited young boy he had always been. After the debacle that was his investigation of the Blightwood, Gerhold realized how helpful it would be to have someone with him who could replenish his supplies and ensure that the hunter always had what he needed. Nethrin was a servant of the Vilheim church but, with a little convincing from Gerhold, the other priests came to the conclusion that it was more important for the young man to help Gerhold on his quests than sweep the dusty floors of the chapel. The young man still had much to learn about being a priest and the study of the Chronicles, but even Brother Francis agreed that Nethrin was needed at Gerhold's side. Along with Roland, the three had been traveling across Midland, slaying bog stalkers, hunting ghosts, and taking on whatever odd contracts they came across along the way.

Perhaps they had been travelling too much, but Gerhold could not help it. Everywhere they went new rumors sprang up, new stories of monsters and creatures of darkness, and with every story and rumor, he had a renewed feeling of hope. Perhaps the next city would bring the key piece information he needed to find Harkin. Maybe the next time they spoke to a travelling merchant he would hear a tale that would lead him to the vampire. Hope was all he had now, for he knew that if Harkin wanted to remain hidden, then there was very little Gerhold could do about it. It was like an irritant in the back of his mind that could not be scratched, a wound that would not heal. So, he traveled and dragged Roland and Nethrin along with him, trying to distract himself from the desperate feelings and cling to whatever hope he could find.

Gerhold made his way out of the little room and down a short flight of rickety steps that creaked and groaned in protest with every step. The shack was

A Dawn of Death

made of three levels that were covered in equal amounts of dust and grime. The wooden walls were cracked and aged, and the windows were impossible to see through as they appeared to have not been cleaned in decades. Gerhold reached the bottom floor and passed through an open room. A small furnace stood in the far corner, flanked by a small counter, that one could only guess was the kitchen, and an ancient wooden table was at the center, covered in all sorts of nick-knacks and tools that belonged to Nethrin. He continued past the jumbled pile of odds and ends and entered the next room where he saw Roland sitting in an uncomfortable chair, ready to open a fresh bottle of wine. There were empty bottles strewn across the floor and the dull stench of alcohol lingered in the musty air.

"Good to see you made it back. Did you get the money?" Gerhold asked, and Roland reached into his coat and tossed a small leather pouch across the room.

"I already took out my part," Roland said and raised the bottle before taking the first sip.

"Of course, you did. Glad to see you are still wasting your pay on drink," Gerhold responded sarcastically.

"Well, these pesky memories won't get rid of themselves, now, will they?"

"You are as talented as you are foolish," Gerhold said and Roland smiled at him.

"Why? Because I drink?"

"Because you could be even more than you are now, but instead of honing your skills you waste your time on drinking and waking up amidst a pile of your own vomit."

"You know, I used to think that way, back when I was a Paladin." He took another drink and laughed. "And what a fool I was. That young idealistic boy who thought that the Vigils were chosen by the Gods to guide their fellow mortals. You know it is taught within the churches that they can do no wrong? How pathetic to believe such nonsense and to know that I once believed it."

"And now you are superior? Falling asleep amidst your own filth? Drinking until you cannot tell your hands from your face? You have truly come a long way from that awful person you used to be."

"You would be doing the same if you were in my place," Roland answered with a sneer.

"I was in your place, the moment I became what I am."

"If vampires could get drunk, I'd bet every one of you would be found dead the morning after you turned from drinking yourself into a stupor and passing out in some ditch covered in your own drool and vomit. Regret, it seems, is something our two kinds share. You just can't do anything about it."

Gerhold stared at his young friend for a moment. Ever since their time in the Blightwood, Roland had become increasingly depressed over the betrayal and his excommunication. He had already been disowned by his family when he joined the Paladins; he had passed through years of training to become the youngest member of the Vigil's Guard in over a thousand years, only to have all of it taken from him. The beliefs that had made up the foundation of Roland's life had been shaken, and now he did not know what he believed. He was a ship without a sail, being tossed about by the waves with no direction or way to guide his journey.

"Feeling regret is not a choice, but how you respond is," Gerhold said and turned to leave.

"Are you telling me you did not have any struggles when you turned? Did you ever stop to wonder why the Gods would do something so horrible to you if they cared for you the way the Chronicles and the priests tell you?" Roland set his bottle down and stood. "I have been traveling with you for over three years now, and the more I see of this world the more I start to believe it was all some sort of accident. How could all-knowing Gods create such a horrible place?"

"Did you ever stop to wonder why the world is as it is? Everything we see, all the demons we slay, every monster we kill, they are all the product of our greed, our hatred, our own malicious desires. You stand here and tell me that the Gods made a mistake, but it is us who have made the mistakes," Gerhold said and Roland scoffed.

"Why would a caring group of Gods allow that woman to die? Or allow that demon to slaughter so many? If they are so powerful, then why did they not stop it?"

"The same questions can be asked of us," Gerhold answered.

"And yet we did something! Not the Gods, just us. Why should I worry about what the Gods think when they cannot protect the weakest of us?" Roland returned to his seat and spat on the dirty stone floor. "Either there are no Gods or they do not care."

𝔄 𝔇𝔞𝔴𝔫 𝔬𝔣 𝔇𝔢𝔞𝔱𝔥

"We humans have been given great power, Roland, the power of choice. Every choice we make affects the world around us, whether we wish to admit it or not. You think that your drinking and moping about affects only you? Half the time I do not know whether you will be fit to fight or not, and there is Nethrin. The boy sees what you do."

"The boy is old enough now to do as he wishes; he does not need you to watch over him."

"He is, but you need to understand that there was a point when he looked up to you. Now, I am not sure what he sees. The count was the one who made the decision that led to his wife's death, not the Gods. It was men who decided to take the gold and jewels from Arden despite what the Gods asked of them. Everything we have seen, all the evil, the corruption, the death, it is all because of actions of men. We must take responsibility for what we can control and help where we can. We must be the ones to make the right decisions."

Roland bit his lip as if trying to fight back another retort before grabbing his bottle of wine and taking another large gulp. Just then there came a soft knock at the front door, and Gerhold heard Nethrin come sprinting down the creaking steps to answer it.

"That's not the City Watch, is it?" Roland asked and reached for his spear.

"Of course not, they do not knock so kindly before entering," Gerhold answered and calmly made his way over across the room.

He heard the sound of muffled voices and then more footsteps as Nethrin came walking into the little room.

"Master Gerhold, sir, I think there is someone here to see you," Nethrin said as he entered, and Roland relaxed his grip on the spear.

"Who is it?" Gerhold asked and the boy shrugged.

"I have no idea. He is well spoken, though, and does not dress as though he is from these parts. I asked him his name, but he said he had to speak with you and that it was urgent."

Gerhold glanced at Roland for a moment, who returned his quizzical look, then nodded at Nethrin and motioned for him to lead on. Just before he exited the room, Gerhold turned, whipped out one of his small crossbows, and fired a bolt that shattered the bottle Roland was still holding, sending shards of glass in all directions and red wine spilling across the floor.

"Hells and hell fire!" Roland roared. "What was that for?"

"I need you sober in case there is a fight," Gerhold answered and closed the door behind him.

Gerhold could still hear Roland cursing as he made his way across the dingy little kitchen and towards the front door where their guest now stood. He was a thin man with white hair that had been slicked back and wore a fancy-looking overcoat. In his right hand was a long silver cane. Gerhold paused and stared, recognizing the man immediately. A name he had not heard in years sprang to mind: Lorick Dren.

"Gerhold of Vilheim, it is good to see you after all these years," the man said in an old gravelly voice.

"I wish I could say the same, Lorick," Gerhold answered, and the other man smiled.

"Still holding on to that old grudge, eh? What has it been, thirty years since our run-in in Kingsport?"

"Nearly that, I imagine. You will understand if I am not entirely happy to see you then," Gerhold said and rested his right hand on the hilt of his sword. "Not since you tried to have me killed."

"The other Seekers wanted you dead, not I," Lorick said. "Besides, we're not here for you, if that is what you are thinking," the man said with a reassuring smile. "After we cleaned up that mess in Kingsport, the Seekers realized you were only trying to help. I had your name expunged from the book. That's why you haven't seen hide nor hair of us for the last thirty years."

"And the mercenaries that were sent after me in Myrthia? That was only a few years ago."

"A minor misunderstanding, I assure you," Lorick answered. "Everything has been fixed since then."

"Glad to hear you figured things out. Now why are you here?" Gerhold asked and Lorick took a few steps forward before setting himself down on an old moldy chair.

"I have a proposition for you," he said.

Gerhold held up his hand.

"Then save your breath. I wish to have nothing to do with you or the Seekers."

"It would be wise for you to hear what I have to say, Gerhold," Lorick answered.

Just then the door to the back room opened and Roland came stomping

A Dawn of Death

out, still as angry at Gerhold destroying his bottle.

"Turning down another job, are you?" Roland said and sat across from the silver haired man.

"This does not concern you, Roland. Let me handle this one," Gerhold said.

"Taking on partners, now are we?" Lorick said with a smile before turning to face Roland. "My name is Lorick Dren. I represent a certain group of people who deal in the same business as the two of you."

"And what group is that?" Roland asked.

"We call ourselves the Seekers," Lorick answered, and Roland raised an eyebrow.

"Never heard of you."

"That is because they live in the shadows. They use spies and secrecy to gather information and then hire out the jobs to hunters and mercenaries, an expensive business that requires a hefty amount of funding from noblemen and criminals alike," Gerhold responded and glared at Lorick.

"We do what we must to protect the people of this world, same as the two of you. Master Gerhold here likes to make it out as though we are some sinister group with dark intentions, but the truth is we do what is necessary to fight evil, nothing more. Sometimes that means allying ourselves with some rather unscrupulous characters, but it is always for a purpose." The man leaned back in his chair. "The Seekers have performed a necessary task for centuries now, a task that you are well acquainted with."

"We do not gather political power and favors for performing such tasks," Gerhold said.

"Yes, but you collect gold, which is far less useful," Lorick answered. "Every lord who is indebted to us and every king who sends us word is doing so to protect those who are innocent. Surely you can see how such things are far more effective when compared to running around the countryside assisting a backwater village with every bog lurker and barghest that happens to pop up."

"You are all corrupt," Gerhold muttered under his breath.

"Whatever you think of our organization can be put aside for now, we have more important business to attend to. I didn't spend the past week searching for you to discuss the morality of the Seekers finances," Lorick said and pulled a sealed envelope from his jacket pocket.

"I told you, I want nothing to do with the Seekers," Gerhold said, but

Roland stood and took the letter.

"What is this?" Roland asked.

"It is the last report we received from our men in Vilheim. You should read it."

"Vilheim? You have men in Vilheim?" Gerhold asked suspiciously.

"We have informants in every city," Lorick answered as Roland tore open the envelope and began to scan its contents. Gerhold watched warily as Roland's eyes narrowed and his expression changed. "When did you get this?"

"Just over a week ago," Lorick answered. "Belick was one of our most trusted informants, but I am afraid we have heard nothing from him since the arrival of that letter."

"What does it say?" Gerhold asked and Roland handed him the hastily scrawled note.

Send help immediately. The situation has deteriorated, and the guards are quarantining the slums, maybe even the entire city. The outbreak has been contained but we do not know for how long. The dark fog has not lifted and every day it seems to grow deeper. Send whomever you can, Vilheim is under siege.

-Belick

Gerhold stared at the paper for a moment and then at Roland; he could tell that they both had the same questions running through their minds.

"You see now why I brought this to you?" Lorick said, and Gerhold shifted his gaze to the older man.

"What is this?" Gerhold asked and handed the letter back to Lorick.

"I told you. That is the last report we received from out informants in Vilheim. That is over a week ago now and we have heard nothing since, and all of our efforts to uncover what is happening have been to no avail. The entire city has been closed to everyone; even the river has been barred."

"We have heard nothing of any of this. The entire city being closed? This must be a mistake," Gerhold said and Lorick shook his head.

"The rumors are just now starting to spread."

"Then what is happening? What else do you know?" Gerhold asked and Lorick stood.

"We know little more than you do, I am afraid. We received a message less than a month ago saying that strange things were occurring in the city, plague

A Dawn of Death

victims turning up across the city, especially in the slums. Then we received another, saying strange fog had settled over the city and surrounding countryside, and that the plague was getting worse," Lorick said and set two more letters on the table.

"A plague? What sort of plague?" Roland asked.

"The people took to calling it the weeping death. That is about all we know of it."

"What did your servant mean when he said the city was under siege," Gerhold asked and Lorick shrugged.

"He meant that something is attacking the city, something evil." Gerhold looked from Lorick to Roland, who seemed to be as confused and worried as he was. "There is little more I can tell you about this, but I thought it would be a good idea to let you know. The other Seekers have already hired a group of mercenaries to investigate, but I believe you are more fitting for this job."

Gerhold rubbed his forehead and paused for a moment before answering.

"Let me speak to my companions in private," he said, and Lorick nodded before returning to his seat. Gerhold pulled Roland aside and the two men stepped quickly into the other room, followed by Nethrin.

"What in the six hells is going on here? Who is he?" Roland asked as soon as they entered the room.

"You do not need to know," Gerhold answered.

"Don't try that this time. I need to know who this man is and if what he said is true." The two men glared at each other. "What is this all about, Gerhold?"

The vampire took a step back before nodding.

"Fine," he said curtly and walked to the other side of the room. "He is part of a sect that that call themselves the Seekers of Light. They were founded in secret after the fall of Dalloran by a group of powerful scholars, mages, and even Paladins. Their goal was to hunt down and destroy dark artifacts and practitioners throughout Tyriel."

"They don't sound too bad to me," Roland added.

"That was a thousand years ago. They have changed now; they have come to believe that their end can be justified by any means."

"And you know all of this how?" Roland asked.

"Because I worked for them, many years ago, long before I turned," Gerhold answered and Roland raised an eyebrow.

"And how do you know they have not changed since then? That had to be over a hundred years ago now," Roland said and Gerhold shook his head.

"They have not. If anything, I imagine they have only gotten worse."

"Be that as it may, what is happening in Vilheim? What do you make of those letters?"

"I am not sure. We spent the past few weeks hunting that demon, not gathering rumors like we usually do," Gerhold answered.

"So, what do we do?"

Gerhold paused for a moment to think before answering. He did not want to get involved with the Seekers, never again, but if what Lorick had said was true then they had to get back to Vilheim. What did the letters mean about a dark fog? And what was this strange plague, this weeping death?

"Roland," he said finally. "Go to the nearest tavern and start poking around; see if you can come up with anything about Vilheim. We will see if there is any truth to Lorick's story. If there is, you should hear something,"

Roland nodded.

"And if his story is true?" he asked.

"Then we will be making our way to Vilheim with all haste," Gerhold answered.

With that Roland left the room and disappeared into the crowded streets. Nethrin and Gerhold reentered the open living space where Lorick still sat nearby. Nethrin returned to the little table and began gathering up his things while Gerhold made his way towards Lorick.

"So how did you find me?" Gerhold asked and Lorick gave a wry smile.

"We have informants in nearly every town and hamlet in Midland; it is not hard to find one of the only vampires in existence who is sympathetic to our cause."

"So, you knew I was in Vilheim then?" Gerhold asked and Lorick nodded.

"After our run-in in Kingsport we searched for you. Once we found out that you had helped our men, I convinced the other members of my organization to leave you be. Some wanted to recruit you and others wanted you dead, but I was able to get enough support to ensure you were left to your business without interference. We did keep tabs on you, from time to time of course." Lorick stood.

"Of course, you did. Is there anything else you need, or have you said

A Dawn of Death

everything you need to?" Gerhold asked gruffly and Lorick shook his head.

"No, that is about all," Lorick responded and slid his hand through is white hair.

"Good, then I think it is time for you to leave," Gerhold motioned to the door.

"You know you should really consider working with us. Between our knowledge and connections and your abilities and experience we could do more for this world than either of us on our own."

"I already told you I am finished with the Seekers," Gerhold answered.

"Well then, just in case you end up making your way back to Vilheim, do take care," Lorick said and turned to leave. "Oh, and Gerhold? Do not throw our offer away so lightly."

With that Lorick exited the dingy little shack and closed the door behind him. Gerhold frowned at the now vacant room and made his way back upstairs as quickly as he could and started to gather up his things. A minute later Nethrin came striding into the room.

"So, we are leaving then?" he asked and Gerhold shrugged.

"Not yet, but I would like to be ready all the same. I do not trust Lorick Dren or those he works with, but I doubt he is lying about the messages. If what they are saying is real, then we need to return to Vilheim as soon as possible," Gerhold answered as he tied his bedroll to the side of his pack.

"If something was happening there, then why did we not hear anything from the other priests? Surely my brothers would have sent us a message," Nethrin said.

"Perhaps they tried. We have been on the move so often, as of late, it would be extremely difficult for a letter to reach us. Either way, I sense something is amiss." Gerhold slung the pack over his shoulder and led the way downstairs.

It was another hour before Roland returned with information and Gerhold spent his time re-reading the three messages Lorick had left for him. The first two were dated and titled and were written in great detail, while the third was hastily scrawled, though, lacked the organization and tone of the others. It had been written quickly and without the thought and preparation of the others. What bothered Gerhold the most was the cryptic and vague descriptions that had been used to tell what was happening. The writer mentioned a dark fog that had settled over the city and the plague, but it felt as though something were missing. Gerhold knew that there had to be other messages and he knew that Lorick was holding something back. The Seeker knew more than he had told them. Finally, Roland returned and Gerhold was more than eager to hear what he had to say.

"By the Gods, it is colder out there than it was last night," Roland shivered and slammed the door.

"What did you find?" Gerhold asked as Roland pulled the grey scarf from around his face and tossed it onto a nearby chair.

"Well it took me a bit to find someone who would know. The bartender was no help at all, but he was able to point me to a recently arrived merchant ship. I got in on a game of breaks with them, but they didn't seem too keen on telling me much at first." Roland grabbed a nearby water skin and took a drink. "But after a few drinks they started talking about their trip from the south. Apparently, they were supposed to have stopped off in Vilheim along the way, but they got word that the city was denying docking privileges to most ships. Seems the entire place is closed off now, but no one knows why."

"Anything about the plague or the strange fog?" Gerhold asked and Roland shrugged.

"They said they ran into some fog, but it didn't seem out of the normal for this time of year. I did not hear anything specific about the plague, but there are rumors," Roland took another drink and tossed the empty skin on the table. "So, what do we do?"

Gerhold stood for a moment and pondered what Roland had told him. It was clear that Vilheim was closed, whether it was to quarantine a plague or not was yet to be determined, but if what Roland had heard was true, then there was a very real chance that the messages from the Seekers were real.

"Both of you gather your things; we are leaving as soon as the sun sets. Roland, can you barter us passage to Vilheim?" Gerhold asked and Roland nodded.

"Of course, but if they are not allowing ships to land, then we may have a problem."

"We will deal with that when it comes. Do your best to get us a fast ship, all right?"

Roland nodded and threw his scarf around his neck once again. A moment later he was gone and Gerhold was helping Nethrin gather whatever they could. Two days of rest was enough for him; now it was time to get back to work.

A Dawn of Death

Chapter 3: Heading Home

Gerhold of Vilheim, Journal Entry: February 5, 5947 of the Common Age
We are nearing Vilheim and should be there within the next few hours. Roland was able to find space aboard a merchant ship headed for Morovia that also plans to stop at Vilheim along the way, if they can, that is. So far, the only rumors we have heard about the city are that it has been closed to all visitors, but the ship's captain wishes to see for himself. Vilheim is the only major port between Breganwarf and Morovia, so he has little choice if they wish to stop and rest.

I have read through the letters given to us by Lorick at least a dozen times, but I have learned nothing more from them, though I am convinced that there were other letters the Seeker did not show us. Was he hiding something? And if so, then why would he want us to return but not give all the information? Either way we will be at the city before nightfall, and then we shall see what all these rumors and messages are about. I have never heard of this weeping death and there are no details about it in the messages from what I can tell. Whatever it is it cannot be a common affliction or else the Seekers would have paid no attention to it. Only a few more hours to wait, then I can start to uncover just what lies behind this mystery.

The little merchant ship sailed through the air high above the snow-covered hills and valleys of Penland while Gerhold sat below deck, calmly rereading the messages for what felt like the hundredth time. Roland stood nearby, leaning quietly against a stack of heavy wooden crates containing various goods and equipment. The soft whistle of the cold winds could be heard blowing about the deck above, along with the clinking and clanking sounds of Nethrin working with his tools in the far corner of the room. They had spent the past day and night below deck after convincing the captain to allow them passage, which had cost them a gold sovereign apiece, and Gerhold was more than ready to be out of the confined space. He hated flying, though being kept below deck meant he did not have to look down and see the vast space between the airship and the ground below.

Suddenly Gerhold heard a voice above cry out, echoed by others, and soon the entire deck was alive with activity. Heavy footsteps could be heard as men clamored about and more voices could be heard. Gerhold looked over at Roland as if to ask what was happening, but the other man just shrugged.

"What's all the noise about?" Nethrin asked.

"No idea, we can't be back yet. Roland?" Gerhold said.

"I'll see what's going on," he answered and made his way over to the stairs leading to the upper deck.

A minute later he came bounding back down the steps with a look of urgency on his face.

"You need to hide, now," he said and motioned for Gerhold to follow.

"Why? What is happening?"

"A Paladin airship is stopping us, looks like they are planning to board," Roland answered as Gerhold quickly began gathering his things.

"Just another reason why I hate flying."

Just then the airship shook violently as something else slammed into the side, and more footsteps could be heard as the Paladins leapt aboard. Gerhold dodged between the stacks of boxes, searching desperately for somewhere to hide. If the Paladins found a vampire aboard, then he would be forced to defend himself, though even he could not defeat a ship full of Paladins. He heard the sound of clinking armor and a harsh voice call down the stairs before the first line of silver clad soldiers appeared. The merchant ship was small and there was nowhere for Gerhold to hide. Finally, he stopped at the back end of the ship where more crates were stacked. There was nowhere else to run and Gerhold's heart hammered as the Paladins drew ever closer, searching the ship for anything out of the ordinary. With no other alternative, Gerhold took a deep breath and slowly opened the circular window along the starboard side and wiggled through.

Immediately his stomach dropped as he hung on the side of the swaying airship, staring down at the seemingly unending space beneath him. He climbed as quickly and quietly as he could until he was hanging from a loose piece of rigging along the bottom of the ship and was able to swing himself beneath it just as a Paladin poked his head out of the open window. Gerhold held his breath and

A Dawn of Death

said a silent prayer that he would not be caught, and his hands would hold steady as the wind whipped violently about. A moment later he heard a *click* as the window closed. Gerhold let out a sigh of relief and began trying to make his way back up along the loose boards and rigging. The wind was strong, but he could still make out the voices of men speaking on the deck above as he tried to open the window again, but it had been locked from the inside. He swore under his breath while trying to figure out what to do next. Thankfully the sky was covered in a layer of grey clouds, which gave him some protection from the burning sun, but still he could feel the heat on his back even with the hood of his cloak pulled up. The other windows had been closed and Gerhold did not want to risk attracting the attention of the Paladins by forcing his way in.

Trapped outside with no way back in, Gerhold pulled himself along the side of the ship and then up towards the deck. The last thing he needed now was for a Paladin to look over the side of the ship and see a vampire hanging off the rigging. He could hear voices coming from above and did his best to stay as quiet as he could while climbing, before chancing a glance in between the spindles along the side railing. Across the deck he could see a second airship that was tied to the little merchant vessel, and multiple long wooden planks had been laid across the railings to bridge the gap between the two ships. At least twelve Paladins patrolled the crowded deck and their commander stood near the helm where Gerhold could hear the man arguing with the merchant captain. The ship's captain, Mister Barrington, was a large man with a fancy coat and a polished demeanor. He was a man who wished to be part of the aristocracy but who was instead forced to settle for being moderately rich, a status he felt was necessary to remind everyone about. Gerhold did his best to catch what the two men were saying, curious as to why a Paladin patrol would have stopped such a small merchant vessel.

"I have already told you; we are on our way to Morovia and plan to stop in Vilheim to rest and replenish our supplies," the large man was saying.

"Have you not heard that Vilheim is closed? Neither visitors nor ships by sea or air are allowed in until the city has been reopened for trade. Why then were you on your way to a city that has been quarantined?" the commander asked.

"As I said before, we were unaware that anything was going on in the city at the time we set out," Barrington answered again. "There were rumors of course, but I had no idea if they were reputable or not. As Vilheim is the only major port between here and Morovia, we did not have much of a choice." The merchant was obviously frustrated, but the commander cared little for the inconvenience he was causing.

"What are you carrying aboard this vessel?"

"Bolts of cloth from Calloria, dyes from northern Drakar, and a few crates of furs we picked up on our last trip north. Nothing out of the ordinary, I assure you."

"Your assurance means little to me," the Paladin said and turned to one of his men. "Did you find anything below?"

"A few passengers but nothing more," the man answered.

"And who are you?" the commander asked, and Roland stepped forward.

"He is a travelling tinker and I am his bodyguard," Roland answered and motioned to Nethrin.

"You look familiar, though I try not to spend my time in the company of brigands and mercenaries. What is your name?"

"Restrard, though I doubt a Paladin would know my name," Roland answered confidently, and the commander sniffed in disgust.

"And you are heading for Vilheim?" he asked Nethrin, who nodded nervously.

"Yes, I was planning on offering my services to the smiths there before making my way north," Nethrin answered.

The commander stared at the two men suspiciously before turning and walking back across the deck to the captain.

"So, you picked these men up in Breganwarf?" the commander asked, and the captain nodded.

"Just the two of them?"

The captain nodded again and Gerhold sighed again. Apparently, the gold had paid for more than just their passage.

"It seems as though everything is in order, then. I apologize for the delay, but Vilheim is closed to all visitors and any ships heading that way must be searched by order of the Regent and the Council of Vigils." The Paladin commander handed Barrington a small scrap of parchment. "If you are stopped again, you may show this to the patrol, and they will let you pass without another search. You must head north or south and avoid Vilheim."

"What is this all about? Why is the city closed off?" the captain asked.

"That is none of your concern. Right now, you need to press on and avoid the area all together. Heed my words merchant or next time we will not be

A Dawn of Death

so kind."

With that the commander motioned for the others to follow as he led the way back onto the other airship. A moment later the hooks and ropes were removed, and the two vessels drifted apart, and Gerhold watched warily as the Paladin airship turned and headed off in the opposite direction. As soon as he was sure he would not be seen, Gerhold hauled himself up onto the deck, much to the surprise of a few of the nearby crew members, and made his way across the deck to where the captain was speaking with Roland and Nethrin.

"Where in the blazes did that other fellow go, eh? Is he some wanted bandit or something?" the captain was saying. His fat neck wobbled back and forth as he blustered on. "I should have turned you all in and avoided the trouble entirely, I lied to a Paladin for the three of you, so I better get some sort of answer."

"You lied because we paid you a week's wage," Gerhold said as he approached.

"Now where in the six hells did you come from?" the captain said with surprise as Gerhold stopped in front of him.

"You need to land this ship as soon as the Paladins are out of the way," Gerhold said and the captain puffed out his chest in offense.

"Now see here, this is my ship and I will not be taking orders from some bandit or criminal, or whatever you are," Barrington said with a scowl.

Gerhold pulled down his gray scarf and smiled, revealing his elongated fangs, then stepped forward and grabbed the little fat man by the front of his fancy coat. The captain's eyes seemed to double in size as he was lifted off his feet and the other crew members gasped in horror at the vampire's strength.

"Land the ship now," Gerhold said and the captain nodded.

"Of course, please—please don't hurt me!" he cried and Gerhold released him, causing the merchant to fall to his knees and hastily crawl away.

Immediately the ship began to descend as Gerhold stood by Nethrin and Roland while the crewmembers and captain did their best to stay as far away as possible.

"I am so glad you dealt with that issue in such a diplomatic fashion," Roland said with a smile.

"We do not have time for diplomacy. Nethrin? Hand me our bag of coins please," Gerhold said, and the young man handed him a small leather bag from which he removed two more gold coins.

"So, what is your plan?" Roland asked.

"We walk the rest of the way," Gerhold answered and handed the leather pouch back to Nethrin.

"But we are still hours from Vilheim, and we have no horses," Roland added.

"Then it is a good thing we travel light. We will make it there by nightfall," Gerhold added and Roland shook his head in frustration.

"It can never be easy can it?"

The airship made a slow twisting arc downward towards snowy ground. Open plains and frozen lands had now been replaced by rolling hills and clumps of trees that dotted the countryside. Gerhold watched as the nervous crew milled about, pulling at the rigging, and the navigator directed the airship lower and lower until they hovered only twenty feet above the treetops. The ship came to a halt above a small hill and two ropes were lowered over the side.

"There you are. I did as you asked, now leave us be," the captain said nervously as Gerhold approached.

"Thank you. This is for the detour, and for not turning us in to the Paladins," he said and handed the man the three coins.

The captain took them without a word, and a moment later Gerhold was over the side and sliding down the rope after Roland and Nethrin. Not a second after he hit the ground, the rope was pulled up and the airship was sailing back off as quickly as the crew could manage. Gerhold knelt and pulled a set of folded maps from his pack and began trying to orient himself using a small compass. There was a little village only a mile or two to the east that he had seen on their way down and a small river that ran along to the west. His eyes scanned the map of Penland, knowing that they were at least ten miles to the west of Vilheim, until he found a spot that looked very much like the landscape that surrounded them. Satisfied with the assessment, Gerhold replaced the map and walked down to the bottom of the hill where Roland and Nethrin stood.

"Don't tell me, it is going to be further than you first thought?" Roland asked sarcastically as Gerhold reached the bottom of the little hillside.

"A little closer actually. Less than ten miles at the most," Gerhold answered.

"Only ten miles? How encouraging," Roland said again and spat.

"At least we have a decent cloud cover," Gerhold said and pulled his hood a little lower. His skin was already starting to feel raw and uncomfortable even with the protection from his coat.

"Well I suppose we should get moving if we want to reach the city by nightfall."

Together the three men set off, heading east in the direction of Vilheim. At first the trek was difficult with Gerhold leading them through groves of twisted trees, over and between steep hillsides, and across frozen creeks and fields. After a few hours of walking they reached a small dirt path and Gerhold used his map to find their location. They turned north and finally reached the main road that would take them all the way to the eastern entrance to the city, and all three were relieved to no longer have to fight their way through the brambles and twisted branches of the wilderness. Of course, using the road meant there was a much higher chance of running into someone, but Gerhold hoped that the rumors of Vilheim being closed would deter most travelers from using the road.

To the east the road twisted and turned between the sloping hills, until it disappeared into a thick wall of mist that ebbed and skirted along the landscape like an approaching wave. The three men stared off at the seemingly impenetrable wall of dark fog, and all that could be heard was the soft whisper of the wind passing between the leafless trees. There were no travelers along the road and nearly every cottage or farm was deserted, save for a few malnourished animals that had been left behind while their owners fled in haste. Without a word Gerhold started down the path, followed by Roland and Nethrin.

After only a few minutes of walking, they came to the wall of mist that stretched out in either direction as far as they could see, its wispy tendrils reaching out across the frozen landscape like the spindly fingers of an old crone. They entered the shifting mists without hesitation, and soon the only things visible were the next few feet of the poorly paved stone road and the gnarled tips of tree branches that grew out of the fog. Roland held his spear with both hands as if at any moment something would spring out from the shifting veil of gray and attack, but Gerhold continued forward with his same calm demeanor, sensing nothing out of the ordinary. As a vampire he could feel when a creature of evil was close by, as if they held some grotesque bond of kinship, but he did worry about other things that may lie within the mists. Men held the capacity for great evil, just as a vampire did, but he could not sense men the way he could sense dark creatures. He had to rely on his true senses to detect humans, and even though his keen eyes could not penetrate the fog that surrounded them, they did nothing to decrease his hearing and smell. If there were any bandits or highwaymen lying in wait, then he would know.

They continued moving as quickly as their limited sight would allow, but after another few hours of walking, Gerhold held up his hand for the others to halt. Immediately Roland raised his spear to the ready position and Gerhold calmly pulled his crossblade from its holster across his back. He took a deep breath through his nostrils and focused on the unusual smell that he had only just sensed. It was a familiar smell, as no vampire could ever fail to recognize the scent of their prey. Somewhere ahead there were humans, hidden by the layers of shifting fog. Gerhold led the group forward slowly, and soon voices could be heard coming from the path ahead. Whether these were travelers, merchants, or bandits, he could not tell, but he was not willing to be taken by surprise. They stopped a moment later and moved off the path only a little, making sure to keep the line of stones in sight to not get lost. Gerhold knelt on the hard ground and listened.

The voices were gone, but the stench of human remained fresh. Every so often he would hear what sounded like a footstep or a whisper, and yet nothing could be seen through the murk. Suddenly the sound of a cracking branch came from somewhere just off the path and Gerhold turned to see the outline of a tall man moving through the trees. The vampire leapt forward and drove his shoulder into the man's mid-section, sending him sprawling across the frozen ground. Two more silhouettes appeared between the trees and four more from the path behind. Gerhold twisted his weapon and aimed it at the new arrivals.

"Hold, or the first one that moves will breathe his last!" Gerhold threatened. The line of attackers halted as one of the men held up his hand for them to halt.

"We have you surrounded," the man said and took a step forward. "Judging by your weapons you are not travelers. So, who are you and what are you doing on this road? Speak now, or you shall not get another chance."

Gerhold heard the familiar sound of bowstrings tightening.

"We are escorting this tinker here to Vilheim. Who are you to bar our way?" Gerhold answered.

"Have you not heard that Vilheim is closed? The roads are deserted for a reason, tinker. Return the way you came; these mists are no place for merchants and travelers," the man responded and motioned for his men to lower their weapons.

A Dawn of Death

Gerhold did the same, but something about the man's voice and the way he carried himself were familiar. They stood in place for a few tense seconds before the man stepped forward and lowered his hood, revealing a mass of dreadlocks that were pulled back. A well-trimmed mustache and dash of scruff across his chin only added to his dashing appearance, and he wore a worn blue long-coat and a quiver of arrows was thrown over his shoulder. Gerhold smiled and took a step forward.

"Most people turned around when they saw the fog, and they were wise to do so, so how come the three of you didn't do the same, eh?" he asked. He had a smooth, roguish voice and a suave smile to match it. Gerhold recognized the accent as one from Myrthia, a nation of pirates and brigands alike. "There are plenty of other places for a tinker to go."

Gerhold slowly pulled back his hood and watched as the sly grin disappeared from the man's face.

"Perhaps I was not honest about that," Gerhold answered. The man stared at him for a moment and his eyes narrowed suspiciously.

"I know you," he mumbled and held his bow at the ready.

"I would have been disappointed if you have forgotten my face, Valaire," Gerhold responded, and a look of recognition passed across Valaire's face.

"Bloody hell, you were at Kingsport, weren't you?" he asked, and his grin returned. "Eh, gents, get a load of this one," Valaire said and motioned for the others to move in closer.

"As I live and breathe…" one of the men said as soon as he saw Gerhold.

"Gerhold of Vilheim?" Another echoed.

"Vampire scum," the first man said again, but Valaire held up his hand for silence.

"Of all the roads in all the world and we both find ourselves on this one, eh?" the man said and smiled again. "Been a long time since we ran into you, and it looks like you've finally hired some help," he said and laughed at Roland and Nethrin who stood nearby.

"We should 'ave killed 'im when we was in Dirge," another man said. He was tall and had a bald head that was covered in tattoos, and a large axe was held tightly in both his hands.

"Or when we caught him in Drethdin," a short-haired woman said.

"Bolin, Leandra, calm yourselves. The Seekers called off the bounty years ago. Of course, we have killed monsters for free before," Valaire said smoothly.

"I save your lives and this is how you plan to repay me, Anton?" Gerhold responded.

"You are lucky I have not already taken your head, vampire," Bolin said and fingered the sharpened edge of his axe.

"I said that is enough, Bolin," Valaire said and rounded on the big man, who glared at Gerhold one last time before spitting at the vampire's feet and turning away. "Sorry about that but being hailed by the Seekers as the only vampire who fights against his own kind may not be accepted by some."

"I take it you are the mercenaries the Seekers hired?"

"We are, and now I know why you're here. The Seekers told us you might make an appearance if we were unlucky enough."

"We are here to help Vilheim, nothing more," Gerhold responded and Bolin snorted in disgust.

"That is commendable, but you're not needed. Perhaps you should shove off and go dally about somewhere else, eh? Let us take care of the important business."

"You of all people should know what I can do, Valaire. Besides, without me there will be no one to pull you and your friends out when you make a mess of things," Gerhold answered.

"And how do you plan on getting into the city? See, that's the nice thing about working for the Seekers now, you get a few advantages," he said and held up a sealed scroll bearing the sigil of the Regent of Penland.

"We can find our way well enough," Gerhold answered again.

"Good luck with all that, then; in the meantime, we'll be on our way. Try not to run into us again, eh? I don't think I can hold Bolin back a second time."

Anton Valaire gave a flourished bow and turned to continued making his way down the road, and the other six members of his crew followed in a line, each giving one last glare in Gerhold's direction before disappearing into the fog. Gerhold placed his crossblade in its holster once again and wiped the dirt from his pant legs.

"First Paladins and now a band of bloody mercenaries," Roland said. "Who in the six hells does that puffed up codpiece think he is anyway?"

"Anton Valaire, he is a Myrthian pirate turned monster hunter. I met him ten years back. Has a bit of a flare for the dramatic, too much for my taste," Gerhold responded.

A Dawn of Death

"Why would the Seekers hire a pirate?"

"Do not let the fancy attire and smooth talk fool you; the man is deadly. Not a bad hunter either, but they tend to be a bit too loud for most situations. I guess the Seekers are more worried than I thought if they called them in to deal with this. If the whole city is quarantined, then a few mercenaries making a little noise will more than likely go unnoticed as the Watch will have far greater concerns."

"How did he get that paper, though? A sealed letter from the Regent?" Nethrin asked.

"The Seekers are very powerful, and they have followers in many places. A few gold coins in the right pockets can get more done than words or a sword," Gerhold answered and started down the path. "Forget about them for now, though; we need to get into the city and speak with the priests as soon as we can. I have a feeling that things are worse than we feared."

"We can use the tunnels to get into the city unnoticed, but if we run into those mercenaries again, we may not be able to avoid a fight," Roland said as he followed behind. "I am all for bravery but seven on two are poor odds even for us, and that big one looked like he knew how to handle that axe. I doubt you will be much help, Nethrin. Not against that lot anyway."

Nethrin nodded in agreement.

"We will worry about that if we have to," Gerhold said. "For now, let us focus on reaching the city before nightfall. It is already growing darker and I do not want to be caught out in this fog when the sun goes down," Gerhold said and continued down the path, pondering just what might be happening ahead in the city of Vilheim.

Chapter 4: A Siege of Darkness

Gerhold led the way through the mists as the light of day began to fade. Visibility amidst the fog grew even worse, but the coolness of night was a relief to the weary vampire, who was already feeling his energy being sapped by so long a time in the sun. Soon a line of orange lights appeared ahead some twenty feet in the air like floating lamps in the dark shifting clouds. They had finally reached the outer wall of the city, and both Roland and Nethrin were visibly relieved with a respite from the deepening gloom. The soft glow from the lights was amplified by the ever-changing blankets of fog that drifted about lazily through the breezeless night sky. It was much cooler now that the sun had all but disappeared, and both Nethrin and Roland pulled their cloaks closer and shivered in the cold, while Gerhold was finally able to remove his protective scarf and gloves.

The main gate was straight ahead, but he knew there would be no chance of getting into the city that way. There was a large camp set up just outside of the front gate; many of the tents could be seen through the fog. The Paladins had blocked every entrance and exit to the city and would kill anyone who tried to get in or out without express permission, such as Valaire had. Even if the city was not closed, Gerhold risked being spotted by the Paladins who would undoubtedly be patrolling the streets, and all of whom had been alerted to his possible presence in the city after the debacle in Blightwood three years ago. This was another reason why they had spent so much time away as Gerhold could no longer move about freely in the city. However, he was able to now bypass the city gates altogether, thanks to Nethrin, who had designed and built a series of passages that led from the old chapel undercroft into the sewer tunnels that led in and out of the city. Not the most preferred way of travelling through the city, but it did allow him to come and go as he pleased, without fear of being discovered by the Paladins.

They made their way around the wall, searching for the nearest entrance

A Dawn of Death

into the Vilheim sewers. Their first stop would be the chapel where they would speak with the priests and find out just what had been happening in the city and where to start their search for any clues about what caused the mysterious plague. It did not take long to find the large metal grate that led to the foul smelling tunnels which ran beneath the city, and Gerhold kept a wary eye on the barely visible ramparts above in case a watchman happened to catch a glimpse of them while passing by. He doubted whether a guard would even be able to see the ground through the fog, let alone the three crouched figures, but he had learned long ago that it was better to be safe. After a few moments of fiddling with the metal grate, it swung open and Roland led the way into the cramped dark space. Nethrin and Gerhold followed, the latter quietly closing the grate behind them.

Once inside, Roland pulled an old torch from the wall and Nethrin poured a small amount of pyrite oil over the top before igniting it. The firelight cast an orange glow throughout the reeking cavern and illuminated the thousand-year-old architecture that was now barely standing. Cracks and crevices crawled up and down the walls, and piles of fallen stone were strewn across the floor, blocking the flow of now frozen sewage. Most of these old tunnels were no longer used to transport waste as a new and more efficient system had been built, which now dumped into the Voldar River, which ran through the center of Vilheim. Sometimes though, these new sewers would leak into the older tunnels, causing a slow buildup of frozen sludge that had to be removed.

Because of this, few ever ventured down into this forgotten labyrinth of stone and rotting mire, making them the perfect highway for thieves, brigands, and those who wished to avoid attention. The City Watch did their best to patrol or collapse the old entrances to these dark places, but for everyone they removed, another would be found or missed. Nethrin had somehow uncovered an old set of architectural plans that had been stored in the undercroft of the chapel, and using these maps, he had discovered secret ways to move about the city unnoticed. These decaying, stinking, collapsing holes were Gerhold's most efficient way of moving about the city without drawing the attention of the Paladins that now roamed the streets.

Roland stopped at a junction ahead and Nethrin briefly glanced at his folded map before motioning to the right. The little torch in Roland's hand bobbed up and down in the darkness as they continued on through the dark passages, and after a few more turns and a brisk walk down a long corridor, they finally came to a halt in front of a well-disguised door that would lead them to the basement of the Vilheim chapel. Nethrin pulled on a nearby lever and the door swung inward with a loud screech of metal on metal which reverberated off the cold, cracking stone of the tunnels.

"Well at least the priests will know we are here," Roland said before giving the door one final push and entering.

Roland led the way up a flight of stairs and Gerhold made sure to seal the hidden door behind them. The steps climbed upwards until ending at the foot of an oak door, held closed by a thick iron lock. Nethrin whipped out a long brass key, and a moment later the door opened, revealing a crowded storage room full of crates, crammed shelves, and piles of odd trinkets and rubbish. Thick layers of dust covered the floors and cabinets while the soft pitter-patter of little rat feet could be heard as the rodents scurried about and away from the torchlight. A few barrels of old pyrite oil stood at the other corner of the room, and Roland made sure to keep his torch as far from them as he could. Voices echoed from the other side of another door at the other end of the room, and both Gerhold and Roland traded suspicious glances as the priests rarely spent their time in the musty undercroft.

"Sounds like everyone in the whole chapel is down here," Roland said as he approached the door.

"That is strange; my brothers rarely spend time down here, not since we completed the tunnels," Nethrin added.

Roland opened the door and they were immediately met with a chaotic sight. Throughout the dingy and poorly lit undercroft were crowds of people, too many for Gerhold to count, all of them shabbily dressed and crammed together into the dark space. Most were closely gathered around what little warmth they could find, whether it be a ring of candles or a few open lamps, while others leaned wearily against the stone walls and pillars, wrapped in filthy cloaks and whatever scraps of cloth they could find to provide some semblance of warmth. Mothers pulled their shivering children as close as they could, trying to provide their little ones with some form of comfort amidst the dismal scene. Gerhold quickly pulled his hood lower and wrapped the scarf around his face once again to prevent anyone from getting suspicious as they picked their way through the crowds.

"What in all the hells is going on here?" Roland muttered and Gerhold shook his head.

"I have no idea."

A Dawn of Death

Just then Gerhold caught sight of a man in long brown robes, one of the priests who tended to the chapel, and started in his direction.

"Brother Martin is cooking up a new batch as we speak. I will do my best to bring as many loaves as I can, but you must understand that grain is scarce. There is not much more we can do," the priest was saying as Gerhold and the others approached.

"But my family is starving down here," a ragged man pleaded and pointed to a woman and two small children who sat huddled in a nearby corner.

"I understand and we are doing all we can."

"Brother Hagar, I didn't realize you were looking to bring in so many replacements for Nethrin here, wouldn't one man have done the job?" Roland said and the old priest turned with a shocked expression.

"Ser Roland? Master Gerhold? Why, where did you all come from? When did you get back?" he asked in surprise and clutched his chest.

"Just now in fact," Gerhold answered. "We heard rumors of something happening here, and it looks like they were right."

"Thank the Gods for that. We tried sending you a message, but the entire city was closed before it could get out. The divines are finally answering our prayers," the priest said and motioned for them to follow. "Brother Francis and the rest of us have been doing our best, but there has been little we can do for these people since they quarantined the city. Since then things have gone from bad to worse."

"What is happening here?" Gerhold asked and the old man looked at him with a confused expression.

"You mean you do not know? I thought for sure that everyone knew what was happening."

"The Paladins are keeping things from getting out it seems," Gerhold answered.

"We heard something about a plague," Nethrin said and the old man nodded while leading them up a flight of stairs to the ground floor of the chapel.

"Yes, it started a few months ago in the slums, but for a time it seemed to be confined to that area. The City Watch closed it off and refused to let anyone in or out, which stranded many of the poorer folk who had nowhere to go. Brother Francis opened the chapel for those in need, but by the time the plague began to spread throughout the city, we were already filled to bursting." The priest shook his head and sighed.

"So, the plague has spread throughout the entire city?" Gerhold asked and Hagar shrugged.

"The affliction can be found in every district, even amongst the nobles. But it is not only the plague that has the city in isolation; it is the fog," he said and frowned. "The fog settled over the city only a few days before the first of the outbreaks was discovered. Some believe it is some sort of dark magic causing the blight and that the fog is poison. All we know is that more and more cases are popping up all across the city, and now the watch has locked every gate and quarantined every section of the city. I do not even know if there is anyone left at our chapel in the Gold District."

"They do not want anyone who has been infected to escape," Gerhold added as they passed into the crowded sanctuary.

More of the priests moved here and there, assisting whomever they could while Hagar led them through the masses of people towards the little stairwell to the upper floors. Neither a single man nor woman was smiling; there was no laughter, nothing but the same desperate looks and agitated posture that they had seen in the basement. It was a depressing, sunken atmosphere that seemed to permeate the very stone of this supposedly holy place. Brother Francis was in one of the upper rooms which held more displaced townsfolk, sitting behind his desk with his head resting wearily on his hand. As soon as they entered the old man raised his head and waved for Hagar to enter.

"Brother Hagar, have you heard from Brother Erik? Will the City Watch find us more grain?" he asked in a weathered and exhausted voice.

"He has yet to return, but I do have other news," Hagar motioned for Gerhold and the others to approach.

As soon as they entered, the old priest rose to his feet and moved to meet them.

"Gerhold? Roland? By the Gods it is good to see you both," he said and clasped their hands. "I cannot tell you how fortuitous it is that you have come back. I am afraid Vilheim is in need of your services."

"We left Breganwarf as soon as we could, once we heard what was happening here," Gerhold answered.

"And it is a good thing that you did. The Paladins have lost control of the slums and the entire district has been cut off. The rest of the city is doing only marginally better, but food is running low and the Paladins refuse to let anyone venture outside of the city by order of Count Leofric," Francis said.

A Dawn of Death

"The count? He has never been the most helpful, but I have never thought he would be one to let the inhabitants of his city starve and die," Gerhold said and helped the old priests back to his seat. Hagar gave a short bow before making his way out of the room.

"No one has seen him in weeks, and some believe he has been stricken with the plague as well. If so, then I do not know what we will do."

"What do you know of this plague?" Roland asked.

"Not much. I myself have only seen one case up close," Francis said and shuddered. "They call it the weeping death for a reason. At first the afflicted complain about pain in their head and stomach, followed by profuse bleeding from the eyes, ears, and nose. The pain drives them mad, causing them to lash out at anything, leading to most of them beating their hands and arms to a bloody pulp, or others, if they are unfortunate enough to be nearby. Most of the infected have been locked away in makeshift asylums, or at least that is what the Paladins call them. They are nothing more than prisons for the sick, places to lock them away to die."

"What of this fog?" Gerhold asked and Francis rubbed his forehead.

"That is the strangest thing of all. It came only a month ago, rolling in during a cold night, and since then it has neither left nor dissipated. Some believe it is what is causing the plague, some form of dark magic or judgement from the Gods for Vilheim's decadence. It is unnerving, but I know very little other than that."

Gerhold nodded and exchanged glances with Roland.

"Anything else you can tell us? This is not much to start with," Gerhold said and the old priest shook his head.

Gerhold stared out the dirty window into the empty grey abyss. The mists were so thick that even with his keen eyes he could barely make out the deserted streets far below. The glow of only a few lamps could be seen in the dimness, like islands in the middle of a sea of shifting clouds.

"I wish I could offer more assistance," Francis said. "The Paladins have come asking questions as well, even about you. As you know, I appealed to the Vigil of Truth a few months ago to have your protected status renewed, but I heard no response. No one else knows, of course, but I am sure you have little to worry about other than the City Watch, though I would be careful around the Paladins here."

"The entire city is going to hell and they still want to hunt me," Gerhold said and shook his head in disbelief.

"Apparently, Pontius Urban's influence is still widespread, in spite of his disappearance."

"And do they come here often?" Gerhold asked.

"No, they spend most of their time harassing the poor and hiding inside the headquarters of the City Watch. They are not all bad, but their commander is more warrior than priest I am afraid," Francis said and frowned.

Just then there was a loud commotion downstairs and Francis stood and exhaled wearily. The sounds of cries and voices rang out from below, and both Gerhold and Roland gripped the hilts of their weapons a little tighter. They walked out of the little room and onto the expanded walkway that looked down over the crowded sanctuary and entrance hall, where a line of five silver-clad men had just entered through the front doors. Men, women, and children were pushed aside as the Paladins passed, causing even more unrest as the soldiers pressed in.

"Where is the head of this chapel?" one of the soldiers called out. He was a tall man with a bald head and a thick beard.

"Sers, how can the servants of the Three assist you?" a priest answered.

"Which of you is the head of this chantry?" he asked again in a gruff, stern voice.

"That would be Brother Francis, you met with him last time you were here," the priest answered again.

"Then bring him to me at once."

"Commander, if I may speak to you in private," one of the Paladins asked and the commander waved his hand in dismissal.

"I have already heard your concerns, Ser Owyn," the commander said in a firm tone.

"But Ser, we do not know if any of this is true. This chapel has been given the protection of the Vigil of Truth, we cannot disobey their orders," Ser Owyn protested.

"Return to your post, Ser Owyn, or you will be relieved of your duties," the commander threatened. Ser Owyn hesitated but then bowed and made his way back to the door, where he stood and glared at the back of his commanding officer. "Bring this Brother Francis to me now."

The priest bowed low and began making his way up towards the stairs to the upper levels. Five more Paladins entered and Gerhold exchanged a worried glance with Roland.

A Dawn of Death

"Speak of the devil," Francis muttered. "What does he want now?"

"Who is it?" Gerhold asked.

"That is Commander Rodrick; he is in command of the Paladins here in Vilheim. As I said, he has taken an interest in our chapel as of late, but I do not know why. I suppose I should go meet with him," Francis said as the other priest came bustling up the stairs.

"Brother Francis, Commander Rodrick is—" the priest said, but Francis just held up his hand.

"Calm yourself Brother Gendal; I heard the commander."

The priest gave another bow before following Brother Francis back down the steps.

"What's going on?" Roland asked curiously. "Why are there so many Paladins?"

"I do not know. Be ready to leave, though. I have a very strange feeling about all of this," Gerhold answered, and the two men ceased their conversation just as Francis approached the Paladin Commander.

"Commander Rodrick, I welcome you to this holy place," Francis said, but the commander's look did not soften.

"Save your breath, priest, I am here on official business. As of now your chapel is under my control and you are under arrest for the crimes of heresy and desecration of holy ground." The commander's words were met with gasps from the surrounding crowds and fellow priests.

"Arrest? Heresy? Is this some sort of a jest?" Francis asked as two Paladins approached and locked the priest's wrists together with a pair of irons.

"We have evidence that you have given sanctuary to a creature of darkness, a vampire, and have even gone as far as to let him perform his foul rituals in this very building," Rodrick said. The men and women in the chapel reacted with cries of support, some yelling that such a thing could not be true. "Do you deny it?"

"I deny your accusations that I allowed a creature of darkness to remain here and perform dark rituals," Francis answered and held his head high.

"Then you are a liar as well as a heretic," Rodrick turned to the people of the chapel. "This priest has betrayed you all. The plague that now festers within this city's walls was spread by the very creature that he allowed to rest and live beneath this hallowed roof. The Vigils may have granted you sanctuary from our purges, but now that we know of your deceit, I am sure they will approve of our decision. You and your ilk are finished here."

"That is preposterous!" Francis exclaimed and the other priests added their agreement.

"Gerhold has not been here in almost a year," another priest said, and a silence fell over the crowd.

"So, it is true!" the commander exclaimed, a look of triumph spread across his face. The entire chapel was silent now. "You see? These priests have been corrupted by the very darkness that has laid siege to this city. It is they who conspired with this vampire to spread the weeping death to the followers of the Vigilant, to those of us who remain loyal to the Three, and it will not go unpunished or unanswered." Rodrick pointed to the other priests. "The rest of you will be interrogated throughout the night. By mandate of the Order of the White Hand, this chapel is now under the control of the Paladins."

"You have no such authority! You think that because we cannot contact the Vigils that your word is now the law?" Francis said. Rodrick rounded on him, slamming the back side of his mailed fist into the old man's cheek and sending Francis sprawling to the floor.

"I have all the authority I need, heretic. Take him away, and prepare one of the upper rooms for interrogation." The other Paladins saluted their commander and set about gathering up the other priests, while others pulled poor Francis to his feet and began dragging him towards the stairs to the upper rooms.

"That son of a whore," Roland muttered under his breath and readied his spear.

"We need to leave, now," Gerhold said.

"What about the others? What about Brother Francis?" Nethrin protested.

"There is nothing we can do," Gerhold said.

"So, we just leave them to their fates at the hands of these Paladins?" Roland asked furiously.

"Roland, you and I cannot defeat twelve Paladins on our own," Gerhold answered.

"But we can sure try," Roland added. "I bet these bastards are as corrupt as the rest."

"We have more important things to deal with. We need to find out what is causing this fog and the plague. There is something else at work here."

Roland glared at Gerhold just as the sound of heavy footsteps came from

A Dawn of Death

the stairs. Gerhold motioned for them to follow, but Roland had already turned and was sprinting towards the stairs.

"Hells and hellfire," Gerhold cursed under his breath and took off after his young friend.

Roland leapt over the edge of the stairwell and landed squarely on the back of one of the Paladins who was holding Francis, sending the man crashing down the steps. The second man turned in surprise, but before he could react, Roland slammed the butt of his spear into the Paladin's face and sent him careening over the side of the stairwell, where he slammed hard into the stone floor and lay still. The other Paladins looked from their unconscious ally to the stairwell where Roland and Gerhold now stood.

"Roland, we need to go now!" Gerhold yelled and lifted Brother Francis to his feet.

The Paladins down below charged towards the stairs, their commander on their heels bellowing for his men to not let the attackers escape. Gerhold dragged the old priest into a nearby room and leaned him against the wall.

"I am sorry, my friend, this is my fault," Gerhold said.

"No, there is something else at work here. Evil is afoot in Vilheim and only you can stop it. Leave me be. My fate has already been written by the Three. Who am I to go against their will?"

"You must come with us. They will kill you if you stay here," Gerhold said. The sounds of battle came from the hall as the first of the Paladins engaged Roland.

"No, I would only slow you down. You have a more important mission than protecting an old man. Go Gerhold! Go and free our city from this siege of darkness."

Without another word Gerhold dashed back out to see Roland locked in combat with two Paladins and Nethrin cowering in a nearby corner. The vampire dashed forward and drove his foot into one of the attackers, sending him flying down the stairs where he slammed hard onto the stone floor. Roland knocked the feet out from under the other opponent and then followed Gerhold as the two men ran back down the balcony just as more Paladins reached the upper floor. Gerhold grabbed a chain that held one of the many chandeliers that hung high above the chapel floor and motioned for Roland to do the same. Then with a hard strike from his longsword, the chain snapped, and he lifted Nethrin off his feet before leaping over the side of the balcony. The people below screamed and ran in all directions as they came hurtling down from above, and Gerhold braced himself as they slammed into the hard stone floor. Roland landed only a few feet from Gerhold and Nethrin, and both released their hold on the chains before darting off towards the stairs to the basement. Just as they reached the steps the chandeliers came crashing down in an explosion of glass and candles that spread out in all directions, adding to the confusion and chaos that Gerhold hoped would distract their pursuers.

Down the stairs they ran two-by-two until they came to the undercroft which was bustling with activity as people ran back and forth, trying to figure out what all the commotion was. Gerhold led Roland and Nethrin through the throngs of confused peasants back towards the secret entrance to the old sewers.

"Just a moment!" Nethrin yelled and darted into one of the side rooms.

"This is no time to be sentimental, you fool!" Roland called back.

"Hurry! The Paladins will be on us any moment," Gerhold yelled but could not make out what Nethrin called back over the cacophony of noise.

A moment later Nethrin reappeared with a larger leather backpack and another bag which he tossed to Gerhold. It was heavy and its contents clanged and shook as Gerhold threw the bag over his shoulder.

"Now we can go," Nethrin said. "Trust me, you will thank me later."

They reached the little storage room just as the first of the Paladins appeared at the bottom of the stairs and darted in their direction. Gerhold motioned for Roland to go first and then Nethrin, before using his sword to smash a hole in one of the small barrels of pyrite oil, causing the contents to leak out across the floor. A thin layer of pyrite oil was enough to hold back a shadow demon, and now Gerhold hoped it would be enough to keep the Paladins distracted so they could escape. Just as the first of their pursuers turned the corner, Gerhold pulled the still burning torch that Roland had left behind from a nearby sconce and threw it into the puddle of oil. Immediately the pyrite ignited and sent burning hot flames in all directions, and Gerhold dove through the secret entrance and rolled down the stairwell.

Gerhold could feel the heat of the flames as he rolled down the flight of twisting stone steps. The fires would be enough to hold the Paladins off, and with how many people were in the chapel the flames would be dowsed before any major damage to the upper levels would occur. It hurt Gerhold to do such a thing to his home, but they had to escape, and he knew they had few options. As soon as he reached the bottom, Gerhold sprang to his feet, grabbed the heavy bag, and

A Dawn of Death

dashed off after Roland and Nethrin into the labyrinth of dark tunnels, leaving the smell of burning oil and cries of furious Paladins far behind.

Chapter 5: A New Plan

Nethrin led the way through the twisting tunnels, glancing every so often at the folded map, with Gerhold and Roland in tow. The sounds of the chapel had long disappeared, but Gerhold wanted to be sure that they were well away from the Paladins, who no doubt would be in pursuit. They climbed over piles of rubble and squeezed through tight holes between collapsed areas of the tunnel, until finally Nethrin stopped and slumped against the wall, his chest heaving from the effort of running. Roland kept his spear at the ready while trying to catch his breath and Gerhold doubled back a few paces to make sure they were not being followed.

"Anyone behind us?" Roland asked between deep breaths.

"Nothing; I do not hear anything," Gerhold responded and returned his crossbow to its holster.

"What in the six hells was that about? Where did those Paladins come from, and how did they know we were there?" Roland asked and Gerhold shook his head.

"Someone must have been waiting for us. There is something else going on here. Someone knew we were coming and informed the Paladins." Gerhold took another look down the long tunnel behind again.

"Perhaps it was someone in the chapel? One of the priests?" Roland suggested.

"It is possible, but we need to remain on our guard from now on. We must assume that there are no safe havens in Vilheim any longer," Gerhold answered and drank a small amount of blood before tossing the empty vial away.

"And did you hear what that Rodrick fellow said? He blames you for the outbreak," Roland added.

"But why?" Gerhold rubbed his forehead, trying to make sense of the situation. "Here is what we know; someone from the chapel, perhaps one of the priests, informed the Paladins about me. When we returned tonight, they must have then informed the commander of my return."

"But why would they think you had started all this? Surely the informant knew you had been gone for some time. Why would they try to convince the Paladins that it was your doing?" Nethrin asked.

"Maybe it was the Paladins who came up with that theory on their own. Or maybe it is a lie altogether. If a Vigil can be corrupted then so can any of their servants," Roland said and spat in disgust.

Gerhold leaned against the wall, frustrated by the turn of events. The priests had always been a reliable source of information and the chapel a haven, but now they were on their own, alone in this city filled with enemies and Gods knew what else. He had been forced to leave behind a friend, someone who had helped him for years. Brother Francis was a good man and now he was in the hands of the Paladins, and whether they were corrupt or not they would treat the old priest as a heretic. They would take the old man with them to their headquarters in the home of the City Watch, and there they would interrogate him. Gerhold could not let that happen, but he also had to worry about the plague. The Paladins were not known for their kindness when it came to dealing with heretics, especially if they were supposed to be leaders in the church of the Vigilant. Brother Francis would not last long once they started torturing him.

"What is all this anyway?" Gerhold asked and let the heavy bag fall to the floor.

"Those? Just some things I had been working on before we left. I did not realize we would be gone so long, so I did not think to bring them," Nethrin said excitedly and undid the straps that held the bag closed. "These are some new bolts I created, sleeping darts you could call them. I based them off a Drakari design, but I was only able to make a few before we left. They are coated in a special toxin that can render a man asleep in seconds. Just do not aim for the heart." Nethrin listed off the contents as he pulled them out. "We also have some extra ammunition, flash bombs, pyrite oil, and a few other things I thought we would need."

"I suppose that was worth the delay," Roland said as he pocketed two of the flash bombs.

"What do we do now?" Nethrin asked and both he and Roland looked to Gerhold for the answer.

"We have two choices. We can try to make our way to the slums and hope to uncover where the plague started, which seems unlikely, or we can make our way to the northern end of town and see what we can find in the headquarters of the City Watch," he finished and both men stared at him with muddled expressions.

"You want to sneak into the headquarters of the City Watch and the Paladins?" Nethrin asked in disbelief.

"Do we have any other choice? Francis said that the Watch and the Paladins have been investigating the plague for nearly a month now, and both can be found in that fort. Where else do we stand a chance of finding the information we need?"

"So, your plan is to break into the most heavily fortified area of the city save for the count's keep?" Roland asked.

"Do you have any better suggestions?" Gerhold asked.

"I just don't think heading into a den of serpents is the best idea."

"We do not have a choice, not if we want to have a hope of unraveling this mystery. The City Watch will have answers, and even if they do not, we can still try to rescue Brother Francis," Gerhold said.

"Why didn't you just let me save him back at the chapel?" Roland asked irritably.

"There were too many of them for the two of us, but now we will have the element of surprise on our side," Gerhold answered. "Besides, we may need their help by the end of this and I doubt either the Watch or Paladins will be willing to assist us if we spill any blood. These should help with that if they work the way you say they do, Nethrin." Gerhold loaded one of his smaller crossbows with the sleeping darts. They looked like his regular bolts but had a long needle-like end.

"We are going to rescue Brother Francis?" Nethrin asked and Gerhold nodded.

"The Paladins will take him back to their headquarters to interrogate him, which means we may be able to get him out while also finding what we need." The vampire held his hand out for the map. Nethrin handed it over and Gerhold began scanning the maze of intersecting tunnels and passages.

"How do you know they will take him there? I thought they were going to do the interrogations in the cathedral?" Roland asked.

"They already believe that Brother Francis is guilty, so he will be taken to a place where they can be more thorough with their questioning. Let us hope we

A Dawn of Death

can get there before they can begin their work on him, though we need to get moving if we wish to accomplish that," Gerhold said and traced a line on the map with his finger. "Nethrin? Is this passage the quickest way to the northern district?" Gerhold asked.

Nethrin took a moment to examine the map before nodding and tucking it back into his pack.

"That is the fastest way, but these old tunnels are starting to fall apart, even more so than in previous years. I think it may have something to do with the water leaking down from above and freezing in the cracks and crevices that are already here. We need to be very careful and hope that there are no collapses ahead," the young man said and set off down the dark passage.

"You sure this is what you want to do?" Roland asked as they walked and Gerhold nodded.

"Yes, but you need to promise me you will keep ahold of yourself this time."

Roland raised his eyebrows in surprise.

"What do you mean?" he asked.

"You attacked those Paladins without restraint as if they were just another enemy. Not only that, but you looked like you enjoyed it," Gerhold said and Roland snorted. "Do not be so easy to dismiss me. We both know how your feelings towards the Paladins have deteriorated over the years."

"For good reason," Roland interrupted.

"Perhaps, but we do not need another reason for them to hate us. If you kill one of them, then there is nothing that will stop the rest from hunting us, not even the protection of the Vigils."

"Those corrupt officials? Those men who sit behind their piles of gold and pretend that the gods have blessed and chosen them to lead? Bah! I want nothing to do with those fools," Roland added angrily.

"Whatever your feelings may be, you must ignore them. We have more pressing matters to deal with tonight and we do not need the Paladins hunting for us with any more vigor than they already have," Gerhold said.

"And sneaking into their headquarters to rescue a prisoner will help?" Roland asked sarcastically.

"Not if we get caught, but that's why I need you to prioritize stealth over revenge."

Roland halted and sighed. He stared at Gerhold for a moment before nodding.

"Fine, no deaths, and I will try not to hurt anyone," he said finally and began to move again. "What do you expect to find there anyways?"

"I am not sure, whatever information they have. Hunting demons and dark creatures is not always as easy as finding their lairs. First, we must find the trail then follow it," Gerhold answered.

"And if there isn't a trail?" Roland asked.

"Then we rescue Brother Francis and make a new plan," Gerhold said, and Roland laughed at this and shook his head.

"You always make it sound so easy."

"Focus on the closest goal; we already have enough to worry about trying to avoid a small army of Paladins."

They continued through the murky tunnels, following Nethrin and hoping they were not too late to save Brother Francis from his fate in the clutches of the ruthless Paladins.

A Dawn of Death

Chapter 6: The Break-In

"Wait here," Nethrin said and halted as they came to another intersection of tunnels. He knelt and motioned for Gerhold to come closer as he looked over the folded set of maps. One was of the mess of tunnels and sewers, and another was an outline of the old fort that served as the headquarters for the City Watch.

"What is it?" Gerhold asked and held his torch a little higher. He did not trust these tunnels. There could be anything just outside the firelight, hiding in the darkness. The tunnels were often home to criminals and the like, men who would not hesitate to kill.

"How did you get ahold of a map of the City Watch fort?" Roland asked and Nethrin shrugged.

"There were hundreds of these old things in the basement of the chapel and thankfully I grabbed these before we left almost a year ago. Gerhold had asked me to study the tunnels and I assumed it would be good to know where these old sewers linked together. Apparently, that is where the old counts stored their architectural plans. There are no Great Libraries in Penland and the closest would be the one in Calloria, which is too far to be of any use. I suppose they felt the chapel was the best place for such things along with the religious texts. They knew the priests would take care of them and few thieves would ever consider stealing from a church," Nethrin answered and then shifted his focus back to the maps. "The tunnel to the right will take us beneath the walls of the fort. We can come up in the courtyard, but there is another way in as well," the young man said with an amused smile.

"What is the other way in?" Gerhold asked.

"I do not think you are going to like it," Nethrin said and held up the map before pointing to a little marking near one of the tunnels.

"What does that mean?" Roland asked.

"Those are the latrines found in the servant quarters" Nethrin responded.

"Then I am taking the courtyard," Roland answered.

"What about over here?" Gerhold asked and pointed at another symbol on the map.

Nethrin glanced at the symbol and then at the legend.

"That is a drain of some sort, perhaps a bathhouse," he answered.

"I doubt anyone would be found in the bathhouse this late at night."

"But I do not know if we can get in that way. That drain may not be large enough, and even if it is, it may not be openable," Nethrin added.

"Can we even get into those tunnels? I thought these older sewers were separated from the new ones?" Roland asked.

"They are, but in many places the stone has collapsed, and we should be able to make our way up through one of the larger cisterns. Those are the only choices we have, other than trying to make our way in from the outside, which I doubt we would be able to do with the place guarded so tightly." Nethrin shuffled the folded map and stood.

"The bathhouse is our best option. If we come up in the middle of the heavily patrolled courtyard, I doubt we would make it a few feet without being seen. If we take the other way, we will need to sneak through the servant quarters, which are right next to the barracks. The bathhouse should be empty this late, and it looks as though we can make our way either upstairs or down with little in between," Gerhold said and traced his finger along the old, wrinkled map.

"As long as it's not the toilets," Roland added. "Where do you think they will be keeping Brother Francis?"

"In the dungeons below would be my best guess, and the information would be in the Commander's quarters. Finding that could be difficult." Gerhold rubbed his chin.

"I'll find Francis," Roland said. "You just worry about getting whatever information you can. If we come out of here with nothing, then searching the slums is going to be our next task. Maybe we can find some information from the beggars there, though I doubt it. They are notoriously tight lipped, but I am sure we can figure something out. A little coin goes a long way with those who are desperate." Roland hefted his spear over his shoulder.

"Lead the way," Gerhold said, and Nethrin nodded before taking off down the tunnel to the right.

It was not long before they reached the end of the next corridor and

A Dawn of Death

continued on, turning this way and that with only Nethrin and his maps to guide them through the maze. Without them, Gerhold and Roland would have been lost for days down in the dark and twisting passageways. Gerhold kept an eye out for any signs of movement amidst the shifting shadows that surrounded them, as his sight extended far beyond the meager light provided by their torches, and though he had rarely encountered anyone down in these abandoned shafts, he did not wish to be caught unprepared. The going was slow as they were forced to take various detours as they came across more and more blocked passages.

Soon Nethrin slowed and motioned for the others to be quiet as he led them down a long tunnel and then up a pile of rubble into a larger and newer-looking sewer space. The soft trickling of water could be heard as a small stream flowed between the layers of ice that covered the stone floor. This corridor ended at a tall open cylinder. Ten feet above them was a small circular grate through which a few dim shafts of light could be seen. The ground was soaking wet and a steady drip of water came from the opening high above.

"Now how do we get up there?" Roland said just as Gerhold darted back into the passageway and came back carrying an armful of broken stone.

"There is plenty of debris in the passages; we can use it to reach the opening." Gerhold set the pile of stone down beneath the opening as quietly as he could. "Hurry, we do not have time to waste."

The three men began moving back and forth, gathering up as much of the collapsed stone as they could and piling it up at the center of the room until they could reach the grate above. After a few minutes of work Gerhold was able to reach up and grab the cold metal, which did not budge even in the face of the vampire's physical strength. Nethrin stepped forward and pulled a curved metal tool from his pack and fit it around one of the iron bolts that secured the grate.

"Try that," he whispered and Gerhold gave the tool a hard twist, causing the bolt to snap in half.

"Excellent, and quiet too," Gerhold said as he snapped off the other three bolts that held the grate in place.

"I'll never understand how you come up with these things," Roland said.

"After Reichberg, I thought it would be good to have something like this is case we ever got stuck again," Nethrin answered. "Making it out of that dungeon would have been a lot easier if we had had one of these."

Nethrin placed the tool in his knapsack and set his larger pack down away from the pools of water. Gerhold touched his finger to his lips to signal the other two men to be silent, and then he slowly pushed the grate up. The metal made a soft squeaking noise as it was pushed up and slid across the tiled floor of the bathhouse. Gerhold grabbed onto the lip of the opening and threw himself up, his crossbow in hand, loaded with Nethrin's sleeping darts and ready to fire. He reached down and pulled Roland up while Nethrin stayed behind. The young man was a brilliant tinker and engineer, but he was worth very little in a fight and was as stealthy as a lumbering auroch. Gerhold moved silently through the bathhouse and crouched near the door at the end of the room.

"The stairs to the dungeons should be to the left when we exit this room," Gerhold whispered. "I doubt you will run into many guards as most are patrolling the walls and courtyard; they are more worried about what is outside of the walls rather than inside. Once you find Francis bring him back here as quickly as you can. Wait for me below, but do not hesitate to flee if you must," he said and cracked open the door.

On the other side was a long hallway that led off in either direction. A lone guard stood at the far end of the hall to the left, watching the only entrance to the dungeons. It was dimly lit, and the guard looked half asleep already. Gerhold dashed around the corner, and after two long steps he lunged forward with his foot outstretched, driving his heel into the man's stomach before he even knew what had hit him. The guard slammed against the stone wall with a dull thud and then slid to the floor unconscious. Gerhold threw the man over his shoulder and hid the unconscious body in the empty bathhouse.

"Make your way down, but be quiet about it," Gerhold said.

"What if he is not there? What if they kept him at the chapel?" Roland asked.

"Then we will have to deal with that later. For now, just do as we planned and then return to the sewers with Nethrin. I will be there when I can."

With that, the vampire turned and continued down the hallway as Roland moved in the opposite direction. He heard the footsteps of a second guard and crouched near the end of the hall until the man appeared around the corner. One swift punch to the side of the head and the man collapsed to the floor. Gerhold quickly grabbed the body and stashed it in an empty room nearby. Commander Rodrick's quarters would be found upstairs; most likely he would have taken over the Watch captain's room and office, and Gerhold made his way through the empty hallways towards a small stairwell that was used by servants while trying to recall the crumpled map that Nethrin had shown them. He climbed the stairs two

A Dawn of Death

at a time and then peered into another long corridor at the top. Two more guards stood at the center of the hall, flanking a large oak door which Gerhold knew led to the captain's quarters. He paused for a moment to see if any other guards were patrolling the floor, then crept silently out of the darkness and charged the two guards.

Both men turned, but it was already too late. Gerhold lunged forward and struck the first man with an elbow to the throat, then used his momentum to spin and swing his opposite fist into the next guard's stomach. Both men collapsed to the floor where Gerhold made sure they were knocked unconscious before listening to see if anyone heard the commotion. Suddenly the door to the captain's quarters swung open and Gerhold saw a stunned Commander Rodrick staring right at him. Before the Paladin could move, Gerhold struck him across the shoulder with his right hand and then kneed Rodrick in the stomach, sending the commander flying back into the room where he crashed into a table.

"So much for being stealthy," Gerhold mumbled as he dragged the two unconscious guards into the room and then locked the door behind.

Rodrick lay sprawled on the floor amidst the wreckage of the table and mess of paper that had once been organized into neat piles. He stepped forward and pulled the Commander to his feet and threw him into a nearby chair.

"You, I know what you are, creature," Rodrick said between deep breaths. Gerhold bent down and took the Paladin's sword and tossed it across the room. "You dare attack me here?"

"You attacked me first," Gerhold said and started searching through a pile of paper on a nearby desk. He made sure to keep his crossbow aimed at the man's chest. It likely that Rodrick knew some magic, most Paladins did, but Gerhold was faster. If Rodrick even raised is hand to cast a spell, he would end with a sleeping dart to the chest before he could utter a single word. "I need to see whatever you know about this plague, and quickly. I doubt my presence here will go unnoticed for long."

"And why would I help you?" Rodrick said.

Gerhold tightened his grip on the crossbow and aimed it at the Commander's head. It was only loaded with sleeping darts, but Rodrick did not know that. The Paladin froze and relaxed his grip on his sword hilt.

"I would stay still if I were you," Gerhold said, and motioned towards a nearby chair. "Sit," he commanded.

"I never expected you to be so bold as to show yourself here," Rodrick said and spat on the floor near Gerhold before sitting in the chair.

"You have information I need," Gerhold responded.

"You want to know about the plague, do you not?" Rodrick said and laughed. "You will find nothing here."

"I thought you were investigating it?"

The commander laughed again.

"Investigating? Yes, that was what I wanted it to look like," Rodrick's face contorted into a malevolent smile.

Gerhold looked at the man for a moment in confusion.

"What do you mean?" he said and grabbed Rodrick by the front of his tunic.

"It is amusing actually, even you might be able to see the poetry in it. You see, I was tasked with ensuring that the plague continued to spread, if you can all it a plague. Ironic that the very man given the task to investigate the plague is the one who helped start it. It is as if I am hunting myself."

Gerhold lifted the Paladin out of the chair and slammed him against the wall.

"What do you know if this? What evil has settled over this city?" Gerhold asked through gritted teeth.

"You have no idea what is happening here, Gerhold of Vilheim. You think that this is a mere plague? A sickness?" The man laughed again. "A fool for sure. There is more occurring here than you can imagine."

Gerhold raised his crossbow and set it against Rodrick's head.

"Tell me what you know. Who hired you?" Gerhold asked again.

"And spoil the surprise? I think not. Pull the trigger; go ahead. You will be guilty of killing a Commander of the Paladins," Rodrick smiled. "You are off the edge of the map, vampire."

Gerhold slammed Rodrick against the wall again, causing the commander's head to bounce off the wooden wall. Rodrick slumped to the floor unconscious as Gerhold set about searching for anything that would help him, any clues that could lead him to whatever conspiracy Rodrick was involved in. Suddenly there came a loud bang on the door and a man called out for the commander. Gerhold ran towards the door, but then stopped as the sight of an open letter caught his eye. It was lying on the floor between pieces of the broken table, and Gerhold snatched it up as a second and louder knock came at the door.

"Commander, are you in there? I heard a disturbance, and I cannot find

A Dawn of Death

Ser Tory anywhere," a man said.

Gerhold quickly glanced at the top of the letter which was addressed to Rodrick and signed by a man named Morvin. Gerhold had heard the name before since Morvin was a powerful criminal who made his home somewhere in the slums. It detailed some sort of shipment that had been delivered to a warehouse in the slums. But why would Rodrick be dealing with someone like Morvin? The city docks were heavily guarded, while the landings in the slums were in poor repair and usually crawling with unscrupulous characters to say the least.

"Ser Bellin? There is something wrong, we need to get through this door," one of the soldiers yelled from the hallway.

Gerhold knew he was out of time and quickly pocketed the letter before sprinting across the room. A loud crashed echoed from the other side of the door as the soldiers slammed something heavy against it, and Gerhold waited until the door had been weakened before throwing himself against it. The door splintered and flew off its hinges as the vampire crashed through it, sending the soldiers on the other side staggering out of the way. Gerhold grabbed one of the nearby guards and hurled him into the other two before running back down the hallway towards the servant stairwell. The cries of the men behind him continued as he hurried down the steps to the hallway below. A fully armored Paladin appeared around a corner, and Gerhold quickly dropped him with a sleeping dart, which caught the man in the shoulder and immediately knocking the man unconscious. Gerhold ran past the man's body and turned down the corridor leading to the bathhouse where he hoped Roland was waiting for him.

A loud horn rang out as the entire fort was alerted to their presence, but by the time anyone had even entered the corridor, Gerhold had already closed the door, entered the opening to the sewer, and was sliding the grate back into place. He glanced around the cistern to see Nethrin jogging towards him and Roland supporting a clearly exhausted Brother Francis with one of his shoulders.

"Gerhold? Thank the Gods. We thought you had been caught," Nethrin said breathlessly as they moved out of the room and into the smaller tunnels.

"Not quite, but it was closer than I would have liked. We need to get moving, no telling if the Paladins will discover how we entered. If they do, this area will be crawling with them," Gerhold said and rushed over to see Brother Francis. "My friend, are you alright?"

The old man looked up and sighed, and Gerhold could smell the blood before even needing to see the wound on the old man's side.

"As well as I can be, I suppose," he answered with a grimace and held a mass of bloody cloth against his wound. "Roland got to me before they could set in on their interrogations, but one of them caught me with an arrow as we ran," he answered in his raspy voice. "Gerhold, they believe the plague was started by you. Rodrick has spread the word that you are to be hunted and captured alive."

"That means the City Watch is going to be looking for us," Roland commented and swore under his breath. "We have the plague, the fog, and now the Paladins and City Watch after us."

"We can worry about that later. Can you walk?" Gerhold asked and the old man nodded.

"With help," Francis responded with a smile. "If I start to slow you down, then leave me."

"That will not be a problem," Gerhold said and turned to Roland. "Let me know if you get tired and we can trade. Nethrin? We need to head south and find a place where Brother Francis will be safe."

"There is Mister Quinn; he is a poorer merchant who lives on the edge of the slums not too far from the chapel. I know he would be more than willing to take Brother Francis in," Nethrin said, but the old man waved his hand in dismissal.

"No, I will not have you endangering someone else for my sake," he protested.

"You are going whether you like it or not," Gerhold responded. "This Mister Quinn sounds as good a place as any for you to hide."

"And where are we headed after?" Roland asked as they started to make their way back down the tunnel, Nethrin at the lead with his torch in one hand and his maps in the other.

"To the slums. I may have found a clue," Gerhold said.

"Good, at least we have a bearing now. You will have to tell me about it on the way," Roland said.

"There is more to tell than you know," Gerhold responded and continued after Nethrin.

A Dawn of Death

Chapter 7: Unscrupulous Characters

They moved slowly, due in part to Brother Francis, back through the twisted passages that ran beneath Vilheim. The poor old priest leaned heavily on Roland and seeming to grow even more tired the further they went. Gerhold moved about like a shadow, ensuring that their path was clear, while Nethrin continued to guide them through the maze, all the while Brother Francis seemed to grow paler by the minute. Finally, after a half an hour, the old man could go no further, and they were forced to stop. Gerhold kneeled next to the old man who leaned wearily against a nearby wall and gasped for breath.

"Come on, old man, we are nearly there. Once we get you to the merchant's house, we can find someone to heal that wound for you," Gerhold said.

"I am sorry, Gerhold, but I think it is a little too late for that," he said with a smile.

"We are not leaving you behind."

"You would only be leaving behind a corpse," Francis said and coughed. Gerhold noticed a small spatter of blood on the old man's sleeve from his cough. Roland stood nearby with a concerned look on his face.

"I can carry you the rest of the way; there is no need for you to walk," Gerhold said and the old man shook his head.

"No, my time is nearly up now. I am too old for this sort of thing."

"I will be the judge of that," Gerhold said and lifted the man in his arms. "Nethrin? Lead on, as quickly as you can."

Nethrin nodded and dashed forward. Finally, they reached the small exit tunnel, and as soon as they emerged, they were engulfed in the swirling mists that prevented them from seeing anything beyond a normal torch's light. They were standing in an open muddy area between the skydocks and the edge of the slums. This area was known as the Bronze District, a place where you would find the highest of the lower class and the cheaper merchants of the city. Gerhold carried Brother Francis in his arms out through the tunnel, followed by Nethrin. Roland stayed behind in the tunnels since it would be much easier to spot a group of four, even in the mists, and with the curfew in effect, they wanted to remain as inconspicuous as possible.

The streets of Vilheim were abandoned and almost completely silent. Every so often a cry would emanate from somewhere off in the distance, muffled by the fog. Nethrin helped guide them through the mists, watching for the patrols that the City Watch had sent out. They passed through the empty streets quickly and reached the merchant's house, which was built against the thirty-foot-high stone wall that separated the slums from the Bronze District, without incident. It was barely more than a basic tenement though it was far better than the shacks and dilapidated houses found in Breganwarf or the Vilheim Slums. Gerhold carried the priest forward and set him down on the cold steps as Nethrin rapped on the door. A few moments later a light came on inside and Gerhold retreated into a nearby alley, hidden by the darkness and the churning fog.

"Who is it?" a man called down from above. "Who be knocking on my door at this hour? I cannot see a bloody thing with this fog."

"Mister Quinn? It is Brother Nethrin, from the chapel," Nethrin answered.

"Nethrin? What in the blazes are you doing out here at this hour? Don't you even know what is happening in this city?"

"I do sir, but I have Brother Francis with me, and we need your help," Nethrin called back but there was no response.

Gerhold was almost ready to leave when the little front door opened, and a small stream of light spilled out into the darkened street. The vampire stood at the ready, hoping they would not attract the attention of the City Watch patrols. Mister Quinn was a heavy man with a scraggly beard and balding head. He held a crossbow in his hands and looked suspiciously from Nethrin to Brother Francis, who looked as though he was ready to collapse.

"By the Gods, what are the two of you doing out here?" he asked.

"The chapel was attacked, and we need your help," Nethrin responded.

"Attacked? By whom?"

𝔄 𝔇𝔞𝔴𝔫 𝔬𝔣 𝔇𝔢𝔞𝔱𝔥

"The Paladins, they came and accused Bother Francis of being a heretic," Nethrin said and Gerhold heard Quinn scoff.

"I wouldn't believe that even if the Vigils themselves came and told me. Why don't you both come inside? It's not safe being about at night or day in this city no more," the man said and helped Nethrin carry the old priest inside.

"He has been wounded. Can you help him?" Gerhold heard Nethrin ask but did not hear the answer.

The door closed and once again the street was dark. Gerhold huddled in a nearby alleyway for a few minutes, hoping that Nethrin would decide to stay and remain safe, but after about ten minutes the young man came sliding out the door, which was closed and locked behind him. Nethrin darted across the street to where Gerhold was waiting.

"Is everything all right?" Gerhold asked as Nethrin approached.

The young man had tear stains across his face, and Gerhold immediately knew what had happened.

"Brother Francis was already dead by the time we entered," Nethrin said and closed his eyes. Gerhold felt his stomach drop. "Mister Quinn said he would take care of the body as long as we need him to."

They stared at each other for a moment in silence, allowing the death of their friend to wash over them. Gerhold saw flashes of the old priests: the first time they had met, and the many times Francis had hidden him from the Paladins and lied for him.

"He was a good man, a true servant of the Three," Gerhold said and Nethrin nodded.

"He was the best man I have ever known," Nethrin said with a weak smile. "You know he took me in when my parents abandoned me."

"He had a knack for taking in those who the rest of the world did not want," Gerhold answered and put his hand on Nethrin's shoulder. "What did you tell the merchant when you left? I imagine he asked you to stay."

"He did, but I told him I had to get back and help clean up the chapel after the attack. He thinks I am brave," Nethrin responded and wiped his eyes. "Not the best judge of character I must say. I hide while you and Roland do all the real work."

"You serve your purpose, Nethrin, and there is nothing shameful in that. We were not all made to be warriors," Gerhold answered and led them into the mists.

"I suppose you're right. Sometimes, though, I wish I could do more," Nethrin whispered as they snuck through another alleyway.

"Perhaps Roland and I can start training you. But it will have to wait, though."

They moved quickly now that they did not have to worry about Brother Francis, and in no time they had reached the muddy open area that separated the skydocks from the rest of the city. After climbing back through the small drainage tunnel, they made their way back to Roland.

"Is Francis all right?" he asked as they approached and Gerhold shook his head.

"Francis is no longer with us," he answered, and Roland slammed his spear against the wall angrily.

"Those bastard Paladins are going to pay for this!" he roared and turned to head back into the tunnels.

"Vengeance for Brother Francis can wait; for right now we have other things to attend to," Gerhold responded, in spite of his own desire to head back to the City Watch and kill Rodrick himself.

"Wait? For them to kill more of my friends. They are all corrupt, each and every one of them." Roland was shaking with anger. Gerhold grabbed him by the front of his leather armor and pinned him against the wall.

"There will be time for that later, but for now we have work to do," Gerhold said and relaxed his grip. "Killing Paladins who had nothing to do with Brother Francis's death serves no use to us now. We must stop this plague and save this city. That is what the priest would have wanted."

Roland exhaled slowly and nodded before Gerhold released him. The young man bent down and picked up his spear.

"So what did you learn?" Roland asked and Gerhold pulled the folded letter from his pocket and handed over.

"Seems like our friend Rodrick has been receiving shipments at a warehouse in the slums," Gerhold said as Roland scanned the page. "He has also been making sure no one finds out about how the plague has been spread; however, he hinted that it was not a plague at all."

"You mean he is part of all this?" Nethrin asked.

"That is what he said," Gerhold answered.

"Did you kill him?" Roland asked hopefully, but Gerhold shook his head. "A pity, sounds like he deserved it. Just like the rest of them."

A Dawn of Death

"If I did then we would have even more problems," Gerhold said. "You do not just walk away after killing a Paladin Commander, and we have enough to deal with right now as it is."

"Who is this Morvin the note mentions? I've heard the name before, but I don't know where," Roland asked.

"He is a criminal, makes his home in the slums. That is about all I know. Sounds like Rodrick has been dealing with him for a while now," Gerhold answered.

"So, this warehouse in the slums, what do we know about it?" Roland asked.

"I am guessing it is owned by Morvin. Do you have any plans for the building, Nethrin?" Gerhold asked and the young man shook his head.

"There are no plans for the upper areas of the slums. The streets and buildings are a mess and the plans I have look nothing like the slums do now, and the ones I have for the sewers are poorly drawn and faded. We may not be able to use the tunnels once we pass beneath the wall or else risk getting lost."

"We will take to the streets once we get there. The slums are always bustling with activity, and I bet even more so now. Besides, the City Watch closed off the area over a week ago, which means no patrols. We will find this Morvin and see what he knows about our little Paladin friend," Gerhold answered.

"Well then, I say we investigate this warehouse; it is all we have to go on at the moment anyway," Roland said and motioned for Nethrin to lead on.

"It will only take me a few minutes to guide us from here. Let us hope none of the passages are destroyed, though."

With that Nethrin moved on once again with Gerhold and Roland in tow. It was a solemn walk, a silent one as each man reflected on the loss of their friend. Gerhold had always liked Francis; he had been a loyal ally and as patient, honest, and disciplined a priest as there could be. He had helped a vampire and been true to his word in spite of what most others would have done.

It did not take long for them to pass beneath the wall and enter the slums, where they immediately searched for the nearest route up to the surface. Without an adequate map there would be no way for Nethrin to guide them through the darkness, and though Gerhold's eyes saw perfectly in the darkness, it still would be impossible to not lose their way. They finally made their way to the end of a corridor and found a rusty ladder that climbed up to the surface. Gerhold was the first to the top and pushed open the stiff iron cover before pulling himself out of the claustrophobic hole. They were in a thin back alley, between two tightly packed buildings made from old, splintered wood and strips of metal. While Roland helped Nethrin up, Gerhold moved down the alley to figure out just where they had come out.

He had spent most of his life in Vilheim, and even in the mess of twisting streets and tightly packed shacks that made up the slums; it was likely that he would recognize something that would tell him where they were. The slums of Vilheim were where the poorest of the city's inhabitants were force to eke out their existence, usually working on one of the nearby manors or at the docks for pittance of pay. These shacks were all they could afford without starving. Years ago things had been better, but as time went on the heirs to the nobility became more and more greedy, paying their workers less and less while they themselves lived in increased extravagance. As the years went by, life in the slums deteriorated until it resembled places like Breganwarf where the poor lived in squalor while the nobility enjoyed their luxuries.

Gerhold walked to the end of the alley and peered out into the streets. Contrary to the silence of the rest of the city, the slums were teeming with activity. Men and women bustled through the crowded paths that wove in between the tightly packed and poorly built structures, and the sounds of crying could be heard echoing down the street. The City Watch had all but abandoned the slums, and now the streets were controlled by the gangs and criminals, however, Gerhold doubted they would be harassing their fellow peasants while the plague was about. Most of the people wore rags or strips of cloth over their mouths and noses, hoping to keep the plague at bay, but something that Rodrick had said still festered in the back of Gerhold's mind. What if this was not a plague? And if it wasn't, then what could it be? What sort of evil magic could cause such a thing?

Roland, Nethrin, and Gerhold wrapped their scarves around their faces, and Gerhold led the way into the throngs of peasants heading in the direction of the docks and warehouses that lined the Voldar River. Many of the shacks had been boarded shut and some had words painted on the doors such as *Afflicted* or *Plagued*. Men pulled carts through the streets that were piled with bodies that had been wrapped in burlap and linen which were being taken to the center of the slums and burned, or else being tossed into the river. Gerhold saw a woman crying in front of one of the quarantined buildings, calling for her husband, but the only sounds coming from within were screams and moans. Roland looked over and Gerhold knew that they were both thinking the same thing; this was far worse than they had envisioned. A group of rough looking men were leading a line of people down the street, all of whom had been tied together with lengths of rope.

"You, boy," Roland called to a skinny child with messy hair. "Where are they taking those people?"

The child stared at the people who had been tied together and frowned.

"They be takin' 'em to the old church at the west end; that's where they been takin' all the sick ones," the boy responded.

After the boy left, Roland turned to Gerhold.

"The old chapel?" Roland said and rubbed his chin.

"I guess that is where they are locking up those who are sick with the plague. We should probably avoid the area then; I do not want either of you catching the sickness," Gerhold said.

"If we haven't caught it already," Roland said with a shrug.

They continued through the crowded streets and passed more boarded up buildings, and Gerhold saw even more carts carrying wrapped bodies, some of which were still moving. The smell of death and blood was strong, almost as strong as it had been in the foul caves of the necromancers beneath Altandir. It wasn't the sweet enticing smell either, it was rotten and disgusting. Gerhold had never smelt such a thing before. It was vile, and strange. Bad blood. Gerhold felt a twinge in the back of his mind, as if the monster were repulsed as well. The vampire did his best to ignore the stench as he led them through back alleys and side streets to avoid the crowds as much as they could until finally reaching the docks. Ahead was a small wooden gate, which appeared to have been hastily constructed.

"Hey, you three, where do you think you're going?" a man called as they approached the gates.

Gerhold turned to see a tall burly man approaching them, flanked by two rough looking fellows.

"To the docks, why? What's it to you?" Roland answered.

"The docks are off limits; you should know that by now," the man growled.

"Under whose authority?" Gerhold asked and the man rounded on him.

"What da ya mean on whose authority? The docks are under the control of Morvin now, and he said that no one is allowed in without his permission," the man spat and glared at Gerhold.

"Morvin controls all of the docks?" Gerhold asked.

"That's what I said, now shove off."

"Would this change your mind?" Roland said and tossed the man a small bag of coins.

The big man opened the pouched and poured out five silver coins and a gold sovereign. Immediately his mood changed, and he turned to look at his fellow guards while showing off the glittering coins.

"Now that's something else; perhaps I misjudged the three of you. What is it you want?" he asked through his toothy grin.

"We need to speak to Morvin," Roland said with a wry smile, and the guard raised his eyebrow.

"Why do you want to speak to Morvin for? He won't just allow anyone in ta see him, ya know."

"We have a few questions that need answering, and Morvin is the only fellow in town who can do that for us."

The man looked them over for another moment before shaking his head.

"Sorry lads, but I can't do that. Morvin would have me skinned alive if I let a couple of random blokes in to see him," the guard said and turned to leave.

"Tell him Rodrick sent us," Gerhold said and the guard halted.

"Who'd you say?" the guard asked suspiciously.

"Commander Rodrick of the Paladins sent us. Tell Morvin or we will return to our employer and inform him that Morvin has refused us audience. I doubt that will help their business relationship much," Gerhold said.

Again, the man paused before finally nodding and heading towards the docks. They waited another ten minutes before the guard returned and beckoned for them to follow. Gerhold nodded to Roland and tapped Nethrin on the shoulder.

"Relax; Roland and I will take care of everything," Gerhold whispered as they walked.

"I just hope this Morvin does not realize we do not work for Rodrick. This may not go over too well if he does," Nethrin added.

"Let me and Roland worry about that. If things go wrong, you just find a place to hide, all right?" Gerhold said and Nethrin nodded.

They followed the man through a small wooden gate and then onto the long wooden platforms that were built along the Voldar River. Large warehouses

A Dawn of Death

lined the docks and old piers stretched out into the freezing waters. Chunks of ice and frost covered the old walkways and made slipping and falling into the river a very real danger. The guard led them down to one of the larger warehouses, and after a brief conversation with another pair of guards, he opened a door and let them in.

"Wait here; Morvin will call for you when he is ready," The guard said and closed the door behind him.

"Well I am surprised that worked," Roland said cheerfully. "And they didn't even take our weapons."

"Which means we should be all the more cautious. I doubt a criminal like Morvin, with his reputation, would be so careless as to allow armed strangers into his presence," Gerhold answered just as another door at the other end of the empty room opened.

"You are the messengers from Rodrick?" a man asked. He had a pointed nose and his hair was slicked back. He wore a nobleman's clothes, though, these were dirty and looked as though they had been worn for quite some time.

"We are," Gerhold answered.

"Good, come with me." He turned and motioned for them to follow.

"I must say we are surprised to hear from you since the Commander's last shipment arrived last week," the man said, though Gerhold could detect a hint of suspicion in his voice. "Would you mind telling me why he sent you?"

"We were told to speak to Morvin only," Gerhold answered and the servant smiled.

"Ah, of course. Right this way then."

The servant led them down a short hallway and then turned and opened the door to a large room at the center of the warehouse. To one side were stacks of boxes and shelves, barrels and pallets, and hundreds of other things that were haphazardly organized so that they would all fit. To the other side was a raised platform that resembled a lord's throne room, though this was far from the grand spectacle of a castle or keep. Guards stood at either side of the steps, and at the top of the stairs sat a tall man with wavy blonde hair and an amused smile. Next to him stood a beautiful woman with long dark hair and pale skin. As they approached four more guards pressed in, each with their weapon drawn, and Gerhold looked up to see four more crossbows pointed at them from the catwalks above.

"Thank you, Penard," the man said and waved for the servant to leave.

"Is this how you treat all your guests?" Roland asked and the blonde man laughed.

"Guests? You are no guests. Guests do not lie in order to gain entrance. I know that Rodrick did not send you." Gerhold and Roland traded concerned glances. "So, this raises the question, who are you and why did you lie in order to speak to me?"

"We need some information and unfortunately your guards were not cooperating," Roland said.

"That is what I pay them for, to keep the rabble and the City Watch away from me. So why are you here then? Well-armed, obviously, not of the common riffraff we usually see in this hell hole, so I am guessing assassins perhaps? Or spies?"

"Neither we are only here to speak with you about your business arrangement with Commander Rodrick," Roland answered.

"And what business is that of yours? You are not his servants and I know nothing of you. If anything, I should kill you right now and dump your bodies in the river."

"Did you know that Rodrick has something to do with the plague?" Gerhold asked and suddenly the smile faded. "I thought not. And now you are afraid that whatever you were helping him smuggle into the city was being used to help spread the disease."

The room was silent. Morvin stood and made his way down the steps and took a seat at one of the nearby tables, and in his place the dark-haired woman now sat. Roland looked confused for a moment.

"Now that is something that I find interesting," she said and pursed her lips at their obvious shock. "I am sorry for the deceit, but you know, running a criminal enterprise is not the safest line of work, especially for a woman."

"You're Morvin?' Roland asked.

"I am," the woman said a smile. "It is much easier for me to move around the city and run my operations when my enemies do not even know who I am. I spread the rumors that my friend here, is Morvin. It gains me respect and allows me to be much more secretive with my dealings."

"I imagine so, and it also gives you protection," Gerhold added.

"It does, and now that you know who I am, I would like to know who I am dealing with." Morvin shifted her eyes to Roland and Nethrin. "Who are the two of you?"

A Dawn of Death

"You can call me Roland, and this is Nethrin, one of the priests from the chapel," Roland responded and tapped Nethrin on the shoulder.

"And what about you?" she asked and pointed to Gerhold.

"Hired muscle," Gerhold answered without pulling down his scarf.

Morvin looked him over suspiciously before continuing.

"A mercenary, no doubt. Now, what is this about Rodrick?" she asked.

Just then another group of people entered the room and Gerhold sighed as he saw the grinning face of Anton Valaire.

"And a good decision that would be," Valaire said with an even wider smile. "Two times in only a few hours? Gerhold you should know better than to waste your time following us."

"How did you get in here?" Roland asked and glared at the impeccable smiling face of the ex-pirate.

"Oh Morvin and I have a history; don't we, love?" he said and brushed his hand along the woman's shoulder. She gave a disgusted look and quickly slapped his hand away. "Besides, if you want to know about anything shady going on, always go to the dirtiest source."

"So you know these men?" she asked.

"Aye, I know these men. Well, I don't know those two men, and that one isn't even a man, are you Gerhold?" Valaire asked and Morvin raised an eyebrow.

"He doesn't look like a woman to me," Morvin said with a laugh and the others followed suit.

Gerhold undid his scarf and threw back his hood, making sure to show his elongated fangs as he smiled.

"No, I am not a man," he said.

The others in the room started to shift uncomfortably at the sight of him.

"A vampire? And what would a vampire be doing in Vilheim?" Morvin asked.

"We are here to stop the plague that has settled over the city," Gerhold answered.

"And you said you are a priest?" she responded and pointed to Nethrin. "A priest working with a vampire?" She raised an eyebrow.

"Things are not always as they seem. You should know that better than most," Gerhold answered.

"Very true, but it is still a rather strange partnership. Besides, there is a rumor going around that the plague was started by a vampire, a vampire who was, until recently, taking refuge in the chapel here in Vilheim. That is a strange coincidence."

"No more unusual than a renowned criminal working with a Paladin Commander," Roland retorted and Morvin laughed.

"Also, true, I suppose," she leaned back in her chair. "It seems you both have a common purpose then," Morvin said and glanced at Valaire. "Now tell me again why I should not have you all killed?" Morvin raised her hand and the crossbowmen took aim.

"Because we want to help keep your city from falling to pieces, that's why," Roland said.

"I care very little for this city, only what I can take from it, and since this plague has started to spread, business has been rather good for me," Morvin said and smiled. "However, what was it you were saying about dear Rodrick?"

"We don't know; that's why we came to you. What was he having shipped here?" Roland asked in return.

"Before I divulge any information, I want to know why you think he has anything to do with this. I mean, it is not every day that a Paladin, much less a Commander, is involved with such darkness as has settled over Vilheim."

"He admitted it to me when I threatened to kill him," Gerhold answered.

"And did you kill him?"

"No, I did not think it was prudent to have the Paladins after me for killing one of their own. Not until I can prove he is a traitor at least." Gerhold locked eyes with the woman.

"You should have, I doubt anyone would have really missed him. Of course, if the Paladins do not know of his treachery, then that would put you in a very precarious position. Of course, this also makes me look as though I am part of the plot."

"That is the same conclusion I came to," Gerhold answered.

"So, let us say I believe you. What then?" Morvin asked.

"You tell us what you know, and we find a way to stop this plague," Gerhold said.

Morvin stared at him for a moment, debating what to do. Valaire stood nearby, staring at Gerhold with great interest. Finally, Morvin rose and started to speak.

"Information is a commodity, and commodities have a price," she smiled wryly.

A Dawn of Death

"Fine, you tell us what you know, and we stop this plague. I doubt people dying makes for good business," Gerhold said.

"I suppose you are right, and besides; I was about to tell Anton here the very same thing. For the past few months, I have been sneaking in shipments of various things for the Commander. Many of them were large boxes and crates. They were always retrieved by the same men in the dead of night, who took them to an unspecified location. I offered to deliver them for a small fee, but that was declined, so I had one of my men follow them," she smiled and shifted her gaze to Gerhold once more. "They were taken to the keep, to the count himself."

Gerhold looked from Morvin to Roland, who seemed almost as shocked as he. The count had been working with Rodrick? What were they smuggling in? Could it have something to do with the plague? Or was it a poison?

"Count Leofric is involved in this?" Roland asked and Morvin shrugged.

"Edgar is not as clean as he would have his citizens believe, but I have no idea if he is involved with these things or not. That is all I know of the matter."

"Do you know what they were shipping?" Gerhold asked and Morvin shook her head.

"No, it does not make for good business to be searching through my customers things. However, if you want to find out for yourself, the last shipment is still sitting in count's storage barge anchored just across the river."

"How do you know the shipment is still there?" Gerhold asked.

"Because I have had the area watched and no one has come to pick them up yet," she answered again. "Is there anything else? If you cannot tell I am a little busy at the moment."

"And the name of the ship?"

"The *Drolgin*, you should be able to find it off the shore of the Gold Quarter. It's the largest of the lot, so it shouldn't be too hard to find, even in this weather."

"What can you tell us about the plague?" Valaire asked.

"The first case was discovered here in the slums and they seemed to multiply with each passing day. One of my rival gangs took it upon themselves to start gathering up the infected and locking them away in the chapel at the southern end of the district," she answered.

"What are the symptoms?" Gerhold asked.

"Bleeding from the eyes and ears, graying of the skin, and violent outbursts," the imposter Morvin answered and Gerhold turned to face him.

"Outbursts?" he asked quizzically.

"Yes. As the disease progresses, they begin to moan and act irrationally, complaining about sounds and noises that no one else can hear. Soon after, the afflicted will randomly attack anyone or anything close to them, spouting unintelligible words and inane babble. Also, we have noticed that they fear the sunlight, or at least they avoid it and prefer places that are much darker. It is almost as if they seek out the darkness," the imposter answered and appeared visibly disturbed just from describing the effects of the plague.

"Is there anything else you can tell us?" Valaire asked.

"No, there is not," she answered curtly.

"You have more contacts throughout this city than the City Watch, my dear. Have you heard any other rumors?" Valaire asked again and Morvin scowled.

"Do not try your charms on me, Valaire. That may have worked a few years ago, but now I know exactly what type of man you are. You are lucky I haven't had you stripped down and tossed into the Voldar."

"Are you still angry about that misunderstanding with Marian? I told you many times there was nothing between her and me," Valaire said and grinned. He took a step towards Morvin, whose expression seemed to soften. "You were always the only girl for me."

"Is that what you told her as well?" Morvin said. "You are a charming fellow when you want to be, Anton, but that only works on those foolish, starry eyed women who have very little going on up here," Morvin said and tapped the side of her head.

"They worked on you well enough," Valaire responded, and was immediately met with a slap to the face.

Roland and the other people in the room began to laugh and even Valaire seemed to find it amusing.

"You see? She still loves me," Valaire said with a laugh.

"You are an insufferable fool," Morvin answered, but Gerhold noticed a small smile as the woman turned.

Just then one of the doors burst open and one of Morin's guards from the front gate came bustling in, his eyes wide with fear. Morvin shook her head and cursed under her breath as the man crossed the room while mutterings and worried looks followed in his wake.

"Could I have any more interruptions?" she said in frustration as the

A Dawn of Death

guard stopped in front of her.

"I am sorry, my lady, but there is an emergency," the guard said between deep breaths. "The chapel has been broken open, the afflicted are free!"

Gasps echoed throughout the room.

"What?" Morvin yelled and her eyes grew wide with fear.

"The gatherers were bringing in a fresh group of infected when the doors gave way! The weepers are running through the streets, attacking anyone they see. We must flee!" the guard cried and the others in the room immediately began moving about, gathering things and preparing to leave as quickly as they could.

"It was good to catch up, my lady, but I am afraid we must leave now," Valaire said and waved farewell.

"Run away as soon as things get hard? Why am I not surprised?" Morvin yelled back sarcastically.

"My lady, we need to leave with all haste. Who knows how long it will take for the weepers to get here," the imposter said and grabbed Morvin's arm.

"Fine! Ready the barge; we will anchor it just off the docks," she responded before turning to Gerhold and Roland. "I hope the information I gave you will help; things are getting worse by the minute."

With that she followed her men out of the room, leaving Gerhold, Roland, and Nethrin behind while the sounds of panic started to grow in the distance. The afflicted were free and now the boiling pot was beginning to spill over. They had little time now before the entire city would be overrun with the plague. Gerhold looked at his comrades, both of whom were wondering the same thing: could they stop the plague in time?

Chapter 8: Escaping the Flood

"Looks like it's time for us to leave," Roland said and ran towards one of the opened doors.

"Do you think it is as bad as they say?" Nethrin asked as they passed through the next room.

"We are not staying to find out," Gerhold answered as he kicked open the last door.

Now that they were outside, the sounds of screams and panicked cries were clearer. Hundreds of people were running through the already crammed streets, and the soft orange glow of firelight could be seen through the haze of fog. The makeshift gate that led to the docks was broken inward and more people were cramming onto the wooden walkways, searching for some way to escape the chaos. Gerhold watched as an older man tripped and fell, only to be swallowed by the growing horde and trampled. The swirling fog only added to the confusion, and Gerhold could see no way through the growing throngs of pandemonium.

"Where to now?" Roland asked and Gerhold darted off towards the other end of the warehouse, trying to put as much distance between them and the rioting crowds.

Just then a group of people came sprinting out a nearby alleyway, muttering and crying out. At first Gerhold thought they were just frightened peasants, but as soon as the crowd drew nearer, he noticed the streams of blood that coated their faces and ears. The weepers caught sight of them and howled in anguish as they surged forward.

"Run!" Roland yelled and took off down the boardwalk.

Gerhold grabbed Nethrin by the scruff of his shirt and took off after Roland as the crowd of infected gave chase. They ran as quickly as they could, past warehouses and rickety shacks that lined the docks, before turning down

A Dawn of Death

another side street. Ahead was another alley that passed between two of the larger buildings and Roland turned as soon as he caught sight of one of the rusty metal ladders that would lead to the roof. They climbed as quickly as they could, and once at the top, Gerhold helped both Nethrin and Roland up just as the flood of infected weepers slammed into the wall below. Gerhold jammed his silver sword in between the last rung and the wooden wall and snapped the ladder off before any of their pursuers could make their way up. More screams rang out from below and there was a large explosion followed by a jet of flame that illuminated the misty night sky somewhere off in the distance.

"That was too close. What in the six hells is going on?" Roland yelled as they jogged across the long open rooftop.

"Morvin said that those infected demonstrated outbursts of violence." Gerhold answered. "Well, if they have been locking up infected people in the chapel for a month, then who knows how many of them are pouring through the streets now."

"What of the rest of these people? The City Watch has closed the gates and they have nowhere to run," Nethrin said as they reached the opposite edge of the roof.

"We need to worry about getting ourselves out of here. Think you can guide us through the tunnels?" Roland asked and Nethrin shook his head.

"I have no maps of this area; it would be far too dangerous to chance it. It might take us hours to find our way out and I doubt we would exit where we wanted to," Nethrin answered.

Gerhold halted by the edge of the building and saw another roof only a few feet across from them. Roland was the first to leap across, followed by Nethrin and Gerhold, and soon they were leaping their way from rooftop to rooftop while the slums descended into complete chaos below. Men and women crammed into the streets and fires raged unchecked as men did what they could to slow the flood of infected. Gerhold led them across the rooftops of the shanties and shacks, hoping he was heading in the right direction of the western gate that would lead to the Bronze District. If they could stay on the rooftops, then they could avoid the crowds and the weepers and maybe even find a way to climb the wall that surrounded the slums. If not, then they would have no choice but to reenter the sewer tunnels and try to find their way back.

The front gate came into view ahead, just barely visible in the mists, and Gerhold could see hundreds of people banging against the wooden doors. Above the crowds, members of the City Watch stood along the wall, calling for the crowds to disperse and threatening to fire their crossbows. The threat of the weepers now gave the peasants the courage to attack, and soon a large group managed to drag a large wooden cart near the gates and started using it as a battering ram. The guards above the gate fired off a few quarrels before they were forced to duck behind the ramparts as the crowds below began hurling rocks and burning pieces of wood at them.

"The whole place is has gone mad," Roland said as they watched the chaos unfold.

"Can you blame them?" Gerhold responded and leapt across to another roof.

"After what we just saw? Not one bit," Roland answered.

The farthest end of the western wall was now visible, and Gerhold hurried along until they came to the last few buildings that leaned against the thirty-foot stone barrier. The ramparts were still too high to reach, and the three men set about looking for some sort of rope or piece of wood that could be used to boost them high enough to climb over the wall. Suddenly the crowds near the gates began to shriek even louder as blood weepers began streaming into their midst. Gerhold searched frantically for anything that could help them get over the wall, but as he looked, he caught sight of a small battle taking place below in one of the cramped alleyways. It took only a moment before he noticed that Valaire and his crew were trapped in the alley, surrounded by weepers that pressed in from both sides.

"Gerhold, I found a rope," he heard Roland yell and turned to see the young man running back towards Nethrin.

"Bring it here!" Gerhold yelled back before leaping off the edge of the roof and landed on top of two weepers who were charging Valaire and his men.

In once swift movement, the vampire whipped out his silver longsword and began hacking at the oncoming horde, sending severed limbs and heads flying. Bolin, the larger fellow with the axe, looked at him in confusion and surprise, not sure where Gerhold had come from. Suddenly a rope fell from above, and Gerhold looked up to see Roland holding the line and screaming for them to start climbing. Gerhold slashed at another weeper and sent its slobbering head spinning off in the opposite direction, and he turned just in time to see one of Valaire's men dragged off by the horde, his screams drowned out by the insane jabbering of the blood weepers. The line of enemies seemed to falter as they were

A Dawn of Death

distracted by Valaire's fallen comrade, and the survivors quickly took advantage of the lull in battle to climb the rope. Gerhold was the last one to begin climbing and not a moment later the alleyway was filled with the babbling and bleeding infected.

"Never thought I'd be happy to see a vampire," Valaire said and helped Gerhold onto the rooftop.

"Save it for now; we need to get over the wall," Gerhold said. "Grab the rope."

Bolin started winding up the long coil of rope and then the group jumped back across to where Nethrin stood. After a few tosses they got the rope to hook onto the side of the battlement and began scaling the wall as quickly as they could. Once they reached the top, Gerhold noticed that the guards had abandoned the wall and the gates had been broken open. The residents of the slums poured forth through the opening and into the Bronze District, scattering in all directions and searching for a way to escape the infected that followed. A group of silver clad Paladins appeared at the end of the street, leading a small army of watchmen, and together they ran forward and began pushing back the horde of insane infected. Carts, crates, barrels, and whatever stone they could find was then piled up in front of the broken gates, sealing in whoever was unlucky enough to be left behind with the weepers.

Gerhold led the way across the wall and back down the other side onto a tall flat roof of a nearby building. Here they stopped and tried to catch their breath, while the screams of the infected and survivors alike echoed throughout the streets.

"How long before they break through that mess, eh?" Valaire asked and pointed to the pile of rubble and carts the Paladins and City Watch had set up.

"Not long I imagine," Gerhold responded.

"I suppose I should thank you for getting us out of that mess," the man added with a grin and stuck out his hand.

"We are going to need your help if we want to stop this madness."

"That you are. Looks like we have a trail now, at least if my dear Morvin's information is correct." Valaire wiped his curved sword clean and slid it back into its sheath.

"Two trails, the barge where she said the last shipment is and the count himself," Gerhold answered and the mercenary smiled.

"Aye, two trails. Looks like we're going to need a plan then, eh?"

J.S. Matthews

Chapter 9: A New Plan

The city was stirring now as lights and lamps were being lit. Even the fog could not hide the sudden glow of the fires that seemed to erupt all across Vilheim. Word that the slums had been overrun had spread quickly and now people in the rest of the city were becoming worried. The panic was spreading like the plague itself. Gerhold stood looking out over the rooftops as the fogs shifted.

"We are running out of time," Valaire said as he moved to stand next to Gerhold.

"I know, but perhaps between the two of us we can solve this riddle before it is too late," Gerhold responded. "I am sorry about your comrade. That was not a death I would wish on anyone."

"I barely knew the man. He only joined up with us a few weeks ago. A bit of a toss pot really, know what I mean?" he said with a smile. "If it had been Leandra, then I'd be a bit more upset."

"You two are close?" Gerhold asked.

"As close as siblings can be. I promised our brother I'd take care of her after he bit it in Dirge; you remember that of course." Valaire said and Gerhold nodded. "He was a good man and Leandra has done all but take his place."

"Still we could have used another man," Gerhold said.

A Dawn of Death

"Quendi was worth half a man, maybe less," Valaire answered with a chuckle. "Besides, he knew the risks. Should have been more careful, eh?"

"Gather the rest of your men; we need to figure out what to do next," Gerhold said and Valaire nodded.

"If I can convince them to work with a vampire."

"I just saved their lives."

"And as appreciative as I am, I cannot speak for my friends. See, they think you're still the enemy and all those rumors about you starting this plague haven't helped 'em much, right? Now you show up and help 'em out once and that may do the trick, but then again it may not," Valaire finished with his toothy grin and set about bringing his followers together.

It took a few moments but soon the entire group was gathered at the center of the rooftop. Roland and Nethrin stood next to Gerhold, while Valaire and his five remaining crew stood opposite them. There was Bolin, still cradling his axe and cleaning its blade, Leandra, a thin woman with short hair who was casually leaning over Valaire's shoulder, but Gerhold did not recognize the other three men. One was a dark-skinned Nurrian who carried a curved sword similar to Valaire's. The other two men were identical, and judging by their accents, they were from Myrthia like Valaire.

"All of you, listen up," Gerhold said, and some of the group turned to face him while Bolin and the other Nurrian seemed to pay him no mind at all. "Our time is running out if we want to stop this plague before the entire city tears itself to pieces. I do not care how you feel about me or what you think I am, because right now we have more important things to worry about. If you want to help me stop this evil, then put aside your petty grievances and work with us." Gerhold paused to see if his words had any effect.

"Petty grievances you say?" the Nurrian laughed. "Do you have any idea what your kind has done to me and mine? Do you know the history that you and your blood-letters have in my home country?"

"I think it would be obvious that I do," Gerhold responded.

"Really? How long has it been, vampire, since you have visited the homeland? Fifty years? Longer? You know nothing of our struggles against your kind," the man spat and cursed in the Nurrian language. "You ask me to put aside the death of my brother and his family at the hands of your ilk? Never."

"Calm yourself, Ke'var; you have no grudges with Gerhold here. Besides, he did just save our lives, eh?" Valaire interrupted.

"Since when have you been a friend of the night kin?" Ke'var asked with a sneer.

"Since he saved our lives for the second time. Did you forget what happened in Dirge?"

"So do I owe the creature something, then? I did not ask for him to help us and I do not ask for it now," the Nurrian glared at Gerhold.

"Any other objections?" Gerhold asked and Bolin let his axe head fall to the ground.

"I don't care for you, vampire, but you saved our lives for a second time, and that isn't som'thin' I take lightly. I'll work with you, as long as you stay on our side," the big man said and Valaire nodded in agreement.

"Good, and you two?" Gerhold said and gestured to the twins.

"My brother and I will follow you, Captain. We have since the beginning," one of the men said.

"Aye, it won't ever be said that Jarok and Jahntu disobeyed you," the other added.

"You already know I am with you, brother," the woman said.

"That leaves just you, Ke'var," Valaire said and stood in front of the Nurrian. "Are you with us, or are you going to walk?"

Ke'var glared at the circle around him before turning and looking out into the mists. The soft sounds of cries and the rare scream could still be heard, along with the crackling of distant fires. A soft breeze had kicked up and carried the smell of burnt wood and corpses with it, inundating the entire city with the stench of fire and death. The Nurrian sighed and turned again to face the group.

"I hate your kind, vampire, and I always will. I joined your group, Valaire, to hunt and kill these creatures, not to work with them as if they are allies. For now, I will stay, but once this is over, you are just another creature for me to kill," Ke'var finished and spat again at Gerhold's feet.

"That will work for now, as long as you are not planning on sticking a knife in my back," Gerhold said.

"I will not have my honor questioned by a night kin," Ke'var responded.

"Then do not give me reason to question it."

The group stood for a moment in silence while Ke'var and Gerhold continued to glare at each other. This sort of behavior would usually not bother Gerhold, but with so much at stake it was frustrating to have a man who was so short sighted. Ke'var would not be someone he would rely on and he planned to watch the Nurrian very closely.

"Now that we are all one big happy family, would you mind telling us what you plan is?" Valaire asked and Gerhold nodded.

"We know two things now. One, the count and Paladin Commander Rodrick are somehow involved with this sickness, and two, the count has yet to retrieve his last shipment, which may or may not have anything to do with this. We need to split up and investigate both." The others said nothing, and so Gerhold assumed they agreed to the plan. "Valaire? You and your men go and investigate both the count and Rodrick. See if you can come up with anything."

"The count has shut himself in his keep; how are we to learn anything of him?" Leandra asked.

"Stick with Rodrick then, that traitor will lead you to something sooner or later," Roland responded.

"Nethrin?" Gerhold said. "I need you to return to the chapel. The Paladins have no idea you are with us so you need to do your best to find out whatever you can and then pass the information on to Valaire and his men in case following Rodrick comes up empty." Gerhold saw a slight smirk on Valaire's face.

"Priests, eh? The second-best source of information, behind beggars that is. Those religious old sods are usually hard to get anything out of, but I guess it's different when you are one," he said and smiled at Nethrin. "Where can we find this Rodrick fellow?

"At the City Watch headquarters, at least that is where he was last we saw him. He has no idea we are working together, so he may even be willing to speak with you. You still have the support of the Seekers I take it?" Gerhold asked and Valaire nodded. "Good, use it if you have to and see what you can find out."

"It shouldn't be a problem," Valaire said and then turned to face his men. "Bolin? I want you to take the twins and see if you can find anything out about this count. Start with a bit of spying, eh?" The big man nodded. "Ke'var, you and Leandra will come with me; we'll see what this Rodrick fellow knows."

"It would have been much easier if Quendi was still alive," Ke'var added.

"But he isn't, so we make do with what we have," Valaire responded.

Ke'var was obviously still upset with the arrangement and with the death of their comrade, but after a brief look of contempt passed over his face, the Nurrian nodded in agreement.

"Fine, but if we are going to proceed then let us do it as soon as possible. I would prefer to be out of the company of this thing," Ke'var said and pointed to Gerhold.

"Is there anything else you know?" Valaire asked and Gerhold shook his head.

"No, but perhaps we will know more after investigating those shipments," Gerhold answered.

"I'll have Bolin and the others see what they can find out about the count. It may not be much if the keep is locked up as tightly as they claim it is, but either way, we can find out something."

"Whatever they can find will help. When you are finished then meet us behind the old Iron Horse Tavern in the Gold District. Do you know where that is?" Gerhold asked and Valaire laughed.

"I know every tavern in every city in Midland," he said and smiled.

"Good luck then; hopefully, we will meet up with you within the next few hours," Gerhold said and they shook hands.

"Let's hope we have something to show for it, eh?"

Valaire made his way down from the rooftop along with his comrades, and a minute later only Gerhold, Roland, and Nethrin were left.

"You really think we can trust them? They're mercenaries for the Gods' sake," Roland complained.

"For now, we need them. There is more going on here than we can handle in one night and judging by how quickly the slums were overrun I would say that is about all the time we have." Gerhold turned to Nethrin. "I need you to go back to the chapel and see what you can learn. Speak with the other priests and the poorer folk who have taken refuge there."

"You mean if Rodrick hasn't had the Paladins execute them," Roland added.

"Rodrick may be corrupt, but I doubt the others are. They are just following orders," Gerhold said and glared at Roland for a moment, reminding him that he was once in their place. "We may need their help before the night is through, if we can prove that Rodrick is a traitor that is."

"There was that other Paladin, Ser Owyn, I think his name was. Maybe he would be willing to help?" Nethrin asked.

"Do your best to learn what you can about Rodrick and the count, if anything. If you want to speak to the Paladin then just be careful; I do not need to worry about rescuing you as well," Gerhold answered and Nethrin nodded.

"I will be careful. Shall I meet you behind the tavern as well?"

𝔄 𝔇𝔞𝔴𝔫 𝔬𝔣 𝔇𝔢𝔞𝔱𝔥

Gerhold nodded.

"Yes but be careful with Valaire. I am not sure we can completely trust him yet," Gerhold responded.

"Why did you tell him our plans then?" Roland asked as Nethrin darted off down the side of the building and disappeared into the mists.

"They won't betray us, but I do not intend to trust anyone who works with the Seekers with more than I have to." Roland nodded and moved to the edge of the roof.

"That puffed up Myrthian," Roland muttered. "Valaire better not betray us, because if he does—" he made a slicing motion with his spear.

Together the two men made their way back down to the fog-filled streets, which were now bustling with activity as men and women began to evacuate the Bronze District. They had no need for travelling through the tunnels now as even the paths and alleyways were crowded with panicked citizens. The City Watch and the Paladins were far too distracted to notice the two men as they passed quickly along through the throngs of people, impossible to pick out amongst the chaos. Vilheim was falling to pieces around them, fires raged unchecked in the slums; the populace was about to riot, and all the while the fog was growing ever thicker. The City Watch and the Paladins could hold back the plague victims in the slums, but how long would it be before it spread to the other districts? How would so few hold off so many? Gerhold knew that time was short, and if he wanted to save his city from annihilation, then it had to be done tonight. If he could not, then the sunrise would signal Vilheim's destruction. A dawn of death.

Chapter 10: The Barge

Gerhold and Roland made their way through the streets as the confused masses took to the streets. The City Watch was now overwhelmed as the rumors of what had occurred in the slums continued to spread, and soon the citizens were marching on the gates, begging to be let out before the plague took them all. The chaos allowed Gerhold and Roland to move throughout the city without any worries of being seen by the Watch, and even the heavily-guarded bridge between the Gold and Silver Districts was crammed with peasants and merchants, all trying to escape the plague ridden slums. There were two bridges that spanned the Voldar, one of which had already been raised to prevent anyone from the slums making it into the Gold District.

Now only the northern bridge remained, and it took Gerhold and Roland very little time to reach it. The throngs of townsfolk barred the way but with a bit of shoving they were able to pick their way through the crowds. Thankfully, they made it across without incident and started heading for the docks that lay along the southern rim of the Gold District. This was fanciest part of town where the richest of merchants and business owners mingled with the lower levels of the noble class. Tonight, though it was being overrun by the desperate folks seeking safety on the other side of the river, hoping the bridges would protect them from the plague victims.

Little did they know that the plague did not care how much money or power someone had. There were most likely weepers that had been locked away by their families, hidden from the purges, kept alive in hope of finding a cure. How long before those infected broke loose just like in the slums? Where would the people go when there were weepers on both sides of the river? Would they break out of the city? If this were a plague then that would be the worst thing that could be imagined, as the citizens would spread the sickness as they ran. But was this a plague? And what did the never-ending fog have to do with it? Gerhold

A Dawn of Death

believed it was not a coincidence that both events seemed to coincide with one another, and he hoped that whatever they found on the count's barge would answer these questions.

"I hope that woman can be trusted; if not, then we may be walking into a trap," Roland said as they pushed their way through the crowds.

"We have no other leads, so we have no other choice," Gerhold responded.

"Maybe she knew we had nowhere else to go? Perhaps she is working with Rodrick a little closer than we thought?"

"Then we should be cautious."

"Like mice going for a piece of cheese, if you hadn't noticed, it rarely works out well for the mice."

They passed through the crowds that had started to gather in the open squares and beautiful markets of the Gold District while the City Watch was doing its best to keep the tide of fleeing peasants from disturbing the more wealthy denizens. Many of the streets had been blocked off or barred by the Watch and by the private guards that were employed by the various wealthy families who lived in the area. Tensions were running hot, and Gerhold wondered how long it would be before the townsfolk began to turn on each other. Gerhold led the way down a side street and then up the side of a tall three-level house. The doors and windows had been boarded shut and Gerhold wondered if this was to protect those on the inside from whatever wanted to get in, or if it was to keep something for getting out.

They made their way along the rooftop and avoided the nearby barricade on the street below, where Gerhold saw a large crowd of peasants gathered. The guards stood nervously on the other side of the makeshift barricade as the crowds continued to chant and call out angrily at the men barring their path, but soon the cries and voices began to die away as Gerhold and Roland descended the back-side of the house to an empty alley below. Now that they were on the other side of the barricades, the streets were deserted with nothing but a few lit lamps and the shifting mists for company. Gerhold and Roland remained wary as they darted in between the fancy gardens and well-kept streets, until finally they reached the docks.

Unlike the derelict and disorganized area in the slums or even the main piers that could be found in the Silver District, these docks were built specifically for the use of the count and the other noble families who lived in the city. The boardwalk was well-maintained, and nearly every pier had a personal warehouse owned by one of the city's wealthy citizens. Tonight, however, they were deserted and not a ship could be seen at any of the piers, as most had either fled before the quarantine or were now anchored offshore in the center of the river.

"What did she say the name of the ship was again?" Roland asked as they paused near along one of the docks.

"The *Drolgin*," Gerhold answered. "It means river serpent."

"Now we just need to find it, which in this fog seems a bit of a problem. Looks like they took every boat, even the smaller ones," Roland added.

"The Watch probably sank them to keep others from using the boats to pass across the river."

"So how do we find this barge?" Roland asked. "It could be a problem with this fog, not to mention the fact that it is not the only ship to be anchored in the Voldar."

"If we find the count's pier, then the barge should not be far away." Gerhold moved down the walkway and glanced at the various signs detailed with fancy lettering and gold emblems. "Look for the ship house marked with the Leofric's name and sigil."

Roland nodded and jogged in the opposite direction while Gerhold moved down the line, searching for the count's dock. Thankfully the City Watch and the guards of the noble houses were far too distracted with the rioting peasants to worry about patrolling the piers, which made searching easier as Gerhold did not have to worry about being seen. It took some time, but soon Roland came sprinting down the boardwalk in his direction.

"I found it, just this way; hurry!"

Gerhold followed as quickly as he could until Roland halted in front of a large warehouse and dock that was protected by a stone wall. The metal sign on the front had the Leofric family name and crest impressed upon it.

"Good work now let's hope we can find that ship," Gerhold said and slapped Roland on the shoulder.

"Any ideas?" Roland asked.

"Just one." Gerhold kicked a nearby door that splintered and burst open from the force.

"Glad we are being subtle," Roland said.

Gerhold stepped into the large ship house and paused to make sure it was abandoned. Inside was a long rectangular pool of water that was separated

A Dawn of Death

from the river by a metal gate, and around the outside of the room was a wooden walkway that stood ten feet above the rippling water. The metal gate could be raised and lowered by a mechanism to allow ships to pass to and from the river. The soft rushing of the Voldar could be heard echoing off the interior of the building and mixed with the clinking of chains and groaning of the wooden walkways. Along the walls were lines of wooden shelves that held various shipping supplies, coils of thick rope, large bolts of cloth for sails, and other tools and equipment. The pool was empty save for two smaller boats that bobbed up and down in the shifting waters.

"Looks like we found our transportation," Roland said and jumped down into the first of the two boats and began to untie the mooring line.

Gerhold grabbed a coil of rope and moved across the walkway, where he tied one end to a wooden post, and then he used the wheel like a crank to raise the metal gate before dropping into the skiff next to Roland. Immediately the swirling mists began to fill the ship house as they passed beneath the gate and floated out into the slow-moving current of the Voldar River. Gerhold and Roland each held an oar and propelled the little craft through the fog, being sure to keep a keen eye out for signs of any ships. Not only did they want to find Leofric's barge, but they also did not want to accidentally run into another ship or be seen. Gerhold double checked the coil of rope every so often to make sure it was still firmly attached to the ship house, as the last thing he wanted was for them to get lost in the fog.

As they continued, little orange and yellow lights started to appear above the wavy surface of the water, floating in the mists like stars. They pushed their little boat forwards, as quietly as they could, until the nearest ship came into view, and Gerhold used his superior night vision to check for any symbols or writings that would identify the craft. They passed by four vessels, none of which were the one they were searching for, and then were forced to double back as the current began to pull them off course. Gerhold used the long coil of rope to try and guide them back to the shore, and on the way another ship came into view. At first, he thought it was one of the ships they had already passed, but as they drifted by, he caught sight of a line of gold letters that spelled out *Drolgin*. Gerhold tapped Roland on the shoulder and together they were able to guide their little skiff next to the barge.

"Keep it quiet, all right?" Gerhold whispered and Roland nodded. "We find out what Rodrick was having brought in, and then we get off as quietly as possible."

"Something doesn't feel right. Why are there no lights? All the other ships had their lamps lit," Roland said.

"Maybe they do not want to be seen?" Gerhold responded, but Roland still looked concerned.

After ensuring their boat would not drift away with the river's current, Gerhold began climbing up the side of the ship. The barge bobbed up and down in the river, making climbing the soaked wooden frame even more difficult, but soon they reached the top railings and Gerhold silently pulled himself over and landed catlike on the deck. It was difficult to see through the fog, but Gerhold could tell that there was something very wrong. Debris and equipment lay strewn about the deck, and the vampire immediately recognized the stench of death that was easily identified even with the soft breeze. Gerhold crept forward and caught sight of a prone figure lying across the deck, a pool of dried blood staining the wood beneath it. As they moved about the deck, they found even more bodies, some were obviously the bodies of crewmembers that had been infected with the weeping death.

"What in the six hells happened here?" Roland whispered and tightened his grip on his spear.

"Looks like some of the crew caught the plague and attacked the others," Gerhold responded while examining one of the bodies.

"Trapped on this ship with those things," Roland shook his head. "I would have rather thrown myself into the river and taken my chances."

"I imagine that is what many of them did," Gerhold responded.

He knelt next to another body and noticed a long trail of crimson that had dried across the wooden deck, as if the body had been dragged. Gerhold followed the trail to a stairwell that led below deck into a corridor of pitch black.

"Following a blood trail into the bowels of a ship covered in bodies? What could possibly go wrong?" Roland whispered sarcastically as they started down the stairs.

Gerhold held his crossbow at the ready as they moved down through the darkened corridor until it ended and opened into the spacious storage area below deck. Stacks of crates and barrels were carefully organized throughout, with only a few narrow paths that passed between them. More bodies could be seen below, huddled in the gloom, and Gerhold stopped at the last step, surveying the darkness for any signs of movement while the ship slowly drifted side to side. He moved forward slowly, motioning for Roland to cover his back while he started looking over the crates and barrels.

"See anything?" Roland asked and Gerhold shook his head.

"Nothing, just ale and wool here."

"That woman better not have sent us here for nothing."

"There are other crates to search, just make sure you keep an eye out for anything that moves, the Gods only know what could still be alive on this ship," Gerhold whispered back and continued down the narrow path between the boxes.

They moved throughout the storage area, glancing at the various crates and barrels, not sure what they were supposed to be looking for. Gerhold halted near a line of long rectangular boxes, all of which had been stamped by the Callorian Trading Company and addressed to Count Edgar Leofric. Out of curiosity, he drew his silver dagger and used it to pry open one of the crates, and as soon as the wooden top slid off Gerhold jumped back in surprise. Inside was a body, a person wrapped in a long black cloak, and it took Gerhold only a moment to realize that it was no normal body. He raised his silver dagger and drove it through the vampire's chest. The body lurched for a moment and the creature's eyes bulged as the silver dagger pierced its heart, leading to a soft high-pitched sigh as its skin began to smolder and burn away.

"Vampires?" Roland said in surprise as Gerhold stepped back, revealing the now ashy remains of the creature. "This is what the count has been bringing in all this time?"

"There are more here, so let us hurry and deal with them," Gerhold said and prepared to crack open the next crate.

Just then he heard heavy footsteps above and voices echoing down from the upper deck. Roland darted down the rows of boxes while Gerhold finished off the second creature. He moved on to the third but instead of finding a slumbering vampire, he found carefully packed vials of blood, and there were at least four other crates that he could see. How many more were on the ship, and how many of those contained more of the creatures? Roland came running back through the darkness and motioned for Gerhold to follow him.

"There are Paladins on board and Rodrick is with them," he whispered. "I bet that pirate, Valaire, betrayed us. We need to get off this ship right now."

"How many of them are there?" Gerhold asked.

"Too many for us to handle by ourselves. I counted at least eight but there could be more, so we need to leave right now."

"What about the crates? We cannot let Rodrick free these monsters," Gerhold protested and Roland shook his head.

"Then what do you want to do? Have me hold off the Paladins while you search through all of this?"

Gerhold stared around at the seemly innumerable number of crates and realized that even if Roland could hold off the Paladins, he would never have enough time to search them all. Then Roland smiled, reached into his pack, and pulled out a shiny silver sphere with a short wick that stuck out to the top.

"How about we leave old Rodrick a few presents on our way out?" he said and placed the pyrite bomb on one of the nearby crates. "We'll sink the whole damn ship."

"You have two bombs; I still have three. Do you think five bombs are enough?" Gerhold asked and Roland shrugged.

"Let's find out."

Together they ran down the aisles hiding bombs in the crates as they went. They replaced the usual wicks with slow burning ones that Nethrin had created, which would allow them more time to get off the ship before the explosions. The soft hiss of the wicks could be heard while little puffs of smoke drifted out from underneath the lids. Soon the footsteps reached the bottom of the stairs and the shiny silver armor and torches of the Paladins could be seen.

"See anything?" one of the Paladins asked.

"Not in this darkness," another answered. "See if you can get a few more men down here to help us search. We will need to carry up the cargo for the count anyways, so we might as well get the help now."

"How many do you think he brought in this time?" the other guard asked.

"Who knows? But that is not what we are being paid to worry about."

"Looks like Rodrick isn't the only corrupt one," Roland said with a hint of satisfaction.

"Then it looks like our no killing rule can be put aside," Gerhold answered.

Roland smiled before turning and heading for the far side of the cargo hold.

Gerhold hurried behind Roland towards a second stairwell that would lead up to the decks, but just before they reached the doorway a light appeared as

A Dawn of Death

another pair of Paladins came striding down the steps. Roland leapt to the side and Gerhold ducked behind a nearby stack of barrels just as the men appeared in the doorway. They stood for a moment before spreading out and starting to search between the stacks of cargo. Gerhold watched as a Paladin drew nearer to one of the crates that held a pyrite bomb, hoping the man would not see the little trail of smoke that wafted up from beneath the lid, but as the guard moved closer he immediately noticed the strange sight. The Paladin halted and stared at the box before reaching for the lid. Gerhold reacted without thinking.

    He darted forward from his hiding place without a sound and drove his dagger into the Paladin's neck. The man flailed about for a moment, but a second stab finished the job and the Paladin collapsed to the floor in a heap. Gerhold grabbed the body and tried to stash it between the stacks of barrels, but the other guard heard the disturbance and was already on his way to investigate.

    "Tamron? What was that? You better not have dropped one of the Leofric's crates or Rodrick is going to let the blood suckers have a go at you," the guard said as he approached.

    Just as the Paladin turned the corner and saw his comrade's body lying on the floor, Roland lunged out of the darkness and thrust his silver spear through the guard's neck. The man fell to the floor with a loud thud and Roland yanked his spear free from the corpse. Two more Paladins saw them from across the room, and Gerhold grabbed Roland and took off in the direction of the second stairwell. They dashed up the steps two at a time until they reached the top and emerged onto the deck of the ship. At least six Paladins stood on the ship, swords at the ready, but they held their ground when they saw Roland and Gerhold.

    "You weren't leaving without saying hello, were you?" Rodrick said as he approached, a smug satisfied smile etched across his face.

    Gerhold looked at Roland as if to ask how much time they had before the bombs exploded, but from the look he received in return it was clear that Roland did not know either.

    "Sorry to be rude, but we have other places we needed to be tonight," Roland answered.

    "And look who is, Roland Lucer, son of Lord Brendin Lucer. Disgraced Paladin, a fallen brother," Rodrick said with a laugh that was echoed by the other Paladins.

    "Seems I'm still more loyal that you lot," Roland responded.

"I am very loyal, loyal to those who pay me what I am worth," Rodrick said and tossed a gold coin into the air. "Anyways, it is good to see you found your way here as now I can clean up all the loose ends in one swoop. This is much easier than searching for you throughout this entire city, especially now that the rioting has started."

"So, the count hired you to bring in vampires and spread the plague?" Gerhold asked, knowing at any moment the bombs would be going off. All he had to do was stall for a few more moments.

"You still can't see the entire picture, can you? And to think I was told that you would be the only thing standing between us and our goal. I suppose they overestimated your abilities, so much for all the great tales," Rodrick said and raised his hand to signal his men to attack.

The first Paladin took a step forward and Roland readied his spear while Gerhold drew his sword, but suddenly an explosion rang out and a fiery blast ripped through the floor of the ship, sending Rodrick and his men flying in all directions. Gerhold and Roland were both hurled backwards, where they rolled across the shaking deck, but both rolled back to their feet ready to fight. One of the Paladins nearby regained his balance and ran at them, only to be met by Roland's spear as it flashed this way and that. The two men dueled as a second explosion rocked the ship and sent wood splinters scattering through the air. Gerhold drew his crossbow and fired a bolt at one of the Paladins who had begun to conjure a ball of fire, sending the man tumbling over the side of the ship.

Out of the corner of his eye Gerhold caught sight of Rodrick who was still struggling to find his footing as the ship swayed violently back and forth. Another explosion and the ship began to list to one side, just as Gerhold charged forward, sword in hand. Rodrick saw him coming and pulled his sword free, just in time to deflect the vampire's powerful blow that knocked him to his knees. Gerhold moved in for the killing stroke when a fourth explosion knocked him off balance, and he was forced to dive out of the way as Rodrick sent a jet of flames in his direction. He ducked behind the foremast as another jet of flame slammed against it, then pulled one of his smaller crossbows out and fired off a few shots in Rodrick's direction before charging again.

Their blades met with a resounding clash and Rodrick stumbled backwards as he did his best to parry Gerhold's whirling strikes. The ship began to tilt, slowly at first but then Gerhold found himself stumbling as the entire

A Dawn of Death

barge started to sink sideways into the freezing river. Gerhold knew he had to stay on the offensive and keep Rodrick's focus directed at him so that the commander could not continue to cast his spells. Though Gerhold was no mage, he knew that spells took focus. Experienced Battlemages could fight in melee while maintaining their focus, but Paladins were never the most accomplished spell-casters. If Gerhold could keep Rodrick's attention on his blade, then he would not have to worry about the man's magic.

Rodrick raised his hand and prepared another spell, but before the flames could be conjured, Gerhold rushed forward and swung his blade in a wide arc. The commander raised his sword just in time to deflect the blow but was thrown back by the force of it. Gerhold knew he had the upper hand now, and the vampire easily deflected one of Rodrick's off balanced blows and slammed his foot into the Paladin's stomach, sending Rodrick tumbling into the frozen waters below. Gerhold watched as the man struggled to swim but the Paladin armor was too heavy, and soon the commander slipped beneath the waves and disappeared into the depths. Gerhold saw a brief glimpse of Brother Francis in his mind as Rodrick vanished into the darkness, and then he struggled to pull himself atop the sinking barge and saw Roland running in his direction.

"Looks like the boat is gone," he said as he helped Gerhold to his feet.

The barge lurched violently beneath them as the rest of the ship began to slip slowly beneath the water. Gerhold had little to fear here. If he drowned, he would wake up again once the water was clear of his lungs, and since vampires could not feel cold the icy temperature of the water meant little. Roland, on the other hand, had far more the worry about. The ship had been blown to pieces and fiery wreckage lay strewn about, floating farther away with the current and disappearing into the fog. Gerhold snatched up a small piece of rope and then reached into his pack for a small vial of orange liquid, which he handed to Roland along with the other end of the rope.

"Drink this and hold on!" he yelled as the river began to surge over the last vestiges of the barge.

Roland looked at the little vial for a second before downing its contents, just as the first wave swept their feet out from under them. Gerhold held onto the rope as they were tossed into the water, feeling the strong current starting to pull them down river. He pushed his head above the water, unable to see the shoreline, and he decided it did not matter which side of the river they ended up on as long as Roland was alive when they did. Together the two men swam as hard as they could, perpendicular to the current, until finally, after minutes of intense exertion, he saw a stone wall appear out of the mists. Soon they were dragging themselves up out of the river and onto one of the city streets.

A Dawn of Death

Chapter 11: Out of the Mists

Gerhold pulled Roland along the street until they came to a small alley where they slumped against the cold stone walls. Roland tried to catch his breath while Gerhold checked to make sure the river water had not gotten through his pack. After a minute of respite, Roland started to laugh.

"I have no idea how we made it out of that one, but I think we just used up the rest of our luck for the night," he said and leaned his head back in exhaustion.

"And we are still on the right side of the river," Gerhold added.

"Better than having to cross that bridge again." Roland shook his hair to get most of the water out. "What was that potion you gave me?"

"Elixir of flame, it warms the body for a short amount of time. It should last long enough for us to find you some new clothes," Gerhold answered.

"Let's hope it does, otherwise I am going to freeze to death out here." Roland's smile faded as he got to his feet. "Did you kill Rodrick?"

"Unless he found a way to breathe water, he is dead," Gerhold answered, a small hint of satisfaction in his voice.

"Good, looks like we avenged Brother Francis after all," Roland added with a smile. "So, the count was having vampires smuggled into the city. Why do you think that is?"

"No idea," Gerhold lied, as he had already started to formulate a theory from the moment, he saw the first slumbering vampire. He did not want to admit it to himself, not yet. Not until he found more proof. This had happened before. Gerhold had gotten his hopes up about finding Harkin, only to see those hopes dashed.

"That's codswallop; I know you're thinking the same thing that I am." Roland glared at him with those fierce eyes, the same kind of fire and passion that Gerhold had once felt within himself at a young age. "Vampires? Corrupt

Paladins? Who does that sound like to you?"

Gerhold wiped the water from his face with a rag and then shoved it back into his pack.

"You think Harkin is behind this?" Gerhold asked.

"Could be, didn't he promise to come after you? And who can manipulate Paladins in such a way? It would have to be someone powerful, more powerful than Count Leofric at least."

"Do not jump to any conclusions; we do not know if Harkin is involved here or not," Gerhold said, even though Harkin was in the very front of his mind. "Now that Rodrick is dead, we need to focus on finding the count."

"And Valaire, I bet that two-faced pig tipped Rodrick off about us," Roland said and Gerhold nodded.

"More than likely I suspect," he answered and got to his feet.

"We better find Valaire and his men before Nethrin does. There's no telling what they'll do to him."

"Let us make sure you do not freeze to death first," Gerhold responded and took off down the alleyway.

They did not have time to make the trip all the way back to the chapel for Roland to get a new set of clothes, so instead they searched for an abandoned house. Many of the nobles and wealthy merchants had already abandoned the Gold District long before the quarantine had been declared, so finding an empty home would not be too difficult. As soon as they came across one, Gerhold quickly picked the lock and kept watch on the streets while Roland entered. It took a few minutes but thankfully he was able to find a set of leather-braced clothing that had belonged to one of the guards, and though they were a little large it was better than walking around in wet clothes as they slowly froze in the bitterly cold night air.

Next, they hurried off towards the Iron Horse Tavern, where they hoped to confront Valaire and his men. It would be six on two, but both Gerhold and Roland were confident that they could handle the mercenaries if it came to that. There was the chance, though, that Valaire would not show at all, thinking that Roland and Gerhold had been killed, and if that were the case, then Gerhold would continue his pursuit of the count and worry about them later.

Suddenly Gerhold came to a stop and motioned for Roland to hide. Ahead they could hear chants and cries of the townsfolk who were still trying to push their way through the barricades that had been set up. Gerhold crept

A Dawn of Death

through one of the alleys to get a better look at what was happening. Through the fog he could see the back side of the barricade at the other end of the large open square, which was lined with City Watchmen and guards from a few of the nearby noble houses who had decided to stay in Vilheim. On the other side of the wooden wall Gerhold could hear the crowds of peasants getting louder and angrier by the minute, but there was another sound mixed with the angry chants. Gerhold focused his hearing, trying to ignore the crowds and the calls of the guards to get back, and caught the faint echoes of screams coming from somewhere in the distance. The screams grew louder and travelled along the lines of refugees, like a tidal wave approaching the shore, until all of a sudden it was all that could be heard.

"What's going on?" Roland asked, but Gerhold only responded by drawing his crossbow.

Somewhere deep inside him, Gerhold felt a faint tremor, a disturbance, as if there were some sort of evil creature nearby, giving off a faint pulse of darkness. Just then Gerhold heard something pass high overhead, followed by a piercing and terrifying screech, and he watched as whatever it was came hurtling out of the mists and snatched up one of the guards standing atop the barricade. It was gone as quickly as it had appeared, but the man's agonizing screams echoed through the city streets as he was carried off in the mists, only to be suddenly cut short. The creature was roughly the size of a man but covered in thick, leathery, black skin and had a pair of great wings that jutted out of its back. Its hands were razor sharp talons and its face was distorted and grotesque with teeth and large fangs sticking out from its mouth. The screeching died away, but the panic had already started.

The crowds were thrown into a frenzy, and soon men and women were trying to scale the makeshift wooden walls as panic began to spread. The guards tried to hold them back but were soon overwhelmed by the sheer numbers. Suddenly the screeching started again, only this time there was more than one. Gerhold saw another creature swoop out of the mists and grab a woman as she was trying to climb over the barricade, while another pulled a man at random from the crowd. The creatures seemed to be everywhere, flying out of the fog like wraiths and then disappearing once more. The barricade started to fall apart as more and more men and women came climbing over, filling the city square as more of the monsters came screaming out of the darkness.

Gerhold grabbed Roland and together they took off into the fray. All around them people were screaming and running, and even the guards had abandoned their posts in the face of the terrifying monsters. Gerhold leapt over a fallen man and fired his crossbow just in time to catch one of the creatures as it swooped in for the kill. The monster crashed to the ground with an agonizing cry, and before it could move Roland was on it, slamming his silver spear through its throat.

"What are these things?" he asked as Gerhold fired at another.

"I do not know; just hold them off as best you can, we need to protect these people," Gerhold yelled back as another creature attacked.

Gerhold spun and pulled out his two smaller crossbows, relying on his keen senses to pick out his targets as they flew about. Two more fell to the ground, where Roland finished them off with his spear. Suddenly Gerhold was ripped from his feet as one of the monsters slammed into him from behind, sending him sprawling to the stone ground, where it leapt upon him, slashing with its talons. He quickly flipped out his crossblade and deflected the creature's rapid blows before decapitating it in one stroke. Roland ran forward and hurled his spear into the mists, and Gerhold saw another creature fall with a glint of silver protruding from its chest. As soon as the monster hit the ground, Roland rolled and yanked his weapon free, and spun just in time to impale another of the flying attackers.

To his right, Gerhold saw another of the winged demons grab onto a man as he tried to run, but before it could get off the ground, the vampire sent a silver bolt into one of its shoulders. It screeched and let go of the man just as Gerhold lunged forward and stabbed it through the heart with his crossblade, then spun the weapon around, loaded another bolt, and slew another creature just as it swooped out of the mists.

Roland came jogging over through the crowds that were now pouring in through the destroyed barricade. They remained alert, but no other monsters could be seen and most of the screeching had died away. The city was now in complete chaos, and there was nowhere to hide. What had started in the slums had now spread to the entirety of Vilheim, but was it already too late? How could they hope to stop the plague and these creatures, not to mention whatever Leofric had in store for them?

"You all right?" Roland asked and Gerhold nodded. Both men were breathing heavily and Gerhold took a moment to reload his weapons and find where he had dropped his smaller crossbows.

A Dawn of Death

"I wish I knew what these are," he answered and kicked one of the dead monsters. "I have encountered almost every monster this world has spawned, but never anything like this."

"These things could be all over the city."

"Which means we have even less time than we thought," Gerhold responded and started to jog across the square, avoiding the masses of fleeing peasants.

"Where do they think they are going? Do they think the count will offer them protection in his keep?" Roland asked as they sprinted towards one of the streets that led north from the square. "They would have better luck trying to break down the city gates and flee this place completely."

"The Paladins outside would slaughter them before they stepped a foot outside the gate."

Roland stopped running as soon as they crossed the square, the faint echoes of screeches could still be heard further off in the city.

"Gerhold, what are we going to do? It is just the two of us now. We are fighting a plague, Valaire, the Paladins, monsters, and a small army of vampires for all we know. I don't know if we can handle this one alone."

Gerhold paused to catch his breath and thought about what Roland was saying. It was only the two of them; they had no support from the Paladins and City Watch. This was not like hunting a lone demon or a pack of werewolves; they were facing something he had never faced before.

"This is not a choice we can make my friend; the Gods have already given us this task." Gerhold heard Roland scoff.

"The Gods? Since when do they give a damn about us?"

"Whether they do or not, you and I are all that stands between this city and complete destruction," Gerhold answered. "We do not have a choice."

Roland stared at him for a moment, pondering any alternative to the seemingly impossible task ahead. He wiped his spear on a dirty rag and then hurled the cloth to the side.

"Gods or no Gods, I suppose you're right," Roland said, and Gerhold nodded and patted the young man on his shoulder. "Let us pay Valaire a visit, shall we? Then we deal with Leofric."

Gerhold smiled and led the way down the street. The smell of death and smoke permeated the air and even the stone seemed to absorb the stench. Vilheim was falling, but as long as they still lived, Gerhold was going to fight.

J.S. Matthews

What other choice did he have?

A Dawn of Death

Chapter 12: A New Alliance

They passed down a few more empty streets before reaching the open square near the Iron Horse Tavern. It was an old building from the times when Vilheim was found on only one side of the Voldar, and it had become a favorite for travelling merchants and sailors. Tonight, though, it was abandoned, much like the rest of the Gold District, and it stood at the end of the dark street barely visible in the fog. Gerhold paused for a moment and knelt in the shadows of a nearby building and did his best to see through the veils of mist. A faint screech from one of the winged creatures could be heard somewhere off in the distance, but Gerhold paid it no mind, his focus was on the traitor Valaire.

"See anything?" Roland whispered and Gerhold nodded.

"The girl, she is on the roof," he said and pointed to the top of the old tavern.

"An ambush?" Roland asked and Gerhold nodded.

"Possibly, why don't you go and find out. I will give them something to look at while you sneak around. Make sure if it is an ambush that she cannot help," Gerhold said and Roland before dashed off into the mists.

Gerhold stood calmly and started to jog across the open square. As soon as Leandra caught sight of him, he heard her give out a shrill whistle to alert the rest of her comrades. Gerhold tightened his grip on his crossblade as he entered the little back alley behind the old tavern. At the other end of the way stood Valaire and the rest of his companions but Nethrin was not to be seen, which Gerhold was thankful for as the boy would just get in the way during a fight. As soon as he saw Gerhold, Valaire turned and took a step towards him.

"About time you arrived. Where's your friend, eh?" he asked with that same smug smile, and Gerhold halted a few steps from Valaire before raising his crossblade.

"Why did you do it, Valaire? Are you involved in this too?" Gerhold said threateningly.

The other members of Valaire's crew leapt to their feet, weapons at the ready, but the Myrthian just raised his hand for them to hold their ground.

"What in the six bloody hells are you going on about, eh?" Valaire asked in a confused tone.

"Why did you send Rodrick after us? You were the only one who knew where we were headed, and I think it is too much of a coincidence that he arrived right when we decided to investigate the barge." Gerhold kept his crossbow aimed at the mercenary's head, but Valaire only stood there.

"I haven't the faintest idea what you're talking about, mate," he said and took another step forward. "We went to the City Watch headquarters just as you said, but your friend wasn't there. Seems he left right before we came."

"Then how did he know where we were?"

Just then there was a commotion above and the entire group looked up to see Roland holding Leandra by her neck in a choke hold. Valaire glared at Gerhold.

"What are you two doing? We're on the same bloody side here, remember?" he yelled and tightened his grip on his sword hilt. "Tell your mate here to get his hands off my sister."

"Tell me why you betrayed us or she dies," Gerhold threatened.

Valaire's eyes narrowed.

"I already told you we had nothing to do with that, you rat bastard. Now let her go!" Valaire yelled again and drew his sword. "This whole city's going mad and the two of you with it."

"You're a liar," Gerhold responded and prepared to pull the trigger.

"Wait, Gerhold stop!" a voice yelled and Gerhold turned to see Nethrin running down the alley in his direction. "Stop, it was not him!"

Nethrin halted next to Gerhold, out of breath and noticeably dirtier than he was earlier. Gerhold lowered his crossbow slowly before turning to Nethrin.

"What is going on, Nethrin?" Gerhold asked while the others looked on.

"Gerhold, it was not Valaire that told Rodrick about the barge; it was me."

Silence followed as Gerhold let the crossbow fall to his side and he stared in disbelief at the young priest. He had told Rodrick? Why would Nethrin go to a man he knew was a traitor? Why would one of his most trusted comrades betray him?

A Dawn of Death

"Why? Why would you do such a thing?" Gerhold asked.

"Because I had to." Nethrin stared at Gerhold with a defiance that he had never seen before in the young man.

Roland released Leandra, who responded by socking him hard in the stomach. Both eventually made their way down and the others relaxed the grip on their weapons.

"You better explain yourself," Gerhold said and Nethrin nodded.

"I was on my way to the chapel, but I was forced to use the streets when I found out that there were infected roaming the old tunnels. I ran into a group of Paladins who offered to escort me to the chapel, but one recognized me from when we escaped and placed me under arrest. I thought they would take me to Rodrick, but instead it was Ser Owyn. He told me I was going to be tried as a heretic unless I helped him, so I told him everything, about you and Roland, and what we do. At first, he did not believe it, nor did he believe that Rodrick was a traitor without proof, so I told him I could prove it," Nethrin smiled.

"So, you told Rodrick what we were up to?" Gerhold asked.

"Yes! I lied and told him that I had come to confess, that I had been led astray and I wished to seek redemption, and he believed me. I knew he would go after you, so Ser Owyn offered assistance. Rodrick denied the request and instead told him that they were following a lead on your whereabouts, but that they were heading for the slums, not the docks." Gerhold still looked confused and so Nethrin continued. "You see? Why would Rodrick lie to his own Paladins if he was trying to help? He did not want Ser Owyn to know about the count's shipments."

"Why would Rodrick showing up at the docks prove anything? Perhaps he was just trying to work things out before telling the others?" Gerhold said. "I doubt it took that little proof to convince them."

"Once Rodrick left, Ser Owyn and I searched his quarters and found the other letters that Rodrick and Morvin had used to communicate. That and there were letters from Count Leofric asking about his shipments but not what they contained. It was enough evidence for him to convince the other commanders to place a warrant of restriction on Rodrick. They are planning to arrest him on sight, and Ser Owyn has been promoted to his place for now," Nethrin said with a wide grin.

"Well, I doubt they will find him unless they do a thorough job of dredging the Voldar," Roland responded with a laugh.

"You mean, he's dead?" Nethrin asked and both Gerhold and Roland nodded.

"That was a thrilling tale and all, but you mind telling me why my men and I shouldn't just gut the three of you right now for what you tried to pull?" Valaire asked and Gerhold traded guilty looks with Roland.

"I think we owe you an apology; we thought it was you all who tipped off Rodrick," Roland said with a sideways glance at Leandra, who was still not very happy about being ambushed by Roland.

"Oh, you're sorry eh? Well that just makes everything better now doesn't it?" Valaire said angrily.

"Rodrick has been dealt with and now we know that the count has been smuggling vampires in through Morvin," Gerhold said, trying to change the subject from their mistake.

"Leofric was bringing vampires into the city?" Ke'var asked.

"We found his last shipment," Roland said and drew his finger across his throat.

"You killed 'em?" Bolin asked and Gerhold nodded. "A vampire who hunts 'is own kind? Never thought I'd see that."

"Did you learn anything about the count?" Gerhold asked and Valaire nodded.

"Aye, he hasn't been seen in over a year by almost anyone; even the closest and most powerful families haven't seen a glimpse of him. And he took to hiring a bunch of strange guards to watch his keep, and then he sent all his others to the City Watch. No one knows what's happening on the other side of his walls," he said.

"I think we know who those guards are," Roland responded.

"We do; they are the vampires that he had smuggled in," Gerhold added.

"Great, well from here on out we'll take care of things. I don't need you lot trying to kill us all again." Valaire sheathed his sword and turned to leave.

"Valaire, wait. The misunderstanding was my fault, but we need to work together if we are going to finish this," Gerhold said and Valaire rounded on him.

"Need each other eh? We'll do just fine without you, what can a few vampires and the count do?"

"It's not just the Count you have to worry about, we think he is working with someone else," Roland interrupted.

"Really? And who's this then?"

A Dawn of Death

"His name is Harkin Valakir, he is a powerful vampire." Valaire shifted his gaze to Gerhold.

"And how do you know this?"

"I do not know, but I have a feeling it is him," Gerhold answered and the pirate laughed in response.

"Well thanks for warning us about the person who may or may not even be in the damn city and all, but I think we will take our chances."

"Don't be stupid, six of you versus a small army of vampires and the Gods know what else?" Roland stepped forward so that he was nose to nose with Valaire. "You'll all be slaughtered, all of you. You need us, Valaire. That, and there is no way you're getting into the keep without our help."

"Well I don't trust you to not stick a knife in my back," Valaire responded.

"We could have left you to die in the slums," Gerhold said and sheathed his crossblade. "I am sorry I thought you betrayed us, but right now the only thing that matters is getting inside that keep."

"The vampire is right," Ke'var added and everyone turned to the Nurrian in surprise.

"You're with them?" Leandra asked with look of contempt. "Not two hours ago you were threatening to kill him, and now you want us all to be best friends right after he tries to kill us."

"Since when did you start siding with the night kin?" one of the twins asked.

"Do not question my hatred for his kind," Ke'var glared at her and muttered under his breath in the Nurrian tongue.

"Then why side with him?"

"Look around you, woman. The plague, the flying beasts, vampires! We cannot face this challenge alone, and even with the vampire and his companion, we barely stand a chance. We must focus on what is needed now, and right now they are needed," Ke'var said and pointed to Gerhold and Roland.

"If he wanted to kill us, why didn't he just leave us all in the slums?" Bolin asked.

The others looked from the big man to Ke'var, some seemingly agreeing with them, while one of the twins and Leandra seemed irritated that the two men dared to side with the vampire. Valaire appeared torn between the two sides.

"You think we can trust them then, eh?" he asked, and Bolin shrugged.

"Saved me life once today. I still owe 'im for that."

"Curse all Myrthians and our foolish morality," Leandra muttered. "We'll rob and steal, but all someone has to do is pull us onto a roof and we'll forgive them for anything."

"Enough," Valaire interrupted before Bolin could respond. "As much as I hate to admit it, Ke'var is right. We need them, for now."

"Have you lost your mind?" Leandra said, her mouth agape in disbelief. "You want us to still work with this creature? Even after what this one almost did to me?" She pointed angrily at Roland.

"You think we can handle a small army of vampires on our own, eh?" Valaire answered.

"I'll take my chances over working with this scum."

"You would rather die?" Ke'var said. "The enemy of my enemy is my friend. That is the oldest saying in this world, and I suggest you think on it, woman, or stay silent."

"This bickering is pointless and is only wasting time." Gerhold stepped forward. "Choose now, work with us or not. Either way, we are going to make our way into the keep."

"And how do you purpose we do that?" Leandra smirked. "Kindly ask the guards to let us in? I'm sure the count wouldn't mind."

Gerhold turned to Nethrin.

"You still have your maps?" Nethrin nodded. "Good, find us a way in, then you head back to the Paladins and tell them to come to the keep. We are going to need their help."

"What if they do not agree to come? They think Commander Rodrick was just involved in illegal smuggling, not vampires and dark magic." Nethrin said.

"You need to convince them; use me as bait if you have to."

"But what if they come for you?" Nethrin asked.

"Do not worry about that; just make sure you can get as many Paladins as you can, maybe even the City Watch. Who knows what the count has planned for us?" Gerhold said and Nethrin nodded, though grudgingly.

"I will do as you ask," Nethrin said and shuffled through his stack of maps before handing one to Gerhold. "That should help you find your way but be careful in the tunnels; there is no telling how far the infected have spread through them."

A Dawn of Death

"So, we have a way in?" Valaire asked and Gerhold nodded.

"These should help us find our way beneath the wall," Gerhold said and held up the map.

"Just so we're clear though, you both are going in first, wherever we're headed. I'll not have either of you at my back," Valaire responded.

"Fine," Gerhold answered and turned to Nethrin. "Good luck and stay safe. I still do not trust the Paladins, not completely anyway."

"I will, but I think you will need more luck and care where you are going." They shook hands. "Be careful in the tunnels, Gerhold. No telling what is down there now."

"We will, now off with you. The sooner you can get the Paladins to follow us the better."

With that Nethrin turned and was off into the mists once again. It was strange to see the young man going off on his own for a second time, as Gerhold and Roland rarely let him out of their sight. Things were changing now; Nethrin was becoming more than just a tinkerer. Gerhold was still stunned by how quickly Nethrin was able to come up with his plan to convince the Paladins of Rodrick's deceit, and now the boy was off on his own in the city as it bordered on complete anarchy. He was not worried anymore, though, as Nethrin had proved tonight that he could take care of himself and no longer needed to be watched and coddled.

"We ready to go?" Valaire asked and Gerhold nodded.

"Let's hope that boy is right," Leandra added as they started off after Gerhold.

"That map better have a way for us to get in," Roland whispered as they walked.

"It will," Gerhold answered, hoping he was correct.

Chapter 13: The Catacombs

    Gerhold glanced over the map that Nethrin had given to him as he led the group through the streets and towards the keep at the eastern end of the city. It was hard to tell what the lines and scribbles meant, but it was obvious that there were few routes that passed beneath the keep. Apparently, the ruling count at the time had the old tunnels collapsed during the construction of the newer sewers, which meant the tunnels might not be an option. The group ducked into a nearby alley as a pack of the screeching monsters could be heard echoing from somewhere above in the mists. The streets were becoming more crowded now as the thousands of people from the western side of the city continued to poor in, filling the Gold District to bursting. Gerhold took a moment to take a closer look at the map while they hid from the creatures above.

    Nethrin had spent time trying to find a way beneath the walls of the keep, but from what Gerhold could see of the young man's notes, it was going to be harder than they had originally thought. Gerhold read through Nethrin's hastily scrawled notes which indicated there was only one other way into the Keep other than the front gates.

    "Did you find anything?" Valaire asked while keeping a close watch on the swirling gray clouds above.

    "There is only one other way in besides the front gate, but I do not think you are going to like it," Gerhold answered and handed over the map. "Here, this is it."

    Valaire glanced where Gerhold was pointing and then showed it to Leandra.

    "Through a crypt?" she asked warily and Gerhold nodded.

    "The nobles grew tired of having to travel across town to the chapel, so they built their own chapel here in the Gold District. There is a smaller cemetery where the nobility would bury their dead, but soon they had to start storing the coffins in a vast series of catacombs beneath the church," Gerhold said and traced his finger over the outline of the building.

"Looks like those catacombs are half the size of the keep itself," Valaire added.

"So we leave behind the monster infested city streets for the cramped and crowded corridors full of the dead. Just lovely," Roland said.

"It is the only way." Gerhold pocketed the map. "Looks like Nethrin found a spot where the old tunnels intersect with the crypt. If it is still there, then that is our only way of getting in, short of laying siege, that is."

"We better get moving; we don't want those creatures swooping down on us. The sooner we get to this church the better," Valaire said and motioned for Gerhold to lead onward.

"Stay close and as quiet as you can. It is not far from here, but we do not want to attract any unwanted attention," Gerhold whispered and then darted off down the street.

They made their way through the Gold District, heading north towards the chapel. Their journey through the streets was tense and unnerving as they dashed from back alley to back alley, doing their best to avoid the larger open areas and main streets. Every so often they were forced to hide between the tightly packed houses or beneath the large awnings that stretched over the street as one or more of the winged monsters could be heard overhead. The side streets were starting to fill with desperate men and women as they tried to hide from the creatures that still swooped about in the fog. Only once did Gerhold catch a glimpse of one as it flew down through the darkness and nearly grabbed a small child. But otherwise the monsters remained invisible haunting specters calling out from the mists.

Finally, the white stone walls of the church came into view and Gerhold saw that the little square was deserted. The walls were ten feet high and made from fine white stone. The building at the center was a little church with three elaborate white towers that rose high into the mists. They quickly made their way across the open area and stopped in front of the barred gates. Roland stepped forward and inspected the gate.

"It's locked, think you can pick it?" Roland asked and Gerhold examined the thick iron lock.

"Possibly, but it will take time," Gerhold answered.

"Can you break it?" Valaire asked.

"I could, but it would be loud. Besides, it's a church," Gerhold answered again.

"Piety? From a vampire?" Valaire said and laughed.

"Maybe we should try ringing them then? So glad to see we are putting your superstitions ahead of saving the city," Leandra said sarcastically.

"I can jump over," Gerhold added.

"And what about the rest of us?" Valaire asked.

"And I doubt whoever is in there would be willing to speak with a vampire," Roland added.

"Then I will have to break it down," Gerhold drew his silver sword.

Without waiting for the others to answer, Roland pulled on the little string near the gate and the faint echo of a bell could be heard from inside the chapel. Immediately the others ceased their discussion and listened. They waited but no one came, and Gerhold could feel the uncomfortable eyes of the others upon him. Roland pulled the string again, only a little harder this time and Gerhold's keen senses picked up the sounds of movement coming from inside the little chapel.

"Try again. There is someone in there," Gerhold said and Rolland started yanking on the string, causing the jingling sound of the little bell to become even louder.

"You're going to draw every one of those beasts to us if you keep this up. Might as well have the vampire break open the lock if we plan on making this much noise," Leandra whispered.

Suddenly the doors to the chapel opened and a thin yellow light could be seen as someone came creeping out. A moment later a little priest came shuffling towards the gate, a scowl visible on every inch of his face.

"What in the name of the Three are you doing? Do you want to draw every monster in the city here?" the old man said in a raspy voice.

"We'd prefer if you opened the gates. We have business in the chapel," Roland answered, and he heard the old man snort.

"Bah! Be gone you vagabonds! We have no room here for the likes of you," the priest answered.

There was no time to argue with the old man and Gerhold knew it. He bent down low and then leapt high into the air with all his might, clearing the ten-foot-high gate with a flip and landing calmly on the other side right in front of the stunned old priest.

A Dawn of Death

"Open the gate, priest," Gerhold said and flashed his fangs.

The old man stumbled back while fumbling in his cloak for something.

"Here, take it and leave me be!" he cried and tossed a little brass key at Gerhold's feet.

A moment later the little gate creaked open, and the others darted in before relocking the gate behind them.

"We need to move inside. Now! No telling how many of those things heard all this noise," Valaire said and made for the entrance to the little church.

Roland grabbed the old priest and pulled him along as they ran up the steps and passed into the chapel. As soon as they were all inside, the doors were closed and locked behind them by three other priests who had come running over to see what was causing all the commotion.

"What is going on here?" one of the priests said.

"Sorry for the intrusion, priest," Roland said as they entered. "We have need of your chapel."

"You brigands think you can just barge in here? This is a house of the Gods, a holy place," one of the old men said.

"Holy you say? Then where are all those who are less fortunate? Why have you barred your gates and offered no help to those who flee the evil that has beset this city?" Gerhold asked and the priests backed away in fear once they realized what he was.

"Vampires? Creatures of darkness come for us," one of the priests cried and started to mumble a prayer for help.

"Just the one actually," Roland said and stepped forward. "Good to see that working for the nobles has turned you into a bunch of selfish old codgers. No room for people like us?" he said and glared at the ring of men.

"We are watching over the sacred chapel of the Three, that is as noble a charge as helping the poor," one answered.

"More like hiding behind your walls while the city falls apart around you. A bunch of cowards," Roland responded and grabbed the priest by the front of his robe.

"As much as I want to spend my time pointing out the hypocrisies of priests and the like, don't we have a city to save?" Valaire interrupted.

"That we do," Roland said and released the old man, who cowered away in fear. "How can we reach the crypt?"

"The crypt? Why do you want to go in there?" one of the priests asked.

"Grave robbing, I suspect. They have come here to rob us," another added.

"Just tell us how to get down to the crypt, eh? I really don't want to have to watch Bolin here pull your arms out of their sockets," Valaire said and motioned towards the big man who growled menacingly. "Trust me; it's not a pretty sight."

The group of old men looked fearfully at Bolin before one stepped forward.

"Through that door and down the stairs. The crypt can be entered through the undercroft. But you may not want to go in there," the priest said.

"Why not?" Gerhold asked.

The priests traded worried glances before another answered.

"The nobles were afraid of the plague, and there were a few cases here in the Gold District. They did not know what to do with the victims," the priests said and stared awkwardly at his feet.

"So, you let them throw their family members into the crypt?" Roland asked.

"Only those that could not bring themselves to kill them. We did not have a choice," the priest mumbled.

"How many people did you trap down there?"

"Maybe twenty, no more than that. No one has gone down there in years, so we thought it would be a safe place for the afflicted while we searched for a cure."

Another priest stepped forward.

"The doors have been locked; you will need this," he said and held out another brass key.

"Great, now we have to deal with more of those things," Valaire cursed under his breath.

"Some servants of the Three you all are," Roland muttered. "Sad that men like Brother Francis die while you scum get to keep on living."

"Just take the key and leave," one of the priests added with a terrified look at Gerhold.

"Come, Roland, we do not have time for this," Gerhold said and pulled on the young man's shoulder. Roland resisted for a moment but then stepped back.

"Lead on vampire, you're the one with the map," Valaire said and

A Dawn of Death

Gerhold nodded.

Roland shot one last venomous glance at the line of priests before following the others into the next room. Gerhold led them down the long flight of stairs, which opened up into a large room of white stone corridors and elegant pillars. They moved to the far end of the room where a large oak door stood alone along one of the walls. Gerhold slid the brass key into the lock and gave it a hard twist while the others readied their weapons. The door creaked open, revealing a long tunnel that disappeared into a wall of pitch black. Gerhold held his sword at the ready, expecting something to come darting out at them from the darkness, but nothing came.

"How big did you say this place was?" Valaire asked.

"Maybe a few city blocks, give or take," Gerhold answered.

"Better not lose that map then, eh?"

"You sure you can guide us through this?" Leandra asked and Gerhold nodded. "Let's hope so, because if we get lost, we'll be wondering around here for a very long time."

"Not to mention the weepers," Roland added.

The other members of the group grabbed a torch a piece, though, Gerhold, with his keen vampire eyes, did not need one to see.

"Let us hope our presence will go unnoticed," Gerhold said and led the way into the darkness.

The catacombs were a maze of tall twisting corridors that were only five feet wide. Spaces for coffins lined the walls and were occupied by the hidden remains of the various wealthy inhabitants of the city over the past thousand years, while the more powerful families had their own rooms and long corridors dedicated to their family lines. There were few unused torches along the walls, and as they were lit they cast a rare amount of light across the blackened corridors, and though Gerhold had very little trouble seeing through the darkness, these islands of light brought a small level of comfort to the others who followed. The vampire tuned his ears and listened for any sounds of approaching weepers, but there was nothing other than the soft crackling of the torches and their echoing footsteps. Gerhold took a deep breath and noticed something odd as they continued. The catacombs smelled of death, as expected, but now there was something else. After a few minutes more of walking through the empty hallways, Gerhold held up his hand for the others to stop.

"What is it? Weepers?" Roland asked and Gerhold shook his head before stepping forward.

He paused in front of a dark stain on the floor and knelt to get a closer look. Dried blood streaks and puddles spread across the ground as if a large battle had taken place in the corridors. Long smudges of black blood moved off down one of the corridors and disappeared around another corner. Someone or something had dragged one of the bleeding victims further into the catacombs. A few rotting limbs and entrails could be seen in the firelight, and one of the twins retched when the rancid smell of blood and decomposition finally hit them.

"What in the six hells did all this?" Bolin asked and held his torch up a little higher.

"Perhaps the weepers killed each other off," Roland said.

"They don't attack each other, remember?" Leandra added.

"Whatever happened here occurred some time ago. The blood is dry, and I can barely catch the scent, but it is rotten and putrid," Gerhold said.

"Which means what?" Roland asked.

"This blood belonged to someone who was infected," Gerhold answered and stood.

"Maybe someone came down here and cleared the place out?"

"I do not think so," Gerhold answered and sniffed the air again. The corridors smelled of death, but there was also something else, something he could not identify. "Keep your eyes and ears open. There is something else down here."

Gerhold started off again down the blood-stained corridor but as the others followed so did their whispers of fear. The darkness seemed to grow the further they went into the winding mess of hallways, and Gerhold could tell the others were becoming more and more nervous.

"What did you mean, something else is down here?" Roland whispered.

"Something attacked those weepers, and it was not a human."

"Any ideas what it was?"

Gerhold shook his head and Roland gripped his spear a little tighter. As they continued, Gerhold noticed a few more bloody stains on the floors from bodies being dragged, but he also saw something else. Many of the coffins and caskets had been opened and their contents removed, but it was not until they came to a larger open room that Gerhold realized what was happening. The area was a large chamber with a single unlit brazier, and its walls were lined with hundreds of opened coffins, some that had been yanked unceremoniously from their shelves and spilled across the ground. The room had four entrances, each of

A Dawn of Death

which had a long line of dried blood leading into chamber. Gerhold also noticed that the floor was littered with bone fragments and shattered skeletons, some still with rotting flesh clinging to what was left of the bodily frame. He knelt down next to one of the corpses and noticed that the weeper's bones had been ripped out.

"What in Azaral's name…" Leandra trailed off as her torch light passed over a pile of bones.

"Where in the six hells did you bring us, vampire?" one of the twins asked, his voice laced with fear.

"Bone-eaters," Gerhold muttered as he picked up a cracked femur.

"What did you say?" Valaire asked.

"Bone-eaters," Gerhold responded and tossed the bone aside. "Creatures that live near graveyards and cemeteries in the more remote regions. They dig up dead bodies and crack open the bones and suck the marrow, but they have been known to attack the living as well."

"So now we have to worry about the weepers and these things?" Valaire asked.

"Judging by all this," Gerhold said and motioned to the surrounding piles of bones and dried blood, "I doubt there are any weepers left alive."

"How did these Bone-eaters get down here?" Roland asked.

"I doubt it was by accident," Gerhold answered. "First the winged creatures and now this? I do not think they are a coincidence."

"So, what are we dealing with here?" Roland asked again.

"Bone-eaters are reclusive, but they tend to appear in packs, and judging by these bones there are many living down here." Gerhold walked across to the other side of the room. "We need to keep moving."

"How dangerous are these Bone-eaters?" Valaire whispered.

"In these close quarters, very dangerous," Gerhold answered and started down the dark hallway at the other end of the room. "Stay close and keep your ears open. You will be able to hear them before you see them."

Gerhold moved forward into the dark passageway followed by a line of torches and nervous mutterings. Worrying about the weepers had been bad enough but Bone-eaters were much worse. He had only encountered the creatures a few times, but he had used traps to snare and kill them rather than fighting them head on. In the cramped hallways of the crypt though the fighting would favor the monsters with their razor-sharp claws and needle like teeth. He had heard of stories where Bone-eaters would drag their victims off and tear them apart while still breathing, and the vampire did not want to have to face off against a pack of the creatures in the claustrophobic hallways of the crypt. But what choice did they have? This was the only way to reach the count and Gerhold was not going to let fear get the better of the group with the entire city at stake.

Deeper into the bowels of the dungeon they went deeper into the darkness. Soon the only light that could be seen was that of the few torches the group carried with them, while only Gerhold could see through the growing gloom. Bolin stood at the back of the group with his large axe in one hand and his torch in the other, watching and listening for anything that may come at them from behind. Every so often Gerhold would stop and glance at the crumpled map to make sure they were still heading in the right direction, and only once were they forced to double back to find their way. Soon the hallways became more and more empty as less of the shelves were filled with coffins.

"Halt," Gerhold whispered and the others stopped.

They had reached a four-way intersection of tunnels and were getting very close to the end of the catacombs, but Gerhold had heard something off in the distance. The fifteen-foot-high hallways seemed to distort whatever sounds that happened to echo off the stone, but Gerhold was sure he had heard something, something that sounded like the cracking of a bone.

"What is it?" Roland said quietly and Gerhold shook his head.

They listened intently but all that could be heard were the crackling of the torches and nervous breaths. They stood for nearly half a minute in the anxious silence, listening for any sounds that would signal an attack, but again nothing came. Gerhold had better ears than the others, and although he did not hear any more of the strange cracking sound, he did hear the soft echoes of footsteps somewhere off in the darkness. He moved forward slowly and past the intersection, still listening intently for any sounds and watching for any signs of movement in the tunnel ahead, then paused again so the others could catch up. Once Bolin had passed the intersection Gerhold started forward again, his heart racing as the sound of shifting and sniffing began to grow louder.

"Do you hear that?" Roland asked and Gerhold nodded.

"Sounds like they are all around us," Leandra said and Gerhold could see her bow hand shaking.

Gerhold listened as the sounds of clicking and hissing started to draw nearer, and he kept his eyes forward but could see nothing amidst the darkness.

A Dawn of Death

Suddenly the sounds stopped, and all was silent again. The others shifted back and forth, frantically searching with what little light they had for the source of the disturbance, while Gerhold stood calmly fingering the trigger on his crossbow. He caught sight of movement, not in front or behind him, but above. Gerhold quietly motioned for Roland to shift his torch a little higher so that it would illuminate the ceiling high above them, and as soon as the light reached the stone ceiling Gerhold saw a shifting mass of fleshy creatures. Roland cried out as the first of the bone-eaters leapt down from above and landed on top of one of the twins.

    In that instant the silence gave way to pandemonium as more creatures dropped from above, landing between the confused and horrified members of Gerhold's party. The creatures were the size of a human but hunched over and lacked eyes. They had oversized nostrils and large mouths that jutted out with lines of hook-like teeth that were made for tearing bone from flesh, and at the end of each of their four arms were long talons meant for slicing through their prey. Gerhold fired his crossbow before flipping out its blade and slicing through two of the lunging creatures. Out of the corner of his eye he could see Roland stabbing back and forth with his spear, but the long silver shaft was almost useless in the close corridors, forcing Roland to rely on his foot-long dagger.

    All around him the battle raged as the Bone-eaters lunged and slashed at their prey and Gerhold slew as many as he could before ordering the others to try and follow him. He pushed forward, relying on his enhanced strength and speed to fight off the growing number of monsters. Roland used his spear to keep the Bone-eaters in front of them while Gerhold slashed and hacked his way through throngs of hissing beasts, leaving body after body in his wake. He turned and called again for the others to keep up, just in time to see two of the creatures yank one of the twins off his feet and begin to sink their hooked teeth into his arms and side. The man screamed as the flood of monsters flowed over him, but there was nothing to be done. They ran past another intersection, which soon filled with more of the creatures, and Gerhold did his best to keep the group moving quickly, knowing that Bolin would only be able to hold the back line for so long.

    Finally, they reached an open room and the monsters seemed to disappear in front of them as they dashed into the vaulted chamber. Gerhold slashed at another creature and finished off a second before entering the open chamber and turned to see the others fighting off the wall of monsters. Ahead Gerhold could see a metal gate that barred the way to the keep's sewers and he ran across the room as fast as he could and slammed his foot against the metal bars, causing the chain holding it to snap and the door to swing open.

"Hurry, through here!" he yelled as the others came sprinting into the chamber.

Gerhold whipped out his smaller crossbows and fired off a hail of bolts at the charging bone-eaters and covered Leandra and Bolin as they were the last through the door, but it was not enough as one of the creatures lunged forward and knocked the two of them to the ground. Leandra screamed as two of the monsters wrapped their wiry fingers around her ankles and started to drag her back into the darkness, her screams echoing over the hissing and gurgling sounds of the horde. Valaire and Bolin both dashed forwards, but it was too late as Leandra was already gone, swallowed by the mass of charging monsters.

"Valaire, Get out of here now!" Gerhold yelled and the Myrthian gave one last horrified glance towards the passage where Leandra had disappeared, before turning and running through past Gerhold.

The vampire loaded a large explosive bolt into his crossbow and fired it into the mass of charging monsters. It exploded with a bright flash and a wave of heat. Screeches of pain echoed through the chamber as many of the monsters were burned or ripped apart by the explosion, only to be replaced by others than charged forwards over the mangled bodies. Gerhold ran down the tunnel, firing off more of the bolts as he went until he stopped at a ladder that led up, which he climbed as quickly as he could. Roland reached down and pulled him up the last few rungs and as soon as he was through the others slammed the metal trap door shut, causing the screeching and hissing sounds of the bone-eaters died away.

A Dawn of Death

Chapter 14: The Shadow over Vilheim

Gerhold leaned against a nearby wall wearily, trying to catch his breath while the others did the same. The thick metal trap door had been shut behind them, and Gerhold sent up a silent prayer of thanks to the Gods for the door being unlocked. Roland stood close by, his spear still at the ready while loud thumps could be heard from the other side of the door as the bone-eaters slammed against it. Valaire and his remaining companions stood at the other end of the room, still silently mourning their fallen friends. Of the six mercenaries only four now remained: Valaire, Bolin, Ke'var, and the other twin. Gerhold reloaded his crossblade and cleaned the blade before standing and making his way over to where Valaire sat solemnly.

"We need to continue on. No telling what is happening in the city during the hour we spent down there," Gerhold said and put out his hand to help Valaire to his feet.

Valaire did not answer or move, but instead he just sat against the cold stone wall, staring off aimlessly. Valaire had been a pirate and now a mercenary, and it was strange to see such a man show emotion. He had always seemed so nonchalant and casual in the way he dealt with his work and with death. Gerhold bent down and placed his hand on the Myrthian's shoulder.

"I told our brother I would take care of her," Valaire said and spat on the ground. "Now I got her killed."

"The blame does not lie with you," Gerhold responded.

"Yes, it does. I should never have let her fall so far behind in those damn tunnels. My brother was my first mate, my best friend, and I let him down. Now those things are devouring what is left of Leandra." Valaire shook his head.

"There was nothing else you could do. They were on us too quickly, and we were lucky to make it out as we are."

"I should have watched out for her."

Gerhold pulled on the little gold chain that hung around his neck and held the locket out for Valaire to see.

"Do you know what this is? This is cursed gold; it is why I turned into what so many people hate and despise. I have been alive for over a hundred and fifty years, one hundred of which have been spent as a vampire. During that time, I have been hunted by many for what I am and shunned by the rest," he placed the locket back beneath his shirt. "Every moment of my existence since the say I laid my hands upon this I have had to fight, not just against what others believe, but against what is inside of me. There is an unseen monster living within, one that never sleeps, never stops hungering, thirsting for blood. I have fought myself, this curse of mine, day after day, and yet, in spite of all of that there were some who stood by me. One of those men was killed not five hours ago, a victim of the corruption that has been allowed to fester within this city, my city."

"Why are you telling me this?" Valaire asked and Gerhold stood.

"Because your sister is dead, and those responsible for her death are still breathing." Gerhold stuck out his hand a second time. "The man who killed my friend is not."

Valaire stared at the vampire for a moment before a ruthless smile began to spread across his face.

"Then I say we make it up to them both and end this, eh?" Valaire said and allowed Gerhold to pull him to his feet.

Bolin strode over and grabbed Valaire in a strong one-handed hug, while Ke'var gave a sympathetic nod as he walked by.

"So, what's the plan?" Roland asked and Gerhold traded glances with Valaire before pulling out the map Nethrin had given him.

He smoothed out the crumpled parchment and tried to find where they were. They had passed through the catacombs and were now standing in a small room that was separated from the sewers by a small wooden door, and he found the chamber on the map with little effort as it was the only exit from the crypts. There were only a few ways out of the sewers that they could use to get into the keep, one that led through a drain into the courtyard and another that came up into the servant quarters.

"We are almost beneath the keep now, and I think our best course of action would be to make our way to the servant quarters here," Gerhold said and traced his finger along the map.

"Looks like there's no other way into the castle other than through that courtyard," Roland said. "The servant quarters may be safer, but we don't have time to go traipsing about trying to find a way into the inner keep."

"But we would be too exposed. There are only six of us and who knows how many vampires and guards the count has patrolling his walls. We need to keep the element of surprise as long as we can," Gerhold added.

"What good is that when the city is falling apart as we speak? Who knows how bad things have gotten in the past hour?" Roland responded.

"I say we go straight in. We can handle a few vampires," Bolin said and fingered his axe blade.

"We need to get to this count as quickly as we can. If that means we make a bit of a ruckus while we do it, that's fine with me," Valaire added.

"I agree," Ke'var said and rested his hand on his sword hilt. "Vampires or not, we must not waste any more time."

"Is that worth walking into an army of vampires and Gods know what else?" Gerhold asked.

"I'm sure we can maintain a bit of stealth, at least until we know what we're up against," Roland said.

Gerhold looked at the other men, all of them determined and ready to fight. They had all lost something this night and now it was time for vengeance, but what would they accomplish by getting themselves killed? Gerhold wanted to reach Leofric as much as the others, but he knew the most important thing was ensuring the city was safe. His desire for revenge must come second to that. Still, did they have the time to be as careful and quiet as he wanted them to be?

Count Leofric was no fool, at least from what Gerhold had seen thus far. His plans had been meticulous, almost perfect, which made Gerhold think they were not the count's plans at all. He had known only one person in his life who could manage such feats and that was Harkin Valakir. Could this all be one of Harkin's plans? Gerhold had learned after so many years of failing to find the vampire that he should not hope for such a thing to be true, but he could not help but notice the similarity between what was happening in Vilheim and what he knew of Harkin. Whether it was Harkin or the count guiding this phenomenon, it did not matter, because whoever it was would be ready for them. The vampire sighed and folded up the map.

"The courtyard it is then, but I go first, and we follow my commands." The others nodded.

Gerhold opened the oak door at the other side of the room. The sound of trickling water echoed through the tunnel on the other side, and Gerhold started down the thin, stone walkway that stood above the little frozen stream of water that ran beneath them. The tunnels smelled of waste and rot, but no one complained as they continued, each member of the company focused on what was to come. It took very little time to get through the sewers, but the journey was tense, as even Gerhold was careful about what could be lurking in the awful smelling corridors. Thankfully, they reached the ladder that led up to the courtyard with no issue, and Gerhold motioned for the others to halt.

"I will go up first and make sure it is clear. Follow me only when I say. Understand?" he said, and the other men nodded. "Be ready for anything."

With that Gerhold climbed quickly up the icy ladder and reached the circular metal grate that led up to the surface. Gerhold peered through the metal slats as best he could, but between the limited view and the mists he was able to see very little. Instead, he relied on his hearing and smell, and even with the echoing sounds of the water below and the stinking smell of the sewer, Gerhold could tell there was someone nearby. He pushed gently against the grate, but it barely budged as the ice had settled around it. Gerhold slowly drew one of his smaller crossbows and with his other hand, twisted the metal grate while giving it a slight push. The ice began to crack, and the metal made a squeaking sound. Gerhold froze and listened intently as the footsteps from above drew closer. As soon as the guard came into view Gerhold pushed up the grate and fired off his crossbow, sending a bolt through the guard's throat and causing the man to fall forward. Gerhold grabbed the gurgling guard and let the man's body fall through the opening where it landed with a crunch down below.

"Good to see we're still taking the stealthy route," Roland whispered as he finished off the vampire with his silver spear.

Gerhold listened to see if anyone else came to investigate but heard nothing. As quietly as he could, he pushed the little grate up and out of the way before sticking his head just above the hole. The courtyard of the inner part of the keep was mostly paved in stone with a large empty fountain at the center and was bathed in an eerie green light that seem to emanate from somewhere high above. It was a familiar light, and Gerhold knew he had seen it before deep in the Blightwood. The mists obscured much of his view, but Gerhold could make out the twenty-foot-high wall that surrounded the open yard and the front gate to the outer area of the keep. Two hooded guards stood at either side of the large oak doors that led into the castle itself, but if there were any guards on the walls, he

A Dawn of Death

could not see them. After taking a second glance around the courtyard, Gerhold slid down back down the ladder to where the other men stood.

"Any others?" Roland asked and nodded towards the body at his feet.

"Two more in the courtyard, but there may be some on the walls that I could not see. We need to make our way across the courtyard as quietly as possible and then through the front doors," Gerhold said.

"The front doors? Very subtle," Valaire said with a hint of sarcasm.

"There is no other way in, at least none that I can see. There are two guards, so we need to deal with them first, quietly. As soon as those doors open, all hell is going to break loose," Gerhold responded and the others nodded.

"It's about time we got into a proper fight," Bolin said eagerly.

"Are you ready?" Gerhold asked and Roland nodded.

"Stick close, Roland and I will deal with the guards at the door," Gerhold said and started back up the ladder.

At the top he once again peered over the side of the drain and could barely see through the fog, which had grown so thick that even the doors to the castle had been obscured. He leapt over the lip of the hole and dashed quickly over to the empty fountain, where he ducked behind the stone circle. Roland appeared a moment later, followed by the four other men who took up positions next to Gerhold. The vampire waited for a moment for the fog to thin enough for him to see the guards, but as the breeze picked up and the mists began to shift, Gerhold saw something that made him freeze. The sentries had disappeared and both sides of the wooden doors were empty with only a few dim torches standing guard.

"I thought you said there were guards?" Roland whispered, but Gerhold did not answer.

Just then, braziers all around the courtyard lit up with golden flames, illuminating the entire area. Gerhold readied his crossbow as silhouettes appeared on the walls around them. Hooded vampires stood at the ready, each with a crossbow aimed at the six figures below. Roland and the others stood at the ready, but their enemies did not attack. Instead another light appeared above them along one of the castle balconies, and Gerhold looked up to see Count Leofric standing above them. He had never met the count but had seen him a few times years ago, back when the count left his keep.

"Good evening, Gerhold of Vilheim, I trust your trip here was an eventful one?" he said, and his droning voice rang out across the open square.

The man's voice had an all too familiar sound to it, a hollow empty echo, and the words the man spoke were even more familiar.

"How did you know we were coming? Who told you?" Roland asked.

"I know very little about any of you, only what my master tells me," Leofric responded.

"Save your words, thrall, and bring your master," Gerhold yelled back.

A soft laughter echoed from somewhere in the distance, and it grew louder as whoever it was began to approach. Another figure appeared behind the count, barely visible behind the thick layers of fog.

"Good evening, Gerhold. Are you enjoying tonight's festivities?" a man called from the balcony above, and Gerhold recognized the voice before he even caught sight of who was speaking.

"Harkin," Gerhold said and saw the vampire move into the torchlight high above them. He looked as regal as ever with his shoulder length blonde hair and black silken shirt. A dark cloak hung about his shoulders and a sword hung at his side. "I knew you were here."

"I would expect nothing less from the greatest monster slayer of all time. I told you I had something planned for you," Harkin said with a grin and flourish of his hand.

Gerhold knew what to expect. The beast roared to life at the sight of his most hated nemesis. The snarling and scratching began, but Gerhold was ready for it and he focused on the task at hand, ignoring and repressing the savage monster as if fought to break free of his control.

"How long has Leofric been your thrall?" Gerhold asked and moved to the other side of the fountain to get a better view.

"Years," Harkin said and dismissed the count with a wave of his hand. "Admit it, you are impressed. I have been hiding here in this city for almost thirty years and you were none the wiser."

"Thirty years?" Gerhold raised an eyebrow.

"Did I not tell you back in the Blightwood that I had been watching you? You did not realize how closely, though. While you were out looking for me, I was right here all the time, right under your very nose."

"The safest place to hide is in the enemy camp," Gerhold said.

"Only if your enemy has something else that they are concerned with, something to keep them blind to all else. And you have been busy, haven't you?"

"Obviously not as busy as you have been. I take it this plague is your

A Dawn of Death

doing?" Gerhold asked and the vampire laughed.

"Plague? Please, I would not be so barbaric and antiquated to use something like that. This has taken me years to plan, a song that I have been composing for many decades now, the perfect composition made just for you, Gerhold. A plague? Bah! A fool could unleash such a thing without even knowing it, but I have created something far more impressive."

"What have you done, Harkin?" Gerhold asked.

"I spent many years trying to understand how you won our first engagement despite my plan working to perfection. I had thought that it was flawless, that once you had walked away with that little gold pendant in your hand that I had won. That you would become what you hunted for so long and that one day I would hear of your death at the hands of another slayer." Harkin shook his head. "I underestimated you, though, just like I did when you fought Lord Bram," Harkin said and leaned against the railing.

"What did you have to do with him?" Gerhold asked and Harkin nodded.

"He worked for me of course. Poor Alnor Bram thought it was his job to kill you, and I thought he would, but I should have known better. After you dealt with the werewolves in Morovia, I knew you were a powerful adversary, but I did not know just how strong you were. I underestimated your will to fight, your uncanny ability to push yourself further than your enemies."

"You were behind the werewolves?" Gerhold asked in surprise and the other vampire nodded.

"Oh yes, in fact most of your escapades those two years before we met were manufactured by me," Harkin responded.

"Why? What did you gain from me destroying your servants?"

"They were not all my servants. Some I manipulated, others I created through force. It is easy to understand people after spending so much time watching and learning. As for what I gained, it was information that I was after. Information about you," Harkin said and smiled. "I wanted to know how great you really were. For years I had heard stories about you, how every beast or monster you came against fell without doubt, and that no dark creature was safe while you lived. I wanted to learn about you, how you fought, what you believed, how you thought, and most importantly your strengths and weaknesses, few as they may be."

"So, you wanted to test me?" Gerhold asked and Harkin leaned back a bit and seemed to be pondering something. "And why me? There were other hunters."

"Others? No, Gerhold, there was only you. The stories I heard said that you were the greatest monster hunter the world had ever seen, and the more I watched, the more I realized that those stories were true." Harkin began to pace back and forth.

Gerhold longed to raise his crossbow and end it there, but he reminded himself that saving the city had to come first. Harkin held the key to stopping the sickness, and Harkin would reveal it soon enough. He wanted to test Gerhold as he had done many times before, it was a game to him, and Gerhold knew Harkin would reveal his intentions.

"Just tell us what you want, monster," Ke'var said loudly.

"I will in a moment, but Gerhold asked why I chose him, and I would be a poor host not to answer. You see it has been two thousand and seventy-one years since I turned. Two thousand and seventy-one years this curse has been hanging over me like some dark cloud that I could never escape. Can you imagine what it is like to live for that long and not hear the sound of a single song? To see the sun only to have to flee in fear and hide away from the light? To live in the darkness, day after day, forced to feed on others just to live? At first, I relished the power. I built cathedrals of stone and ruled over my own little kingdom hidden away in the shadows of history. I visited every corner of this wretched world and saw things that few men have even dreamed of, and yet it was all empty. It was as if I was staring at a cup full of clear cool water, dying of thirst, only to have it disappear every time I tried to drink it. I came to a point where all I longed for was death."

"Then why didn't you just off yourself and save us the trouble?" Roland interrupted.

"Oh, I considered it. I once stood atop my castle, staring out over the vast frozen kingdom that was all but mine in name. It was nothing. It was all empty. Life had no meaning and no value to me, so I stood there preparing to just let myself fall over the side and end it all. But to be honest, I was too much of a coward to take my own life. I feared the unknown that comes after death. I craved a release but was too afraid to embrace it, and then you came along," Harkin said and pointed at Gerhold. "At first, I thought you would be worthy of granting me the peace that I so desperately sought, but after a time I realized something. The more I watched you defeat monsters and listened to the stories, the more alive I felt. You were what I had not had in years, a true rival to test my abilities and my strengths, to push me to create, to think, and to do."

Harkin paused for a moment before continuing.

"You see, Gerhold, what I lacked was purpose. Purpose is what makes us what we are. We may not be human anymore, but we still need a reason to exist. Without it this world is nothing but an empty journal, a story without end or form. Without purpose we are like a writer without a pen, a ship without a sail, being tossed to and fro by the waves of time until we are finally dashed upon the rocks. Purpose is what guides us, what drives us, and it is what gives us a reason to exist. Without that reason, we exist simply to continue our existence, which is nothing short of madness. Defeating you became my purpose, but even that was not enough. I did not want to simply beat you or kill you, as anyone could be lucky enough to accomplish such a feat. I wanted to absolutely destroy everything you were and everything you had ever built; I wanted to make you beg for death so that there would be no doubt as to which of us was greater."

"And so, I plotted, and I schemed, until I finally understood how to accomplish my goal. I knew you had some way to detect curses, and I knew I needed to get close to you and uncover your secret. My plan was perfect, even Virgil played his part to the end, a little too enthusiastically, I might say, which is why I had no qualms about killing him."

"He wanted to take your place," Gerhold said and Harkin nodded.

"Yes, but his attempt at betrayal only helped to reinforce my lies and convince you that my little charade was reality. I could not have planned it any better, so you can imagine my surprise when I learned that it had turned against me."

"What did you think turning me would do?" Gerhold asked and he could hear Roland whisper something to Valaire. "Did you think I would join you? That I would turn on those I protected?"

"Something like that. I had hoped you would bring terror down on those who one saw you as their greatest champion, that instead of hearing stories of your heroism I would hear tales of the horrors you wrought upon mankind, and that after any years of such terrible acts that I would hear of your demise at the hands of a new slayer, starting the process over once again. You ruined that of course, and I was furious to say the least," Harkin shook his head. "For years I wondered how you could have resisted the urge to feed when I could not. Were you perhaps stronger than I?"

"I had a friend who risked his life to ensure that I did not become a monster, a priest, just like the one your friend Rodrick killed tonight. I suppose he was our thrall as well?" Gerhold asked and Harkin scoffed at the suggestion.

"Rodrick? No, all that traitorous little whelp wanted was gold, like some everyday bandit. Pathetic really, but he was nothing more than a pawn, no different than Lady Friedrich." Harkin chuckled and Gerhold's eyes narrowed. "After you foiled my perfect plan, I spent quite some time brooding over my defeat. I felt as though you had taken my purpose from me once again, that I was doomed to spend eternity on the precipice of this terrible curse, and then I realized something. Though I failed, I had created an immortal enemy, someone who was now a true rival, one whom I could battle with until the end of time. You are my purpose, Gerhold. Our fates are intertwined, our existences mirrored opposites like fire and ice, east and west, light and darkness. I exist to challenge your existence, as you exist to challenge mine."

"The very second that I get the chance, Harkin, as soon as I can ensure the safety of my city, I will kill you. Make no mistake about that," Gerhold threatened, but Harkin just laughed again.

"Kill me? No, Gerhold, you will not. Because without me you will have nothing to seek after, you will have no goal, no purpose. I am the reason for your existence as much as you are mine. Without me you will succumb to the curse that you so desperately fight against. You know this, do you not? You fear it more than anything else in this world. The scraping and gnawing beast at the back of your mind, threatening to break free at any moment. It is getting stronger, isn't it? You fight it with all your might, but you know, deep down, that you are only one failure of will from being me."

Gerhold said nothing, his thoughts still hanging on Harkin's last few words. He told himself it was not true, but it was a useless attempt to assuage his fears. Was his pursuit of Harkin the only thing that was preventing him from becoming a monster? Somewhere off in the distance Gerhold heard something. The striking of metal on metal, and the screams of men. Faint, but there all the same.

"That is a load of horse dung if I've ever heard it," Roland said but Harkin dismissed these words.

"Oh, but it is true. Without me, you will become me." Gerhold glared at Harkin but still said nothing. "The madness is not all that bad though. Once you let yourself pass over the threshold, you realize that you have been trapped your

A Dawn of Death

entire life and that there is an entire realm of infinite possibilities ready to be explored."

"Enough, Harkin!" Gerhold roared and raised his crossbow. The vampire guards above did the same and shifted their aim to him. "Tell me how to stop the sickness or the next realm you will see will be the Pits of Sargoth!"

Gerhold glared at Harkin, who did nothing more than stare back with that familiar amused grin. After a moment he raised his hand and the vampires lowered their weapons, but Gerhold kept his crossbow aimed at Harkin's throat. Again, the sounds of men yelling, and the clash of steel seemed to echo from somewhere in the distance, though much closer this time. Perhaps the townsfolk were trying to break into the keep.

"So, you wish to know how to save your city? How to prevent Vilheim from becoming a smoldering pile of bones? I think not, at least not yet," Harkin answered.

"Kill him then," Valaire said.

"I mean it Harkin; tell me now!" Gerhold threatened and tightened his finger on the trigger.

"You know me, Gerhold. I would never make it that easy. If you wish to know how to save your city, then come and get me. You will find me in the highest tower. Sound Familiar?"

With that, Harkin dove backwards through the doorway just as Gerhold pulled the trigger. The bolt bounced harmlessly off the stone wall, and he only had a second to react before the other vampires raised their weapons.

Suddenly there was a loud bang, and the world was swallowed by a dense cloud of dark smoke, and Gerhold felt someone grab him from behind and pull him down just as a hail of bolts passed overhead. The missiles clanged off the stone fountain, and Gerhold realized that Roland had set off one of their smoke bombs. They leapt to their feet and dashed forward through the blinding smoke until they were able to see again, and all six men stood with their weapons ready, surrounded by vampires. Gerhold looked from Roland to Valaire but neither man showed any sign of fear in the face of such odds. At least forty vampires had crowded into the courtyard, surrounding the company on all sides. Gerhold knew there would be little chance of a victory, but it this was to be the end then he was determined for it to be an end worthy of remembrance. For a moment neither side moved, but then there came a loud crash against the front gate, and many of the vampires turned to see what had caused the commotion. The wooden gate shuttered and then shattered into a hundred splinters from the force of a fire explosion.

The battle cries of men erupted from the other side of the smoking remnants of the front gate and before the flames even began to dissipate, soldiers in silver armor came running through the opening. The vampires were caught off guard and were so surprised that not even one had time to react before the first wave of Paladins slammed into their ranks. Chaos ensued as Gerhold, Roland, Valaire, and the others leapt into the fray, cutting their way through the horde of confused vampires. Their enemies gave way, and for a moment the monsters retreated, only to surge forward once again as more of the creatures came pouring out of the castle.

Gerhold led the way, slicing at any vampire that crossed his path, while Roland stabbed and twirled his spear with deadly accuracy, until finally they reached the lines of Paladins. The two small armies came together with a thunderous crash, and the sounds of screams and battle cries rang out from all around. Paladin mages sent streams of flames into the ranks of vampires while others fought face-to-face with their swords and shields.

"Gerhold, over here!"

Gerhold could barely hear Roland's voice over the sounds of battle.

Roland was fighting side-by-side with a Paladin who Gerhold recognized as Ser Owyn, and he quickly joined them as more of the monsters bore down upon them.

"Good to see you again, Ser Owyn. Or is it commander now?" Gerhold called as he dispatched two enemies with one swift sweeping strike.

"Acting commander, though I hope to make it permanent," the Paladin answered and slammed his shield into a nearby vampire, sending the creature sprawling to the ground where it was trampled. "Your friend, the young priest, said that you know how to stop this madness?"

"I do, but I must get to the highest tower," Gerhold answered.

"The town has gone to hell and the people are trying to break down the gates and escape the quarantine. We cannot allow this plague to spread, so we need to stop this as soon as we can," Owyn yelled.

"It is not a plague!" Gerhold answered.

"Then what in the six hells is it?"

"I do not know, but I can stop it."

Gerhold slashed one of the vampires across the chest and then cut off

A Dawn of Death

another's arm, while Roland finished it off with a stab through the heart.

"If you can finish this, then do it! We can handle these beasts," Owyn called.

Gerhold paused for a moment, and Roland seemed to notice his hesitation.

"Go, Gerhold! You're the only one who can make it up to the tower in time," Roland said. Finally, Gerhold nodded, and with one final pat on the shoulder he turned to leave. "Oh, and Gerhold?" The vampire halted. "Kill that bastard!"

Gerhold nodded again before darting off between the charging Paladins. He quickly scaled the stone wall and then started down the battlements towards the castle. The highest tower loomed high overhead, hidden by the shifting layers of mist. This would end tonight, he told himself as he ran. Harkin would die.

Chapter 15: The Din of Battle

Roland watched as Gerhold sprinted off into the mists before returning his focus to the battle at hand. He lunged forward and slammed the tip of his spear through a vampire's back as it was fighting a Paladin, then spun his weapon and slashed the long sharp tip across another vampire's chest. The small army of Paladins was now joined by members of the City Watch, and together they began to push the horde of vampires back. The battle was loud and bloody as the two sides continued to duel within the confines of the castle courtyard, but it was clear that the vampires were losing ground. Valaire, Roland, and Owyn fought side by side while Bolin charged forward like a mad man, swinging his axe side to side and sweeping away enemies with each stroke.

Their foes fell back through the courtyard and those that stayed and fought were butchered. The Paladins roared in triumph, hell bent on pursuing their enemies and utterly destroying them, but as the vampires continued to retreat, Roland noticed that something was wrong. He paused and tried to warn Ser Owyn, but it was already too late as doors on either side of the courtyard swung open and out poured a number of babbling weepers that attacked the Paladins from both sides. Roland reached into his pack and pulled out a flash bomb, which he hurled into the oncoming horde of babbling infected. The explosion caused many of the weepers to stumble and cry out in pain as the bright flash of light stung their eyes and caused them to swing their arms erratically as they tried to attack whatever was around them.

"Attack now, while they're blinded!" Roland yelled and dashed forward, slashing with his spear back and forth.

The weeper onslaught was short lived, but then there came more screeches from above, and Roland looked up to see more of the winged monsters swooping in for the attack. Streams of bright white fire leapt up from the ranks of the Paladins and collided with the creatures in midair, and the leathery-skinned monstrosities burst into flame. More of the creatures moved in but were once again repelled by the Paladin mages that continued to illuminate the misty sky with more balls of fire. A monster landed on a Paladin nearby and began snapping at the man's face with its razor-sharp teeth, only to then be stabbed through the back by Roland's silver spear as he hurled it from across the courtyard.

"A good strike," Owyn called as he pulled Roland's spear from the monster's body and tossed it back.

"The vampires have been pushed back inside. I say we finish them off and go help Gerhold," Roland said and Owyn nodded.

"Let us hope he is still alive to help," Owyn said as they made their way towards the castle doors.

"You don't know Gerhold like I do; it's the ones that get in his way that you'll have to worry about," Roland responded and followed a line of Paladins.

"Ser Owyn? The doors are locked from the inside," one of the men said as they approached.

Another bolt flew right over their heads from one of the ramparts above, and a member of the City Watch turned and fired an arrow into the attacking vampire's chest.

"Use this," Owyn said and handed the man a silver orb.

"Where did you get that?" Roland asked after recognizing the pyrite bomb.

"Your priest friend gave us a few to use in case we could not get through the front gates," Owyn answered as they backed away.

One of the Paladins set the pyrite bomb near the foot of the double oak doors and lit the wick before running to join the others. A moment later the bomb exploded, shattering the doors, and sending bits of stone in all directions. The first few Paladins through the doors were met by a volley of bolts that tore through their armor and left most of them dead or wounded. Roland dashed inside with the second wave and darted behind a nearby pillar to avoid being shot by the vampires. The entry hall was a long, wide room with a balcony that ran along the top where the vampires stood at the ready and fired away with their crossbows. Beneath the walkways were thick white stone pillars that the Paladins used to hide from the rain of arrows.

"They have us pinned in this entrance," Owyn said and cursed under his breath. "If only we had a few more of those bombs, we could level this whole place."

Roland chanced a quick look out from behind the safety of the column, only to have a bolt fired from above nearly catch him in the forehead. The vampires lined the balconies and walkways above, firing down upon the unprotected Paladins. Roland looked around the room for another way up, but could see none, and then instinctively reached for his pack. He had used all of his pyrite bombs back on the barge, but he still had a number of flash bombs.

"I have an idea; just cover your eyes," Roland said.

Roland tossed a flash bomb out and called for the others to duck, and as soon as it went off, he and Owyn ran towards the stairs at the end of the hall. Another group of vampires came charging down the steps and Roland met them head on. Vampires were stronger and faster than the average human, but these were just fledglings, freshly turned. Roland had spent years dueling against Gerhold, and not a single one of these younger vampires could compare to the speed and strength of the hunter. The spear was as much a part of his body as his hands and feet, and it darted in and out between his enemy's weak spots, tearing through flesh and leaving behind many dead. Roland danced along the steps, dodging the wild swings of his foes while either killing them outright or wounding them enough for the following Paladins to finish off.

Valaire came flying in from behind, his long, curved sword flashing back and forth and sending his enemies reeling backwards in fear, while Ke'var made his way up the opposite staircase. Owyn and Roland led the charge as they turned down the long walkway and engaged the last group of vampires. The Paladin Commander used his shield as well as his sword to dispatch enemies, slicing them nearly in two or crushing them with the heavy metal guard. Roland dashed forward between two enemies and jumped, twisting in midair before tripping both with the end of his spear. Another monster charged towards him, sword raised and ready to strike, but Roland rolled to the side and leapt into the air. He used his foot to push off a nearby wall and slammed his shoulder into the vampire, sending the monster over the edge of the balcony to the stone floor below, where the other Paladins finished it off.

Roland pushed himself wearily to his feet as a line of Paladins sprinted past him, chasing the last remaining remnants of the vampire defenders. He leaned against the wall, trying to catch his breath as Valaire and Ke'var came striding up with Owyn in tow. He greeted both men with a breathless nod.

"That was a hell of a fight," Valaire said and spat over the side of the railing.

"Thank the Gods you all got here when you did," Roland said and patted Owyn on the shoulder.

"It is not over yet. There are still some stragglers milling about that will need to be dealt with," Owyn answered.

"Ke'var and I can help with that," Valaire said and motioned for the Nurrian to follow.

"What about that large fellow?" Owyn asked and a shade of sadness past over Valaire's face at the mention of Bolin.

"Bolin got it pretty good from those damn weepers. Your men are tending to him in the courtyard, but I don't think he will make it," Valaire said and then the two men walked away.

"I know very little of you all, but you did good work tonight. The Gods will truly smile upon these actions," Owyn added and picked up his shield again. "I better go check on my men."

"Good, you deal with that, and I will go and find Gerhold." Roland slapped the commander on his back, and then turned and made for a stairwell at the end of the balcony.

He sprinted past a small skirmish at the top of the steps between a few vampires and members of the City Watch, making his way as quickly as he could towards the highest tower. The sounds of battle had started to die away with only a few small pockets of fighting, and Roland knew the Paladins could handle the rest without his help. Right now, it was Gerhold he was concerned with and just what Harkin had planned for him. If his friend needed help, then he would be there.

J.S. Matthews

Chapter 16: The True Plague

 Gerhold ran along the battlement until he reached an open door that led into the castle interior. A vampire stood in the doorway and Gerhold leapt into the air and drove his foot into the creature's chest, sending it flying backwards into the empty hallway beyond. Gerhold rolled to his feet and fired a bolt through the creature's heart before it could stand, then made his way up a staircase to the upper level of the keep. At the top was a long hallway lined with windows on one side and doors on the other. But as soon as he started down the hall, three more vampires appeared at the other end. Gerhold drew his crossbow, but before he could fire, another enemy slammed into him from behind, sending the weapon skidding across the floor.

 Gerhold leapt to his feet just in time to avoid one of the vampire's attacks and instead caught the creature's arm and slammed its head into the wall as the other two came running towards him. The first attacker stabbed at him with a long sword, but Gerhold quickly moved to the side and guided the sword into the chest of the creature behind him. He drove his elbow into the vampire's face, pulled the sword from its grasp, and beheaded it with its own blade, before deflecting another blow. Gerhold dodged another swing and parried a blow from the wounded vampire behind him, before quickly slashing the other across its chest and finishing it off with a stab through the heart.

 "Please, please let me go!" the wounded vampire said, as he stared at the fallen bodies of his comrades, whose flesh had just begun to smoke and burn away.

 Gerhold ignored the creature's pleas and grabbed it by the throat, lifting the vampire off its feet, and threw it through the nearest window. Shards of glass danced across the floor as the creature fell screaming out the opening and landed far below with a dull thud. More frantic footsteps could be heard as Gerhold continued down the hallway towards another flight of stairs at the far end, where

A Dawn of Death

more of enemies appeared. Some continued down the steps towards the entry hall while others turned to face Gerhold, but little did they know the wrath that was about to set upon them. In a single smooth motion Gerhold fired his crossbow, blinding the creatures with a brilliant flash of light as the flashbolt exploded, then attacked the disoriented foes with his crossblade.

The vampires fell one by one, screaming in agony as the short, slender blade tore through their flesh, leaving behind a hallway filled with their charred bones. Up the twisting stairwell he sprinted before more enemies could appear, hoping it would not be too late by the time he reached Harkin. He reached the top of the steps and pushed open the door at the top, which led out onto the rooftop of the keep. Many steeples and spires rose through the mists from the stone building, and to his left, Gerhold could see a line of buttresses that resembled the exterior of the Vilheim cathedral. The highest tower of the keep stood at the far end of the rooftop, and at its peak, Gerhold could just make out the eerie green glow between the blankets of fog. Ahead lay the long, slanted expanse of the rooftop and a walkway bordered by a waist high railing and standing at the end of this walkway were two hooded vampires guarding the entrance to the highest tower. They caught sight of him and began to slowly move in his direction while Gerhold calmly reloaded his crossblade.

"Where do you think you're going, kin slayer?" one of the vampires asked.

"I was heading for that door behind you," Gerhold answered and held his crossblade firmly in both hands.

"Were you?" the other said and smirked at his companion. "And how about now?"

"Oh, I am still getting to that door; I am just going to cut the two of you into pieces first."

Just then he heard the soft sound of a footstep above him, and due to his enhanced agility, he managed to roll forward and out of the way as another vampire leapt down from above, slamming his sword into the stone walkway where Gerhold was standing only a second before. The hunter completed his roll and fired a bolt at one the two attackers charging from the other side of the roof, but the vampire dodged the missile with ease. These were not fledglings but full vampires, trained and ready to kill. Gerhold flipped out the crossblade and engaged the lone creature behind him, hoping to finish it off before the others arrived and joined the fray, but it was immediately apparent that the creature was more than capable with a blade. Their swords clashed together, the two vampire's dancing back and forth in a deadly dance. Gerhold heard the sound of footsteps coming from behind and leapt over his assailant to avoid its charging comrades.

With a flip of his wrist, he slashed his blade across the vampire's back and then parried the other two attacks. The wounded vampire fell forward with a cry of agony as the other two moved in to duel the slayer. Gerhold switched his crossblade to his left hand and drew his silver longsword in the other, just in time to catch both attacks. His hands whirled about, blocking, stabbing, and parrying as the other two vampires lashed out at him with their blades. He deflected another strike, but one of the assailants landed a hard blow to his stomach, sending Gerhold against the stone railing. Another attack forced him to his knees, where he spun both his weapons and trapped one of the creature's swords between the blades before avoiding the other's swing.

The three vampires fought along the rooftop walkway, neither side able to gain an advantage over the other as their weapons struck back and forth. The speed and strength of the strikes would have been enough to break a mortal man's arm, but Gerhold held his own against the onslaught, dodging and parrying each strike before following up with a flurry of his own. The attackers moved to either side of him and trying to focus on both enemies grew difficult as fatigue began to set in, and Gerhold knew he had to deal with one of the creatures before he was overwhelmed. He waited for an opening and then drove his foot hard into a vampire's chest, sending the creature sailing across the roof where it landed hard on the stone.

Gerhold launched himself forward at the remaining attacker with both weapons striking out in unison, forcing the vampire backwards in a defensive posture. He deflected one of the creature's attacks and then, with another quick slice, he separated the vampire's hand from its arm. The silver sword clanged across the ground as the monster clutched its severed limb, but before Gerhold could deal the killing blow, the other vampire attacked again from behind. Gerhold blocked the strike, but his crossblade sailed out of his hand and over the railing. The two dueled for a moment before Gerhold caught the vampire with an elbow to the head and then finished it off with a swift stab through the chest. The creature cried out in pain while Gerhold caught its falling weapon and used it to behead the handless vampire that had just retrieved its weapon.

Both bodies collapsed to the ground where their flesh began to smolder and burn away. Gerhold turned to see the last vampire slowly climbing to its feet,

A Dawn of Death

still holding the wound on its back that oozed blood. The hunter calmly pulled out one of his smaller crossbows and fired a bolt through the creature's chest before making his way across the roof to the tower door. He took a moment to catch his breath and to reload his weapon. All he had now was a single half-filled hand crossbow and his silver longsword since there was no time for him to retrieve his crossblade. His pyrite bombs had all been used on the barge and he had given his last flash bombs to Roland. None of that mattered though, as Gerhold knew that Harkin would have a plan for anything Gerhold could come up with.

Gerhold took one last deep breath before opening the door and entering the base of the tower. Inside he saw to his right a twisting stairwell that climbed up through the tower, and to his left there stood the bottom of a lift much like the ones he encountered in the Blightwood. It was a mess of chains, ropes, and pulleys, and Gerhold grabbed onto a nearby lever and pulled it. Nothing happened and the vampire uncorked one of his last vials of blood and downed it in one gulp before turning and starting up the long flight of stairs. The feeling of warmth and strength spread through him quickly as his body absorbed the life force from the blood, allowing him to run quickly up the twisting stairwell without needing to rest. Soon he reached the top and paused before another door while readying his longsword.

He reached out and opened the door, and immediately the stairwell was bathed in a dull green light that came from the center of the large circular room ahead. Gerhold entered slowly, his eyes darting side to side for any sign of Harkin. The circular chamber was tall with a high arching ceiling that had a hole at its center, and large stone pillars stood around the outside. To one side of the doorway was an opening where the lift stood unmoving, but otherwise the room was completely bare. At the middle of the room was a square stone altar, above which floated the glowing green sphere that Gerhold recognized as the Channeling Stone. He moved forward and reached out to take the stone and stop whatever Harkin was doing, but then a voice rang out from the other side of the room.

"I would not touch that if I were you," Harkin said and walked out from behind one of the pillars.

Gerhold whipped around and pulled out his hand crossbow, sending three bolts in Harkin's direction in quick succession. The vampire was ready, and Harkin dove behind another pillar as the missiles bounced harmlessly off the stone wall. Gerhold pulled the trigger a fourth time but the crossbow only gave a clicking sound.

"Empty now?" Harkin said and walked back out from behind the pillar as Gerhold dropped the little crossbow to the floor. "Do not worry, I cannot use my magic, not while I am maintaining that spell," he said and pointed to the glowing orb. "As I was saying, I would not touch that. The stone is drawing an immense amount of magical energy from the nether realm, and if you pull it from the pedestal, the resulting explosion will make your bombs look like little sparks."

Gerhold looked from Harkin to the glowing stone.

"What is this stone doing?" Gerhold asked.

"Look a little closer and you shall see," Harkin said and Gerhold looked at the altar beneath the orb.

Sitting on the flat stone surface was a single golden ring and it was as if the green light was being pulled from the gold itself.

"Cursed gold?" Gerhold said aloud and Harkin nodded.

"Yes, you see I came across a spell many hundreds of years ago that would allow me to transfer magical properties to other objects. My hope was to transfer our curse, the curse of vampirism, to an entire population, effectively creating an army of vampires. Of course, as you have seen firsthand, the spell did not have the exact results I was hoping for."

"You are spreading the curse?" Gerhold asked.

"Yes, through the fog actually. Of course, I could not have my army destroyed by the sunlight so I added a bit of my own flair, which may have been the problem. Somehow the mist carries the curse, though, I do not know exactly how it happens or why only some people are affected. Perhaps it has to do with how long they are exposed to it," Harkin said and shrugged.

"All those people who are sick, you tried to spread the curse to them?" Gerhold asked and Harkin nodded again.

The monster was alive again, its strength like nothing Gerhold had felt before.

"As I said it did not work as intended. Instead of transferring the curse, it only imparts pieces of vampirism onto those affected. Instead of absorbing life essence from blood, their bodies expelled it, and since they are unable to satiate the hunger they are driven into madness, much like we are when starved. Sad that my plan failed, but it still served its true purpose, creating another challenge for you." Harkin smiled.

A Dawn of Death

"All of this, this death, all the destruction, all of this was just to test me. You have truly lost whatever bits of sanity once remained within you," Gerhold said, the anger and righteous fury was audible in every syllable.

The bars were bending, the cage was failing, and Gerhold felt the deep desire to finally let the beast free. To relieve the unwavering pressure in his mind.

"You do not understand, Gerhold. You have no idea what I have done. This curse is more than you can comprehend because you have only lived with it for a short amount of time," Harkin said and took a step forward.

"A hundred years a short time?"

"Compared to thousands of years it is." Harkin's eyes narrowed. "Do you have any idea what an eternity feels like? To exist for no reason. Men were not meant to live forever, and that, Gerhold, is the most devious part of the curse. We fear death but cannot embrace it out of fear, and so we are trapped on this earth forever with no goal."

"Purpose," Gerhold repeated. "You already went off on your tirade to justify your evil. You are no different from a robber or a murderer. They all justify their actions just as poorly as you do. Only a fool would believe such a thing."

"A fool you say. Who is the greater fool: the one who seeks to better his eternal existence or the one who protects those who seek to destroy him?"

"I protect the innocent as I have always done," Gerhold answered and Harkin scoffed.

"Innocent? You mean those who would kill you without hesitation just for being cursed? Those who actively seek your destruction right after you assist them?" Harkin spat on the floor. "I told you before, Gerhold, you are not one of them, neither of us is. You can fight for them, protect them, even spill your own blood for them and they will still see you as only one thing, a monster. That is what you are to them and no matter what you do that is all you will ever be."

"And what other choice do I have? Be like you? A plague upon this world? A leech that seeks to suck away whatever I can for my own sake and pleasure? Never, Harkin. I will fight those like you until my dying breath."

Harkin stared at Gerhold for a moment.

"I see there is no reasoning with you then," Harkin said and Gerhold readied his sword. "You know I was always better than you. You may have willed yourself to resist the curse, but I still managed to turn you into a monster. In the Blightwood you acted as the perfect pawn and could do nothing to stop me. So, what makes you think this time will be any different? I may not be able to use my magic, but I am quite capable with a sword."

"You have lived for far too long," Gerhold responded.

Harkin smiled one last time, then raised his hand and tossed something at Gerhold's feet. A blinding light flashed, and a deafening boom exploded and Gerhold dropped to his knees, disoriented by the bomb. Images of the room flashed in front of his eyes and the intense ringing in his ears felt as though someone had drummed him over the head with a club. He leaned against the altar for support, but just as his hand touched the cold stone, something hard collided with him from behind and Gerhold was sent crashing to the ground.

"Falling for your own tricks?" Harkin said from somewhere beyond Gerhold's blurred vision, the words barely audible over the ringing sounds echoing in his head. "I told you, you will never beat me, Gerhold."

Gerhold climbed slowly to his feet, his vision finally beginning to clear, but Harkin was nowhere to be seen. Gerhold felt his teeth elongate and jut out of his mouth as the desire to rip Harkin limb from limb began to consume him. He could hear the guttural snarls emanating from his own self echoing off the walls. The beast was at the precious of his consciousness. The hunter spun about wildly sword at the ready, but just then the sound of footsteps came echoing up the staircase. He turned in time to see a man come walking through the doorway, spear in hand, and immediately recognized Roland.

"Gerhold, are you alright?' he asked.

Gerhold watched as a silhouette appeared behind Roland, but before he could utter a word of warning Harkin leapt from the shadows and thrust his blade into Roland's back. The silver tip burst through Roland's chest and the silver spear slipped slowly from his grasp as the young man fell to his knees. Harkin yanked his sword free, leaving Roland on his back in a growing pool of crimson blood, before stepping away and motioning for Gerhold to come to his fallen comrade. Gerhold cried out in anger and ran forward, swinging his sword in a wide arch that Harkin dodged with ease before kneeling at the side of his dying friend. The beast was still there, but the sight of his wounded comrade somehow drove it back into the dark, for the moment at least.

"Roland! Roland, hold on," Gerhold muttered while cradling his friend's bleeding body.

"Ah, mortality. Perhaps our plight isn't so bad after all?" Harkin said and laughed.

A Dawn of Death

Roland looked up and gasped for breath.

"Gerhold, I—" he coughed, and blood trickled down the side of his mouth. "I am s—sorry."

"Just hold on," Gerhold whispered and leaned Roland against a nearby wall.

"You are far too sentimental," he heard Harkin say. "He would have died eventually anyway."

Gerhold turned slowly to face Harkin, malice etched upon every line of his face, and his sword clenched tightly in both hands.

"Come now, let us finish this," Harkin said with a laugh.

Gerhold leapt forward and swung his blade at Harkin with all his might, rage emanating from his very being. Their swords came together and Gerhold lashed out with a series of strikes so quick that a mortal man would have only seen a blur. Harkin was no mortal man, though, and he deflected each blow with equal precision before going on the attack. The two danced back and forth, matching skill with skill and strength with strength. Gerhold blocked one of Harkin's strikes and drove his fist into the vampire's stomach, only to have Harkin's elbow catch him under the chin. Their blades met again and Gerhold slid his sword down and spun the blade so that it yanked Harkin's weapon out of his hand. Before Gerhold could capitalize on the advantage, Harkin grabbed his wrists and slammed his other hand into Gerhold's arm, causing him to drop his sword.

Both engaged in hand-to-hand combat, striking out with their fists and feet. Harkin caught Gerhold's arm mid swing and delivered a hard knee into the slayer's side, followed by a fast set of strikes that Gerhold was barely able to block. They locked arms in grapple, and Gerhold pushed Harkin against one of the pillars before connecting with a wild swing. Blood trickled from Harkin's broken nose and he kicked out with his foot. Using the pillar for leverage, he was able to drive Gerhold backwards before delivering a second and strong kick that knocked the slayer to the floor. Harkin grabbed his fallen blade and raised it high above his head, but Gerhold rolled to the side and the blade struck the stone floor at the foot of the altar.

Gerhold dove to avoid another strike and felt the stinging pain as the blade tore into his side. He landed hard on the floor and rolled out of the way as Harkin continued his attack, and as he got back to his feet, Gerhold saw the glint of silver metal to his side. In one motion he used his foot to lift the silver blade off the floor and fling into the air. He caught the blade and spun to meet Harkin, deflecting the blow just in time. Their swords moved back and forth, and even with his wounded side, Gerhold was able to match his foe's ferocity. He was numb to the pain; his only thought was to kill Harkin. Both combatants knew how to handle a sword after so many years, and Gerhold knew that with such skill each was waiting for the other to make a mistake.

That error would happen, and as always, Gerhold was ready. Harkin swung his blade with all his might and Gerhold parried the blow, allowing his foe's momentum to carry him forward, where Gerhold struck him across the face. Harkin's already broken nose spewed more blood as Gerhold's elbow slammed into it, sending the vampire off balance and to his knees. Gerhold wasted no time and struck with his blade, slicing through Harkin's chest with a howl of pain and then drove his foot into the vampire's stomach, knocking the sword from his hand and causing his foe to go skidding across the floor. His side throbbed with pain from the wound he had received, and his eyes and ears still ached from the flash bomb, but Gerhold ignored these feeling and stepped closer to Harkin, who still lay on the floor, holding his bruised side.

"I must admit; that was impressive," Harkin said and moved to his knees while clutching the bleeding cut across his chest.

Gerhold raised his sword, wanting to waste no more time with his words, but just as he did, Harkin stretched out his hand and the Channeling Stone gave a great shudder that shook the entire tower. Gerhold was almost knocked off his feet as the orb glowed with an intense light and the tower gave another great lurch. Harkin leapt to his feet and dashed across the room towards one of the windows.

"There is nowhere for you to run, Harkin!" Gerhold yelled as the vampire stopped at the foot of a tall arched window, the end of a long rope in his hand and the other end tied somewhere outside the window.

"Oh, but there is," Harkin said and opened the glass pane. The orb pulsed with power again and Gerhold felt as though the tower would topple from the strength of the vibrations.

"What did you do?" Gerhold asked and Harkin laughed.

"You have less than a minute before that stone channels enough power to destroy this entire tower. After that, there will be no way to stop it from spreading the fog across this entire realm," Harkin answered and stood on the edge of the window. "You can stop it, but whoever takes ahold of that stone will

A Dawn of Death

be eviscerated by the magical energy, and if you destroy it, well, you remember your pyrite bombs?"

"You will not escape me this time!" Gerhold roared and moved toward Harkin.

The beast roared to life again, finally he would have his revenge. Finally he would kill Harkin.

"Is your vengeance more important than the lives of those in this realm? If so, then by all means come chase me," Harkin smiled again as Gerhold halted and stared at the glowing orb.

The beast snarled and lunged a final time, but it was met with an equally powerful blow of will. Gerhold felt the world slow to a crawl, remembering what was at stake. This was not about slaying Harkin, it was about the city and the people. His city. The monster scratched and howled as Gerhold forced it back, as the sunrise slowly drives the darkness of night away.

"That is what I thought. You do not need to take ahold of it yourself, though, there is someone close by who is already dying." Harkin nodded towards Roland, who lay gasping in the corner of the room. "So that leaves you with a choice: sacrifice yourself while I escape and dear Roland here dies, or let him destroy the orb, and you can continue your quest to destroy me."

With that, he leapt from the windowsill and disappeared. Gerhold stared at the empty space, longing to follow, longing to plunge his blade into the vampire's heart and end it all. His chance at vengeance was once again slipping away, Harkin was going to escape. The beast roared again, but Gerhold held firm. How long before he would find him again? How many years of empty searching? The beast was still there, lurking in the darkness, but Gerhold knew what he had to do. The hunter turned and ran towards Roland. He reached his friend's body, Roland's blood staining the ground and his spear lying nearby.

"Gerhold—" Roland gasped.

"Do not speak," Gerhold said and lifted Roland, dragging him towards the lift.

"Use—" Roland coughed, "Use me, let me take the stone." Gerhold laid his friend down on the lift and rested his hand on the young man's shoulder. Roland reached up and grabbed Gerhold around the neck. "Please! I—I can do this."

"Let go, you need a healer now. I will not let you die, not like this," Gerhold answered.

Surprisingly, Roland let go and leaned back against the back wall of the lift. The two friends stared at each other for a split second, the anger in Roland's eyes now replaced with a strange sense of peace.

"Help will come, just hold on until then. Find Harkin and kill him, understand?" Gerhold said and then stepped back.

Before Roland could protest again, Gerhold slammed his silver sword into the chain that held the lift in place, causing the platform to jerk and descend. Gerhold watched as Roland passed from view and then turned to face the glowing stone that once again pulsed with energy. The slayer walked forward, sword in hand, face defiant as ever, and his cold eyes showed more determination than ever before. Harkin had escaped, but Gerhold would not let him win. Never again. If Harkin's only reason to live was Gerhold, then he would take from the vampire that which he needed most. He walked calmly up to the altar where he raised his sword, images of Roland and Nethrin passing through his mind. Poor Brother Francis lying dead, and all those he had been forced to watch pass on as he lived. Death was nothing to be feared; it was only the next great adventure. He was not Harkin and he would never become like that monster. The beast within him was silence for the first time since he had turned. No clawing, no scratching, no wailing attempts or calls for feeding. Just complete and utter silence. He had won the battle.

Gerhold swung the sword with all his strength and the blade crashed through the Channeling Stone, shattering it, and sending glowing shards in all directions. It was as if time suddenly slowed, and Gerhold watched as the green glow of the stone began to dissipate, followed by another bright light that erupted from the remnants of the orb. A bright light, a fierce heat, and then nothing.

A Dawn of Death

Chapter 17: The Final Entry

Journal Entry: February 11, 5947 of the Common Age

    I am sad to say that this shall be my final entry into these journals. It has been five days since the Battle of Castle Neffgard, or at least that is what they are calling it. Many Paladins fell in the courtyard and halls of that castle while trying to drive out the vampire's that had made it their home. Count Leofric was found in his chambers, dead, a dagger through his heart carried by his own hand, and now the castle lies deserted. The Paladins, led by Commander Owyn and along with the chapel priests, are in control of the city, and they are doing their best to administer help wherever needed. Healers from nearby cities are starting to arrive, and those still affected by the sickness are being taken from the city, though I do not know what is becoming of them.

    Few people know of what happened on that night, and I have done my best to record what I know within these pages, but I fear we may never fully understand what occurred. During the battle in the courtyard, Gerhold of Vilheim, the greatest slayer in history, made his way up to the highest tower to confront Harkin Valakir. I know that the two dueled and that Gerhold won, but that somehow Harkin used the channeling stone to try and destroy the castle and spread the sickness throughout Penland (If that is at all possible, it is too terrifying a thing to imagine). All I know after this, is that Gerhold helped Roland escape the tower, who had been wounded, and then the entire building erupted in green flame. The highest point of the tower had been ripped apart by the force of the explosion, and nothing of Gerhold or Harkin could be found. Roland seemed to suggest that Harkin escaped, but unfortunately, he passed before we could learn more.

J.S. Matthews

The mists have disappeared, and the city is safe, but my heart is heavy with sorrow as I mourn the loss of both my friends. Roland lived for only a day after the Paladins found him at the bottom of the tower, barely alive and suffering from a grievous wound. I was able to speak to him for a time, and I was there when he breathed his last. The brothers are going to place his coffin in the cathedral undercroft, and just before his death, he received a full pardon for his previous transgressions which ended his exile from the Paladins. He died as a true warrior.

I do not know what happened to Gerhold, but I can only assume he perished in the explosion. A sad end to such a story. Gerhold was the greatest slayer of his time, a hunter who waged his war within the shadows of our history. Content only to do what he knew was right and never ask for any fame or recognition for what he did. Never have I met a man before such as him and I imagine I shall never again. It should be known, though, that Gerhold of Vilheim — vampire, monster slayer, and friend — defeated Harkin Valakir. I can only hope that my friend has found his peace, and that he has received from the Gods a welcome given only to the greatest of followers.

There is nothing else that needs to be said about those two men, save that they should be remembered in song and writing until the end of this wretched world. The stories and legends of Gerhold will never be forgotten, and I for one shall not forget his sacrifice. To whoever reads these words, go and tell the tale of Gerhold of Vilheim. Spread the news of Roland's sacrifice, and of their deeds. By doing so you shall add a ray of hope to this world and ensure that these heroes are not forgotten. Tell of these tales and remember.

-Brother Nethrin of Vilheim

A Dawn of Death

Epilogue

Jarrell Vorren read to the bottom of the crumpled page and turned to find that it was the last one. He stared at the last page, hoping that somehow there would be another behind it, but there was not. The last signature on the page was etched into his mind, and Jarrell realized why the last few entries had been written so differently and in such strange handwriting since they had been penned by the priest Nethrin. It had also surprised him that the uproar those ten years ago in Vilheim had been because of Gerhold. Everyone at the library had been talking about the vampires in Vilheim and how monsters had taken over the city. It was all very vague and cryptic, but now Jarrell understood. Slowly he slid the little page back into place and shifted the volume on the desk, and only then did he notice that Ernhold was standing at the end of the table.

"Have you finished?" he asked, and Jarrell nodded. "Good, so now you know what happened to Gerhold."

"I am not really sure. The journals did not say exactly what happened to him," Jarrell answered.

"Of course, they did, you read it yourself. Gerhold of Vilheim died at the top of that tower," Ernhold said coldly. "He faced Harkin and lost, just as he did time after time."

"But you cannot be certain, even the priest did not know," Jarrell said again. He was beginning to feel nervous as Ernhold calmly walked around the table and stood directly in front of the desk.

"Oh, but I do know," he said and lifted his hood so that it fell back behind his neck.

Jarrell saw a handsome but somewhat pale face and a long mane of golden hair, and a name sprang to his mind but got stuck somewhere I his throat.

"You recognize me, do you not?" Harkin asked and Jarrell was barely able to conjure up a nod. "We have never met, and yet you knew who I was the moment I revealed myself. That is how it should be."

"W—Why" Jarrell stammered and slid his chair back and away from Harkin. "Why did you come here?"

"I came to bring you these," he said and tapped his fingers on the leather journal. "It took me almost ten years to find these, and as soon as I did, I knew what had to be done with them. You see I tried to track that priest, Nethrin, but he had all but disappeared after that night in Vilheim. However, I was able to track down these. He had given them to another priest, one who sold them to me for only a few silver pieces to raise money for a new chantry he was trying to build."

"But why? What is so important about them?" Jarrell asked, his voice shaking with fear.

"I thought that was obvious. I want the world to know the story of Gerhold of Vilheim. I want every peasant in every borough on every wretched continent to know his tales. I want to hear the bards sing of his feats, to listen to poets recite his victories in turn, and I want every person to know who beat him." Harkin smiled. "I want you to tell everyone the real story. How the greatest slayer this world has ever seen was bested by Harkin Valakir."

Jarrell stared at Harkin, his hands sweating and his knees shaking. He was sitting face to face with one of the most evil and terrifying villains he had ever heard of. Alone in this little dark room, Harkin could do anything to him, and no one would be the wiser. He considered calling for a guard but realized it would be no use, as by the time the words even began to leave his mouth Harkin would reach him. Instead, Jarrell did his best to speak.

"W–what do you want me to do?" he asked.

"It is simple really; I want you to write a story. I want you to tell the world the truth so that the name of Harkin Valakir will forever be thought of whenever Gerhold's name is mentioned. That whenever a minstrel sings of his deeds there will be whispers of my name and how I bested him." Harkin rested his hand on the table and closed the journal. "When I had heard of his death, I did not believe it, as I assumed he would allow Roland to take his place and remove the stone. I had to see the body of that pathetic Paladin to make sure all the rumors were true, and when I did, I knew he had done the unthinkable. In that moment, I must admit, I thought that Gerhold had finally defeated me. I did not think he would allow me to escape his vengeance, but I guess I underestimated him once again. I thought he was so committed to my destruction that he would allow Roland to destroy the Channeling Stone instead of himself, but he was much smarter than I ever gave him credit for. He knew that by ending his own life I would be lost at sea once again. Doomed to live an empty life of

A Dawn of Death

eternal madness."

Jarrell swallowed as Harkin moved and sat on the other side of the desk. Jarrell's hands shook and his breathing came in short quick gasps.

"I thought he had won, until I realized something. If I could show the world that he had been beaten, that I had forced him to end his own life, and that ultimately, he had lost, then I could destroy his legacy. I could prove that even the greatest slayer could not challenge Harkin Valakir, and I could destroy the myth that surrounded him. I could show that ultimately his life was a waste." Harkin stood again and made his way around the desk.

"What are you going to do with me?" Jarrell asked, though dreading the answer.

"Do with you? Nothing of course! I need you to pen the story, to tell the world of this. However, if you do not, then perhaps I shall return," Harkin said with an evil smile and tossed his hood up over his head once again. "You may keep the journals as a thank-you for being so attentive during our little meetings, but do not disappoint me, Apprentice."

With a flip of his cloak Harkin turned and strode across the room before opening the door and exiting without another word. Jarrell watched as the door closed and let out a loud sigh of relief as he felt his muscles begin to relax. For a few moments he just leaned back in his chair and took deep breaths, trying to calm his rapidly beating heart. He had spent three nights in the same room with the most powerful vampire in history and survived. Jarrell felt his stomach do a somersault at the thought and felt as though he may retch, but before he could, the door to the little room creeped open again. Thinking it was Harkin returning, Jarrell froze.

"Good evening, Apprentice," the High Keeper said as he entered. He saw Jarrell and must have realized how close he was to throwing up, because the old man promptly made his way across the room and picked up a small basket that was filled with old papers and handed it to him.

Jarrell leaned over it and felt the rush of foul-tasting bile as he retched into the bucket. For a few moments he just sat there, feeling sick and leaning over the smelly container while the High Keeper patted him on the back. Finally, he sat up and took a long drink of water from a nearby cup.

"Feeling better?" the High Keeper asked, and Jarrell nodded. "I cannot imagine what it must have been like to realize you were in the same room with him."

Jarrell looked up at Yorlan in confusion.

"You knew?" he asked, and the High Keeper nodded. "You knew all along that I was sitting alone in a room with the most dangerous vampire of all time and you let it happen?"

"I did, and I am sorry for that. It was necessary, though," Yorlan said and rested a comforting hand on Jarrell's shoulder. "To be honest you were never in any real danger. You were under the protection of more than just the Battlemages."

"So, the guards got him? Please tell me the Battlemages have him?" Jarrell asked and the old man shook his head.

"No, he is gone now."

"But why? If you knew, then why would you let him go? He cannot be powerful enough to fight all of the Battlemages," Jarrell said in a panicked voice, but Yorlan just motioned for him to sit.

"Do not worry about Harkin Valakir. There are things occurring here that you have not been made aware of. You have been a part of something very important, and it was imperative that you were kept unaware. Now, I think it is time for you to make your way back to your room. I imagine you could use some sleep?"

Jarrell just stared at the man, dumbfounded by what he was hearing.

"How can I sleep? After what I read and after what I just saw? How can I sleep while he is out there?" Jarrell said fearfully.

"I thought you wanted to go on an adventure?" Yorlan asked and raised his eyebrows. Jarrell did not respond. "I told you; do not worry about Harkin Valakir. If it will help, you may remain here, and I will post a guard to watch over you." Yorlan smiled in comforting manner. "Perhaps it would help to write some?" he said and nudged the journals.

The High Keeper stood and made his way over to the door.

"What do you want me to write?" Jarrell asked.

"Well, since you neglected to copy those journals then perhaps you should start on that? Or, if you feel so inclined, perhaps you should write your own story. You are training to be a Keeper after all. Perhaps you should tell the world the true story of Gerhold of Vilheim?"

Jarrell stared at the High Keeper, still trying to figure out what was going on. Was the old man out of his mind?

"But what should I say?" he asked finally, and the old man shrugged.

A Dawn of Death

"That is up to you, but perhaps you should put off the ending for the time being. I may have a new one for you here shortly," the old Keeper said with a smile and left.

Jarrell sat in his chair for a time, trying to understand what had just happened and to make sense of the past three nights. His mind felt his mind go numb, empty, as if his confusion clouded all thought. Jarrell noticed a little bottle of liquor sitting on the table and took a large gulp of the stinging liquid, which caused him to cough. After a few minutes of sitting in the silent room, he slid his chair forward, picked up a nearby quill, and dipped it into a bottle of ink. Slowly, he penned a few words across the top of a fresh page, then leaned back and looked at the fancy curved writing: *The Lost Journals*. Satisfied with the title, he leaned forward and began to write. His worries began to slowly dissipate with every new word and line, and as he wrote, Jarrell realized the forgotten tale of Gerhold of Vilheim was lost no more.

Harkin Valakir gave his horse a slight kick as it ran down the forested road between the Library and the little town of Eldrith. It usually took around a half hour for him to travel from the base of the hills, where the town could be found, up to the little Library that had been tucked away at the base of the peaks. It was a beautiful area, even more beautiful now that his business at the Library had been concluded. At first, he had been nervous with his plan as the Battlemages guarding the Great Libraries are often trained at spotting dark creatures, but he knew a spell or two that could fool even the most powerful mages and that had proven true. He gave a great sigh and closed his eyes, picturing the years to come when the stories of the great Harkin Valakir would begin to make their way across the realms of Midland.

Although, what would he do now? Surely there would be hunters that would come looking for him as the Apprentice boy would most certainly spread the tale that he was in fact alive. Perhaps he could find another rival? Someone to challenge him as Gerhold had all those years? He shook his head and laughed; there was only one Gerhold of Vilheim, and even he could not best Harkin Valakir. As he approached a bend in the road, the trees parted and he could see out across the vast open plains of western Arendor, but as he was admiring the beauty of it all, a clicking sound echoed from somewhere nearby. Harkin turned just in time to watch as a silver piece of metal slammed into his left shoulder, knocking him from his horse and onto the hard ground.

Immediately he leapt to his feet and conjured a ball of fire in his right hand, unable to lift his wounded arm. For a moment all was quiet, then a second click sounded, and another silver bolt slammed into his opposite shoulder. Harkin fell to his knees and cried out in pain, unable to move either arm enough to pull the silver metal from his body. The wounds hissed and burned as the magical metal melted his skin, and Harkin did his best to stand and remove the bolts, but as soon as he did another came hurtling out of the darkness and slammed into his leg. On his knees again, Harkin listened as the sound of crunching leaves and footsteps of his attacker closed in, until finally the silhouette of a man appeared along the side of the road. He wore a set of silver armor and a full-faced helm of the Battlemages who guarded the library. In his hands was a finely crafted heavy crossbow that looked all too familiar.

"Good evening, Mister Ernhold," the man said. "Not a very common name, but it does have a familiar ring to it."

Harkin looked up at his attacker, wondering why one of the Battlemages had followed and attacked him.

"I borrowed it from an old friend," Harkin said with a grunt of pain. "But congratulations, whoever you are. The last time someone wounded me like this was ten years ago."

"I know," the man responded as he approached and reloaded his crossbow.

Harkin had heard that voice somewhere but could not place it.

"You are the guard that followed that old Keeper around," Harkin said finally as he recognized the Battlemage's walk. The guard nodded in response. "So, the old codger knew who I was after all? Very curious indeed."

Harkin tried to pull one of the bolts out with what little strength he had, but the Battlemage raised his crossbow.

"Don't. Just leave them where they are," he said.

"I highly doubt you would just sit here if we traded positions," Harkin said and gasped from the effort of trying to remove the metal shaft, which did not budge.

"I've had worse," the man said as he calmly undid the strap beneath his chin and removed the helmet.

Harkin immediately recognized the man, the long dark hair, and the handsome face.

A Dawn of Death

"You?" Harkin said in surprise and Roland nodded.

"Surprised?"

"The last time I saw you, you were lying in a pool of your own blood, gasping for every breath, so yes, I am very surprised," Harkin answered. "I must ask, though, how did you live through that?"

"I didn't," Roland said, and his smile revealed a pair of elongated fangs. The young vampire pulled on a little chain around his neck to reveal a familiar golden locket hanging from it. "I lay there on the floor of that tower dying from my wounds and I begged him to let me destroy the stone, knowing full well what it would cost me. I was already dying, and I wanted the satisfaction of knowing I had helped and that Gerhold had survived to continue his war against you. But I also knew he would never let someone sacrifice themselves for him. As he knelt down next to me, I slipped the amulet off his neck. Fortunately for me, it turned out that the curse runs its course even after death."

"Convenient," Harkin responded with another grunt of pain.

"Nethrin was the only one who knew, and once they buried me, he broke into the chapel undercroft and took my body. He performed for me the same service another priest did for Gerhold all those years ago. He prevented me from attacking anyone. I kept my humanity."

"And for the past ten years you have been skulking about in hiding?"

"A bit, yes," Roland said. "When I awoke from death, I spent the first few months searching fruitlessly for you, until I realized that I would never be able to find you. Gerhold had spent years of his life trying to track you, so how was I going to manage such a task that even he could not accomplish? Instead, I came up with a plan to lure you in. I hope you don't mind but I took a few pages from your book for my little charade."

Harkin's mouth spread into a wide smile, and then he started to laugh. At first it was only a low chuckle, but soon he was roaring with amusement and Roland looked on, slightly confused by Harkin's enjoyment. Finally, as the laughter started to subside, Harkin spoke.

"So, all of this was you? The journals, the priest I bought them from, even the old Keeper? All of this was your doing?" he asked, and Roland nodded. "And you waited for ten years?"

"I needed you to believe you were safe, that you had won. It is the same plan you used on Gerhold at Ravencroft." Roland answered. "I also needed you to decide on the Eldrith Library, which is why you found the priest in Osgoroth. I knew you would want the world to know, and I assumed you would go to the closest library."

"Bravo my young friend, bravo indeed. I must say I am impressed, but I must ask you another question. Was it worth it? All your plotting and scheming, all the years of waiting for me to fall into your little trap? All that time spent for this moment, and now it is already almost gone," Harkin said with a sneer. "Was all of that worth the sting of revenge?"

"Every single minute of it," Roland answered. "You always wanted to beat him, but in the end, Gerhold won. He never abandoned who he was. He never turned into you. That's what you wanted, wasn't it?"

Harkin didn't answer.

"If there is one thing this world will remember about you, Harkin Valakir, if is that you were defeated by the greatest monster slayer of all time. His name will be what the folk think about when they hear yours, his tales will be sung, and his legend will grow. Yours will only be a footnote."

The vampire sneered.

"And after I am dead, then what?" Harkin taunted. "You are no different than me or Gerhold for that matter. Without me you just exist to continue your existence. A circle of pointlessness. You will be consumed by the monster that lives within you now, just as it does within all vampires. It is there now, clawing at the back of your mind, screaming and raging. It is only a matter of time before it escapes, and, with you being immortal, it has all the time it needs. Fight all you wish, but you cannot hide from the curse of darkness."

Roland raised his crossbow.

"You've lived for far too long," he muttered and pulled the trigger.

The silver bolt slammed into Harkin's chest and passed straight through his heart. For a moment Harkin just stared at it in shock, then, as the flames began to burn away his flesh, Roland saw the fear in Harkin's eyes, a look that stayed until there was nothing left of Harkin Valakir except a smoldering pile of ash and bones.

"That was for Gerhold," Roland whispered as he bent down to retrieve the silver bolts.

He stood and heard the echoing sounds of hooves coming from somewhere further up the path, and soon two riders appeared on the horizon with a third horse in tow. Nethrin sat atop the first steed wearing his typical brown robes, and on the second horse was High Keeper Yorlan. The two men slowed until they came to a halt.

"How did it go?" Nethrin asked as he leapt down from his horse.

"As well as it could have gone," Roland answered and pointed to the pile of charred bones.

Nethrin bent down to examine what remained of Harkin.

"I only wish I could have been here to see his face when you did it," Nethrin said and shook his head in disappointment.

"Thank you again for your help," Roland said to Yorlan.

"Yes, thank you uncle," Nethrin added.

"It was the least I could do for the nephew I was never able to take in when he needed me," Yorlan said and rested a hand on Nethrin's shoulder. "I am glad that you have finally found your peace."

"We have, and we could not have managed it without you," Roland responded.

"Was it as fulfilling as you imagined?" Yorlan asked.

Roland chuckled.

"Revenge never is."

Yorlan nodded and pulled himself slowly back up onto his horse.

"Well then gentlemen, is there anything else I can do for you?" the old man asked.

"You have already done more than enough for us already," Roland answered.

"Then I suppose I shall bid you both farewell. I still have a library top run after all, and I believe there is a certain Apprentice of mine who will be more than excited to hear this news," Yorlan said and turned his horse around. "Oh, and Nethrin? Do not wait another twenty years to come and visit me again. I cannot promise I will still be alive if you do."

"Of course, uncle," Nethrin answered and the two men shook hands.

With that the old man nudged his horse forward and began his short ride through the hills to where the library was tucked away along the mountain slopes. Roland stared out over the moonlit plains. Far below he could see the twinkling lights of the little village of Eldrith and the dark outlines of the few trees that dotted the open plains. A soft breeze blew down across the mountainside and he heard it pass through the branches of the tall pines. He had spent ten years planning and working towards this moment and now that it was done, he felt strange, as if a great weight had been lifted from his shoulders. For the first time in many years, he felt free.

"Well, where are we headed now?" Nethrin asked.

Roland stood silently for a moment before answering.

"I don't know. What do you think?"

"How about somewhere warm?" Nethrin suggested.

"Like Drakar? Plenty of monsters to hunt down there in the desert," Roland answered and heard Nethrin make a disgusted sound.

"Absolutely not, too much sand."

"Nurria then?" Roland Suggested.

"No, Gerhold always said it was a terrible place," Nethrin answered again.

"Well, you're a hard one to please all of a sudden," Roland responded with a laugh.

"We could see if Commander Owyn has anything for us?" Nethrin asked and Roland shook his head.

"I don't feel like dealing with the Paladins right now, not if we can help it anyways. Owyn is a good man, but I get tired of all the strange looks I get working with him."

Nethrin chuckled.

"Now who is hard to please?"

The silence returned before the young priest spoke again.

"Valaire and Ke'var are still in Calloria."

"They are hunting Snatchers, so I hardly think they would need our help," Roland answered.

"Yes, but it may help us get on better terms with the Seekers, and we need to after what you pulled last time," Nethrin said and grinned.

"I let a vampire go; they will get over it eventually," Roland answered and frowned. "But I suppose you are right. It would be nice to get a few more contracts from them again."

"Besides, maybe it will turn out to be bog lurkers or something more interesting, and it is never boring being with Valaire," Nethrin said and leapt up onto his horse.

"Calloria it is then," Roland said and climbed onto the other horse where his silver spear hung in the saddle.

The two friends started off down the path, but Roland could not help but glance one last time at the remains of Harkin. He watched as the ashes were

A Dawn of Death

picked up by the light breeze and taken away with the wind, leaving behind the burned skeleton, which was all that remained of Harkin. Roland closed his eyes for a moment and could see the smiling face of his mentor and friend. Gerhold would be proud of him, he was sure of it. And with that, both Roland and Nethrin headed off into the darkness, unsure of what other adventures lay ahead.

Author Notes - The World of Tyriel

It has now been just over ten years since I started outlining the map that would eventually become my fantasy world of Tyriel. It was in one of my English classes, during my senior year of high school back in 2006, that I first started to draw the outline of what would become the realm of Arendor. Over seventy drawings later, I was left with the following map. This is the first time I have included the entire world map in one of my books, as so far I have only revealed small portions of Tyriel. I thought it appropriate to include this in my final book of this series, as the main goal of these three stories was to introduce you, my reader, to this amazing world.

Tyriel is a beautiful place, full of wonder, excitement, and mystery. It holds fantastic tales of courage and honor, sadness and tragedy, and acts of both great good and evil. *A Curse of Darkness* is but the first step into this magical world. It was the beginning of an incredible journey into this universe, and one that I intend to continue. Every realm in Tyriel has its own history, its own reason for "being", and my goal is to explore as much of this world as possible.

I want to show you the amazing underground world of the Hammarites, the splendor of the Callorian cities, the arid and dangerous deserts of Drakar, and the beautiful mountains of Arendor. Gerhold's story was only one of hundreds this world holds, and I promise that the best of these tales are still to come. Thank you for taking the time to explore this world with me, and I hope you enjoy the stories to come as much as I do. For now, though, I hope you enjoy your first look at Tyriel, and don't forget to leave a review of Amazon/Goodreads if you enjoyed my story.

- J.S. Matthews

TYRIEL

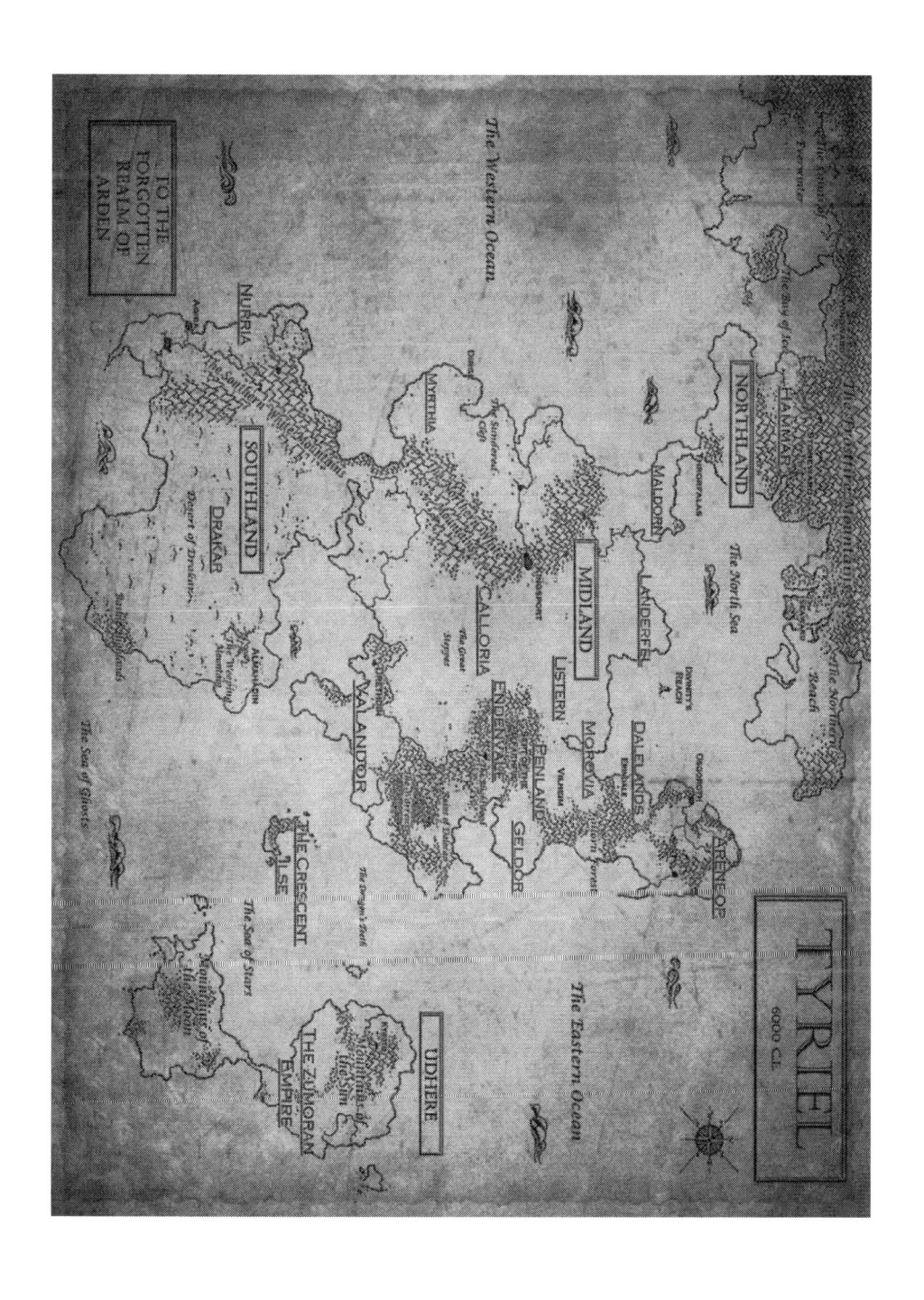

Made in the USA
Columbia, SC
09 March 2023

0a3d8887-6b52-4b99-830d-59e2b86e6f9aR02